INLAND

INLAND

A Novel

Téa Obreht

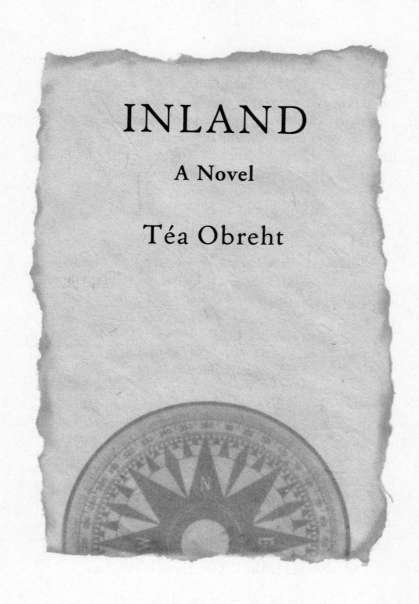

RANDOM HOUSE LARGE PRINT

Copyright © 2019 by Téa Obreht

All rights reserved.
Published in the United States of America by Random House Large Print in association with Random House, an imprint and division of Penguin Random House LLC, New York.

Cover design: Jaya Miceli
Cover art: Tamara Ruiz

The Library of Congress has established a Cataloging-in-Publication record for this title.

ISBN: 978-1-9848-9090-0

www.penguinrandomhouse.com/large-print-format-books

FIRST LARGE PRINT EDITION

Printed in the United States of America

10 9 8 7 6 5 4 3 2 1

This Large Print edition published in accord with the standards of the N.A.V.H.

For my mother, Maja,
and her mother, Zahida

Time doesn't change,
Nor do times.
Only things inside time change,
Things you will believe, and things you won't.

—James Galvin, "Belief"

INLAND

THE MISSOURI

WHEN THOSE MEN RODE DOWN TO THE fording place last night, I thought us done for. Even you must realize how close they came: their smell, the song of their bridles, the whites of their horses' eyes. True to form—blind though you are, and with that shot still irretrievable in your thigh—you made to stand and meet them. Perhaps I should have let you. It might have averted what happened tonight, and the girl would be unharmed. But how could I have known? I was unready, disbelieving of our fate, and in the end could only watch them cross and ride up the wash away from us in the moonlight. And wasn't I right to wait—for habit if nothing else? I knew you had flight in you yet. You still do; as do I, as I have all my life—since long before we fell in together, when I first came round to myself, six years old and already on the run, wave-rocked, with my father in the bunk beside me and all around the hiss of water against the hull. It was my father running back then, though from what I never knew. He was thin, I think. Young, perhaps. A blacksmith perhaps, or some other hard-laboring man who never caught more rest than he did that swaying month when night and day went undiffered, and there was nothing but the creak of rope and pulley somewhere above us in the dark. He called me **sìne,** and some other name I've struggled lifelong to recall. Of our crossing I remember mostly foam veins and the smell of salt. And the dead, of course, outlaid in their white shrouds side by side along the stern.

We found lodging near the harbor. Our room overlooked laundry lines that crosshatched from window to window until they vanished in the steam of the washhouse below. We shared a mattress and turned our backs to the madman across the room and pretended he wasn't a bit further gone each day than the last. There was always somebody shrieking in the halls. Somebody caught between worlds. I lay on my side and held the lapel of my father's coat and felt the lice roving through my hair.

I never met a man so deep-sleeping as my father. Dockwork will do that, I reckon. Every day would find him straining under some crate or hump of rope that made him look an ant. Afterwards, he'd take my hand and let the river of disembarking bodies carry us away from the quays, up the thoroughfare to where the steel scaffolds were rising. They were a marvel to him, curious as he was about the world's

workings. He had a long memory, a constant tooth-
ache, and an abiding hatred of Turks that tended to
flare up when he took tea with likeminded men. But
a funny thing would happen if ever some Serb or
Magyar started in about the iron fist of Stambul: my
father, so fixed in his enmity, would grow suddenly
tearful. **Well, efendi,** he'd say. **Are you better off
now? Better off here? Ali-Pasha Rizvanbegović was
a tyrant—but far from the worst! At least our land
was beautiful. At least our homes were our own.**
Then would follow wistful reminiscences of his boyhood village: a tumble of stone houses split by a river
so green he had no word for it in his new tongue,
and had to say it in the old one, thus trapping it
forever as a secret between the two of us. What I'd
give to remember that word. I could not think why
he would leave such a town for this reeking harbor,
which turned out to be the kind of place where praying palms-up and a name like Hadziosman Djurić
got him mistaken for a Turk so often he disowned
both. I believe he called himself Hodgeman Drury
for a while—but he was buried "Hodge Lurie"
thanks to our landlady's best guess at the crowded
consonants of his name when the hearse came to
take his body away.

Our mattress, I remember, was stained. I stood on
the stairs to watch the Coachman load my father
into his wagon. When they drove off the Landlady
put her hand on my head and let me linger. The
evening downpour had withdrawn, so a sunset

reddened the street. The horses looked ablaze. After that, my father never came to me again, not in the waters, not even in dreams.

That Landlady prayed night after night before a cross on the wall. Her mercy got me hard bread and a harder mattress. In return, I took to praying with my palms together and helped tend her lodgings. Ran up and down stairs with buckets of soapwater, hunted rats, wedged myself up chimneys. Staring men who sat in the shadows sometimes lunged for me. I was a skin-and-bones kid, but unafraid enough of stairwell drunks to kick them while they slept, so they learned to leave me alone. Another summer, another plague, another visit from the Coachman and his black horses. Another and another. A mess of script appeared on our curbpost. **Can you read that?** the Landlady asked me. **It says "pesthouse"— do you know what "pesthouse" means?** It turned out to mean empty rooms, empty purse, empty bellies for us both. When the Coachman next came around, she sent me away with him. Just stood there, staring down at the coin he put in her hand.

I bunked in the Coachman's stable for a year. He was the cleanest man I ever knew. Couldn't get to sleep without his house just so and his slippers side by side under the bed. The only unevenness to him was an upper tooth that had come in a tusk, giving him the look of a fancy rat. Together we went round the dens and fleahouses on Bleecker Street to collect the dead: lodgers who'd passed in their sleep, or had their throats cut by bunkmates. Sometimes they were still in their beds with the sheets drawn over them when we arrived. But just as often we'd find them folded into trunks or stuffed under floorboards. Those with cash and kin we took to the undertaker. The nameless we drove to uptown hospitals and delivered through back doors so they could be tabled before wakes of looming young men. Their innards laid out. Their bones boiled white.

When trade was slow, we'd have to pull them from churchyards. Two dollars to the gatekeep to look the other way while we walked among the crosses searching out newly turned mounds. The Coachman would start a tunnel where he guessed the head might be, and I would wedge down, shoulders and arms, all the way into the cold earth and stab forward with my iron until I broke the coffinboards. Then I'd feel about with my fingers till I found hair or teeth, and ease a noose over the head. It took both of us to pull them out.

"Still easier than digging them up," was the Coachman's reasoning.

Sometimes the mound fell in on itself, and sometimes the body caught and we had to leave it there half-dug; and sometimes they were women and sometimes kids, too, and the graveyard earth couldn't be got out of my clothing no matter how hot the washhouse kettle.

Once, we found two people sharing a coffin, face-to-face, as though they'd fallen asleep in it together. Once, I put my hand in and felt only the give of earth and the damp velvet of the pillow. "Someone's beat us here," I said. "It's empty."

Once, I broke through the boards and moved my fingers over coarse hair and skin and was just getting the rope past a reef of jawbone when fingers grabbed my wrist somewhere in the dark. They were dry fingers, hard-tipped. I started and dirt flew down my throat and into me. I kept kicking, but the fingers held on till I thought I'd disappear down that hole. "Please, I can't do it again," I sobbed afterwards— but I could, it turned out, with a broken wrist, and a twisted shoulder, too.

Once, a great big fella got stuck halfway out his coffin. I sat there in the dirt with his pale arm on my knees until the Coachman handed me a saw. I carried that arm all the way uptown, wrapped in its own burlap sleeve, on my shoulder like a ham. Some evenings later, I saw that same rent sleeve on a one-armed giant who stood unmoving in the fishmarket crowd. He was pale and round and stood smiling shyly at me, as though we were old friends. He drifted closer, hugging that empty sleeve, till he stood at my side. It seems an odd thing to say, but a thin tickle spread around me, and I knew he'd put his ghost arm about my shoulders. That was the first I ever got this strange feeling at the edges of myself— this want. He let forth a rueful sigh. As if we'd been talking all the while. "God," he said. "God I've an awful hunger. I'd love a nice cod pie. Wouldn't you, little boss?"

"Fuck you," said I, and fled.

I did eventually stop glancing over my shoulder for him—but that feeling, that strange feeling of want at the corners, it stayed. For days afterward, I would wake to whorling hunger and lie in the dark with my heart in my ears and my mouth running. As if something within was digging me up. Ordinary rations couldn't sate it. The Coachman sat counting my spoonfuls at mealtime. "That's enough, goddamn it," he'd say. But it wasn't enough—and what he berated me for was only the half of it. He wasn't around to watch me scrounge for apples fallen from the fruitcart, or wait till the grocer's back was turned to steal rolls. He wasn't around, either, when the bakergirl came down the street with that basket on her arm, so huge it listed her to one side, shouting, **fish pie, fish pie.** Whenever someone stopped her, she flipped up a checkered napkin to reveal a mountain of doughy knots. **Fish pie?** she asked me, like she knew about the want going sour in me. I sank five whole pies, crouching in an alley with the laundresses shouting to each other above me, and as I ate the want grew and grew in me till it ran over, and was all gone.

I wouldn't feel it again till years after we'd been caught. After the workhouse, after the judge passed sentence and sent the Coachman upriver and me to the railhead with six or seven other boys, westbound, with papers in my hand that read only: LURIE.

We were a week on the train, past farms and yellow fields and cabins smoking on gray hummocks, all the way to where the Missouri shallowed to mud. Town was a strip of stockyards and houses. The surrounding hillsides bristled with tree stumps. Wagons burdened with massive boughs harrowed the road.

They took us to a townhall that smelled of cattle and sawdust and got us up on a crateboard stage. One by one, the other boys were called down the stairs and into the dark. The old man who raised his hand for me was named Saurelle. He had frowsy ears and a hitch in his step, and a Mercantile that boasted dry goods and whiskey. His upstairs rooms were always overrun, every last soul westbound. His other hirelings were a pair of brothers: Hobb and Donovan Michael Mattie. Hobb was just a kid, four or five maybe, with a temper that could set grown men shaking in their boots. He was lightfingered, too—he could lift anything from anybody, and was pretty brazen about it. Saurelle didn't dare lay a hand on him for fear of Donovan, some twelve years older, a man already, rangy and redheaded as a fox. The proud tender of a new little beard Hobb and I mercilessly thorned him about. Sunday afternoons, he slipped out to smash his fists against the noses of bareknuckle challengers from every corner of the state. No matter the damage to his own face, there he'd be the next morning: brewing coffee, smiling stiff. When the old man thrashed me for miscounting coin, it was Donovan who gave up his meat to cool my ruined eye; Donovan who stitched me up when yardfights went sideways; Donovan who said, "Don't ever let nobody touch you, Lurie, no matter what."

For two years, we shared an attic room. We scrubbed floors and ran the faro layout. We hauled freight and boiled tea to muddy Saurelle's water into whiskey. We laughed through the gray winters, searched for privy-bound lodgers who'd blundered off in the snow. If one of us took fever, the other two followed into illness and back out again like we were going up and down stairs. In the summer of '53, Donovan and I climbed up out of typhoid, but Hobb did not. Old man Saurelle was decent enough to pay for his casket so we wouldn't have to make it ourselves.

Hobb didn't come back around till a few months later. He came soundlessly and without warning. He'd lost his voice in death, it seemed, but not his itch for pickpocketing. I would roll over from wakeful dreams to find his little hand already on my shoulder and some trinket on my pillow: a needle, a thimble, a spyglass. When his want overcame me, it drew me to similar objects. I would stand at the counter while some traveling woman adjusted her spectacles to better study our wares, and my fingers

would ache. Donovan, by this time, was prizefight-
ing in the grip of ceaseless and blinding rage. How
to put to him that his little brother was alighting at
the foot of my mattress in the dark eluded me. So
did any reasoning for why a haul of rings, spectacles,
thimbles, and bullets was massing under my bed. "I
stole them," I lied when Donovan found the box.
"For Hobb." He struck me, then held my head till
my ears stopped ringing. We took the box out to
Hobb's grave and dug a shallow hole to pour all that
theft into—which made Hobb furious, and for long
nights his want kept me awake. I only minded a little.
I hoped that if Hobb's death had made me an older
brother to him, it might also have made Donovan
an older brother to me.

I started another box. The want never seemed to
go away. Sometimes I'd give in to it and lift a watch
or a book, which gave Hobb no end of glee. Later
on, I wondered if his want had gotten into Donovan
the way it did me. If that was what emboldened us
both to robbery. At the outset, our mischiefs were
bored doings, heists only in name. Roadside holdups
of travelers who happened through the clearing
where we shared our midnight whiskey. We had one
sixgun between us, but our quarry didn't know that.
I would follow Donovan out of the bushes and stand
behind him while he aimed the barrel at fat bilks
and jabbering drunks, and every once in a while
some cleric who tried to turn us godward. Pretty
soon, we had a good haul under the bunkhouse floor:

watches, coin purses, papers that probably meant something to somebody. Hobb eased off sitting on the edge of my bed and busied himself sifting through this junk. It was an all right way to go on being together.

Round about that time, Donovan caught a prize-fighter in the brow a little too hard. When the kid roused up, his speech was all cotton and his eyes couldn't fix on a point. The Sheriff came round, asking questions about the fairness of the fight and was Donovan packing his gloves? To Donovan's claim that he wasn't wearing gloves at all came an answering kick in the ribs and the question of what we could offer to make him look the other way. I sacrificed a silver watch from my haul, but a few days later here came the Sheriff, back again, asking, "How come 'Robert Jenkins' is etched on the back of my new timepiece? Ain't he the man who were robbed just last week out on the Landing Road?"

This time, Donovan broke his jaw.

We were on the run all summer before our likenesses began showing up on bounty handbills. In Breton, in Wallis, in bayou camps, we peered into the charcoal renderings that bore our names and laughed at the lack of resemblance. "Might as well meet all this head-on," Donovan said. So the next time we stood up a stagecoach, he made it known that we were the Mattie gang. "Say it back to me now," he told the whip, who mumbled it around the gunbarrel in his mouth.

The next poster offered twice the reward.

We hid out in the barn loft of some laundress half in love with Donovan, who called us gentlemen in company till her neighbors softened up to the idea of having us around. This got us invited to a few suppers. We ranged, hatless and bewildered, through strangers' kitchens. Held hands round the table with curiously smiling whitelace daughters and mumbled our thanks to God for his bounties and mercies. Somehow, nobody turned us in. "Who'd've thought," they all said, "that Peyton County would be lucky enough to hide two boys willing to show the Federals just what Arkansas thinks of northern law?"

We joined forces thereafter with distant Mattie cousins, Avery and Mathers Bennett: dull, happy-cabbage boys from Tennessee. They had more muscle than sense, but Donovan reasoned that two Matties hardly made a gang. With four we could knock over a waystation. We could even knock over a packtrain—and we did, pouring in amongst the wagons in the dark, so the screams lit up like candles around us.

Knocking over a stagecoach in Fordham one night, we ducked an errant pistol-shot from an overbold New York kid. His second try winged Donovan's shoulder. Next thing I knew, I had the kid by the hair and halfway out the cab and the others weren't even stopping me. Newspapers two counties over called it "savagery." It must've been, though I hardly remember anything save wiping my boots after and wondering when I'd started the kicking.

The next poster said:

Wanted:
The Mattie Gang
Contact Marshal John Berger,
Peyton County

"Well, goddamn," Donovan said, with no dearth of pride. "You got the marshals after us now. This is worth celebrating."

My heart was all sour, but celebrate we did. At a bonfire in our honor, I met eyes with a dark-haired girl whose name escapes me now—if I ever knew it at all.

She knew mine, though. Sat right up out of my arms when she heard it later on in the barn. "You the Turk that rides with Donovan Mattie."

"I ain't any sort of Turk."

"People say that New York boy you beat mightn't live."

"Boy?" I said. "He was a man. He wore a suit."

That Donovan was my brother, had saved my life just about every day since he tipped back my hat to study my sorry carcass coming through his door, seemed not to make any difference to her. She climbed down out the loft, and I was left half the night in a heave of terror, alone and missing Hobb almost more than I could bear.

Later that week Donovan led us all into town to get a look at Marshal Berger's posse mounting up to hunt us. The Marshal seemed, even then, older than his years, his brow like a newly turned field. He had a naked upper lip three shades lighter than the rest of his face, and we could tell he was regretful of shaving his mustache by the way he kept covering his mouth with his hand. Donovan and me and the Bennett brothers ranged ourselves in back of the crowd and clapped at the speech he made about the ills of sheltering outlaws.

"These ain't good boys," was his gist. "They're bad-men. Rough as hell. You're doing evil to hide them. Ask yourselves if it's bread and shelter you'd be giving them, were it your kid done for like the New York boy: every rib broke and one eye gone and his teeth kicked down his throat."

I remember wondering what the New York kid's want would be, if he should happen to die and find me. Would he bind me up in the sorrows of all the things he hadn't lived to do? Or press in on me till I gave myself up to the Marshal? Or avenge his death by sending me to my own?

Marshal Berger went on staring out at all our sun-reddened faces. At least half the crowd knew us by sight, but it was Lewis Riffles, the miller's idiot son, who broke silence. "You sure you got good pictures of the Mattie gang? You sure about they height, they weight? Couldn't they be anybody? Couldn't they be right here among us?"

Smiling all the while, Lewis Riffles, and growing brasher with each syllable till titters shot across the square, from one end to the other.

The Marshal stood looking into his own shadow in the dirt, and answered wearily, "Yeah, we got good pictures. Yeah, I reckon they could be among us now." When he'd had enough play, he came down the stairs and took Lewis Riffles by the ear and dragged him to his knees. "All right, all right," Lewis was saying, but anyone could've told you it was too late, his ear a whitening bud vised between the Marshal's fingers. Suddenly he got to squealing and thrashing, and right there in front of us the whole lobe rent off in one long strip, and a bit of red side-burn with it. The Marshal stood over poor Lewis, who lay in the dirt, face-to-face with his ear-bits all dusted as if for a fry-up. Berger said: "Any man stands between me and one of them Mattie animals, I'll do him this way and worse."

He tried hard for us in one ambush after another all year long, as if he didn't know the whole county was holding out on him on account of that broken, earless Riffles kid. They hid us in their henhouses and cellars. They passed us off as kith and kin. Whenever we managed another escape, I thought it must be Hobb, somehow, looking out for us from wherever he was when he wasn't stinging my finger-tips. A bit of miracle every day, sent by our little brother, who only wanted us home and settled.

But then at last came the evening when Donovan's temper finally played out, and the cab of a Butterfield stage we were holding up filled with brief thunder and the blue light of his sixgun. A scream erupted in

all that confusion, and followed us all the way back
to town.

It's funny how you can dance with a certain line,
back and forth, for years—but once you're over it,
you're over completely and for good. A man can get
away with a lot in Arkansas, but not blowing a mag-
istrate's brains out all over his little daughter's lap.
That particular misstep earned us a handbill stuck to
the barn-door:

Wanted for the Murders of
James Pearson of New York
&
The Honorable Magistrate Colin Phillips
of Arkansas:
Donovan Michael Mattie, of Missouri
&
His Small Hirsute Levantine

"Fuck," Donovan said. "That New York kid up
and died after all!"

I was in a dread I hadn't felt since my grave-robbing
days. "Why'd they go on like that about the way
I look?"

"Because being a weird little monkey, you're easiest
to peg." This from Mathers Bennett, who himself
had been born looking like a walleyed carrot. "I say
we give you over, Lurie. We're an easy fucking make
with you tailing us around."

Donovan told him there'd be none of that. Come

evening, he'd shaved my hair down till I was bald as a cane rattler. I looked like one of them madmen that the Jesuits were always leading around.

"But not like any hirsute Levantine, at least," Donovan said.

We rode into the hill country. Split up to blur our trail and slept fitfully in the ditches. Overhead the black trees went creaking and groaning. Sometimes, we passed days without seeing one another. Sometimes Berger's men got close, and the woods filled with the red twilight of their torches.

Well, Mathers caught typhus in a Greybank whorehouse. We emptied our pockets to bribe the madam to keep him hid till he was well again, but she didn't wait two days before giving him up to the Marshal. Mathers hanged without trial, of course, right there off a Greybank beam. We heard about it from a newspaperman in Drury City, who went on to talk about Mathers's last words—a prayer for the cause—and steadfast refusal to give up his accomplices. "I'm a loyal fella," was the gist. "And Matties is my blood. But with them rides, so help me God, a rough little killer Turk what lately shaved his head to evade the law. He goes by Lurie, and though kicking that New York kid to death was just about the closest he ever came to any kind of worth, he definitely ain't a Mattie. Amen."

When Donovan heard this, all the life went out of his face. He bade me put my hat on right away. "You know, he ain't even half-wrong about you."

"What do you mean?" I said desperately. I figured he was fixing to tell me I wasn't a Mattie.

"Well, you're a rough little killer Turk all right. And your head is shaved."

In the green hills above Texarkana, Berger came close. He had hounds, and a keen eye up a tree who clipped me almost right out the saddle. Donovan washed what mud he could out my shoulder and stitched me up in the dark, but I took fever all the same. He laid me in a ditch and covered me with the saddle blanket and packed me in with hearth-heated rocks. "Goddamn," he kept saying, with this strange little faraway smile, "but you can't die when you never even seen the ocean."

What a strange thing to say. Was that where we'd been headed all this time? And would that have been my want—to see the ocean? I couldn't tell. And would it be Donovan I put my want into if I went in the night? I managed to keep myself up on that thought alone almost till morning. But not quite. For when I came round, Donovan was gone. I thought at first it must mean I'd come over the other side—and I remember thinking I didn't feel much want for any damn thing, and certainly not the ocean, and wasn't that funny?

But then I found the bread and water Donovan had left behind for me, and I knew he'd ridden on. I wished I'd been right before: that I'd be dead before he left me. Tracks in the mud where he had ridden quietly away, Hobb's brother and mine. Nothing to remember him save a crust of bread and this old canteen and my fear.

I first filled the canteen in Iron Springs, and searched for him there. I searched for him in Greenwood, too. But it was futile dodging around the truth of his appearance, describing him one way here, another there, lest someone recognize me and put together our association. I slept in alleys. I fed in churches where parish priests got after my soul with all the fire of their convictions, as though they knew I was carrying that little thief Hobb around, along with my own sins, and maybe they could nab us both for God.

I was sitting in a boardinghouse at Miza Ridge when Marshal Berger shambled in with eight men and eased himself into a chair that creaked like it was giving voice to all his own aches. That wily old wolf met the eye of every soul present, and held mine so long I knew he was asking himself how come I looked so familiar. Where did he know me from? I waited till the dance-floor crowd thickened up, and then slipped out a back door and by morning was headed south again.

I aimed to keep moving till the faces on all the bounty bills were strangers to me. One fishing town after another spread its pale lights before me down the coast. I bedded in skiffs, sea-tossed and wondering what would be worse: drifting oarless beyond the breakwater, or waking to find Marshal John Berger looming over me. River barges south of Matagorda offered steadier lodgings. But the brimful stores of ships' holds tempted Hobb. His want grew and grew. He wanted after hooks and bells and sailors' goodluck charms. He closed my hand around coins and boot buckles. His rage, whenever I traded his trinkets for meals, was feverish. For all the weighted jangling of my coat pockets, he thought us empty.

On I went, south along the bays. This succession of weeks, of raggedy people fishing the shallows and squalls loosing streams of black rain, might have continued if, in the spring of what must have been 1856, by the light of a burning sunset, I hadn't climbed the rope ladder of a creaky full-rig with a swordfish prow berthed at the longdock in Indianola. The wind was rising and a final green blaze narrowing out above the waves. I have since wondered whether I remember it so clear because I somehow knew it would be worth remembering, or whether the intervening years have given my memories a sheen of Providence.

Whatever the case, seeing the deck deserted, Hobb got his hooks into me. I searched bivvies and saddle-bags for something to quiet him. He didn't want the strange coffee cup I first laid my hand to, nor a silver bridle. No: what he wanted was a glass bead, deep-water blue, painted up with a dizziness of receding circles, which I drew from a small pack and recognized at once to be an eye, something very like the **nazar** my father had kept in his pocket. I let Hobb have it. I wandered the deck. I filled my canteen at the waterbarrels. Near the stern, a crude barn had been erected, and, making sure I moved unseen, I let myself in, thinking I might shelter till morning.

And there of course—sightless, blundering into a fog of stink and breath, terrified suddenly beyond reason—what should I find but you?

MORNING

AMARGO

Arizona Territory, 1893

TOBY CAME RUNNING BACK FROM THE creek, empty-handed, to tell her he'd found more tracks—down by the creek this time.

"All right," Nora said. "Show me."

She reined up and followed her youngest into the gulch. The trail narrowed between high bluffs and let out among the black imbrications of an ancient riverbed before winding for a quarter mile through cottonwoods and down to the shore. Little remained of the stream now save glossy September mud and the wakes of what few salamanders had managed to evade Toby.

He pointed to where his bucket had dropped. "Them's the tracks."

"Those are," Nora said.

It relieved her to see his hair growing back. Through three sons and seventeen years of motherhood,

shaving had borne out as the only successful campaign against lice, but its effects were decidedly
punitive—Toby looked like a deserter from some
urchin militia, sentenced to bear the badge of his
dishonor. What if, this time, history should fail him,
leaving him bald forever? He made a sorry little man
as it was: too thin for seven, soft and golden and
clewed-up with doubt. Prone to his father's wilding
turn of mind.

This business with the tracks had rooted deep, displacing all his other worries and earning him the
derision of his brothers, Rob and Dolan, who
wouldn't brook a child's ghost story now that they
were so-adamantly men. The only solution they were
charitable enough to entertain—"Just say the word
and we'll bait it, Tobe!"—ran thoroughly against his
inclinations, for Toby had no great wish to **see** the
beast; merely to be believed in the matter of its existence. Last week the boys had taken him out to the
abandoned Flores claim, site of the tracks' initial
manifestation, to cure him of his nonsense. (By what
means Nora could not guess, though she had managed to refrain from warning them to mind his bad
eye. They were her boys. Emmett's sons. Recent out-
bursts aside, they were upright and vigilant, careful
with others in general and with Toby in particular.)
Still, she had waited on the porch until they reappeared in the red boil of twilight, two horses dragging
long shadows. Dolan bobbing stoutly along, Rob a
few yards ahead and so starved-looking at sixteen that

she wondered how he was managing to keep Toby upright in the saddle before him with just one arm.

"Well?" she called. "Did you bare your teeth to whatever's out there?"

Rob lifted him down. "Weren't nothing out there but some grouse and an empty old turtle shell. And we're all agreed that none of them's fixing to haunt Toby ever again."

A tiny smile dragged the corner of Toby's mouth. The matter seemed at an end. But then followed morning after morning of Toby at breakfast, his eyes red with sleeplessness. Chin slipping from his hand. Mishandled eggs staining the henyard in his wake. Nights—while Emmett hunched over his **Sentinel** drafts in the kitchen, and Rob and Dolan lay dead to the world upstairs—Nora put her ear to Toby's door and listened to the restless rasp of his body under the covers.

Predictably, Emmett traced their son's distress to what they were now calling "last year's mischance." Anything that went sideways with Toby could be explained away by it: a fall from horseback last March, indistinct, by all appearances, from any of the dozen Toby had brushed off over the years—so very ordinary in its course that Nora hadn't even bothered to go to him when he fell. "I doubt it could have been helped," Doc Almenara had assured her later, having declared it a miracle that Toby wasn't blinded outright. They had been waiting ever since on the sight in his left eye to return, and for reprieve from some of the accident's other miseries: headaches that set him retching; lightning that streamed through his field of vision; an inability to distinguish waking from dreaming.

He had come to fear the dark and the shapes that roared out at him from the electric chasm of injured sleep. To make matters worse, he mistook Nora's tenderness for pity, which she found unfair—she could not help wanting, on those frequent occasions when he bumped a wall or missed a cup-handle, to seize his little head and hold it in both hands. Had he been too young to question her, or old enough to understand, Toby might have grit his teeth through such attentions. But he was just the right age to find them unbearable.

Luckily, however, it was past him to question why she might be crouching streamside with him now, making a big show of hearing him out.

"Look," he said. "See?"

She looked. Familiar disturbances marred the bank: a crisscross of skunk and quillpig trails, the smooth sidewind of a snake crossing the wash.

"There," Toby said, "and there. See how it's sunk-in at the top?"

He was pointing to a dent about the size of a small plate. The drag of his finger through the mud succeeded only in making it look like a picturebook heart.

"Anything else?"

He showed her where he thought he could see a

few more scuffs scraping off into the sage, and up the old game trail with its trim of heat-withered grass.

"Must've gone up that way," Toby said. "Loosing these rocks as it went."

"Care to offer a thought on what it is?"

"Well, it ain't small." To prove this, he beckoned her to the overgrown hackberry stand just up the shore. Its branches were stripped bare all the way around. The few remaining berries, a withered orrery of orange globes, were all packed way back against the bole.

"See?"

"Not a creature alive won't make quick work of hackberries in a drought, Tobe." She grew irritated. "Save for Josie, it seems. Didn't I tell her come and get the rest of these picked before the birds beat her to it?"

She shouldered in for a fruit and offered it to Toby, but he only squeezed it until its skin snapped and the grit ran between his fingers. Then he wiped his hand on his trouserleg. He was sulling.

"What's the matter?"

"You think I'm telling tales," he said. "You won't even look around."

"Aren't I looking?"

"Not like you really think you gone find anything."

She seized her trouserlegs and shoved into the thicket, pretending to look for sign. The boys still called this hillside "the antelope trail"—though any namesake antelope were long gone, having wised up quickenough to the shoddy little blind Emmett had built at the top of the gulch back when they were newcomers here. These days the slope was a scald of dead grass, one switchback after another twisting all the way up the red face of the bluff. The only heart-beat around might belong to the occasional chaparral cock scurrying from shrub to shrub. Here was one now, of course. It took off the moment her shadow touched it.

She stood in a drowse among the new ironwoods, still pretending. The sun had got into her. Damn near all morning, she had gone without thinking of her thirst. Something miraculous had happened while she slept to make it seem as matter-of-fact as breath-ing. She was slow and warm, and glad now that Toby had delayed her going into town. She could take less frenzied stock of matters. That Emmett was three days late returning from Cumberland with water was not so unusual. He could be no later than this eve-ning, and there was a little water yet in the rainbarrel to last until then. Nor was it unusual to find Rob and Dolan's beds empty. They had managed to pack up in the dark and make their way to the printhouse, as they often did, without waking her. As soon as she had put Toby's fears to rest, she would ride into town with their lunch—the long way, calm and unhurried. She might even feel brave enough to stop by Desma's place and pick up the elk steaks, after all. Call on Harlan, perhaps, and see if the Sheriff's day was slow-going.

"There's nothing up here, Tobe."

"You ain't gone but ten yards."

"Toby." He wouldn't look at her. "When do you figure I can turn back? Once I'm snake-bit? What'll you do then, all alone, and your brothers way out in town?" She had drifted somehow into trying to coax a smile out of him. "You gone throw your mama over your shoulder, carry her all the way back up the draw by yourself?"

His voice was ruinously sad. "That's all right, Mama. Please come back."

She went on. Stowaway burrs dimpled her hem. She climbed the narrowing trail to its first hairpin, where the undergrowth lay flattened over the path. A huge, brown grasshopper sailed from stalk to stalk, becoming a distant rustle. Some twenty yards above her, snags of moss were outspread across the brush. As sun-burnished and red as the dead girl she and Emmett had dragged out of a cave down in the hollow their first summer here. Kindling crisp. In the places where her muscle had dried out, the skin had stiffened and dented. A thatch of orange moss, just like this, capped her skull. No sign of how she'd got there, though Emmett had notioned she must have crawled in to get away from the heat and never crawled out. Grinning to herself for a hundred years—or a thousand, they hadn't been able to tell.

"There's nothing, Tobe."

Below, her son was back to frowning at the bank. "Don't it look—well—**cloven** to you, Mama?"

"No." She watched him. "Why would it?"

He shrugged a little, but his real concerns were finally loose now, and there was no pretending otherwise. Interest in cloven hooves, like every other recent absurdity, could only point back to Josie, Emmett's ward and occult cousin.

"Pig hooves are cloven," Nora said. "Remember what those look like?"

"I don't hardly."

Nora held up two fingers. "They leave a trail like moth wings." She went back down to him, and they looked at the red mud together. "It's not cloven, Tobe. No matter what Josie's been putting in your head."

"She ain't putting nothing."

"Well she certainly isn't helping your elocution."

All the way back along the creekbed, the empty bucket clanked against his thigh. His free hand was stuffed in his pocket, out of her reach.

BACK AT THE TOP OF THE GULCH, TOBY stopped. "Where's the dogs, Mama?"

She was hot and out of breath, and she didn't know. But his question had finally flushed out the strange sense of absence that had goaded her all morning. It wasn't just that the boys had already fared off, or that Emmett's ongoing delay had forced her to brace for yet another wretched, waterless day. No, there had been something else, too, something under or around it all, and now it struck her: the dogs. The dogs were gone—four of them, possibly five if that old amorous one had survived his latest dalliance with whatever coyote bitch had most recently turned his head. Their din—feral and ungovernable as they were, sounding off from every corner of the farm at every hour of the day, and driving Emmett to empty threats of execution—was her constant companion, and in its absence stretched a stillness so vast the small music of the grasses could not rise to fill it.

"The boys must have taken them," Nora said.

"Where?"

She thought about it. "Hunting?"

For the first time all day, Toby laughed. "Mama," he said. "How silly."

He went on ahead of her toward the house. It sat against the bluff with the melted sun in its windows and a black cloud—the telltale sign of Josie's fried eggs on the make—sieving through every crack around the door. Of late, Nora had found herself envisioning what might become of the place when the Larks, too, finally played out. When Rob, his patience overdrawn, finally joined some north-bound cattle drive; and Dolan lucked into an apprenticeship—perhaps, with God's mercy, under the benevolent hand of some patient judge; and Emmett inevitably got his way, abandoned the newspaper, and bundled Nora and Toby and his ancient mother into the wagon and set course for his next venture in some nameless camp, if there still existed such a thing in this world. The house would fall silent. Mice, having prospected every last crumb, would nest in the eaves. Rattlesnakes would follow. The scrub oaks, with their thirsty roots, would wander down the hill, creeping, by and by, over the jackfence and over Evelyn's little headstone and down toward the outbuildings. The yard would go to seed, all those hard-fought grasses returning in their prickly mats to outman the descendants of Nora's cabbages. Perhaps a late summer storm might blow the barn down. Perhaps a prickly pear, small and round, would begin its slow ascent through the floor in one of the downstairs rooms. Soon some quiet autumn evening would find the farm just another massif of slanted roofs, and the lightless windows would draw some desperate neighbor to probe their well, as she and Emmett had done when the Floreses—Rodrigo and Selma, and Toby's little friend Valeria—had pulled up stakes last year without warning. Gone without goodbye, in the custom of surrender.

Watching Emmett stand in the Floreses' dusty foreyard and guess how long their well had been dry had been bad enough—but then came the greater mistake of going into the house, where a host of small heartbreaks lay waiting. The beds all made up. Boxes of old cards and letters still in the drawers. Pictures left by the front door because they had obviously been considered, deemed too frivolous or heavy, and jettisoned on the porch. The silence that overwhelmed Nora and Emmett in that house had lasted through their evening chores and followed them to bed, where they had nevertheless set about each other with uncharacteristic vigor. Some hours later, sleepless despite her exhaustion, Nora had watched Emmett raise himself from their twisted blanket and balance on the windowsill to reach the ledge high above their headboard.

"What's got into you?"

"You'll see," Emmett said. He was still unclothed and a little out of breath. He worked a nail loose and began scratching something into the wood.

"What are you writing?"

He surprised her with a smile that shed ten years from his eyes. "Emmett, Nora, and their boys lived and were happy here."

"What about Evelyn?" she'd wanted to ask—for sure enough, Evelyn was already in her ear, muttering: **Yes! What about me?** She sounded more incredulous than hurt, which was fitting for a seventeen-year-old girl—as she would have been, as Nora imagined her. Seventeen and incredulous and asking a not-unreasonable question: What about her? Hadn't she, too, once lived in this house? Hadn't she gone on living in it, persisting as she did in Nora's imagination? And if she'd been a real spirit, rather than the imagined manifestation of their long-dead child, would the decampment Emmett now seemed to be planning not leave her to haunt this place, horribly and unimaginably alone?

Over the last year this idea had grown in Nora, and its growth had crept between them somehow, like ice between planks. Perhaps, if she had mentioned it to Emmett that night, this would not have happened. But Emmett had seemed at such blissful remove, so pleased and absorbed by his scribbling, that Nora couldn't bring herself to pierce him with such questions. Instead, she had drawn the covers around her chin. "That's a fine glut of nonsense, Mister Lark."

"I reckon it's a damn lovely truth," he said. "We should remind ourselves of it more often."

It was so unlike him to be this extravagantly wistful. There was no recourse save to tease him. "I'm sure you're not writing one damn thing, Mister Lark."

"Of course I am."

"Well, if you are I'll bet you're only writing 'in this house, Emmett Lark brooked a lot of nonsense from his wife, God help his soul.'"

"Here, look for yourself, if you don't believe me." She let him help her up, but even standing on tiptoe brought her nowhere near eye-level of the ledge. She persisted in teasing him about it. In the intervening months, whenever some quarrel erupted between them, or he disappeared like this, she became more and more convinced he hadn't written anything there at all.

What a thing to say—"Emmett, Nora, and their boys lived and were happy here." Well, the living could not be denied. But she doubted whether any of them could stand before the court of heaven and truthfully lay claim to happiness.

Except Toby, of course. The eerier and more inhospitable a place, the happier he seemed. There he was in the foreyard, cheerfully waving her down.

"Look!" he cried. "Gramma's escaped again!"

Emmett's mother, Missus Harriet, sat on the front porch with her face tipped sunward. Her wheelchair—older than the Territory, and on loan to them from Doc Almenara for so long Nora figured they must own it by now—had truly

disintegrated into something monstrous. Cane curls
fanned out from its wicker back in all directions.
Where they met the fingers of whoever happened to
be pushing it, they drew blood. The huge, rusted
forewheels gave the whole conveyance the look of
some bedraggled survivor of Pharaoh's army. Its
present charioteer—sixty now, perhaps a little older,
and still the battle-ax she'd been when she came to
them from Kansas—had been immobilized two
years ago by a stroke. Robbed, if not of her appetites
and aversions, at least of the means to voice them.

Toby backed the old woman carefully into the
kitchen, where Josie was prodding a skillet of pulver-
ized corncakes in the midst of the usual bedlam:
charred eggs and smoke; the wide-flung oven belching still more heat into the kitchen. Two breads, left
to rise overnight, had burst out of their pans like
dancehall girls leaning over the rail. The sight of
them sent a bolt of panic through Nora. She
had mixed them last night in the grip of optimism,
still listening for Emmett's wheels on the drive—still
counting on all the things water would allow, a long
drink and laundry, perhaps even a bath—and now
here they sat: two bloated mistakes that had brought
the entire household not one, but two, cups closer
to the bottom of the bucket.

Not yet seven in the morning, and already she was
shouting at Josie.

"Didn't I tell you get that bread baked?" In one
swift motion, the girl threw the pans in the oven and

kicked the door shut. "And didn't I tell you never leave Missus Harriet out on the porch? People die sundrowned here."

Josie looked aghast. "I'd never leave her, ma'am—she must've escaped again."

"Don't lie, goddamn it."

"She keeps doing it, Mama," Toby put in. "She manages it somehow when nobody's looking."

"Lies cut holes in the fabric of Heaven, Toby, and make all the little angels fall out."

"So does saying 'goddamn.'"

"Look." Her mother-in-law's face was beginning to glow around the furrows. "She's sunstruck."

Josie bustled in to wipe the old lady's brow. "May I give her some water?"

"I suppose you'll have to."

"You mustn't keep getting away from me, Missus Harriet." Her anxious little face was stern. "You'll get me in Dutch."

The dram of water she measured out mercifully hadn't reduced the bucket by much—there was still enough to cover the bottom of the ladle, enough for a small drink, perhaps for everyone, perhaps even Nora herself.

"How much is there left in the springhouse?"

"I hardly know, ma'am."

"Well don't be giving her any more until you find out!"

Josie hurried into her hat. She was "that sorry, ma'am"—she was always that sorry, and there were countless transgressions to be that sorry for. Josie had the hazel eyes and broad forehead of Emmett's far-flung Scots kin. Her cheeks and throat were scattershot with freckles that flared an obscene pink after half a second in the sun. A triad of clefts fissured the bridge of her nose whenever she was under duress, and Nora was beginning to feel sorry for these hard-working lines. They might as well stake up for keeps for all the rest they got between admonitions.

Passing Toby in the corridor, the girl grazed a hand over his bristly head. He seized at her and said in what he thought was a whisper: "Mama don't think the tracks are cloven. They don't strike her as tracks at all."

Josie stooped down to him. Dark lines laddered the back of her dress—a rare sign of mortality, Josie sweating. Born of woman after all. "How do they strike **you**?" she said. She, too, thought she was whispering. She thought Nora couldn't see the small shrug of Toby's shoulders, or the way Josie's hair met his stubbled little forehead.

"They're tracks," said Toby.

"Well, then, that's so. What we see with our hearts is often far truer than what we see with our eyes."

Having wafted this profundity, Josie took her leave. Her ridiculous hat, crowned with turgid burlap sunflowers, presented almost too great a temptation when it came bobbing by the window moments later. It could be dislodged with the mere flinging of a shutter. But then the hat's occupant might be knocked down or, given Nora's luck, knocked out. And the day would fall to waste: confusion, reproach, water wasted on cleaning her up, hours wasted on summoning the doctor, tears wasted on patching up that pale forehead. And hadn't they all had their fill of stitches last night?

Nora resumed her calculations. There were two, perhaps two and a half cups of water left in here. Filling at least one bladder in town and boiling a little more from the rainbarrel would restore the bucket to almost half-depth. They had gotten by on less all day. For now, she had only to go on resisting thirst herself—a feat more easily managed when she was not watching others drink.

Perhaps inevitably, Toby came in frowning. "I'm thirsty."

"Want some water?"

"No, Mama. I know you're awful worried."

"There's a drop of coffee left."

He made a face. "It's two days old!"

He stood on tiptoe anyway and peered into the kettle.

"Are we square about those tracks, Tobe?"

"Yes ma'am."

"Toby."

"Well, Pa would believe me."

Of this, she had no doubt. "Why not show him when he gets back?"

"Dolan says he ain't ever coming back."

He clapped the coffeepot shut and began thumbing hunks of corncake apart, one for himself, one for Gramma. Whatever nascent glimmer of forgiveness Nora had been brooding since the previous night dissipated. No amount of entreaty or admonition could make the boys understand that careless talk could not be had around Toby. Nothing escaped him. He was always listening, always mulling—especially when he appeared not to be. A perceptive child, she'd told them, casting about for a diplomatic way to put it— **perceptive**. Yes, more perceptive than any of them: more perceptive than Papa; more than Josie; more even than Dolan, who by his own esteem was the very paragon of perceptiveness, declared himself perceptive in the way of Greek poets, really, capable of perceiving for the county, and happy to tell you all about it. Well here was the harvest of their ongoing underestimation of their little brother: he had overheard last night's racket. In frightening him, it had naturally resurrected all the other things he found frightening, with cloven hooves, and all the devilry they bespoke, right in the vanguard.

"Missus Lark!" She was in such froth she almost failed to notice the premature return of Josie's hat, which shot past the window again and reappeared moments later in the doorway—with Josie wilding under it. "Missus Lark! Something's got into the springhouse."

"THERE." JOSIE TUGGED AT HER ARM. "You see?"

The springhouse crouched in a copse of scrub oaks at the far end of the yard, but nothing was visible for all the branches, save a glimpse of light-stippled tin Nora supposed must be the roof, and a sliver of door, which jawed a little on its hinges, first this way, then that, clattering faintly where it slapped back off the jamb.

"What is it?"

"I don't know, ma'am. Something's stuck the door."

"Well is it man or"—she veered at the last possible moment—"animal?"

But it was too late. "Beast," Toby said. He had gone very still in the tangle of Josie's arms, his whole mien more reminiscent of some thunderstruck little dime-novel urchin than a real child now, all of which deepened Nora's unease into irritation.

"Between the pair of you," she said, "we might as well be living on Herschel's moon."

She seized the shotgun from behind the kitchen

door and crossed the yard, sunblind. Two agonizing courses of sweat had begun to race down her ribs. She could feel each distinctly, and really smell herself besides, a needless reminder of how long this entire household had gone unlaundered.

The springhouse was a hopeless early construction: an adobe half-dome that had supported a succession of failing roofs before Emmett finally settled on this ill-fitted tin sheeting that all but defeated the structure's purpose. The door, which came into view as she rounded the **huerta**, was indeed open. There was something lodged in the jamb. She couldn't quite make it out. But from here, it looked like a boot.

"Hullo?" She cocked the hammer. "Come out slow, you're stood down."

It would turn out to be a man, of course. Trespassers never failed to be. Women—even the Indian ones—were good enough to come by the front door. Roughnecks, on the other hand, were only ever surprised in transgression: sleeping in the barn loft, or breaking for the woods with an armful of eggs or—once—forcibly accosting one of Nora's sheep. Time and time again, she had managed to keep her voice firm and her aim steady, knowing all the while that she was more afraid of these bummers than they were of her—a truth made glaring on the single occasion of Rob's encountering one such drifter. A smallish man with a mustache so dirty it appeared almost green, he had emerged from the wreckage of their henhouse and stood staring at Nora with sullen, impassive eyes, and then advanced as though the shotgun she pointed at him were a fistful of flowers. But when Rob burst, hollering, from somewhere behind her, how that ugly little bastard had lit out! She'd never seen a fella so small take such bounding strides.

This, however, was different. Rob was not here. He was in town. He would not be putting in a sudden, timely appearance to rout this sonbitch. It was just herself now, and the gun—which she prayed had not been discharged since she'd last checked it—and the owner of whatever footwear her springhouse door was thumping against.

She tried again. "You'll find nothing to rob here." And then: "I can fix you a meal if you'll only come out."

Desma would be tickled by this ruse. Town stories had it that a dusty badman had shambled in off the flats one roasting afternoon and surprised Desma in the act of washing her linens. The roughneck was ball-jointed and thin as a cur, and looked like whatever had happened to him out there in the desert had been a hell of his own making. So when he fell to his knees and begged for a drink, Desma just said, "Hold up—can't you see I'm on my way through something? You just wait one goddamn minute while I finish what I'm doing, mister, and then you'll have my attention." And went right on slapping her sheets against the washboard until the roughneck slumped over and died. "It weren't my intent to kill him," was all she had to say in the aftermath, "but I only had that last bit of water I needed to finish up the washing, and he didn't frankly look like the caliber of man you'd waste spit on."

But even the promise of sustenance did not prompt this enigmatic obstruction to budge from the springhouse door. Minutes went by. Nora shielded her eyes and looked back toward the porch. Josie still had her son strangleheld in the shade.

There was nothing left to do but go forward. A few more steps brought the object to view: not a boot after all, but a leather cinch of some kind, worn as hell, though ordinary enough, and wedged sideways so that its buckle caught the light. She nudged the door with her foot, and a triangle of sun yawned across the springhouse floor. She took in the unremarkable shambles of the place—the hooked sausages in slow, perpetual rotation, the tins crammed along the rear shelf, the jerking motes that cohered finally into flies—and for a moment nothing seemed out of place. Then a sour blast of whiskey and rot gusted at her, and she saw: sometime in the night, the shelf nearest the door had been dislodged, and an avalanche of bottles and jars had met their demise on the ground.

Before her eye found the rainbarrel, she saw its lid on the floor, and knew, without seeing, that it was on its side.

Before it lay the carcass of some small, desiccated bird.

The water, Mama, Evelyn said. **It's gone.**

***

THE SIGHT OF HER TEARING OUT OF THE springhouse took them both by surprise—but they scattered all the same. Nora was only fast enough to manage a single swipe at the hem of Toby's shirt before he sprang out of reach and scrambled up the porch.

"Come here," she said.

"I can't see, Mama." He hovered, glaring reproachfully down at her. His bad eye flitted like a jarred moth. It never seemed to do this when he wasn't being asked to account for some grave mistake.

"That latch was wide open. Weren't you meant to lock up last night?"

He shook his head. "Josie was."

But Josie, too, had already flown out of reach. "I latched it, ma'am," she called from across the yard. "I know I did."

Of course. It had been Josie sent out for whiskey last night after Dolan's overwrought suppertime eruption. An odd, appalling moment that needn't have happened if he had just left off badgering Nora about his father for once—if he'd given up bewailing how long Papa had been gone, and that Nora seemed angrier about the lack of water than what folks were saying in town about Papa and the Sanchez boys and the suspicious wagon, and all the rest of that over-cooked nonsense, till eventually he was shouting. He'd called Nora—what? Unseeing and foolhardy. "I see you've learnt some new words," Nora shot back, pleased with how readily the reply had come to her, at least for a brief, triumphant moment. "Unseeing and foolhardy," Dolan had said again, of her—and then put his fist through the door. It was so absurd she would have laughed if she hadn't been laughing already. But then his knuckles turned out to have been rutted to the bone, and the entire household found itself rooted stupidly there in the gloaming of his rage. It struck her that leaving Dolan to twist in mangled distress might caution any onlookers against similar displays. But then her sympathies got the better of her. This was Dolan, after all. More taken aback than anyone by his own outburst. Welling with confusion and what turned out to be a great deal of blood. So out Josie went for the whiskey, and the rest of the evening had devolved into the candlelit stitching of flesh.

Perhaps it was inevitable that some part of Josie's already tenuous judgment should lapse in all that confusion. But no, Josie insisted. She had locked the door, ma'am. Last year's run-in with that bear had righted her for good, cured her of assuming any doors were fastened or windows latched. She was real careful about locking up now. She could remember the feel of the bolt against her fingers. Yes, yes she could. In the lifeless air of the springhouse, she raised her fist as though it still held the evidence that might exonerate her.

Nora gave her a little shove toward the rainbarrel. "Then how did this happen?"

"God preserve us, Missus Lark."

"We will need His preservation now more than ever, Josie, since we hardly seem capable of preserving ourselves."

She could picture it so clearly: the door creaking on its hinges all night, tempting the dogs, who were always prodding and scrounging around anyway, to nose it open and down the rainbarrel trying to water— like every other damn thing in this drought—and then flee to wherever they were currently waiting out their masters' retribution.

"Goddamn, Josie, but what a mess."

"I did lock it!"

"Don't lie."

"I did, ma'am. I know I did."

"Then account for this. Did the dogs hop up on each others' shoulders, circus-like, and unbolt the door? Or did I go sleepwalking and open it myself?"

"I really don't know, ma'am."

"Perhaps your 'lost man' left it open to spite you, then."

She felt, before the words even left her tongue, the

cruelty of conjuring this particular apparition. But it was too late now. She was rewarded with having to watch Josie's face tighten into a rictus of misery. "I beg your pardon, ma'am—but it's just plain wrong to hoot at the other living."

An uneasy silence lengthened out. "I only mean to say: this is not an act of Providence, Josie. The door was left unlocked."

Toby was crouching over the dead bird—a windhover, perhaps, or some other insubstantial raptor—so close that his nose might brush at any moment against its dry, flattened skull.

"Leave off that thing."

"Don't you think it's some sort of omen, Mama?"

"Certainly—of our worsening prospects." There was a crust of something in her hair, just above the nape of her neck, and she scratched at it until her nails came away pink. "That was the very end of our supply. Josie—do you understand?"

At last, Josie did. You could always tell a Damascus moment was upon her when her hands went to her forehead. "Almighty God, Missus Lark—the water! I am just **that** sorry."

Now commenced a drawn-out treatise, of which Nora absorbed very little. She was thinking gloomily of the depleted kitchen bucket. She was thinking, too, suddenly and viscerally, of her mother, and the gusto with which Ellen Francis Volk had committed herself to the thrashing of servant girls. Whatever solace her mother seemed to find in throwing these sapling women over her knee had mystified Nora—until now. Now, she understood perfectly that her mother's rage—a twisting, gasping, biting thing, indigenous to the Reilly women of her maternal line—must have loosened a little as the girls' bare bottoms and her own hand turned the same blistering shade of red. Nora could well imagine herself in the teeth of that impulse. But she could remember, too clearly, witnessing this punishment, feeling her own face tickle until it had contorted into a kind of hysterical awe, laughing and crying in simultaneous horror of the executioner and sympathy for the condemned. None of that could happen here— not with Toby standing by, pretending to study the ground but listening, all the while, to every detail of Josie's protestation. Which was winding down now, thank God, for Josie seemed to have got herself into a knot. "What I mean, ma'am, is that I can't imagine how I could have left it open, since I remember my own hand on the latch. I do. But—if I did ma'am, if that happened to happen, I am **that** sorry. I suppose you'd be right in telling me that I should have gone out to make certain, but I didn't think of it. And even if I'd thought of it—well—I doubt you would've let me, ma'am."

Let her? Nora didn't understand. "Why on earth not?"

"Well—it had fallen dark."

"And?" She glanced back at the house. It was, at most, thirty yards. Hardly the Panama crossing. She turned around just in time to catch a guilty exchange of glances between her youngest and her ward disintegrating like the tail of a comet. "Why wouldn't I let you, Josie?"

"Well, ma'am," Josie said. "On account of the beast."

＊

AT THE TOP OF THE DRIVE, NORA FOUND herself turning to look right down the empty road. An old habit, frustratingly revived since the Floreses' flight had made the Lark place, once more, the northernmost habitation for miles. The last known point before the page went blank. Then she spurred old Bill left and rode toward town along the canyon road. It was just coming on fall, and the valley was making a brilliant spectacle of its own death. Yellow detonations stood like signal fires above the sub-ducted creeks where the cottonwoods, at least, had managed to find water.

Toby had vowed to have the springhouse righted by the time she returned, and Nora had left it at that. It was enough for now—any further sanction-ing would fall to Emmett, who could always be counted on to mete out the crushing blow of his disappointment. Nora would stay out of it. She had gone too far already in barbing Josie about the lost man—though she would not, now or later, be cowed into making amends for having done so, no matter how the boys felt about it. The most recent of Josie's apparitions, the lost man was naturally likewise the most tiresome. He had manifested on the ridge some weeks previous as a hollow, lingering redness that closed around Josie and stopped her picking any more of the season's last piñon. "I had to flee home right away," she had announced rather tremulously to the entire kitchen. "But I can't say he didn't follow me."

Dolan, ever the first to take her at her word, sprang to his feet and made a big show of looking out the door. "Did he mean you harm?"

Josie was already wilting into a chair and reaching for a cup of water—an unnecessarily generous one—outheld by Rob. "No. But he did fill me with sorrow. He don't know where he is at all."

An interminable, wasted afternoon's interrogation revealed that Josie had no sense of the lost man's aspect or intentions, nor the nature of his demise. She knew only that he was not gone for good. Talking of nothing else for days did little to steel her for his return—which surprised her, quite conveniently, while she was clearing snakes' nests from the overgrowth at the top of the claim. Josie was mid-swing when she felt him arrive. Into the bushes went her machete. Down went Josie, face-first into the thickets, hurrying to make contact. As Nora understood this carry-on—which she had personally witnessed once or twice, usually at parties when revelers pickled enough to welcome a bit of nonsense had goaded Josie to reach across the great divide to their dead kin—séance involved a great deal of sing-song and mumbling. But it was the hand-holding where Nora's belief ran aground—for whose hand did Josie hold when she was all by herself?

"Perhaps if we went out with you," Nora said, "and stood around in a circle, morning and noon, you might induce him to reveal his desires."

As this had earned her a look of general outrage from every man in the room, Nora had kept all further suggestions to herself. And in any case, the lost man had not returned since.

"No doubt he will reappear the first instant she is tasked with something more arduous than sewing," Nora had concluded a week later, climbing into bed.

Emmett shook his head. "It's a wonder to me that you can be so taken in by Rey Ruiz's water-witching, and yet treat our poor Josie with nothing but contempt."

The comparison was absurd. Rey Ruiz had made a science of divining water. Perhaps his implements were a bit crude—but willow sticks aside, he was more reliable than any cloud massing in the distance. Countless people owed their livelihoods to his proficiency at reading sign.

Josie, on the other hand, had been born to absolute chicanery. She was the daughter of Emmett's cousin Martha and the mesmerist Reverend Kincaid, whose five other wives she had grown up likewise calling "mother." As Nora understood it, Josie was the only child of that entire dubious coven and the sole heritor of the Reverend's celestial gifts. These withdrawn, enigmatic people extorted money from nitwits in a dark house on Mott Street. All their séance and card reading and divination, however, had failed to predict the typhus outbreak to which they succumbed within days of each other when Josie was but thirteen. Alone in the world, Josie found herself the custodian of a ramshackle townhouse and all its attendant debts. She refused to set foot outside. For a few lean years, she performed readings by mail, and in this manner struck up a correspondence with a certain Mister George A. Hamill of San Francisco. Friendly letters quickly turned to betrothal. But he, being a gentleman, insisted that such a union be superintended by the appropriate parties: in this case, Miss Claver's Heart & Hand Club, which connected Atlantic State brides with reputable men of the West. The necessary arrangements had somehow managed to cost Josie her remaining inheritance—which disappeared, along with Miss Claver, all evidence of her Heart & Hand Club, and Mister George A. Hamill himself—while Josie was writing verse about the landscape on a train somewhere east of Cheyenne.

These facts had been remitted to the Larks in a long letter from Emmett's sister, Lenore, the day Emmett brought Josie home from the Prescott station. Lenore was raising cattle and eight children on the Powder River, and her patience with Josie had played out. The girl was, in her words, "a gentle soul." But Lenore's husband preached the gospel. He did not think it fitting to tolerate communion with spirits under his roof. The loss of more than half his herd to a calamitous winter was as plain a sign from the Almighty as he needed. Josie would have to live elsewhere.

Nora had looked up from six crammed pages of Lenore's atrocious penmanship to see Emmett smiling sheepishly at her. He drummed his hat. "We can scarcely turn away another pair of hands," he whispered. "And I thought—well. I thought you might like a girl about the place."

You have **a girl about the place,** Evelyn huffed in her ear.

Dwarfed by hat and carpetbag, and managing, by virtue of her pinched face, to look simultaneously anxious and contented, Josie Kincaid had hovered in the corridor like the chaff of some sad dream.

The sight of her filled Nora with dread. But Emmett was already seizing on her silence. "At least we'll have spared her from the whorehouse. Can there be any doubt it's where she would have ended up, had she made San Francisco?"

"You always were a soft touch for lost causes."

Josie's demerits manifested right away. Six months with Lenore in Wyoming had done little to harden her up for country life. She slept lightly, ate little, and swooned often. Ordinary ranch implements confounded her. She was likelier to use a hammer the wrong than the right way around. She had an aversion to killing anything, especially mice, which she caught and freed in the evening fields with the help of Dolan—who laid eyes on her, decided that theirs was a love preordained, and quickly became the world's most knowledgeable and benevolent mouser. Her belief in the oracular power of birds enkindered her at once to Toby, who took to following her around as if she had just stepped forth from some storybook. Churning around in Josie's mind was an almanac of tincture remedies, Oriental magic, occult notions, absurd natural histories—especially those detailing the monstrous lizards unearthed by Cope and Marsh—all of which she talked ceaselessly about, making household rides into Amargo unbearable.

But the girl was not entirely without use. For one thing, she talked to Gramma. Not in the way an ordinary person might address an invalid—which, during her lifetime, Nora had learned was similar to the way most people might address a dog—but conversationally: with accommodating syntax, pauses to allow for Gramma's imagined reply. You'd round the corner to find Josie and Gramma in the kitchen, sphinxlike, locked eye to eye in wordless confab. Afterwards, Josie might say, "Missus Harriet don't like the look of the garden this year. Says there's not enough rain in the world to save them cabbages." And for all of Nora's aggravation, the old lady would seem a little more smug in her armored chair. A little more present. This was the sole, undeniable boon of Josie's tenure: she kept the old lady's cogs turning.

Owing to Gramma's age, however, Nora had begun to suspect that this was a gift compromised by its connection to Josie's cardinal power: communion with the dead.

The dead, whom Josie called the "other living," were apparently everywhere. They announced themselves to her in town; on the road; at church. Their sentiments were revealed to her abruptly and unbearably. She might be riding along, content enough, and suddenly find herself so dismal that she would double over and whisper: "I feel a lonely girl here." And then whosoever happened to have the misfortune of accompanying her would be obliged to stand there while Josie felt around for this unmoored soul with her mind, sometimes for hours.

This unwelcome eccentricity was further poisoned by the fact that the dead seemed outnumbered only by living affiliates who wished to commune with them. Word of a clairvoyant at the Lark place had gone roaring through town the instant the girl arrived. To Nora's provocation, visitors began appearing on her porch with pies and pan dulce and other neighborly tributes. They lingered for hours, bashfully sidling up to the subject—could the mistress of the house possibly be persuaded, oh would she ever be so kind as to consider asking Josie to summon a brother, a mother, some friend long-deceased?

"Not in this house," was Nora's general position.

But Emmett was giving. Emmett was curious. Emmett was determined to see the girl in her element. "The Paloma House has offered to host a séance," he told Nora.

"Now what on earth would possess Moss Riley to do a thing like that?"

"I believe he has some words for a cousin who passed on while Moss still owed him money. And God knows he needs the business."

"I'm not sure crowding his parlor with imaginary ghosts will bring the throngs back to Amargo."

But crowd his parlor with imaginary ghosts was exactly what Moss Riley did: first in April, and then again in June. Soon enough, Emmett found himself escorting Josie to town for séance every other Thursday. He would sit against the parlor wall while the lamps were dimmed and the curtains drawn, and watch the candlelit faces of Ash River prominents in their haunted evening finery: the new mayor's new wife; the schoolmaster; even the daughter of one of the Stock Association bigmen. They had come all the way back to Amargo to mill nervously in the creaking ruin of the Paloma House Hotel and make their peace. One after another, they outlaid their regrets to Josie. The mayor's wife had lost a sister in childhood. She longed to explain that she had not intended all those small, daily cruelties that sisters visit upon each other, and for which she'd thought she would have a lifetime to atone. Jack Turner was after a lost compatriot from Gettysburg; he wanted to confess that despite promises to return the dead soldier's journals to the mother who mourned him, he had failed to do so and sent only a letter, and was awful regretful of this lapse now that he was getting too far along in years to travel anymore. And so on and so forth.

More intriguing to Emmett than even the details of these confessions was Josie's occasional, staggering accuracy about intensely private matters: childhood endearments, deathbed confessions. And then there were the sourceless rappings that sometimes erupted around the room while she was in the thick of her visions. Emmett was not too prideful to admit that, having approached the whole thing with an air of skeptical curiosity—either Josie was the genuine article, or he would uncover the means by which she got up to her tricks—he was surprised to find himself still casting about for a conclusion six months later.

Complaining to Desma Ruiz about it, Nora had said: "Emmett started out thinking he would play Seybert to Josie's Fox: trick her into an admission of fraudulence and write it all up for the **Sentinel**." She put down her cup of tea. "But now here we are: he's all but ready to declare her holy."

If there was one person whose disdain of spiritualist practices exceeded Nora's own, it was Desma.

"Want me to try the girl's mettle? I could call down to Amargo next Thursday and ask after my dead husband. Ask her: Do you see a short, bearded bummer, wearing a stolen shirt and sporting a gambler's bullet in his skull? And will he tell you where he hid all that money he stole from me?"

She had meant her first husband, Joseph Gris; her current one, Rey, a smiling colossus of a man, had been standing behind her, still very much alive—at least for the time being.

Rey said: "If she does manage to summon up that sonbitch, make sure and ask him if it's hot enough where he is now."

"Rey," Desma said testily.

His hand vanished among her curls. "Don't reckon the dead can hear me, Desma. And if they can, so—they're well warned of the company they're keeping. Joseph Gris **was** a sonbitch."

Week after week, Emmett and Josie clattered off together, side by side in the dray: he falsely somber but humming with excitement; she veiled in taffeta like some tragic widow in a play, clutching her planchette in its black velvet box.

The bereaved came and went, thinning out until only the guiltiest remained. And all the while, not a word praising or condemning the whole absurd pantomime appeared in the **Sentinel**.

Then April came, and—as the old folks put it—Rey woke up dead.

Doc Almenara declared that Rey's heart had simply given out. It was a surprise to all, though it should not have been: Rey had been tall enough to stoop coming through any door in the county, tall enough to pluck stranded children from trees. The Reverend Miles, who had tolerated all the furor around Josie in staid dismay, used the opportunity of Rey's burial to point out that there were fewer people assembled here—"to send to God a very fine man, a pillar of the community, the finest Mexican who ever lived"—than there had been at the Paloma House on any given Thursday in months.

"I hope you're pleased with yourself," Nora told Emmett afterwards. "You've managed to abet Josie in upstaging the church."

"I can think of no better way to honor Rey. He would have preferred séance over service."

"How can you bear to have us affiliated with a hoaxer?"

"Darling, whether her powers are real or not, Josie is a true believer. She doesn't think she's hoaxing anybody. There's not an ounce of harm in her."

"There's plenty of harm in telling people she can talk to their dead."

He folded his arms. "Don't you talk to Evelyn?"

She had not expected to feel so wounded—but then she had not expected him to sound so gleeful in catching her out, either. He was only aware of her furtive confabs with their dead daughter because Nora had confessed to them in an agitated state, at the very edge of sleep, some distant night when Emmett had returned from town so maudlin with Christmas punch she'd believed him incapable of retaining a single word she said. "She was only just beginning to laugh," he'd whispered through un-expected tears. "How I miss her." It had felt safe, even necessary, to tell him how that laugh had grown and changed with the girl she still imagined roaming this house.

That he had remembered after all, and could now bring himself to fling it at her in defense of Josie, blew through her like cold rain.

"That," she managed, "is not the same thing."

THERE WAS STILL NO ONE ELSE ON THE road when she climbed up out of the valley to the last stretch of hardpan, and urged her horse to the edge of the Cortez **aguaje.** It was a brackish tank, near-empty now and tenanted by a few stranded frogs that peered up at her from the mud. Once, in a summer almost as dry as this one, Nora had carried this brown mire home and the boys had rigged up a sieving line with nothing but two buckets and a silk scarf they'd begged her to sacrifice for this purpose. "Trust me, Mama," Dolan had said, small and newly spectacled, humming with the prospect of replicating a trick he'd read about. "Silk'll work best." It had been a miraculous transformation to watch: the steady fall of the loam in one bucket, the rise of clear water in the other, like a single, interminably drawn-out exchange of breath. "See?" Dolan had said. But that had been years ago. Any surface water she'd passed these recent weeks was true mud, thick and still, fit for nothing but sucking down your boots. No amount of alchemy or patience could turn it into water. There was so much silt in the **aguaje** now that even Bill wouldn't drink. He just stood there dripping foam, looking dazedly around. Still. She could give it a try.

No. It would not come to that. Emmett was likely back at the house by now. And if night should fall to find him further delayed—well. Surely someone would come along. She looked around. Save for the blinding white arses of a couple of antelope bouncing away, the flat lay empty in all directions.

Whoever had thought to instate a watering hole in this spot could not have been a woman. It was impossible to linger here without feeling observed. The goblin barrens rose up on either side of the path ahead: bulbous gnomons; knotted terraces; wedge-headed hoodoos, each a narrows into some otherworld. Eastern dudes were known to pay good money to be brought through here and stand around in their frills, trying to guess where, in this maze of stone, some outlaw or another had laired in the old days.

This seemed to be the place to fall out with other men. The boys had come home as recently as last week covered in this telltale red dust, and waved her off when she pressed them about it, telling her the matter was "settled." There was finality to this summation, a tone that suggested no further inquiry would be suffered—which, of course, only infuriated her. They had taken to cordoning off their affairs, whispering, veering into Spanish when they heard her step in the hallway, as if she were some enemy, and not the woman who had rubbed nettle tea on their pustule-cratered chins for years, or caught them eating elk velvet in a misguided attempt to gain a few inches of height.

All her boys had augured themselves in this valley. Rob—her son through and through, bullheaded and quick-tempered, beloved abroad and withdrawn at home—was a wild and unheeding child of the silver camps. In the eerie, misshapen stones of this valley, he had recognized what he most loved of the world. Today, this rock might resemble the Green River railhead; tomorrow, a buffalo—shapes he had pursued through dime novels and eventually recaptured, many years later, in the wood carvings for which he had become known. For a long time now, she had tried to resign herself to the inevitability of losing him to the life that called out to him. Grassland days and starlit nights. Printhouse apprenticeship ran contrary to his every longing. That kind of work—precise, bookish, slow to glory—came more naturally to Dolan, whom the goblin barrens had presented with the first opportunity to talk down to his wild, lithe older brother. Where Rob saw abstractions of the world, Dolan saw facts, the plain passionless truth of things: stone carved by water and wind, and nothing more. He dismantled Rob's visions accordingly: of a geographic depression resembling a woman's skirts, he had once said, "That's just a bajada, you idiot—can't you see?"

Poor Dolan. An exasperated schoolmaster—one of the dozen who'd fled Amargo—had once called him "a most condescending plodder." The explanation Nora demanded on this point only made things worse: "Well, Missus Lark, Dolan can spell and do arithmetic, and don't he let everybody know it. But I doubt he could find the schoolhouse were it not for the other children. I believe he's never gone anyplace ahead of someone his entire life." She had campaigned against the continued employment of this ill-mannered windbag, all the while privately fearing his assessment might be true. He had high opinions, Dolan, but rarely found the conviction to follow through on them, even if he was right. A second rider all his life. Yet he was more Emmett's son than the other boys: meticulous, measured. He studied a situation carefully before speaking. When he took a position he rarely deviated from it. And he could be a joker on par with any of the funny boys from the big papers.

But too often of late, he had surprised her. Yesterday in particular. That outburst with the door, the force with which he struck.

She didn't like to think about it overmuch, lest she devolve again into rage. It would do her no good to arrive at the printhouse in a mood.

And then there was Toby, of course—a man apart. Where the goblins were concerned, he went in for the old prospectors' stories: the stones were maidens, usually, endungeoned or cursed with immobility, awaiting some providential intercession. He knew them backwards and forwards, while Nora hardly managed to retain even their broadest outlines. No hoodoo ever looked the same to her—which, Toby insisted, was part of their magic.

"This one makes me sad, Mama," he'd once said of a caravan of knotty lumps.

"Why, lamb?"

"It's a lost remuda, and they're trying to get home. And they never will. It makes me sad."

Mournful wonders swirled everywhere he turned. This outlook had taken root in him when he learned that the little block of granite on the hill behind their house did not merely bear Evelyn's name; she was buried beneath it. "Her bones, Mama?" he asked, with a kind of gruesome wonderment that left Nora sleepless.

He wanted to know how his sister had died. Nora told him about heatstroke. About how people could drown in the sun—"which is why you must mind me, or Josie, or anyone else who tells you to come in the shade." Next, he wanted to know where Evelyn's spirit had gone. Nora's answer—"Heaven"—did not suffice. After consulting Josie, he decided the little gravestone itself must be ensouled, and no amount of contradiction could persuade him otherwise. Next thing Nora knew, he had got to making his own weird little hoodoos around the ranch, stacking flat stones to a height of about two feet, naming them after made-up people with made-up demises.

"Are all those folks buried here on our farm, Tobe?"

"Yes, anyplace there's a marker."

"So many."

By his logic, the whole goblin barrens were one sprawling boneyard.

She was thinking about this when she realized the susurrus in the grass had quieted.

She turned around. The road was still empty.

Mama, Evelyn said. **Look.**

Some creature, black and huge, was coming through the distant heat-shimmer on the ridge. Nora mounted back up and laid the rifle across her knees. There were a few trees up there, spaced just inconveniently enough to conceal whatever was moving down toward her. She couldn't tell, in truth, if it was one thing or two, but its slow plodding betrayed an animal dazed by the heat. She waited for whatever was coming to take shape.

What is it, Mama?

A steer, I think. Probably one of Absalom Carter's.

What's it doing way out here?

Looking for water, same as us.

What'd you think it was before?

Before when?

Just now, when you jumped up in the saddle like that. What'd you think it was?

I hardly know.

You thought it was Toby's beast.

Don't be tiresome. Here it comes.

That don't look like the Carter brand, Mama.

It does so. That's a C, ain't it?

But look at the hooks on those C's. That's Crace ranch.

Well so it is. The Cattle King's own runaway. What's it doing way out here indeed.

I thought it was looking for water.

Mister Crace has plenty of water on his own goddamn land. Brazen bastard doesn't even pretend anymore to keep his cattle from wandering wherever they please. Here, let's give it room.

Why should we, Mama?

Papa would want us to, Evelyn. He wouldn't want us being careless.

There's room enough at the water for a horse and a steer, and a good deal more than that.

It will do no harm to back a little ways from it.

I'm staying right here.

Don't let's do anything to stir it up. Or look like we're trying for it. Trying to interfere with it, I mean.

Wouldn't we need kerchiefs for our faces, if it was interfering we intended to do?

Or frown at it, or look at it sideways, or any damn thing.

Ridiculous.

Remember what happened to Fint Colson? Somebody happened to say they saw him on the Almovar

Road, moving a couple black steers that didn't look like his own. And nobody's heard from him since.

There's a wide gulf, Mama, between rustling steers and watering your horse alongside the Crace brand.

Still. I'd not want any onlookers to mistake my intentions.

Besides, Fint had a notorious problem with cards, and it's widely known he ran off to Mexico.

That's just something they wrote in the **Ash River Clarion,** Evelyn.

There's plenty of folks think Mister Crace is a very fine man.

He could stand to talk a little less. And I'd say he's sat astride a horse and looked downvalley at more than one Sioux camp in his day. But he's far pleasanter than any of the other Stock Association bigmen.

Excepting his name is the only one comes up whispered when somebody sells for next to nothing, or takes off in the middle of the night.

Precisely.

But didn't he give account of himself? Didn't he come to Josie's séance and ask her to call up Mister Fint Colson to see if he was dead? And didn't he sit there just as patient as a cloud while Josie fussed and fussed and couldn't find no trace of Mister Fint Colson at all in the firmament—which surely proved he wasn't dead?

Evelyn, you can be so dispiritingly gullible. His

only purpose there was to let everybody know he hears what's said about him in town. That's plain enough to anyone with an ounce of sense. And anyone who thinks otherwise probably hasn't read a thing but the **Ash River Clarion** in a long time.

Mama. For someone who's so down on the papers, you sure have a lot to say in them. I hope you're ready to explain yourself to Desma about it.

＊

JOSIE, FOR ALL HER INTERMEDIARY powers, had turned out to be devoid of the only gift that might have been of use: divination. The girl could call down your aunt who'd succumbed to typhoid eighteen years ago, but she could not, by either occult power nor observation, deduce that last year's poor snowfall might beget this year's poor snowfall; that no arroyos would flow come spring; that every thunderstorm that looked to be massing nearby would veer suddenly or dissipate. She had failed to predict this drought just as she had failed to predict the grasshoppers that ate the paint off Lenore's house in Wyoming. Most damningly, perhaps, she had been as surprised as anyone when the notice came out in the **Ash River Clarion** the previous summer.

The territorial legislature has introduced a vote on whether to move the Carter County seat of governance from Amargo to Ash River. The **Ash River Clarion** cannot endorse any position on this point. But it is our solemn duty to invite our valued readers to debate the matter in the coming weeks.

Emmett had spread the newspaper over the kitchen table for the benefit of Nora and Josie. As they all read it together, he had proceeded to roar with some strange combination of mirth and fury until the boys abandoned their various chores and came to see what all the noise was about. Each in turn edged ahead of Nora to scowl at Bertrand Stills's tiny indecipherable print: Dolan, freshly reeking from some expensive ablution; Toby forever underfoot for fear of being left out; Rob, touchy as a cat and in bad need of a haircut.

"Well," Emmett said at last. "That's the county seat gone."

"Don't be ridiculous," said Nora. "We've had it in Amargo damn near twenty years."

"And it's been a valiant run. But just you wait and see where their valued readers come down in the debate."

The first letter firmly behind the move to Ash River came roaring off the **Clarion**'s front page one week later. Its author was a woman whose name Nora did not recognize. "Says here she lives on the south fork of Inés Creek," Nora muttered. "Where the hell is that?" The boys stood reading over her shoulder. Every so often, Emmett's finger would alight on a phrase outlining some topic he had wagered would

arise: the tide of newcomers lately drawn to Ash
River; the well-stocked Mercantile; the new tele-
phone generously provided, and new road generously
paved, by Mister Merrion Crace of the Crace Cattle
Company.

These merits were echoed some days later by a
geologist writing to support the move for reasons
particular to his expertise. Emmett was so animated
by the write-up that he didn't even bother to come all
the way inside before he started reading. "One must
consider," he shouted from the door, "the degree to
which Ash River's terrain—being flat and navigable—
would improve freighting and transport."

"That's not a bad point," Dolan put in. He had
developed a habit of pausing midway through some
unnecessary labor and standing around until Josie
noticed and remarked upon whatever he was doing.
This time, however, scrubbing spuds at the basin,
she seemed immune to the charms of the ax gamely
cocked on his shoulder. Dolan cleared his throat.
She did not look up. "That is to say: the Amargo
Canyon Road is a terrible mail route."

Emmett went on reading. "Further to my last is the
question of water. Amargo's meager resources sufficed
the founders of this community—the Widow Ruiz,
her late husband and the handful of stalwarts who
first proved up here. But as our ranks swell, and we
face another year of scant precipitation, and consider
annexation to the United States besides, we must
inquire: Will every new emigrant live permanently at

risk of drought? Will the advent of the twentieth century see the United States move on, while we of Carter County continue to rely on the dubious sorcery of well-witches? And, most vitally of all: is Amargo more likely than Ash River to obtain a connection to the new railroad now being extended from Prescott to Phoenix; and, if not, will we go on governing our county from a seat that remains forever inland?"

Even Rob couldn't help hooting at this. "It's some damn nonsense, suggesting Ash River's a surer play for the railroad than we are. Mama—ain't they been promising one since before I was born?"

"They certainly have."

"That's what people do." Dolan, still with the ax, sauntered back in. "They wager you'll forget someone else has already failed on the promise they're making. And people do forget, you know. They surely do."

"Do you intend some use for that thing?" Nora said. "Or is it just grafted to your hand?"

A red tinge blotched Dolan's face. She tried to think of something to lighten the silence, but Emmett was still musing on. "I'm not certain a railroad is so far-fetched for Ash River. Merrion Crace pastures—what? Two thousand head in the valley? Once he manages to wrest the last of the creekfront from Desma, he can add two thousand more. He'll need a ready way to ship them back east. The Stock Association's organized and already persuaded. They could handily fund a little shoestring to the Prescott-Phoenix line."

"I'd like to see him wrest anything from Desma," Nora said.

"You will." She wished he would stop smiling. Nothing was more galling to her than that wistful condescension. "When Ash River wins the seat, Amargo will go bust and Desma along with it. He won't have to send one more clerk to harry her, nor fire a single shot. He'll end up paying pennies on what he offered her three years ago—if he pays her anything at all. It's inspired, really."

"I'm in wonderment that you can endure it so coolly. This isn't chess, you know. We live here, too. If Desma folds, so do we all."

He spoke without looking up from the **Clarion**. "One doesn't fold in chess."

In the intervening months, she had often regretted her inability to summon a smarting enough reply. "Surely not everyone can be in favor of moving the seat."

"You're damn right, Mama," said Rob.

Emmett shrugged. "Of course not. But I told you, they'll only ever print the ones who are."

"Why aren't we printing the rest?"

"What rest?"

"The rebuttals."

"If there's rebuttals, they're not coming in to the **Sentinel**."

This was beyond endurance. Since when had he

ever relied on others' words to fill his pages? Certainly not when he was decrying the miner's plight, or enumerating the sins of the latest Indian agent, or scurrying off to the mountains to ask the old-timers exactly how much snowfall they'd had, and just how much more they could earnestly prophesy. "Then write you something, Mister Lark."

"I suppose I may."

To calm herself, she aimed all the false exuberance she could muster in Rob's direction. "On the bright side, should Ash River become a proper cattle-town, you might consider staying here after all, and not go grumbling off to Montana."

Rob looked darkly from her to Josie, and back down at the boot he was patching.

For a little while, Emmett seemed to undertake the task of drafting some response. He stayed up nights writing, and it heartened her to see his forehead so often in his hand by lamplight. But time went on, and this supposed answer went unprinted. When he'd fared off in spring—hurrying to Flagstaff when the ink delivery failed—she brooded the secret hope that he had left because the article was finally meant to run, and he could not bear to linger and be praised for it. But not a word appeared. Nothing.

The next reader to favor moving the county seat was some Ash River schoolmarm. She feared Amargo's reputation was still too proximate to its lawless early days to make it reliably representative of the county. "We need only consider," Emmett, loudly mirthful, read, "the significant fact that the Amargo Canyon Road seems to remain a haven of villains and badmen, while the Ash River Road is spared these blights."

"We ought to go over there," Rob had said. "We ought to go over there, and give the Ash River Road a taste of what blights really are."

Emmett looked at him. "You leave off that kind of talk."

"But there've been no holdups on the Amargo Canyon Road, Papa. None at all."

"There will be," Emmett said. "Closer to the vote."

Sure enough, in July, a holdup was reported. In what was probably the longest tract of text Nora had ever seen committed to a **Clarion** column, a traveler from Prescott detailed his encounter with two hatted men on "stole-looking" horses who delayed him for three hours near the Cortez **aguaje** before relieving him of his purse and boots. His trials were considerably worsened by the long, barefoot trek into Amargo to notify Sheriff Harlan Bell of this depredation. "Imagine my anguish," Dolan read, in a profoundly nasal mimicry of the writer's voice, "to learn that my reward would be a further three hours' detour to a parched little pueblo, where Sheriff Harlan Bell, a rough man of unsympathetic disposition, directed me to an establishment he referred to as a 'hotel'—which turned out to be a drafty ruin as old as the frontier itself, where the apex of hospitality was being assigned a room whose windows had not been shot out."

"Moss Riley will take exception to that," Nora said. "He's let the Paloma House go a little, sure—but it's still a very fine place."

Emmett's head, fixed in a sour smile, floated around the parlor door. "Ah, poor wretched pilgrim. If only Ash River were the county seat—then the Sheriff's office would be **there**, mere steps from all the new hotels, and not here in this backwater."

Dolan rustled the paper in his father's direction. "I believe their point is: it's a no-water."

This glibness was got from Emmett's side of the family, and it did not suit Dolan at all. Nora found herself unbearably provoked. What were they doing, sitting here in the kitchen, chuckling at the inevitable dissolution of the town—as though that smug pedant, Bertrand Stills, were the sole owner of a printhouse in the entire valley? As though they were powerless to do anything but shrug and be swept away?

"How's that rebuttal coming along?" she said.

"It is, by and by."

"A year ago you wouldn't have slept for writing."

Emmett was a smiling man. Years of sunburn tinged his good-natured creases. In the rare instances his face hardened, the effect was sudden and repudiating. "We'll see."

"We ought to go and show our force," Rob interrupted from his corner, "before the stages reroute to avoid all these so-called depredations."

But it was too late, even for that. Next came a lament penned by Ferdy Kostic, that sniveling, bowlegged little Slav who carried the mail. His duties had been adversely impacted, for the Overland stages were beginning to deliver all freight to Ash River. He supposed this sudden turn rested equally on their fear of depredation and the conviction that Ash River was sure to win the seat. It pained him personally to reflect on this, as he himself called Amargo home. But he could only concern himself with practical matters: if Amargo retained the county seat, he would be obliged to travel all the way to Ash River for the mail, and then all the way back, thereby delaying its delivery.

"He should move there, then," Nora said. "And see how the women of Ash River like it when he starts peering through their windows."

"We'll all be moving soon enough," Emmett said.

What galled her most was that Emmett lacked the decency to sound grim about this prospect. Something thrilled in his voice, the anticipation of new possibilities. Well, of course. Here was a chance to get away from all his mistakes and shortfalls. You couldn't blame a man for losing his lifework to a town going bust.

"If you'd be good enough to finish that rebuttal we might yet stand some chance of slowing the course of this madness," she said.

"I am taking my time with what to say."

"Why not ask someone for whom the matter is more urgent? Desma, perhaps?"

"Desma? She's in mourning. She's got her hands full now with two claims, and all those Land Office bilks coming by to harry her, miles of paperwork. Don't be bothering Desma."

"What about your other readers? Don't you have any?"

"I tell you, nobody has written in about this."

"Because they've learned you won't print it. They're dumbfounded by your silence. They've read nothing these last months but weather predictions and amusing little ditties about who's visiting whom from out of town."

The more heated Emmett grew in a quarrel, the stiller he stood. Even his jaw barely moved. "Nora, that seat was lost the instant Merrion Crace sank his greasy, limey bribes into the legislature's pockets," he said. "It would be useless to stir up something about it now."

"Let me do it," she said. "Let me write something."

"You will **not**."

"Let her, Pa," Rob said.

"I needn't write it under my own name."

The boys were watching closely now. Emmett removed his spectacles. "Mark this carefully: we will not be standing toe-to-toe with Merrion Crace's newspaper three months ahead of a vote he means to win."

"Perhaps if we had enough mettle to, we wouldn't have found ourselves so debt-drowned that it will relieve you to abandon our home and printing press when the town goes bust."

He stared patiently at her. "If you're so damn hot over it, maybe it would do you some good to get it all down on paper."

She took on this recommendation with vigor. Having written nothing save letters in years, she looked forward to ordering her thoughts toward some greater purpose—but they were scattershot by anger. After reading Ferdy Kostic's letter one final time in the drafty gloom of four in the morning, before the pages disappeared forever down the privy, she managed to write a meandering defense of life in Amargo. She wrote of the town's early days, back when it was just a silver camp on the shores of Big Fork Creek; of Desma and Rey Ruiz, weathering drought and depredation; of the small band of first-comers all sleeping under canvas together; of Harlan Bell, post-riding before he ever dreamed of becoming Sheriff; of Doc Almenara, who'd given up a vainglorious life in San Francisco to work good deeds on this little scald of earth.

Nora wondered, given her feelings upon first moving here, how she'd managed to churn up so much goodwill writing about it now. Perhaps the old folks had been right—getting mawkish about one's life, no matter its substance, took nothing but time.

Or perhaps she was a passable writer, after all.

The more she revisited her points, however, the

more their underlying truths seemed to defeat her purpose. You could not speak of life in Amargo without mentioning solitude. Or snakes. Or the unavoidable fact that this valley, once green enough to fool farmers, laid its hopes year after year on the promise of winter snowfall a hundred miles distant, which these two seasons past had failed to revive so much as a thread of clear water in any of the creeks its people had staked their claims around.

And then there was the heat, of course.

Don't bring up the heat, Mama, Evelyn said over her shoulder. **Then you will have to talk about me, and no good will come of that.**

If the truth of their little town was less than Edenic, perhaps the right way to rally her neighbors' hearts was to address what losing the county seat would cost them. Already, they'd lost two stage lines. Their Mercantile, their post office, their freight contracts would follow. Maintown, inevitably, would fall to ruin. People would find themselves forced to travel three, perhaps four days, for mail and flour, for the mere sight of another soul. This would lead to the eventual abandonment of all the remaining homesteads—a decampment far greater than even the drought had induced. And then what? Their claims, which Merrion Crace had been slowly buying off one plot at a time from the defeated and the willing, would be overrun by his cattle without his having to pay so much as a cent to the people who had broken those acres. And the only task left to Merrion Crace would be to wait for the waters to return, and the whole place to green up again—this time without a soul to object, or a fence to get around. Well. Wouldn't he like that?

Her writings descended into profanity.

I doubt this is the way to proceed, Mama, Evelyn said.

I confess I'm beginning to understand why your father gave up.

Perhaps you should consider telling a meaningful interlude about your own life in Amargo?

There was sense in that, of course. But where to begin? Should she detail the great odds she and Emmett had beaten to stake up here? Or start even further back? Was there merit in calling down the spirit of her father? After all, nothing bestirred frontier spirit more than the enterprising adaptability of others—and Gustav Volk, for all his faults, had boasted life enough for twenty people. Following an inauspicious start in dentistry back in Laibach, he'd come over and tried on the mantles of hostler, assayer, and postmaster in just a few short years. His ultimate iteration was as a lumbermill foreman of Morton Hole, a sturdy little burg in the new free state of Iowa, where Nora's mother joined him two years later with those of her children still living.

Of that particular journey, Ellen Francis Volk was

reluctant to say almost anything—save to confess that its duration had felt, to her, like drifting, unbounded and bereft, away from any graspable fact of life, while all around her a featureless and impenetrable twilight gathered, like an evening of the mind.

NORA GREW UP A STRANGER TO THAT feeling. Morton Hole was comfortingly delimited: west of town lay the rich plain, dotted all the way to the Missouri with folk sturdy or mad enough to break it; east lay the Mississippi, with its great log drafts, merging and bumping alongside her father's in their stagnant downriver course.

The Volks opened a boardinghouse, and Nora's earliest memories were of miles of damp linen, acres of bread, the ceaseless music of spoons on tin that attended the upkeep of hungry lumbermen.

She learned letters and manners from the pale, dismayed wives of her father's subordinates, who raised her to defend the hearth and revile a lie—nominally at least, for the older she grew the more she came to recognize falsehood as the preservative that allowed the world to maintain its shape. The lumbermen, for instance, talked of her father as a fearsome man: proud, immense, and daunting. Their reticence about his more vulnerable qualities—his superstitions about the weather, or his habit of leaving a little a drop of something at the bottom of his glass to placate the Devil—allowed him to go through life undiminished. He, in turn, lauded the hospitality and vigor of his wife, blind or indifferent to the well-known fact that years on the trail had made her rheumatic and closely allied to whiskey.

For Nora's brothers, too, duplicity was a way of life. Around town they were known for being decent and upright, the kind of boys who'd help you break acres if you were injured without accepting a cent for their trouble. But at home they were hellions, the gentle Michael lured into instantly regretted misadventures by the head-wild Paul. Hardly a morning arose without some concealment of the previous night's exploits: where they'd been, how late they'd stayed, why they smelled like the cathouse, how much money they'd lost in whatever long-odds prizefight had most recently rattled the barn behind the school. Nora withstood years of her mother's switching for refusing to report their nocturnal misdeeds. Her own knack for deceit surprised her. Lying was as easy as saying nothing.

It struck her at some point that all life must necessarily feed on willful delusion. What else could explain the existence—and still more surprisingly, the persistence—of a place like Morton Hole, this huddle of journeyed lives strung along a thoroughfare obdurately referred to as Main Street? Would it not have been more earnest to call it Only Street? Despite his illiteracy, its founding father (a prospector evangelist now awaiting salvation beneath a stone slab marked A. R. MORTON) was at least forthright enough to call it a hole. Nora's elders, on the other hand, had gussied up their row of shacks as if it were Chicago rising. They built a church with a white steeple, and a clubhouse for town councilors. The Ladies' Association troubled itself with securing schoolteachers, establishing watercolor salons so that Morton Hole's fairer sex might be initiated to the sublimities of portraiture. The storekeeping Fox brothers fit their Mercantile with a huge plate-glass window, which fell victim to howling storms, only to be replaced by new panels from Saint Louis— each after the other doomed to the selfsame fate, year after year, as though the Fox brothers believed sheer determination might alter the odds of glass against an Iowa hailstorm. As though any recent arrivals on these plains had more agency than the cornhusk dolls Nora had wantonly demolished as a child.

Buttressing local delusions were the polite idioms that ruled both print and conversation: women took the waters; men took the air; folks did or did not acknowledge the corn. The only exception was made for Indian depredations, regarding which both newspapers and conversation were pointedly explicit. By the time she was five, Nora had heard just about every imaginable butchery detailed. She spent so much time imagining the wretched corpses scalped and disemboweled and scattered about the plains that she began to feel she'd witnessed it all personally. The town ladies must have shared that illusion, for a great deal of their time was spent debating the extent of God's mercy where self-solution was concerned. It took her a long time to understand that they were wondering whether their Heavenly Father would forgive them if they killed themselves upon being captured by the Dakota. Ten years old when Fetterman rode out on his star-crossed jaunt against the Sioux, Nora had squirmed through a sermon dedicated to outlaying the desecrations those good men had suffered: their eyes torn out, their limbs hacked off, all of it detailed right there in the **Herald,** which the reverend shook at his congregation from the pulpit. Less than a year later, that same reverend would stand graveside at her brother's burial and say that Michael had been "remanded to his Judge"—igniting in Nora a lasting flicker of hatred, because she knew the cleric capable of listing atrocities, and it seemed cowardly of him to talk around Michael's agony. There was nothing genteel about the fever that had denigrated her brother and scorched his brain.

When she first met Emmett Lark, he'd seemed as susceptible to such distortion as everybody else. He turned up at Gus Volk's mill the summer Nora turned sixteen: a rangy, bronze youth with an odd, angular face and a firework of sun-fried hair. Nothing to his name but a chessboard and a gunnysack of old books. He was picking up labors on his way out west, where he intended to become a schoolmaster. The first thing Nora heard about him was that he seemed unprovoked when the other men derided his teaching ambitions. The second was that a mere week on the job saw him entrusted with the notching and tallying of the logs, as no greater pedant had ever come through Morton Hole.

Emmett was a natural fit for the attic, the roasting crawlspace to which Nora's mother relegated all newly arrived greenhorns. Nora, in her Sisyphean stairwell treks, would look around the laundry pile and see him bellied on the floor in a futile effort to keep cool, his finger wandering slowly, back and forth, down the page of some unintelligible scientific guide. Every once in a while, for variety, he would lay the chessboard out and stare at it. More than a month went by before she realized his set was not intact. Hominy kernels were interspersed among the rooks. A huge, cracked bicuspid sat where the white knight should be.

"What's that?" she asked one night, having braved up enough to put her head around the door.

Emmett raised it from the board. "A tooth."

"That's evident enough," she said, flushing with embarrassment now that the conversation seemed fated to continue. "What from?"

"A river horse."

"What's that?"

"Something rather large, I think."

Even in those days Emmett's smile brimmed with a kind of inscrutable half-sadness. It had made her feel very gullible, and therefore very provoked. "I think you'll find that we are not such bumpkins here as you suppose, sir," she said. "I happen to know there's no such thing."

"I'm afraid there is, miss. In Zambezia, I believe."

She went away seething. Zambezia indeed. No smirking attic-dweller better think he could fool her so handily with some bestial invention. It amused her now to remember that the most punishing thing she could think to do was revert to calling him "Mister Lark" and restrict her interactions with him even further. A curt good morning. Clipped thanks when he happened to hold the door. A simple strategy, but one that continued to confound Emmett until Christmastime, when some magazine illustrator lodging with them donated a stack of stereograph cards to the Yuletide bazaar in an effort to impress her father. Tasked with raffle inventory, Nora was shuffling through them before the festivities when she came across the picture of a boatful of outmatched tribesmen, hurling javelins at a tusked and boulder-headed monster, which reared at their vessel from the frothing waters. At the bottom of the picture were printed the words: HUNTING THE RIVER HORSE.

She found Emmett outside, clearing the drive. "You ever seen one?" He stared at her from behind a drift of breath. "A river horse?"

"No, miss, I have not." The tooth had been gifted him by a well-traveled friend of his father's. Nora drew the stereograph from her sleeve and held it out to him. He helped her climb the jackfence, and they angled the card to catch the light sieving out from the party.

Emmett whistled. "If that picture's within a breath of the real thing, some poor fella surely lost his life gaining this tooth."

"From the mouth of a river horse to an Iowa timber camp," she said. "What a journey."

Other people had spring wagon rides and long afternoon walks. Nora and Emmett had the tooth. It reminded them how little of the world they really knew, a fact they strived together to remedy. Whenever he was sent to town, Emmett would buy, borrow, or barter whatever newspapers and magazines he could source, and scour the faded print for any new learning that might swell their mutual bestiary. With an unsteady hand, he cut out stories about Burmese wildcats, or snakes the length of a whole train car that could crush a man's bones and swallow him whole. Nora, in turn, pored over the ancient newsprint that papered ladies' kitchens. She tore out pictures of dome-backed pack mules of the Saharan desert and strange, striped wolves that haunted the islands of the Tasman Sea.

Not long before they fell in together, a traveling circus brought a zebra through Morton Hole. Emmett and Nora stood on the bridge and watched it move slowly down the road on the opposite bank, through the brindled trees and into history.

"They never look in life as they do on paper, do they?" Nora said.

Emmett shrugged. "I guess people don't either."

In November, when the river began to freeze, he rode for Nebraska. She was as sorry to see him go as she had ever been about anything. It was a wretched, drawn-out goodbye, and she readied herself for a wretched, drawn-out wait for his letters. He surprised her instead by reappearing in her father's parlor that same evening, dressed in what passed for finery, heart outspread, dry field nettles in his fist.

The story, as Emmett later told it to their boys, was that he'd gotten as far as Freehold, been thunder-struck by love for her, and turned his horse. The truth, she suspected, was that he'd reached Freehold, realized he had very little notion of what he was doing, and come back for reinforcements.

They were married in her father's house, and set off the following spring. For two years they followed rail-road and rumor. Where schoolmasters were not needed, the frontier flung wild alternatives at Emmett, who was game enough to try his hand at just about anything: storekeeping, clerking for the railway. Dispiritingly, no occupation tolerated greenhorns for very long, even if they were learned. No sooner had Nora warmed to the curtains and mattress of whatever place boarded them than they were off again.

She did not begin to feel the unboundedness her mother had described all those years ago until a few towns along the way. It grew in from the outer corners of her mind. She could not help feeling, as she marked the particulars of each new camp—the view through her window, the way to the Mercantile, the face of whatever woman lived nearest—that a featureless twilight was massing both ahead and behind. With every rearrangement, it seemed to draw a little nearer.

The Larks ended up in Cheyenne. Some years earlier, the Union Pacific had come through and left behind a Babylon maelstrom, a bilious, gray, seething wreck on the plains. Miners and gamblers and pimps, swaggering dudes who'd found themselves lesser men than they believed: all of them, guts laid bare. From the tiny window of their house on Spruce Street, Nora watched the defeated shadows lurching home at dawn and felt this must be the crux of life: everybody blundering around in the full glare of ruination.

No undertaking in Cheyenne was ever completed. Hammers sang day and night. The moment paint gawded a falsefront, the pale blond bones of some new joint sprang up overnight just down the road. If something looked to be nearing completion, there loomed the unspoken understanding that it would likely burn down soon enough and compel more work. Beyond town lay the twin cables of the railway, and the plains, gray and snow-dregged in winter, yellow every other season, scattershot with distant, unseen forts. You could stand anywhere and look off in any direction and feel you were nowhere, and yet somehow perfectly bounded, perfectly surrounded. That was Cheyenne: nowhere, wanting nothing more than to be exactly what it was.

Even Emmett could not escape its influence. At first, he pursued his old schoolmastering ambitions with his usual good cheer. He started small. Set up a tiny schoolhouse he managed to fill with unruly ragamuffins who shouted over him and tumbled about the place. But there was little living in that, and he was flanked on all sides by greater chancers than he had ever been. Of course, that he was surrounded by them in saloons, where they came to weep about how their risks had bankrupted them, made little difference. Nora recognized what was coming—her father had been similarly disposed.

Sure enough, their house became a waystation for the woebegone. She lost track of how often Emmett returned at day's-end, tailed by some low-down, hungry soul, half-crazed with sun and the absolute bleakness of life. She would lie on their cot behind the buffalo hide curtain that divided the room, listening to Emmett defend the sanctity of work and worth until dawn.

One of their more tolerable lodgers was a man named Sandy Freed. He'd got himself sideways in some sort of assaying enterprise, and had just drifted into town in disgrace when he happened to sit beside Emmett's table at the Iron Horse saloon. The two of them were prone to wax poetic about this moment, but Nora could guess at the meat of it. Emmett was probably scribbling in his notebook, and Sandy was not so drunk that he couldn't read over his seatmate's arm. He'd probably said: "May I tell you, sir, what a damn pleasure it is to meet another literate person here? Pardon my profanity, but I must speak my mind. A damn pleasure."

Then they probably shook hands, exchanged pleasantries. Emmett was persuaded to divulge his frustrations with frontier schooling. And then Sandy Freed, gazing wonderingly at him with those big liquid eyes, went on to say something like, "If the frontier were made up of more men like you, sir, I reckon I wouldn't have hit the gargle at all. Yes, yes. And maybe I'd have done all the things I intended to prove up this here territory in the spirit of the coming century."

Once Sandy Freed got upright again, he made himself useful about the house. Nora found he could be marvelous company. His God-given eloquence was buttressed on all sides by charms he'd cultivated throughout a long life of asking forgiveness for assorted transgressions about which he was alternately boastful and ashamed. He'd read the poets, and was happy to talk for hours about them. A life of travel had initiated him to the world's many wonders. Their details varied somewhat from story to story, but hearing him gab on about them while she worked kept the twilight at bay. When Sandy was not crumpled by his chief vices—drink, dice, and balcony women—he could see straight to the beginning of the century. And what a glorious vision it was. "Information!" was his favorite breakfast talk, assuming he had managed to rouse himself from whatever debasement he'd enjoyed the night before. "News, debate! That's what'll help the plowman and the stonebreaker, Emmett. You gone fight a righteous fight? Then spread the written word from here to California."

By this time, the Larks were rounding the bend on their second year in Cheyenne. Emmett had failed utterly in his efforts to redirect the hatred of Cheyenne's schoolchildren from the Indians to the British; and from luckless settlers to cattle barons. He had also served as a pallbearer to strangers—cowpokes and prospectors at whose funerals he was often the only mourner—and had begun to feel that the disadvantages of being a community pillar outweighed the merits. Every hour of the day might bring some distraught new widow to his door, freshly robbed of a husband who'd been cheated out of land or dues or goods by more powerful interests. These women wanted advice, protection, a sense of what to do next. Guilty over the limits of his counsel, Emmett resorted to buying their livestock, mostly sheep, thereby easing a little of their burden as they packed up and returned to whatever life they had most recently abandoned.

"What in goddamn are we supposed to do with all these sheep?" Nora asked, once their rickety little makeshift pen was overrun.

"Sell them, of course," Emmett said cheerfully.

He tried this, and after several half-failures learned from some more knowledgeable entity that he'd managed to get himself a runty flock. Nora's fury failed to even dent his amusement. He threw himself into learning how to right the ship—which was, in truth, what she had most admired about him all along. He learned how to shear them, and then found out little by little that their ongoing deficiencies were the result of needing more grazing land, a place to roam and fatten without the threat of ruinous winters.

By this time, Sandy Freed had taken off for Arizona Territory. Having roamed awhile, he took on the role of town booster for a little mining district between Phoenix and Flagstaff. For a thousand dollars he had acquired a mortgaged plot with a ramshackle house on it and a printing press installed therein. One thousand dollars. A sum Sandy had never seen, nor would ever earn, in his lifetime. But there was his signature on the bank papers, and his name in the banner of the misspelled newsletters that kept arriving at Emmett and Nora's under the heading **The Amargo Sentinel** with charming regularity until the next time Sandy hit the bottle.

Then his correspondence took on more urgency. Oh, Mister Lark, how glorious it is in Arizona

Territory. Cloudless blue skies and green fields for grazing. Fine, hardworking folk unafflicted by the deficits of character that drive men to gold fever, et cetera. And such redoubtable ladies to keep Miss Nora company!

She remembered bristling at this. "Why would I want to keep company with redoubtable ladies? What the hell does he mean to suggest?"

"That you're pretty redoubtable yourself, I think."

"The nerve of him!"

Emmett eyed her sidelong. "What do you figure it means?"

"Of doubtful reputation."

Emmett shook his head. "This is why a writer must always steer clear of words that aren't intuitive. That can't be easily pulled apart. Redoubtable. Means formidable."

Every day, Sandy insisted, the town was filling up with new souls and fresh elation. Why, a Portugee clothier had just opened! Such fine scarves. Sandy's contentment was impeded only by how fiercely he missed dear Emmett and dear Miss Nora—who were denying themselves a real benediction in this earthly course, not seeing the birth of a splendid new town. Wouldn't it be something if they could all be reunited again under the banner of a glorious and worthy newspaper, therewith to bring the Territories into the bosom of the Union?

"Why's he so frantic?" Nora wondered.

"He's in trouble."

"You're not thinking of heading to his rescue, are you?"

They almost certainly would have managed to resist his enticements had their house not been the very last in a row that caught fire one September night when a cook at The Golden Spike two doors down let the bacon go a little too black. One errant spatter, and there went their books and papers, their roof and bed. Nora had been in the family way—or, at least, she thought she might be, despite several years of failing to be. She had stood across the street, with one small ewe under each arm, watching the useless mustering of the firewagon, and known in her very bones that Emmett would take this disastrous turn as an omen of new opportunities. Nothing that felt like reversing course could hold him here. She had seen her last autumn in Cheyenne.

Sheep, fire, and Sandy Freed's silver tongue. Those were the intertwining threads that brought them clattering into Arizona Territory in 1876. They arrived to find Amargo little more than a row of tents along Big Fork Creek, and Sandy Freed already dreaming up new prospects in Montana even as he initiated Emmett to all the exasperations of the Washington press—which, Emmett was flustered to learn, was swiftly growing outmoded and already worth nowhere near what Sandy had paid for it. But Sandy was himself: charming and well-intentioned, though a hopeless writer and editor, and still no stranger to the cardhouse. By November, he was so desperately in arrears that Emmett's signature had to be secured on the bank papers. Not long afterwards, Sandy rode out to resupply in Flagstaff. His last letter had arrived six years ago, and was postmarked from Ontario—a place Nora heard was cold and isolated and overrun with badmen, the kind of place where a person could easily drown or freeze or fall down a steep ravine, or meet with any number of just comeuppances for taking advantage of the blithely good.

Mama, Evelyn said, after Nora had accumulated about twenty pages of this. **You've veered off the merits again.**

"Right," she said. "The merits."

Why don't you write about the house? Everyone's got a house.

The house. Emmett had insisted on building their first one himself. After the August monsoons carried it off, they raised this one together, squabbling over its construction. Emmett was homesick for the white palings and velvet wallpaper of his boyhood. He wanted Nora to have that, at least. But she couldn't help seeing such frivolities as a shortcut to all kinds of ruin. There must be a reason why every **poblador** within a hundred miles of Amargo built **jacal**. Mud walls humbled a house, made it look sturdy and self-contained, removing the impression that it might be occupied by a bunch of vulnerable know-nothings. If they were going to be rubes in every other walk of life, hadn't they better be practical where the house was concerned? Besides. They'd be up and gone within the year.

But Emmett stood firm. So they hauled timber from the mountains; cut back mesquite and manzanita; hammered and measured and sanded until they had raised the very finest, lopsided imitation of a dogtrot she'd ever seen. They built a henhouse that fell victim to every enterprising fox within ten miles of the place, until they wised up and started laying out strychnine—which cost them dog after dog in the bargain. By the end of the year, they had thirty acres broken and their first winter wheat planted—and when that went to hell, they grew doomed greens until Desma Ruiz took pity and gifted them squash and turnip and better notions of how to coax life out of the roasted earth. On their claim papers, they wrote that they intended to "raise wheat & sheep." Emmett could laugh about this now, as though it had been some stranger's distant, pastoral fancy—but the facts stood clear: they had spent years sanding hooves and shearing miles of shit-smeared wool and yanking steaming, blood-clabbered lambs into life. Autumn after autumn, they had brought the flock in off baking summer hillsides, so they could inch forward against the debt of the printing press; so the three boys they raised up on hearthside pallets might have books and pencils; so they could get well enough situated to close off the old porch into two rooms, then three, and build up a floor, and put each boy behind his own door so that each might become his own man.

Should the county seat be lost to Ash River, all this would have been for nothing. All the sores and sunstrokes. All the little details of life. And death, too.

The merits, Mama, Evelyn said. **The merits.**

The merits, the merits. Well, if Emmett could be believed about what was written on that puncheon ledge, the merits were simple enough. They had lived here. Not happily—but more so than some. Emmett, Nora, and their boys. Evelyn, too—for only a few months among the living, certainly, but every day thereafter as well, grown up in every cobweb and mote of dust and pool of sunlight upon the floor. When Nora pictured the empty house, she saw Evelyn coursing through its beams and banisters, through the burled hearts of the logs and the unconquerable window smudges and the oil stains on the counter. Her daughter was as much a part of it as any of them—more so, perhaps, for Evelyn was tethered to its very foundations, buried in the soil on which it stood. She had grown into a fine, pragmatic, if slightly brusque, young woman, and she would not tolerate leaving this house.

But there was no writing this. So what was there left to say?

"For many of us, our gardens are the graveyards of our very hearts. When Amargo goes bust, will we leave our dead behind?"

You'd better not write that, Mama, Evelyn said. **It will only draw people's minds to me.**

She had better not write any of it. She was seized suddenly with the terror of what people would think if the nonsense she found herself committing to paper should ever be read by anybody. Even in its most censored edition, her words could only whet the appetite for gossip that seemed, at this juncture, the only thing Amargo and Ash River still had in common. She did not want to write about Evelyn; and without Evelyn, Nora's story was as matter-of-fact as anyone else's—save that other people's daughters had lived, while hers had not.

Everything she'd written went into the fire.

But the whole endeavor was in her blood now. If only she could find the right standpoint from which to make a single, necessary appeal.

If only Desma were willing to write something. Desma was unassailable. Unlike damn near everybody else, she had come to this place before any hope or delusion had formed about what it might become. Not one soul in this valley had managed to stand on two feet without a little push from Desma—a push she was always willing to give, though it ran against her fundamental inclination to be left alone. To have managed all that, and be rewarded after twenty-four long years with the death of her dearest love and truest friend, and be harried now by a relentless procession of riders and inspectors and agents questioning the legitimacy of her holdings. Well, it was just about beyond endurance.

This was how, a month ago, Nora had finally come to write:

Alas, it seems the word "Amargo" cannot appear in the **Ash River Clarion**'s pages without reference to outlaw depredation, insolvency, and water shortage. We of Amargo are astonished to learn our prospects are so dire. The introduced measure is nothing but the final stroke in a long campaign of malicious denigration of our township and citizenry, prospects, and safety, all to Ash River's gain. The **Clarion** would do well to remember Amargo's near-twenty years of meritorious service as the county seat, owed in large measure to the efforts of good folk like Desma Ruiz, a widow twice over, who settled here twenty years ago and has remained through drought and famine and Stock Association depredations to prove up the land and serve as a reminder that fulfillment and prosperity and fellowship can be got here. We owe her esteem and allegiance—for what will become of her house, her memories, her redoubtable life's work should the town go bust? Amargo must not surrender without contest, no matter how many false reports the **Ash River Clarion** prints; no matter how many dragons' teeth Mr. Merrion Crace and the Stock Association sow.

Emmett was puzzled when she showed him the letter.

"Why are you using the word 'redoubtable' here?"

"Well, I know its meaning now."

"Other people don't. They might run aground on the same misunderstanding as you did before. It's not an intuitive word."

"You haven't much faith in your readership."

Emmett was still studying the paper.

"And here—what do you mean by dragons' teeth?"

"The Hellenes had it that when you sow dragons' teeth, you reap a battle-ready army." Pleased with herself, she watched him make his way through her letter again. "When will you print it?"

"Print it?" He looked up at her with genuine surprise. "Darling, this undertaking was purely for the benefit of your constitution."

Her constitution? Her constitution boiled for days. Worse still was Emmett's inability to comprehend why she was so withdrawn and curt.

But don't you feel released, Mama, having written it?

She did not. All that time, all that effort. Pages and pages written and rewritten, wrung out and reconstituted until she was no longer certain of her own logic. And Emmett—still dragging his feet with a rebuttal he continued to claim he was writing; still dawdling with half-hearted scraps of script he refused to let her see. Where was the pen-wielding cavalier who had protested the Apache Wars outright, and marked every land-grab and unjust closure and extra-judicial hanging from here to Yuma?

Well. Emmett had carted off to Cumberland in search of the wretched Paul Griggs and his damnable water delivery, leaving the boys in charge of the printhouse. And one day later, a little giddy with sleeplessness and determination, Nora had found herself slipping her note to Dolan.

"A last-minute addition," she said.

Dolan read it with widening eyes. "Has Papa seen this?"

"Of course."

"Who on earth is 'Ellen Francis'?"

In a failure of imagination, Nora had put her mother's name to the text. But Dolan had no memory of Ellen Francis Volk, had never met nor written to her. It would surprise Nora to learn that he remembered having had a Grandmother Ellen at all.

"You don't know her. She's newly set up out on the Red Fork."

"And she wrote to **you**?"

"To your father. Last week."

And still there had been time to confess, to

withdraw. Still Dolan had lingered in the doorway, twisting his hat. "You're certain Papa approves?"

Rob, who'd watched all this sidelong from the fence, returned and took the note from his brother's hand. "Come on," he said, "Papa approves."

And so the piece had run—and what had it wrought? A fleeting afternoon's thrill at the sight of her familiar words, ink-fat and coursing down the page, so formal, so lasting. A brief daydream that she and Desma might laugh about all this together. She had even allowed herself to believe—just for a moment, admittedly, for she knew Desma well enough—that after an initial period of agitation, Desma might grow to feel bashfully warm about having been lauded thus for all the virtues she would never extol in herself.

But instead, everything had gone to hell. The very next afternoon, Dolan was waving the **Clarion** in her face. They did not shy from rebuttals, the **Clarion**, and they'd written one up so fast Nora could scarcely believe they hadn't had it lined up long before the whole mess had even begun. Goddamn the might of the daily.

Despite our desire to mount a defense of our publication's character—baselessly maligned by **The Amargo Sentinel**—the **Ash River Clarion** abstains from anything that might invite indictment of our journalistic propriety. Suffer us to dismantle these accusations instead. Firstly: reporting the facts about Amargo's predicaments is a matter of civic responsibility. That once-noble town's inevitable ruination is as wounding to us, its friends and neighbors, as it is to its own fine citizenry. Second: it is well proven that counties derive a great benefit from the movement of legislative seats. The process encourages civic engagement, and will be crucial to our Territory's petition for statehood. Finally: though Mr. Merrion Crace holds a stake in this newspaper, the **Sentinel**'s crude understanding of his involvement betrays divination rather than truth—which is unsurprising, of course, given its publisher's connection to mesmerists and mediums. The facts are as follows: this paper was established to furnish the people of Inés Valley with news and tidings, and Mr. Crace has always been divested from its management. As to Mrs. Desma Ruiz, being widowed twice would require her having been widowed to begin with; and since we have it on good authority that her confederation with the late Mr. Rey Ruiz was not legal—insofar as she was, and yet remains, married to her first husband Mr. Robert Gris—it is the duty of this publication to point out that she is not a widow at all.

"There'll be hell to pay now," said Dolan despairingly. "From Father and the Stock Association both."

"So be it," Nora said. But her heart was whipping. She read the last line again. How perfectly like Bertrand Stills, that desperate windbag, to compensate for his lack of editorial substance by devising utter fictions—and about Desma no less, and so soon after Rey's death. The muckraker.

I reckon she wouldn't be in the muck, Mama, Evelyn pointed out, **had you not plunged her there to begin with.**

It would have been wiser, perhaps, to let the matter lie. Had the slights been aimed at Nora herself, rather than at Desma, perhaps she might have managed to harden herself to them, and the whole affair would have fallen silently from memory. But there she was, not two days later—folding her reply into Rob's hand, because she knew in her bones that Dolan would not make the same mistake twice.

Rob smirked. "This Ellen Francis sure is something. She writes up the news faster'n we do."

"She's got nothing better to do," Nora said. "She's very old and past her time."

"Awful steady penmanship. I damn near recognize it."

"Don't be smart. Make sure it's printed before Missus Francis expires from this world."

And so it was.

If any doubt remains as to the **Ash River Clarion**'s relationship with truth, look no further than its reply last week to **The Amargo Sentinel**. This screed reveals all one need ever know about the **Clarion**'s stance on fact. Though if further proof of duplicity is required, one need look only to the **Clarion**'s recent history. Was it not the **Ash River Clarion** that published, just last summer, a report of two schoolmarms roasting to death in their shack—a quickly disproven fiction whose purpose was to discourage homesteading by professional ladies? And did not the **Ash River Clarion** vastly exaggerate the number of steers that perished in the Brushing fire—claiming it was four hundred head of cattle, when in fact it was thirty, so that Merrion Crace and the Stock Association could claim greater losses? The scores of recent arrivals for whose benefit the county seat warrants removal may not know this of their local paper yet—but rest assured that those of us who have lived with it for years are not so readily fooled. To besmirch a citizen as well respected as Desma Ruiz casts a pall over Ash River and all its citizens. It is well established that Mrs. Ruiz' first husband, Robert Gris, was gunned down in New Orleans in 1868 following an altercation with a gambler about a pony. To those lacking the necessary arithmetic: this means Mrs.

Desma had been a widow for eight years when she wed Rey Ruiz of Carter County on March 25th 1876 in the church of maintown Amargo, whose very pews the county seat relocation would see emptied. As many of you know, she was widowed again following Rey's death this April past.

And thus in the eight days since Emmett had been chasing Paul Griggs and the water owed to them around Cumberland, blows had been exchanged thrice between Amargo and Ash River, and Dolan had lost about a stone of weight agonizing over it. But all the details were now outlaid: dates, locales, the manner of Robert Gris's death. Indisputable to a fact.

Nora had just begun to feel steady again when the next reply came flying through her door. This one froze her blood.

I write regarding a matter of which I have been advised by a gentleman agent who visited me last week. I am that same Robert Gris of New Orleans, the very man married to Desma Gris in that selfsame city. I have not seen my wife, Desma (née Zaganou), since 1868, when she disappeared from our house. Given that she was prone to certain indulgences and had vanished to pursue them before, I presumed she would return in due course. When she did not, I presumed some ill fate had befallen her. I regret to hear of the passing of her friend, Mr. Rey Ruiz, of which the agent has informed me, but the law is clear: we cannot both have been her husband, as she is still my wife. I urge the citizens of Amargo and Ash River not to be taken in by this unfortunate duplicity.

"Well?" Dolan had shouted, tossing all four papers down on the kitchen table, one after the other. "Are you satisfied now? Has anything been helped? Are we apprised of all the facts?"

"Don't raise your voice to me." Nora pinned her hands on the chair beneath her and made a show of reading what was before her again. "What nonsense," was all she could think to say. "Surely nobody believes this can be true?"

"It don't matter. That it was raised will make it true for half our citizenry, Mama. They will never doubt it." He stood with his face in his hands for a very long time. "I don't know how you ever intend to face Desma again."

In his corner, Rob was sanding the edges off a small wooden buffalo.

"All the same," he said. "I'm glad of Missus Ellen Francis. Fuck Merrion Crace and the Stock Association both."

THE SAN ANTONIO

AS FOR THE GIRL, WELL—THAT'S A goddamn misery, Burke. She meant no harm. That's plain enough. You'd know it, too, were you a little less pain-blind. I wish it were within my power to give you some relief. But you seem to be improving on your own—so until we leave this place you must try to get calm again. Rest, and take me at my word. She meant no harm. Of all her kin, she was the gentlest.

You reckon I must be wrong. You want to tell me I have been before. Well, that may be. Perhaps the years have softened me a little too much toward the young and their little well-meaning ways. Or perhaps I'd rather have spared her the sight of you! No, Burke, my affections have not inured me to the frightening wretchedness of your face. Those teeth. The stink. Forgive me, but unlike yourself, I have the benefit of remembering what it's like to be scared to death of you.

For it **was** you gave me the fright of my life that

night on the **Supply**. Had it not been for your hollering, I would have stolen from the ship with the blue **nazar** in my pocket and drifted on, town to town, until some noose found me. I wouldn't have cried out in fear, nor fallen backwards over a tangle of rope, and there certainly wouldn't have been three or four fellas all standing around waiting for me when I got outside.

Nor would I have been grabbed from all flanks and swung onto the deck, while everyone shouted at once "Who goes there?" and "Give it back, give it back!"—though, of course, I realize that's impossible, for they would have been shouting in Turkish or Arabic. They were only shadows, but their gist was clear enough: I was a thieving little interloper, and outnumbered four to one. They began to search me. All Hobb's loot sang in my pockets. Things looked bleak. But then I threw my head into the nearest man and when the shock of his fall loosened the others' grip, I broke free and went over the gunwale and didn't quit swimming till I reached the lower harbor.

My clothes were still drying on me when an afternoon downpour brought three of my harriers into the saloon the following day. To the delight of all present, they wore pantaloons and fezzes, but I recognized them right off by the bruise staining one of their noses. My own was its twin, save for being set a little higher—a difference too insubstantial to make us anything but the two people who'd wounded each other. The men came inside and got themselves round a table overlooking the beach. Thus I found myself in a bind. I'd only come in out of the rain intending to get warm and steal a bit of breakfast. But now I was forced to wait. Back in the darkness of the ship, my captors had seemed hulking. But I could see now that even my bruise-mate was young and slight. It took him a long while to notice me. When he did, he didn't tell the others what he was smiling about.

After a while he advanced to the counter where I sat. "Thief," he said under all the noise.

I told him I was no such thing, and furthermore would be called no such thing by anybody, especially not some son of a bitch in his choice of headwear. He went on standing there with his hands at his sides, not looking at me. "You stole something of great value," he said. "Not to the world in all its workings, perhaps—but certainly to me."

And yes, Burke, I realize my embellishment here. He could barely line up three whole phrases of English in them days, which wrought some tension between his constitutional stillness and the need to wave his arms around in order to make his meaning known. But we understood one another—that is to say, I understood he knew I had the **nazar,** and he understood I was denying this. "You know," he said, "in my mother's house, a wrongdoer was always given three chances to set matters right before punishment. So, seeing's how it's her **mati** now burning a hole in your pocket, I propose to give you three chances to right the wrong you've done me."

"That's mighty of you," I said.

"Will you take this, your second chance?"

That got me going. "Second?" I said. "By my count, this is the first."

"Oh?" Finally he turned my way and counted off on his fingers. "Last night when you were caught, you had ample chance to return it, and you did not. That's one. Here I am again, giving you another opportunity. Will you take it?"

"Take what? I don't know what you mean. All this trouble began with you thinking I took something off you. I'd be crazy to take anything else—chance or otherwise."

A second finger sank into his fist. "Well then, that leaves us one last chance. If, when next I see you, you do not return my **mati**, I will take it and cut your whole chin off besides."

"God's heaven, mister. Was that how your mother punished you?"

This did nothing to alter his smile, which the wide-set eyes made look both affable and murdersome. "Of course not," said he. "But then—she was my mother, after all."

His name, I would later learn, was Hadji Ali— though the sailors who brought him here from the

Levant had given up trying to pronounce it and taken to calling him Hi Jolly instead. Jolly for short. The joke, of course, being that he was anything but: a brooding, handsome, steadfast Syrian Turk whose smile was constant but almost never sincere. The name stuck—sometimes to men who bore him no resemblance, which contributed to his being the only soul I ever knew who could be seen in two places at once. People liked the way the moniker sat on the tongue, I think, better than they liked the man who bore it.

Even in them days he gave the impression that his kinship was impossible to earn, and thus perhaps worth everything. What else could explain why I found myself, by way of this errand and that, still unmoved from Indianola when evening came? I'd managed to lay eyes on him twice during that time: first at the stockyards, where he was undertaking some sort of inspection; and then again at the hostler's, arguing with Hans Wertz about the price of hay. My bruise-mate did not see me— which ran against my aim to show him I was unafraid. Hobb, of course, was eager to have me steal from him again. We fought it out all night, Hobb and I: he wanting after my bruise-mate's fez, buttons, the very shoes on his feet; I rejoining that we knew nothing of this red-hatted stranger or his ways, and perhaps ought not tempt our third chance, having already spent two.

By dawn I had talked myself into making tracks.

I did not want to admit my wrongdoing. But neither did I want my chin lopped off, which seemed
a threat just absurd enough to be possible. I would
go south to the border. And I might have done
it—who knows? just imagine!—had some odd
sentimentality for Indianola's sleeping falsefronts
not drawn me crosswise through town one last time,
along the empty stretch of main street where I found
the only other living soul awake at this hour: a rangy
little old-timer interrupted in his homeward journey
by some vision out at sea. As I passed, he turned
my way.

"Son," he said. "Look there. Can you tell me what
that is, coming ashore?"

Well, Burke, I've never claimed full clarity on all
the turns that threw us together. This is the strangeness of memory: in recalling a moment, I am instantly
reminded of all the details that elude me, and feel
myself making them up even as I say "this is certainly
true; and this, and this." But my first sighting of
you has never been vulnerable to such corruption. I
remember everything. The diluted moon hanging in
the pink confluence of sea and sky. The dock pilings
bared by low tide, tower after tower of stone reef
mirrored up and down in the perfect stillness of
Matagorda Bay. The little fishing boats dragging their
wakes home, and among them a tiny skiff, thinly
manned and light on the waves, inbound from the
grim offshore hulk of the **Supply**. Unremarkable—
save for its cargo.

"That's a horse," I told the old-timer.

"Is it?"

But no—not a horse after all. As those oarsmen pulled for the beach, a strange silhouette began to firm up: a snake neck and frowsy mane. A huge periscope head turning slowly this way and that. A tent-peg underbite. A drumlin back from which the morning wind raised a constant and ethereal fog, the dust of six months at sea.

By the time Jolly and his boys got the thirty-three of you ashore, all of Indianola had taken to the roofs and balconies. The crowd was twenty deep around the corral, and every soul there had gone giddy-mad—you camels in particular, for imagine all that time in a ship's hold! You rejoiced in the fresh air and open sky, roaring, jostling, belching incredibly, dust-rolling, butting necks along wild laterals. All about the corral there rang a song of awed denigrations—what in hell were these jangling monstrosities; these big, toothy, snooded goats? What was their purpose? Nobody dared put one finger past the fence, where Jolly paced with the vigor of a man guarding some dark and delightful charge. It came to drift back to the multitude that these camels were the stock of Henry Constantine Wayne, that handsome devil, gathered from all parts of the Orient by the small handful of Levantine boys who had lately been har-ried around town, and imminently bound for San

Antonio, there to serve as pack animals for the cavalry.
The thought of our brave boys mounted up on these
clownish monsters incited a fresh round of insults,
with special ire now directed toward your smaller,
two-humped cousins. Where, exactly, would our
illustrious horsemen sit? Between the humps? Imagine
the bold Lee on one of these! Didn't matter how
far they'd journeyed, didn't matter if they could fly,
they still didn't look right—like lions uddered the
wrong way up! Wouldn't this just tickle the Indians!

Right around then, Jolly folded to his pride and
sprang up onto the shoulder of your huge white
cousin, kneeling patiently there in the middle of the
corral. Despite all the epithets now flying about
the place, he managed to announce, the beast on
which he stood—name of Seid!—could carry more
than fifteen hundred pounds for nine days without
touching water. And if the present company could
assemble a freight heavy enough to keep the camel
from standing up, he, Hadji Ali, formerly of Izmir,
would gift this, his own mount, to the city.

Well, nothing in memory had moved the people
of Indianola to such frenzy. Out they came from
every doorway, first with their kettles and pans; and
then, as their kitchens emptied, with whiskey kegs
and fireirons and gunnysacks of grain; their cham-
berpots and oil lamps and petticoats. Bales of hay
based the load. Laundry carts were commandeered
and bags of linen run up to Jolly, who stood on Seid's
shoulder, snatching boots and jackets from midair,

shouting encouragement to those below—yes hand me that fiddle, yes sir that bucket will fit nicely here—smiling all the while, working out the puzzle of weight and space while the load bloated like a sail.

In due course, an ancient cannonball was brought up from the beach and dropped into one of the linen sacks that dangled from the teetering hummock of Seid's saddle, with a tiny child counterweighted on the opposite side. Seid just went on lying there like a clenched fist. Each new burden slowed his breathing, but the overladen ribs continued to rise and fall. Jolly circled him, fussing, cinching, pulling, chucking the camel's whiskered chin when it began to foam.

Then at last the storehouses and pantries of Indianola were empty, and Jolly bade the camel stand. It unfolded like a dream making itself up as it went. Falteringly, it rocked forward and up and back, strutted one set of legs, one set of leathery thumb-print knees, and then the other, scaffolding itself, tilting its rider around as though he were just another protrusion of its own damnable anatomy. Up it went, with its mouth foaming and all the blood-courses beneath its skin bulging. The load listed a little to the left, a little to the right. Then Seid gave a mighty sigh, of strain or triumph, and took one step forward, and then another. Breathless Indianola watched this improbable brute, manifestation of a want they had not known until it had drifted within reach, shuffle away under the weight of all their pos-sessions. A few steps more brought the camel past

where I stood at the fence. My heart was guttering.
As they went by, Jolly looked down at me—and,
Burke, I took that **nazar** right out of my pocket
and dropped it into his hand. Unsurprisingly, this
did not topple the camel, which only sighed again
at the touch of Jolly's hand, shifted forward, and set
off down the thoroughfare, rolling steady, like some
great four-legged peddler's wagon under all those
pots and pans and trumpets and boots, fifteen hundred or fifteen thousand pounds of cotton and flour
and hay and linen, while in its wake silence fastened
over the rooftops of Indianola.

It wasn't some great purpose kept me following your
packtrain for so many days after Jolly and his men
took you inland. I suppose I was curious about the
camels and their boys, and the soldiers who led you all
across the marshes, and pleased to see the little black
line of your silhouettes flickering ahead of me while
I walked. And it was a thrill to watch you groomed
and watered at the close of each day, and a thrill again
to watch Jolly fit Seid each morning with his saddle—
a thin, leather-wrapped chair, brilliantly chevroned in
green and white, that fit snug at the shoulder, with its
pommel trident protruding from the beadwork like
the reaching arm of some petrified beast.

And it felt like getting away with something to lie
up in the trees at night, unmarked yet close enough
to hear the cameleers' campfire snap, and discern

from their muted talk a few of the old words that still tugged at my memory—fellow, father, God—all spoken in a rhythm so familiar it felt like trying to remember a dream.

And certainly I was getting away with something that first time I crept into camp and sat the fence—a feat of only modest courage because I was convinced the Levantine night-watchman, being old, couldn't see me. You came to look me over and stretched straight-away for the carrots in my hand and I sat very still and tolerated the coarse prodding of your nose while you pried your supper from me. Having got away with this once, I naturally tried it again, misunderstanding that it was neither the watchman nor the soldiers I should fear, but **your** own kin—for camels are liable to notice being excluded from a feeding and start bellowing like hell, which was how I found myself running blind through the scrub with shouts and gunfire behind me, grateful that the moon had yet to rise.

Well, every night thereafter, Jolly came out and stood at the edge of his camp and called out: "Misafir, are you there?"

And I would press myself into the parched ground, drawing not one breath, and after a while he would return to the fire and the talk would start up again.

Four or five nights out, a few luckless rustlers tried for the corral. By their screams, it was clear that they had failed to properly scout what manner of stock they were robbing, and their poor attempt succeeded only in scattering you camels. Crouching under my tree in the dark, I counted the subsiding rifleshots and urged myself to get up and throw in with the defenders—it'll be a long while, I told myself, before you hear this kind of fellow, father, God talk from anyone again. This all went on for a good while. I was still only halfway out of my bedroll when the raid quieted into the thin shouts of recovery—a camel found here, another there—and after a while what should come sighing through the grass toward me but you? Thud thud thud came your soft and heavy feet, all the way to my shameful bedside. You put your face in amidst my bags as though you'd done so a thousand times before and nosed around until you found what you wanted and dispatched what was left of my supper.

"Well, misafir," Jolly said when he came to retrieve you. "I think you will find this a little more difficult to hide than my mother's **mati**."

After that, I slept at the edge of their fire and did not run again until I had to.

Donovan once told me the world is home to two kinds of folk: those who name their horses and those who don't. Having made off with one or two mounts in my day, I counted myself among the latter. But this obviously proved as untrue of me as it did of Jolly's other cameleers.

Eight feet at the shoulder, Seid was the foul-tempered pilot of the train, the biggest of the dromedaries. He scowled disdainfully down at his lesser cousins. To make matters worse, he had to be hobbled at night—for the score of his contempt was reserved for other males of his species, and Tulli, the Great Red, in particular, whom he kept deferent with constant biting, bumping, and frothing. His fellowship with Jolly went way back to when they rode together against the Germans in Algiers. "Don't let them two get around a German, especially together—they go crazy, hey," the night-watchman told me.

This was Yiorgios—George, with his old-timer's face and wistful smile, forever striking fire into a crooked pipe. Nobody seemed to know if George was really as ancient as he looked or if his harrowed wincing was the result of some affliction, but it gave him the aspect of a patriarch, which drew people to him. Women especially. Half that trip he was lurching on his feet. Drink was not to blame, nor was the uneven length of his legs. Every few minutes he probed his ear and sighed in bliss. **"Mal due débarquement. Tu comprends?"**

I had a little French off the Louisiana balcony girls and I put it together that he was suffering from sea-teeter. I asked if France was where he'd come from. But no, he said: Greece. **"Hellada."** George was a pointer. Always aiming that big-knuckled finger toward the ether or the weather or into the faces of strangers, as though you need only turn in the suggested direction to find some obvious truth. He pointed at Jolly and said **"Grèce, aussi!"** and howled with laughter.

"**Vieux**," Jolly said to me. "A very ridiculous old man."

Always at George's heels was the soft-faced Mehmet Halil—called Lilo by all—the last son of a wayfaring line, a quiet, spindly kid blighted by the stubborn politeness of country folk. Looking at him, I remember thinking his only certain prospect was to come to harm. He preferred camels to people, and a bull he called Adnan to any of the rest of you. He couldn't have been more than twelve, and just having him around made me lonesome for Hobb. It'd been a long while since I'd felt older than someone.

With us, too, was Jolly's cousin, Mico Tedro, a wiry, battlesome kid who likewise spliced his native tongue with French at speed. He was a slight, petulant man, and the journey seemed to have made him slighter and more petulant still. Careful of his toilet, he took pains to outfit himself in a vest embroidered with gold birds—from which I succeeded in lifting a button for Hobb. Mico was just vain enough to notice it gone. He raged about its disappearance, but never did manage to track it to me. He was a passable enough rider, but complained all the time about everything. I couldn't blame him, for he contended daily with a mean, labile old gal called Saleh. He was generally disappointed, George told me, because he had expected more from this adventure: more excitement, more deference, and certainly more pay.

"There's pay?" said I.

"Not for you, misafir."

George liked to say that his camel, Maida, spoke all the languages he did. In truth, she knew a handful of words in three and was learning more as he now made his way through the world's features in English: sun, road, tree, star, plain. It delighted him to hear the few **merhabas** and **mashallahs** I had left over from my father. "Between us, misafir, we'll be asking God to bless every tree and rock between here and the sea."

George was keenest about rivers. He mapped the trail as we went, comparing his scribbles to a stack of ancient charts he'd got off some shoreman in Izmir. At every fording place, George would hunt around for our stream on paper. "This is the Guadalupe, misafir," he said, following the wild crooks of that river with a careful finger. "See how it is one of a few short streams? They all begin here." He pointed to a blank space on the map where the black lines met. "Nobody has drawn it in yet, but here we will find a—how do you say? **Escarpement**."

"Escarpment."

He beamed. "You see, misafir? It's all very easy."

He navigated by thumb as much as by compass, and though Hobb wanted after the sharp gold points of his drafting tools, I knew I could take nothing from George without raising suspicion. Hobb settled for a little silver clasp that dislodged one evening from George's left shoe.

You were a much easier mark, Burke, I'm sorry to say. It was far simpler to rob a tassel or bead from the tack of a nameless yearling. You were a good sport about it, too, pretending not to notice, putting up with my laughable packing practice in the cold blue of three in the morning. I believe you regarded me as a kind of tolerable idiot—but a certain rapport, I thought, was firming up slowly between us. You were patiently benevolent and immensely curious of all goings-on. You lipped the greasewood bushes as we went and announced yourself every quarter mile with a fearsome, gargling **buuuurk.** You had a loathsome habit of twisting your neck back to worry the fleas that worried you. Stirred up, your fleas soon became my fleas. Their bites shot out in angry red blotches all over me. By the third day's riding, I was raging through fever-dreams, visions of standing side by side in an ocean with Hobb, who skipped **mati** after **mati, nazar** after **nazar,** across the glittering waves and bade me follow them into the current.

I've been trying to remember what I said of cameleering to that little writer we met in Nevada some years ago. His name escapes me, but I remember being pleased with what I eventually told him.

"No living man can mount a camel without degradation. No sooner has the rider figured where to place himself than he is pitched overboard. This will happen, to the amusement of witnesses, on at least the first several attempts."

What else? Camels loft a sandstorm getting to their feet. They rise in sections: the front, the rear, the middle. Any one of these on its own feels like being thrown from a wagon, but all three together could make a man rethink his relationship with the Almighty. Firming the reins is useless. Once mounted, the rider finds the gulf between himself and the camel's head tracted only by a steep, descending bluff of neck that offers no protection in the event of a fall.

Camels do not take kindly to spurs. They must be addressed only in soft tones, and struck by nothing save the flat of the hand. They will eat any hard or rough foliage, even greasewood, while in caravan and ought not be discouraged from browsing whenever it pleases them, for it does not slow them to do it. A camel can go seven days without water, after which time it will begin to suffer. This will be evident by the sag of its hump sooner than by any change in its disposition. A watering camel can drink fifty gallons at a time and must be given freedom to revive itself. If interrupted, it will exhibit the less amiable aspects of its nature: profound intolerance and incredible strength.

Camels are not for the listless or lowdown. They are faster than one might expect, and twice as rattletrap. They are frowsy and irate. Their fur sloughs off and drifts, filling the air with a sweet, malty stench that frenzies mules and horses, who scatter to outrun their own terror. Those big, rubbery lips hide purple gums, gravestone teeth with which they try for everything in sight: hats, arms, ears, coyotes dogging the herd.

But camelhair is the softest in Creation. Camel's eyelids are thatched with the finest lashes God ever loomed. They are sturdy from their ears to the soles of their feet. Their hearts belong to their riders. And their great height lays all the horizon to view.

My first day in the saddle, sickened by your rolling, I looked down at our many-legged shadow running out over the grass, lengthening in the dying sun, and found my throat gone tight. It struck me, without doubt, that I had somehow wanted my way into a marvel that had never before befallen this world. And I was lonesome for my father, and for Hobb and Donovan, and for all the flickers of my life before, which seemed to be receding from me now in the wake of this consuming and incredible turn to which they had all led.

The first flat stretch of Texas from Indianola to San Antonio, a corridor of lush river valleys, made for easy riding. We must have still been well east of the Comancheria, but that did not keep us from glassing the hills for hostiles. This was owed to the efforts of our military escort, Gerald Shaw, a sour-faced Irish teamster who was determined to terrify us, and complained endlessly about the smell of the camels, as offensive to himself and his men as it was to their horses and mules. The whole spectacle of our stink and noise disgusted him. "The disgrace of the army," he said. "And the delight of the hostiles." He gloried in detailing what would happen if we crossed the trail of a war party. "Dog meat, my hirsute friends." Our deaths, he wanted us to know, would not be near as terrible as our desecration: our guts pulled out, our heads chopped off, our bravest bits reconfigured, and our camels commandeered only to ride later against Shaw's own brave lads who, he assured us, would not hesitate to cut them down.

But any sign of water brought us only to some small pueblo of tough-living Mexicans. By the time we sighted these habitations, their streets would already be teeming. Old Sam Morse might have rethought the use of his telegraph, had he known the speed at which news traveled out here. No victory or massacre was ever so thoroughly heralded as our arrival. Dogs came running to us. Children, arrested in their games, were stunned into silence. From every doorway the enraptured came to marvel and stare: the old ciboleros in their brilliant drapes, shamelessly amazed; the girls with their sunflecked shoulders; the young cowpunchers making like they'd seen everything worth seeing and wouldn't be stirred to awe by the absurd centaurs now advancing on their town. By and by even they would extend a hand to the passing flanks, and then one of your cousins might flare his nostrils and fire a gob of spit into the crowd, delighting every shoulder-straddling urchin in sight.

But for the most part, you were all as indifferent to the wonder you provoked as you were to the rain.

Our cook was a freedman called Absalom Reading, whom the soldiers called Old Ab—though he was probably no older than ourselves. His chuckwagon—heavy with chicken cages and rainbarrels and the loathed cornmill we called "Little Giant"—groaned along behind the packtrain with Ab following along on foot. He had a mustache so thick it might as well have been ambulatory. Sheening his right hand was a web of scars, got, according to some of the soldiers, in some long-ago altercation with a slaver. Others had it that the wound was self-inflicted so he might keep his hand near a hot pan without flinching when the oildrops hissed against his flesh, an ability that seemed pointless save for being incredibly impressive. Which, in a company of dragoons and roughriders, is frankly purpose enough.

Ab was the warden of our sustenance, and by his hand were wrought the few comforts to which we looked forward at day's end. But he was a changeable provider. He and Jolly became enemies right away, for Ab wouldn't leave off staring at the saltpork left behind, night after night, on Jolly's plate.

"Something the matter with that, boy?"

"Ali don't eat pig," George told him.

"Well. Ain't he just as fancy as the duchess's doilies?"

Few habits could've been more ill-suited to that march than Jolly's abstaining of pig. I'd say it cost him about ten pounds in the first week alone. I remember watching him flush the scrub for quail in clothes loose as a scarecrow's. The few birds he did manage to scare up were dangled furtively over our campfire while Ab's back was turned, in and out, in and out, till they were reduced to ash. There wasn't much eating in them, but Jolly rolled those black bones around his mouth like they were sweet as liver.

No pig, no tanglefoot, nor gambling nor whoring around—all of which accrued distrust from the infantry entire, but Shaw in particular. Jolly didn't give a damn. His indulgences were solitude and the blank page. Riding along, he rested papers on his knees and scratched away. From my place at the back of the train were visible only tracts of darkness, but upon closer inspection whole worlds could be found on those pages. Sunsets. Vistas full of caravans. The ruins of an overgrown homestead.

"Where'd he learn that?" I asked George.

"When he was riding with the Turks."

"I thought all you lads were Turks?"

I'd learn soon enough what calling Mico a Turk got you, but George didn't seem to mind.

Jolly prayed palms up, like my father, but in those

days relied on Lilo to tell him when to pray and how often. It was strange to see him defer to a soft, quiet kid. But Lilo had grown up praying this way, and the details of worship were rooted deep, while Jolly could never quite trust himself with his own devotion. When still a child, he had ended up the ward of a Turkish trader and his family. The particulars of this varied depending on who was telling the story; Mico had it that Jolly was stolen; George said he'd gone of his own will. He had grown up surrounded by the necessary recitations, but never quite one with them—they being led in Arabic, of which he had even less than the Turkish he could hardly read. So, George told me, he bowed and touched his forehead to his carpet, and managed, in this way, years of distant following by the time some bedbound elder bade him to undertake the hadj on his behalf. Whoever that man was, Jolly never spoke of him. But it was the pilgrimage by which his name was got that first bound Jolly to the God he'd worshipped from afar. After that, his devotion was entirely his own. Having found God, Jolly next went looking for silver. He chanced upon some in Syria, but was cheated of his share. So he went looking for gold, minerals, salt. What he found was war: all along the sea, and then in Algiers, where he rode Seid into battle for the French. The summer after this bloody venture he learned the camel trade driving a caravan back to his birthplace, where he found his mother dead and his cousin Mico bankrupt and very aggravated by the changes life had demanded of Jolly.

All that while, Jolly had managed to go forward feeling that he was set right in the ways of Allah—save for those occasions when terror of his own possible ignorance seized him. Thus overcome, he would sull and darken.

"What a thing it would be," he'd said to George one night, in the early days of their friendship, "to go through life believing myself devout and discover only at the threshold of death that I'd gone about it all the wrong way!"

Not long after, Henry Constantine Wayne drifted into the harbor on the **Supply** with talk of deserts of a different kind. Jolly went, never quite able to rid himself of feeling that his recitations were misremembered, his rituals corrupted by some deficiency—and the further his journeys took him from people who seemed to know, the warier he became.

It felt a lifetime, but couldn't have been more than a handful of days of northwesterly travel that brought us to Fort Green, a straw-thatched adobe barracks with a Comanchero hostler who eyed us up with dispassion: as though every hump and jangling bell that now passed his gate had been foretold to him long ago. A rare greeting, but disappointing nonetheless. The fort was a rough, desolate place, particularly distressing to Mico. Walking the ridge with me at sundown, he took in the pockmarked barrens and the distant mesas, and his eyes filled with tears. He flung his hat to the floor. "Is it **all** like this, misafir?" I said I hoped so, for I found it bestirred me. He did not share my feelings. "But where are all the people?" he said. "Where are **les grandes cités**?"

What did he want with **grandes cités**, I wondered? The little I could recall of the ones I'd seen was drear and noise, rank streets and the proliferate dead. "I thought you were desert people?" I said.

He drew himself up and gave me a look that might have reduced me to dust. "I am from Smyrna, misafir. Smyrna. Do you know it?" I did not. This was counted against me. "It's a magnificent city by the sea. The port is full of ships and the hills shine with lighted windows. This." With a disdainful wave of his hand he took in the whole barrens below. "Where **is** everything?"

I didn't know. Some of it was probably in San Antonio. Some of it was certainly in New York. And the rest, I reckoned, might be in California. Around us were just ragged trails and oases greened by underground creeks, the occasional dead flitting across the plains, always searching, always moving on in pursuit of whatever it was they could not see.

You may remember two companies came through Fort Green while we were encamped there.

The first was led by Captain Lee Walden. He was taking his cavalry west to Llano Estacado, there to be soundly thrashed by the Comanche. Jolly laid eyes on him and said, "Look at this clown. There'll be trouble tonight." He got that way sometimes—he believed he was as much an oracle of human rot as aching joints were of rain. Sure enough, after Wayne and Walden took themselves off to a nearby ranch to sup like civilized folk, the new arrivals gathered round the keg of whiskey Gerald Shaw kept stowed in his saddlebags. They were all pretty well away by sundown, and getting louder by the minute. Jolly, I remember, was sat out in front of our tent. His day had gone sideways enough already: Seid had coughed through the afternoon around the foaming bulge of his tongue, and increased by tenfold his usual snapping at the other bulls, so that Jolly'd had to trail along behind us to keep him from derangement. Jolly had taken a fall trying to hobble him, and was now mending the bridle, his whole countenance set like the innards of a fire. "I told you," he kept saying as the drinking got louder and more profane. "I told you." George, laid out under a map, spoke without looking at him: "Nothing's happened yet. Ain't their racket bad enough for you to be inviting their attention as well?"

It was Shaw, of course, that got up Jolly's gall. He began wandering the fence with a clutch of wobbly dragoons on his tail. Drink had made them bold. Every so often, one of these thin, blue-eyed men would leap onto the posts and make a grab for a camel's face—**give us a kiss, honey** being their general chorus. Well I wish you had, Burke—just like the one you gave those prospectors last week. Goddamn them. Anyway, those spry enough not to get knocked back off the fence by the force of the camels' revulsion would then fall to bemoaning your tremendous stink.

"You realize," Jolly said, "that it's us they mean. Not the camels."

That he'd said this in Turkish was not straightaway apparent to me. When it struck me, I felt pretty pleased with myself. But nobody was paying any attention to me, least of all George. "Leave it alone," he said.

But Jolly could not.

"I caution you to stop that," he called to the dragoons after a time. "They are easily provoked."

This led to a raucous survey of the dangers of the camel. Perhaps, if one did not drown in its spit, one risked being blinded by its hideousness. "In any case," Shaw concluded, "I look forward to the day when these formidable deterrents join us in whipping old Lo on the plains. Perhaps their stink will wild the Indians, same as it wilds our mules."

It was the wrong thing to say to Jolly. "You ought to heed your mules—they're wise enough to be afraid."

This led quickly to the arithmetic that one Texan packmule was worth Jolly's whole caravan put together, and so on. Shaw got to pointing out that he'd seen a mule kick a man straight through a stone wall. Jolly told him—in fewer words—that if his way of warfare was to kick enemies, one by one, through stone walls, then no wonder his army was in need of camels. Mico laughed so hard at this he started hiccuping. Lilo's face tightened into a nervous smile. Whatever good nature had underlaid this repartee was thinning fast. George tried to bring everybody round. "We are talking," he muttered, "about mules and camels."

Jolly felt pretty sure we were not.

Half the standoff was drunk beyond disgrace, and the other blind with rage. Next thing I knew, Shaw was leading a mule from the stable, and Jolly had got the hobble off Seid. Our Mexican scout, Savedra, who didn't care one way or another how it went, was sorting bets.

I will admit, shamefully, that once I realized it wouldn't be you sacrificed to this unusual premise, I was quite curious to see it play out. George looked disgusted, which I understood to mean that whatever was to come would be rough as hell. You know yourself, you were there—had certainly seen it before, in your time, having come such a long way with Seid. He was a big, hard locomotive of a thing. Mean as a matter of course, and proud in the way Jolly was proud, to the detriment of all else. I have thought often of that evening, and of my memories of the moments before that black mule, with its wide eyes, and Seid, with his head lowered like a battering ram and his mouth trailing spit, connected. I can think of no words to describe what ensued, but you would no doubt agree: Seid more or less broke the mule in half.

This sobered everybody right up. A general scramble resulted in the communal digging of a very shallow grave. "Didn't I tell you leave it alone?" George kept saying.

We'd got the mule buried by the time Wayne returned.

Some hours before daybreak, a banshee noise startled us from our tents. The jogging light of our torches angled around sleep-gray faces and torn nightshirts and alighted finally on the source of the sound: a battered, raging lion in the corral. Cornered by a forest of camels' legs, it was shipping and roaring for a break in the line. By the time a gun appeared, it had already got its shoulders beneath the fence and we could hear it crashing around in the undergrowth for a long time afterward.

We were ordered back to quarters, but there was no sleep to be had. I lay half-dreaming, with the spyglass I'd lifted off Shaw clenched in my fist, and turned over to find Jolly awake and staring. He seemed to have been waiting for someone to whisper to.

"I'm fair ashamed, misafir."

I asked why. He thought about it in that sullen way of his. "Well," he said, "if there had been no blood earlier, we would not have drawn the lion."

———

The second company, three horsemen who rode in late and unannounced, joined us some days later as we were bedding down. They were somber and quick in their unsaddling, deferent to Wayne's presence when he came out to welcome them. Having said their goodnights, they made a fire a little ways off from our own, and sat there grimly spooning Ab's cold leftovers and talking softly. As the evening wore on, they got to looking over at us again and again, until one of them stood and brought his mottled yellow calfskin boots to our hearthside.

"Gentlemen, pardon me," he said. "We've heard so much in recent days about your charges. Understanding that it's awful late and dark and a great imposition—would you be good enough to let us see them?"

It was a great deal of good English, and spoken very softly. The cameleers looked to me, and without thought or consultation I said, "Sure, friend"—and thus found myself looking straight up into the unmistakable face of Marshal John Berger.

If I'd been shot in the heart then and there, Burke, I would not have been more stunned. He went on looking at me. Jolly was already rising to oblige his request. Everything went to noise and light: George laughing that thick, ridiculous laugh as he, too, got to his feet. Mico whining about something, saying in Greek that he was warm now thank you, and not going anyplace. "Misafir?" George said, but I shook my head, no—which only brought Berger's stare drifting over me again. It lingered this time, before he let himself be led away. They were all gone a long while, during which I reckoned my choices. I could bolt off into the darkness, but I would not get far. I could feign trouble with the language, if questioned, which would only make my companions suspicious.

When they returned, I was still sitting there, unmoved and undecided.

Berger wore a look of total sublimity. It almost made him look kind. "Well, gentlemen, what a thing. Much obliged." He held his hand out to me and there seemed to be no end to his shaking. "Much obliged," he said again, and went back to his fire.

A long while elapsed before I raised my eyes again to watch Berger in smiling confab with his companions. His glances in my direction grew more and more infrequent, and when the fire was down to its embers I rolled myself up and covered my face and lay there hour after hour expecting to look up and find myself beneath his boot.

But all night long nothing sounded but the snap of the embers, and somehow in the morning Berger and his men were gone.

A ragged green town rose at last from the grasslands one gray afternoon not long afterwards. The windows of its ruined church sat empty. A slurry of cloud slanted cooling rain across the Spanish houses and straw-thatched barracks.

An outlaw of some notoriety had been hanged that morning, and the whole place was still hungover from the spectacle. The streets were strewn with colored paper. We passed the scaffold on our way through town to the barracks, but the body had already been taken down. Somebody was cutting up the rope for a keepsake.

Mico, clearly on the rough end of a sleepless night, growled, "Is this **une grande cité**?"

A grand city, thought I. No. "This is San Antonio."

Awaiting us at Camp Verde was a besworded commandant who had hurried from Houston to meet us. He had a smart, clean face and yellow hair, and leaned against the fence with one long leg resting on the bottom rail and a stalk of grass between his teeth. The most remarkable thing about him was the evenness of his haircut. Regimentals always groom to look as if they're just on their way to a wedding feast.

"Do you know who that is, duchess?" Ab beamed to Jolly. "That's my old pal Ned Beale."

"Another clown," Jolly said.

Whether this was a result of Jolly's ignorance, or an attempt to get up Ab's gall, I don't know. Being from the Levant, Jolly could be forgiven for not knowing Beale. But the sight of him sure set the rest of us to swooning and waving our kerchiefs. Edward Fitzgerald Beale: bushwhacker, explorer, lieutenant;

compatriot and brother-in-arms of Kit Carson, who once crossed from Texas to California on foot with nothing but a jackknife and enough grit to turn your teeth to powder. Afterwards, I always said that I knew Beale was a modest man by his grooming: a braggart of his stature would've allowed himself a mustache twice that size.

Hobb goaded me, but I couldn't imagine the risk of thieving off Beale.

By evening, we had the fate of our little Oriental packtrain all laid out on good authority. Beale had been tasked with staking a wagon road to California. He would march from here to Albuquerque and then west from Fort Defiance, into the barrens, through canyons and badlands; through Comanche, Ute, and Mojave territory and to the westernmost crook of the Colorado River, penetrating the Great American Desert along the thirty-fifth parallel.

This news was met with general celebration— though to me it sounded much like our trip so far, except with even less water, and even more Indians. I found myself reluctant to feast in honor of the expedition, for Beale's presence had made everything seem more formal, what with photographers and all, and I had begun to fear I might be asked to leave the company here. Ah, I tried to tell myself, but that would suit me just fine. I'd been long enough with this ludicrous train and could make my way west along some less calamitous route, making far less a spectacle of myself. I could go anywhere. I sat counting out my possibilities and growing sadder by the minute. After supper, I left the Turks and infantry to their contemptible merrymaking and walked into town.

I wish you'd been there, Burke, to see the saloons all lit up in the wake of the hanging. I moved slow along the main thoroughfare, looking through windows, hovering barside, carried on the aftermath of sojourn and execution until I found myself in the plaza once more. The dead were everywhere, flitting in and out of doorways, looking for bits of themselves—for here sat the Alamo, Burke, with its ruined steeples like the peaks cut off a mountain. The flag was slumped on its mast in the courtyard of the governor's house. The windows were filled with yellow light, and shadows of the revelers within were dark against the drapes.

On the courthouse stairs sat a thin man in a ragged coat. A strange sadness swept through me at the sight of him. The man sat with his elbows on his knees, feet slightly spread. His hands were clasped in a way I recognized. His cheeks were staved in, and there was a faraway look about him that prickled my neck before I ever sat down close enough to see the purple choker shining above the collar of that well-worn and familiar gray coat, the one I'd known and followed for years as though the garment itself were my home.

"Donovan?" I said.

It was himself. Donovan Michael Mattie—if not in the flesh, then very recently freed of it. He looked me over for a long while with those eyes I had loved. "It's you," he said. "Hardly recognized you."

"What happened?"

He couldn't quite put it together. The dead never could at first. "I was in the square. Then I fetched up here. But I can't remember how." His sour, maddog aspect was softened by fear. "What do you think it means?"

I told him it meant he was a free man. I suppose I was wincing back tears, because Donovan smiled slantwise at me and said, "You always were a damned fool." He went on looking at me, and then pointed. "That's mine." He meant the canteen, which I'd worn about my neck since the day he left me wounded in the ditch.

"You gave it to me," I said. "That night I was shot." I meant to say "all those years ago"—but how long had it been? One year at most. Perhaps two.

"I remember," he said.

"Why'd you leave me behind?"

"I don't know." He stared off. "Figured it was the last kindness I could do you. Was I wrong? Reckon you're better off now, anyway. That Berger. He trailed me every chance he got and made sure someone else did if he weren't about. He put out word of me in places I ain't never been: Denver and San Francisco and the like, and followed up on every sighting. He didn't quit—as you see. As you see. I wouldn't stick around these parts if I were you. God, Lurie. I'm so thirsty." This name surprised me. I hadn't heard it spoken in a long time. "Lurie," he said again. "To have seen clear enough how my life would turn. To have had sense enough to drink from every stream I passed."

Before I could stop him, his hand was out and on the strap of the canteen. For the moment it continued falling through me, I pictured his fingertips raking my heart. It's not as cold as you would expect, the touch of the dead. The skin prickles like a dreaming limb. It's not the strangeness of the feeling that terrifies you—it's their want. It blows you open.

I passed a ferocious night. No sooner had the dismal apparition of my once-brother left my side than I found myself plunging my face into the San Antonio River. Submerged thus, I saw a flash of desert and a ruined church. I found my way back to barracks and stood by you at the **aguaje.** It would be the first of many occasions I noticed the way you drink—a deep, alert, searching draught; the water observable in its course through your neck, your grunts and slurps ruminative and stern, different entirely from the idle dipping of a horse.

Days passed in San Antonio and still Jolly made no invitation of fellowship to me. Hope failed. I went on grooming you and watched him ready the train, dragging my feet about going my own way. Donovan's

want had got firm hold of me by then. I had taken
to filling his canteen at every watering place and tipping little sips of it all through the day. With his
want came a tight terror of the canteen running dry,
so I could never bring myself to empty it, merely to
fill and fill again, even if it was nearly brimming, so
the water within mixed and tasted of everything:
earth and iron and soil and the rain that spent half
the day threatening and the other half flooding
everybody out of the bunkhouse. Such was San
Antonio.

Donovan's want differed from Hobb's. After that
first night, it seemed to thin out little by little, until it
became matter-of-fact. Perhaps it was calmer because
Donovan had died older than Hobb, which made his
want duller, more self-contained. Or perhaps, because
it had not obliterated Hobb's want—merely moved it
aside a little—it could not be as fierce for contending
with a want already contained in me. This led me to
wonder after want itself—was I permitted any of my
own? Must I now forever fill up with the wants of any
dead who touched me, all who'd come before me? I
knew little, and now know even less, save that every
now and again, if I closed my eyes while drinking, a
vision might surprise me. Most of the time it went so
quick I could hardly catch the details—Donovan's
face or Hobb's, or an old feeling I recognized. But
then, too, unfamiliar sights: a particular evening, a
particular woman, a snowbound street. A girl crumpled by the water's edge. Well, it's clear now what they

were. But it made me uneasy in them days, never knowing if I'd been shown what was, or what might, or what never could be.

Myself, I had only one want: to continue on with the Camel Corps as guest and wayfarer for all time; or, failing that, to cease wanting to.

The night before you were set to depart, Jolly found me. There was a strange thrill to him: what I hoped was a reluctance to bid me farewell. I remember fearing that he would embrace me, and that I would shame myself by weeping. But I needn't have worried. He was all flint: "The lieutenant has need of you." He led me into the quartermaster's place, right up the stairs and into the office of Ned Beale himself. The lieutenant sat behind a huge desk on a chair made of antlers, unblinking, and looked me over. "Who are you, boy?"

I told him I was one of his cameleers. This was, for the time being, still true. He looked from me to Jolly, and held up his hand. "As far as I know, Wayne hired six of you fellas for the caretaking of our stock: Hi Jolly; Mimico Tedro; Greek George; Halil; Long Tom; and Elias. Two of these men decamped at Indianola following a dispute over wages. So who the hell are you?"

Jolly wedged himself in. "They have taken his name down wrong, **efendi**. His name is Misafir. My cousin. Only Elias left us after Indianola."

I stood there nodding. Beale had thick, bushy

brows. One couldn't help but think they bespoke supernatural powers of observation. He lifted a paper from his desk. "I got a letter here from Texarkana. **Please be advised, it says. We have reason to suspect that a man named Mattie has concealed himself among your packers. He is a small Levantine of about twenty-three years in age, and has long been wanted for the murder of John Pearson of New York. He was an erstwhile consort of the outlaw Donovan Michael Mattie, recently hanged in San Antonio. If identified, please detain this man at barracks and send word.**"

By the time he put the paper down, my chest had gone so tight I thought I would fall. Jolly made a valiant go of not looking in my direction, but I could see the veins in his forehead outstanding. It struck me I should never have given him that **nazar** back. What a fool, I thought, to admit thievery weeks before an accusation of murder.

Beale lengthened that frank stare of his till I felt my death come into the parlor and take up all the remaining space. "Are you this—Mattie?"

"No, sir."

He turned then to Jolly. "Is he?"

"His name is Misafir, **efendi**."

"And where did we pick him up?"

"Izmir, **efendi**."

"Gerald Shaw seems not to remember him before Camp Verde."

"Shaw drinks a great deal, **efendi**, and talks a good deal more than he drinks. But that don't alter the fact that this is my cousin from Izmir."

Beale read the letter again. "Ali," he said. "You're known among the men to be an upright sort of person. A little hotheaded, according to some—"

"Who says that? Shaw?"

"—but upright and truthful and hardworking. Think carefully." Beale held up the paper. "If you could write, and it were your name about to be undersigned to a letter defending this man, would you still make the same claim?"

Jolly managed a shrug. "I don't know, **efendi**. Perhaps I'd be a bit more careful about writing 'Izmir.' I'm not sure if he was really born there after all." He turned those wildly smiling eyes to me. "Can you recall the place of your birth, Misafir?"

By some miracle, it came to me. "Yes," I said. "I was born in Mostar."

Afterwards, Jolly and I sat together astride the barracks fence. He said nothing for a good while, only tamped his tobacco.

"You needn't have done that," I said. "But it was awful good of you."

"We have all been called this or that over the years. But now we are who we are."

Whoever he'd been before, he was one of God's

own as far as I was concerned, and I told him so. He didn't seem to think much of that. It occurred to me for the first time what a funny expression that is. I had never much reckoned its meaning. One of God's own what?

"For instance," Jolly said. "I was born Filip Tedro. But when I got to Mecca my name became Ali Mostafa. By making the pilgrimage, I was allowed to call myself a **hadji**. So: Hadji Ali."

"Hadji Ali."

"But **hadji** is an honorific, Misafir. You see?"

I turned this over for some time. It was all gusting through me: not just Mostar—not just my father's birthplace, that tumble of stone houses and the green of the river I couldn't recall, but his own name, too, unthought-of for so long and dredged now from the blackest loam of my mind. Hadziosman Djurić.

I pulled it into its separate pieces.

Hadziosman Djurić. Hadziosman.

"Who's that?" Jolly wanted to know.

"My father, I think."

"Hadji Osman?" He grinned at me as though we'd just struck a lode the breadth of Texas. "But Misafir— are you a Turk, after all?"

MIDDAY

MIDDAY

AMARGO

Arizona Territory, 1893

AFTER YEARS WITH SANTA ANNA'S militias, Rey Ruiz's father was galled to find the very wars he fought had shifted the border south of his own holdings. Anglo officers stood in the plazas of his childhood haunts insisting he would be permitted to keep what was his. Convinced of Mexico's imminent repossession of the territory, he stayed put in this loathsome new republic and raised Rey up with a robust feeling of **vergüenza** that lingered long after the old man had gone to God. When Desma met him on her way west, Rey was hurrying the stragglers of his family's decimated herd out of Chiricahuan territory and beginning to doubt his father's convictions. Mexico was embattled, bust. It didn't seem likely to come back for the people lost to its most recent defeat. So he and Desma traveled three hundred miles in each other's company. He found her no stranger to **pistoleros**. The men of her family had led ambuscades all over the Macedon. When he recounted a hazy childhood memory of sitting at the kitchen table while soldiers bayoneted sacks of flour and his father hid up the chimney, Desma said, "And did your mother then prepare them a meal so splendid they never noticed she hadn't warmed a single pot over the fire?" as though she had lived it herself.

When they got to the Río Rojo, they staked adjoining plots and went a further seven years pretending to be strangers, proving up side by side while Amargo grew up around them. Rey, having studied the **yanqui** bootheel from below all his life, had finally alighted on the means by which to adjust the vantage. He built a reputation as the surest water-witch in six counties. He fenced off his length of the creek and started charging herders and travelers to water at the breaks. Effortfully, he crushed within himself all lingering vestiges of his grandmother's belief that farming was a weak man's work. By the time Nora and Emmett came bumbling in, the Ruizes were only just married, pillars of the camp and stewards of a combined 320 creekfront acres.

"That's a fair bit," Emmett had observed rather nervously during one of their tentative early suppers. "Won't every man coming this way try and take it from you?"

"Do you reckon that'd be a change from what my people grown used to?"

Rey's people were Mexicans and Quechans. But depending on both day and grievance, the unknown tendrils of his line might expand to accommodate fellow sufferers of Navajo and Pueblo and Yavapai blood. Even Apache sometimes—so long as the target of their raids was some inept **yanqui** river fort and not a fatherless ranch.

He had taught Nora and Emmett about the importance of the clerical offensive. One must always know the whereabouts of all paperwork and be able to produce evidence of any agreement, any exchange of goods or services, at a moment's notice. Nothing pleased Rey more than confusing inspectors and fellow citizens with his organization. This went hand in hand with Desma's own proclivity toward order, which extended well beyond housekeeping. The last decade of her life had been given over to subduing every unruly inch of range that adjoined her homestead. It had been a stealthy undertaking. Every year, the wagon road near her place just happened to get a little less crooked. The flowers happened to get a little less wild, the trees a little more uniform, until columns of cypress were growing three abreast all the way down to the bottomland, where her outbuildings sat huddled on the south fork of the Río Rojo, currently a mudsmear that caught the light in such a way that it looked, for a hopeful moment, like clear water.

Desma's foreyard was deserted save for a handful of chickens and Goatie, Amargo's most vaunted citizen, presently enjoying a dustbath. She had first appeared half a lifetime ago in one of Rey's rabbit snares: a small, fat thing with a scrub-brush hackle and a white blaze down her face. That she was of caprine aspect was undeniable—but here town consensus ended. She was so small, and made such a strange racket. Nobody could prove that she was really a goat, and nobody could prove that she was really a sheep. Presented at the county fair on Desma's whim, she had triumphed in both designations, bringing gawkers from all over the territory to debate this crucial point while she tottered primly around at Rey's heels. The appearance of her photograph in the wilderness society newsletter had eventually brought a Prescott bigman to town. He insinuated, among other things, that Goatie was no more than a hoax, and further compounded this mistake by suggesting that the only way to prove otherwise was by necropsy—to which Rey responded by beating him, in Desma's words, "till he couldn't see God," an incident the **Sentinel** neglected to mention, but the **Clarion** decried for weeks.

At the height of Goatie's fame, Rob and Dolan had practically lived at this house. Picture them: six and five, begging to bathe her, walk her into town, sleep in the barn loft overlooking her pen. Did Rob, now, remember warning every passerby that she was a chupacabra, until he half-believed it himself? Could Dolan recall selling wilted greens out of a crate to spare pilgrims the disgrace of meeting her empty-

handed? The only Lark to visit her of late had been
Toby—who, though fond of her, had never held her
in as high esteem as his brothers had, for by the time
of his birth she had already shocked everyone by
growing up to become a burro.

And what an obvious burro she was—ornery
and old now, thirteen, fourteen, perhaps even fifteen
years gone since her county fair debutante days.
White with age now and potbellied, and evidently as
wedded to her particularities as any dowager, for all
it took to bring her indignantly to her feet was a few
shouts of Desma's name.

When Nora went on calling, Goatie shook herself
out and stormed off behind the house.

Perhaps by some stroke of luck Desma might be
out after all, and the questions that needed facing
could be held off for another day. But that scenario
hid another unwelcome concession: no elk steaks for
supper.

Nora braved the house and called up the stairs.
The landing was dark. Ordinarily there could
only be one cause for prevailing silence at the Ruiz
residence—which would continue, to the embarrassment of unexpected visitors, for however
long Desma and Rey required to get themselves
decent and out of whatever hayloft or wheelbarrow
they had fallen into together when the passion
struck them.

But that wouldn't be the case now. It would never
be the case again. That was the funny thing about

death. The wake of its altered mundanities could keep surprising you long after it had swept through.

The fusty damp of the kitchen—worsened considerably by the stovefire's dying heat—was probably owed to the mountain of vegetables that muddied the kitchen table. What extravagant waste, Nora thought. Beets and turnips everywhere. But—damnably, maddeningly—not a drop of water in sight. An empty basin sat on the table. The coffeepot was cold. Inside slapped the black dregs of this or yesterday morning's brew, the sight of which made her so dizzy with thirst she could have tipped the grounds down her throat. And why not? There was nobody watching, nobody here or upstairs or outside the wide-flung rear door through which she could see the back field.

Everything out there struck her as suddenly brown—as though the distant river had swallowed the immediate plane, where flowers and bright-spouting leaves ought to be. The garden had been all churned up. New fenceposts, pink and indecent, retreated uphill alongside the old, which were busted up in one, no, two places—right at the side of the house, and then further down by the shore.

And there was Desma after all, walking uphill and away, a distant speck of black and orange against the woodshed. Nora shouted after her again, but succeeded only in earning another derisive stare from Goatie.

Now that she knew where Desma was, she could

at least brace herself for what was to come. She felt
better about it, somehow. There was a difference,
however small, between calling upon somebody on
home ground and ambushing them there. She would
at least have the element of surprise, a chance now to
think about what she might say.

She fell back to the kitchen. The fire had a little life
in it yet, and for a hopeful moment she lifted the lid
off the cookpot. But no water there, either: only a
little island of parched cornmeal stuck to the scarred
bottom of the pot. That was how Desma had got so
thin, she thought. Cooking so little now that Rey was
gone and leaving little islands of food day after day.
And what did she intend to do with all these vegetables, weirdly green and underripe? How strange of
her to harvest so many and leave them strewn about
like this.

**Do you reckon she tore everything up in a
rage, Mama?**

Desma? God no. The only thing that galls that woman
more than Merrion Crace is a disordered house.

That's why I love it so here.

It's easy to keep order when there's not three boys
and a New York orphan running your place down.

**Sure, but you don't have the Stock Association
haranguing you and calling you whore in the paper,
either.**

What's that got to do with housekeeping? I mean
only that if Desma had her way, the world would
work in perfect symmetry or not at all.

Maybe that's as it should be. Not like our place.

Well, you can damn well stay here, then. I'm sure Desma would welcome the company, and God knows there's enough beets here to feed the whole town twice over.

Wouldn't it be something if she was having a party, Mama? And you weren't invited?

Teach me to rattle off in the paper.

I don't think she's read it.

She certainly has.

I don't think so, Mama. Look.

There it was. Right in the middle of the kindling crate, between the stove and Desma's knitting chair. It took Nora a moment to recognize it—but the inferior paperstock was unmistakable, and there sat the telltale mutilated **A** of the **Ash River Clarion**'s AUCTION section.

Seeing it jolted her as though she'd met the eye of some co-conspirator she had never expected to see again.

Don't look like she's read it at all, Mama.

Oh, she's read it all right.

But suppose she hadn't? It was Rey's habit to devour the news; Desma was more likely to just get around to bits of it whenever she could. Papers, having survived his wringing and over-gesticulation, were relegated to the kindling pile, strategically placed beside Desma's chair so that she might peel pages off into the fire as she read them. A strange habit that confounded Emmett—for what if she had cause to revisit a column, or desire to remember some event she wanted to attend or item she wanted to buy?

Desma found this notion laughable. "Where the hell do I go, Emmett?" she'd say. "What the hell do I buy?"

How often had they sat here, in this very parlor, while she mended trousers on that very chair with her half-moons slung low and laughed her way through the description of some corset or iron before feeding it to the fire?

Yet there it was, the offending daily, sitting insolent and intact in the middle of the pile and offering by its very existence the most absolute proof of having gone unread.

If she'd read it, Evelyn said, **wouldn't it have already burned?**

Perhaps she's kept it to confront me with.

Come now, Mama.

It just seems impossible.

Surely it's easy enough to tell if a paper's been handled or not, Evelyn pointed out.

Perhaps it was inevitable that Nora's attempt to edge out this solitary sheaf should send the whole stack spilling to the floor—but neither Nora nor Evelyn had foreseen this. On all fours now, prairie-dogging to keep an eye on the woodshed, Nora shoveled papers back toward the kindling crate. What looked like recently arrived letters surely belonged at the top of the pile—but then there were the undated envelopes; the scraps of script on which no legible date was evident, but the misplacement of which Desma would certainly note. To make matters worse, every time she righted things, she spotted more stray pages that had flurried away, some under the table, others beneath the footstool, both within crawling distance, but in opposite directions, so that she had to scuttle back and forth like a beetle.

Hurry, Mama.

Desma was coming back. Struggling under an armful of new fenceposts, she would need three minutes, perhaps more, to come in sight of the open door and Nora's guilty red face.

Nora got the **Clarion** out from under the stovebox and opened it. This copy was creased once, only in half, and seemed to have suffered none of the damage that befell papers passed from hand to hand—the worn-out corners and cup rings and sticky vestiges of meals. Perhaps such things did not befall papers delivered to a house devoid of men and boys. Perhaps papers in widows' households maintained only that single, primordial seam.

Or perhaps she just hasn't read it, Mama!

That's not possible.

It would be too immense a stroke of fortune. She glanced outside. Here came Desma with the strides of some Amazon, stout and sunburnt, bosomed like the prow of a ship and crowned with that glorious detonation of hair into which white lines had recently begun to intrude.

Lord, but she moves fast.

Are you going to take the paper?

Don't be ridiculous.

If she hasn't read it yet, Mama, she needn't ever.

She'll hear all about it around town. If she hasn't already.

But the author, Mama. Town gossip won't tell her it's you.

When Nora looked up again, the fenceposts had dropped from Desma's hands. In their place was the derringer out of Desma's pocket, useless at this distance but leveled at the open door as though it might drop a bird at two hundred yards with lethal accuracy.

"Who's there?" Desma shouted. "Come out, you're stood down!"

"It's me, it's only Nora!" She waved her free arm.

"Who?" And then, after a few moments, Desma put it all together. "Praise God." She stood awhile with her hand on her chest. "I thought: here they've come now in broad daylight and me without the rifle like a right fool."

Nora babbled reassurances—no, no, it was just herself, sure.

"I suppose you're here for the steaks?"

"Only if you've a few to spare."

"I ain't gone hunting this week, Nora."

This felt punitive. But it was unlike Desma to lie. Nora gestured to the deluge. "What's all this?"

"As you see."

What was the meaning of that? A rebuke? Quarrel

didn't seem to be in the immediate offing—but neither did an embrace, nor a smile. If only she could remember how Desma greeted her on any ordinary day. Her fingernail tasted of salt. "Do you need help?"

But Desma only waved her off. "Help yourself to what's left of the coffee. I'll be along in a minute."

And as the woman outside dropped from crouch to crouch to gather up the jackknifed fenceposts, Nora tipped the stove lid open and dropped the **Clarion** inside. For a blinding, terrifying moment, she watched it strike the ash on the cold end of the stove, and she thought it might not catch. But then a tiny wisp of flame sprang to life along its edge. The fire did its work, and she replaced the lid.

Her heart was still staggering a little when Desma swept in. "What are you standing around for? You waiting on me to put out the good silver?"

"I'm surprised you think there's any left—I been waiting on you unchaperoned a full ten minutes, and this here's my roomiest thievin' skirt." Nora lifted her hem and swished a little from side to side.

"At least you left the vegetables."

This was better. Here was the Desma she recognized. Desma, whose eyes were always this flat, always this mirthless—perhaps especially when she was feeling mirthful.

"I wouldn't want the folks invited to whatever feast you're planning to go hungry."

"I'm dissolving my garden."

"You look to be fortifying it—that's a hell of a lot of new fence."

"I doubt it'll do much to keep in what belongs to me and keep out what don't."

"Deer?"

"One of Crace's men." Desma opened the coffee-pot and made a face and began looking around. Nora allowed herself to hope that a water bucket might appear from someplace. "I caught them this time. Saw them with my own eyes, horse and rider just yonder. Though not till they'd ate most of my cabbages."

"Good," Nora risked. "With yours out of the running, maybe the rest of us will have hope at the harvest fair this year."

Desma didn't laugh. Nora took her hand. "Let me help."

Fence-raising went no faster with both of them at work. She grappled each post to the instructed angle while Desma grimaced through a mouthful of nails and bent to the hammering. The blows set a garble of panic through Nora's chest.

They moved into the field. Here and there, massacred beets leered up from between the furrows.

"Seems an awful lot of damage for one horseman," Nora said.

"Well, ain't damage Crace's staff of life?"

"Still."

Desma straightened. She was making that face she sometimes made when she was fixing to call you an idiot. "You saying I'm telling tales?"

"Of course not."

"You don't believe me?"

"I do."

Desma dusted off her hands. "You know how you sit up in the night sometimes, but you're still half-asleep and casting about for what woke you? Well. A few nights ago, I came to and lay an age trying to figure it out. Then I realized it was Goatie, calling down the gods. Raving and hollering. She gets that way these days, being half-blind. Sometimes I think she realizes through that fog of hers that she hasn't seen Rey in a while, and wonders where the hell he's got to, and starts crying for him—only she always quits after a little while. That night she didn't. So I went over to the window and seen my little garden fence all busted up and a horse so hard at work in the plot I could hear it chewing all the way up in the house. When I got to shouting, it turned and I could see the rider, clear as day, grinning at me. Grinning, Nora. Like all along, he'd been hoping to get caught. Anyway, as the shouting made no difference, I started shooting instead. I must've hit the horse, for it left a bloodtrail. Not that it did much good. Just look at the damn fence." She pointed to the wreckage on the far side of the yard, where the old poles were blown out like timber behind an avalanche. After a while, she laughed. "If Rey was here, I'd have had to talk him out of giving chase. Lest it was a trick to lure us out here for hanging."

Nora looked down at her shoes. She made the only joke that came to her. "Toby would say you've seen the beast."

Desma shook her head. "The notions that child's mind runs to. You ought to put that Josie right out of the house, like your sister did."

"And break Dolan's heart? He'd never forgive me. None of them would."

"He'd forgive you soon enough. Boys always do."

Desma espoused the kind of easy faith in children only held by people who'd never raised any themselves. And thank God for that, for it was good to be reminded of the merits by someone who lacked the constitution to withstand many of parenthood's most profound rewards: the shying and the sulking and the constant ingratitude, and eruptions like the one last night, which she had intended to detail to Desma, but thought better of now. If her determination to forgive the boys was sincere, Nora must not compound their disgrace by poisoning the neighbors against them.

And anyway, Desma was shading her eyes and looking up the hill. "What's here?"

A rider was coming down the side road. Desma let the hammer sink. Her free hand had vanished in her apron pocket, where her derringer bulged none-too-subtly behind a pattern of faded flowers. Nora drew over to her and they stood together and watched him:

a stringbean in a plug hat that could only be Ferdy
Kostic bringing the mail.

"Lord," Desma said through her teeth. "That hat."

"Emmett calls him '**strawman**.'"

"How come?"

"Because he says Ferdy has all the outer vestments
of a real fellow—but if you ruffle him one bit, the
stuffing comes right out."

It felt good to be laughing together at last. Here
they were, two old friends on the same side of something. Perhaps the Almighty had devised a purpose
for Ferdy Kostic after all.

He drew up at the fence and sat there, surveying
their handiwork. "My God, Desma," he said. "I see
you just about fixing to keep the whole county out."

Desma returned the hammer to her shoulder. "I'm
staking up against whatever bummers been feasting
they horses on my cabbage."

"Well thank God I came by in time to see the last
of our open range," Ferdy said.

"Thank God."

He sucked in his cheeks and made a show of
squeezing through the fence. "I reckon I'll have to
jump my horse from now on."

"You'd do better to leave the mail on the front
porch, like normal folk."

Ferdy said nothing.

Then, at the sight of Nora, his entire face lifted.
"Well hullo, Missus Lark! I'm surprised to see you
here."

She shifted a little. "Yes, I only just came by."

"And here you are," he said. "Well, you're mighty brave. Mighty brave."

The only thing she could think to say—"Ferdy, I hope you haven't been taken in by all that depredation talk!"—dropped thick and lifeless among them all. No change in the postmaster's mien. Not a flinch from Desma.

Still mounted, Ferdy now opened his gunnysack and started rummaging. Nora had long suspected his whole pretense for taking up this work was owed to his desire to make wild conjectures about other people. It had ceased to humiliate her on home ground—in fact, she had surprised herself by the sincere absence of feeling whenever he asked why no young men were ever writing to Josie—wasn't it strange, her being so delicate and lovely and gifted in such a very peculiar way? But to weather this ceremonious fumbling here, of all places, fired her whole being.

"Well, let's see now," Ferdy said. He rested a fistful of letters against his pommel and squinted through them. "Let's see. I got a rather short note from your brother in Philadelphia. What a strange word that is, Philadelphia—ain't it strange?"

"Strange as it was last week, Ferdy," Desma said.

"Who ever heard of putting two perfectly good letters together—and not to make a new one, but one what already exists? Where I come from, our F's are F's. Imagine my name being spelt Pherdy." He was amused enough by this to spell it once or twice, by which time Nora caught herself chuckling in agony. Desma's face was like stone. "Last week's **Ladies' Home Journal**, delayed—and Missus Lark, I have yours, as well. Here it is. What else? Another notice from the Land Office. I see you're still back and forth with them about Rey's claim? I reckon they don't like it when you go awhile without reply. I can stop back through on my way to town, if you want to answer 'em right off. No? All right." He shifted in the saddle. Desma's hand was still out-stretched. "I didn't bring the **Clarion** round—I didn't think you'd care for it after this week."

Desma stood staring up at him. "I pay for the **Clarion**."

"Do you? Better hope the Land Office don't."

Nora's stomach plunged.

"You'd better bring it round later, Ferdy," Desma said.

He looked down at the fan of remaining envelopes in his fist. "What about this letter for Rey? Will I leave it with you?"

"What's the alternative? Leave it on Rey's grave?"

He made a show of looking through the letters again, switching between two and three, as though he couldn't decide how many there were, until Nora finally said: "For God's sake, Ferdy—can't you read?"

His downcast smile was full of confidentiality. "I'm awful sorry these letters for Rey just keep on coming. I reckon it must be hard to apprise ever'one that he's gone and left this world. Can't hardly think of a person who would expect it. A young man, really, at forty-five. But he was awful big, Desma. Not fat, I mean, but big. I reckon he went for the same reasons big dogs go sooner than little ones." He tapped the letter against his pommel. "I'll tell you square, Desma. This note here looks mighty personal. D'you mind if I leave it at Rey's place? I know you'll only go and get it after I'm gone, but—well. I got the law to consider."

"Do what you like, Ferdy."

"All right, then." He tipped his hat. "Missus Lark." And then, disaster. "Missus Gris."

He turned his horse up the rise. It seemed to take hours, but at least, Nora thought, the cold dregs of this moment were fading. He was working his horse over the tumble of rocks by the big juniper, and once they were over it would be up and away toward Rey's plot, and perhaps then she could bring herself to look at Desma—who, in true form, was already back to work, crouching with the letters heaped on her lap. How like her to be so calm. To be stooping already to thumb the dirt from a huge potato with her right hand.

That it was a rock did not become apparent until it was halfway through its arc to Ferdy's head. Even then, there was no time to shout a warning. It thumped between Ferdy's shoulders, knocking him sideways. His horse jerked, twisted out from under him and left him in the dirt. He wasn't on the ground two seconds before Desma was on top of him. Her fist caught him between the shoulders with a surprisingly thin thwack. Without knowing how, Nora had appeared at their side, close enough now to see mud spraying everywhere, and the fact that Ferdy was moving.

"Help me," Desma said. She shifted off him and grabbed his shoulder. Nora stooped and helped roll him. The effort made her head swim. She gasped once, and then again, wondering how long it had been since she'd drawn breath—and there was cause now to go back to not breathing, because Desma was straddling Ferdy Kostic's chest. An arm emerged from the struggling mass of his coat to hold her away. Ferdy was sputtering. Desma forced her fingers into his mouth.

"Say, **Missus Ruiz**," Desma said. "Say it." His whole head followed when she tugged his jaw down. "Say it."

A garbled version of it came foaming around her fingers. Meethuth Rooweez. Rey's letter now appeared in her other hand, and she began tearing it, wadding a flurry of paper into Ferdy's mouth. Her fingers, where they disappeared in the wet, wrenching recess between his lips and tongue, were harrowed with gnawmarks, orange with the same blood that oiled his teeth.

Whatever ideas Nora'd had about how Ferdy might be let up were lost to the vision of Desma pulling him to his feet and then kicking him back down. It all happened so fast she couldn't even say where Desma's boot had connected. He sat there forever, spitting out one piece of bloodied paper after another. Then he was on his feet, retreating to the twitchy withers of his horse, so fast he seemed sped along by Desma's curses rather than his own volition: "Don't you ever lay a hand on a piece of paper with my name on it again, Ferdy Kostic—you hear? You hear?"

A miraculous swing lofted him into the safety of the saddle. He didn't turn around until he was all the way to the fence. His parting words—"You're a right old bitch, Desma—they'll string you up for claim-jumping yet, and won't nobody say a goddamn thing save good riddance"—were shouted over a torrent of Desma's Hellenic expletives.

※

THERE WAS WATER IN DESMA'S KITCHEN after all. It had been hidden in plain sight, in a bucket Nora had mistaken for the slop pail just beneath the wash basin. She watched the tragic last dregs of it decanted into a pot, there to boil while she got bandages and Desma sat on the table with her legs up on the stools and dug through her gouged knuckles for bits of grass and stone. She did not suffer being touched even under ordinary circumstances, and when Nora soaked the rags and brought them over, Desma took them and balanced them on her lap and began cleaning her hands herself. Nora stood back against the counter and listened to the cool crackle of the water wrung back into the bowl. She must not leave here without some—if there was any left, if Desma hadn't wasted the last of it on the ridiculous exercise of beating the postman senseless.

"He bit you," Nora finally allowed herself to say.

"He sure did."

"Reckon he's got madness?"

But there was no coaxing a smile out of Desma. "He's right, you know."

"Don't mind him."

"But he's right. Rey never did make up no will. He could plan on a whole lot of life, but he never was too keen on readying up for the hereafter. I think he reckoned we'd die together in an embrace at the age of a hundred and twenty having spent all our money and salted our fields so the rest of you couldn't take them."

"An admirable dream."

"Though a little rosy, I think, given his tendency to get into fights with stockmen and inspectors and every other goddamn soul, all while spitting in the face of the Land Office besides. And even if he hadn't pointed a gun at every inspector that came this way, won't no Land Office in the world give 160 acres of creekside land to some woman whose porch an angry Mexican left his boots on—even if he did leave them there for twenty years."

"But you're his wife."

Desma had moved on to bandaging. Her apron was spattered with blood.

Nora felt dizzy. Little pinpricks of light dotted the shadows of the kitchen. At length, she tried again. "You have his name, Desma. Nobody's ever known you as anything save Ruiz. Surely that's got to count toward inheritance. Perhaps if we wrote you letters of proof."

"Please, Nora. I'm quite satisfied with what's been achieved by you writing on my behalf already."

There it was. And here was the moment, overtaking her at last. Confess her wrongdoing or disown it. She could outline her reasons for what she had done, right her wheels here and never feel cowed about this again.

But she didn't. She buckled. "What do you mean?" she said.

Saint Peter had sounded more convincing at the break of day.

Desma was laughing. For a moment, she seemed almost sincere. Perhaps it might not be too late to pretend her answer had been a joke. But it was. "Ellen Francis?" Desma said.

"Who's that?"

"Nora. For God's sake. You're the only soul I ever told that Robert got shot up over a pony."

"That's hardly true."

"It is."

"You told plenty of people. You told Emmett, you told Rey."

"Was it Rey wrote that letter? Being dead for some time now, I doubt it—though it seems nothing can be put past dead husbands of mine." Desma shook her head. "All I ever said to anybody else was that Robert Gris was buried back east."

Nora stood for a long time, watching Desma bandage her hand. "Why would you say anything different to me?"

"Because you ask and ask in that way of yours. And we known each other seventeen years."

"How did he really die?"

"I guess he didn't."

"So it's true. You're not his widow."

"Perhaps," Desma said finally. "Last I saw Robert Gris, he was sitting up under a pile of boards at the bottom of our staircase, which had fell through as he was coming after me with a broom. The whole staircase went, right down to the bottom. Like something godstruck. Took me a stretch to realize I weren't dead myself. Then I just ran. Didn't look to me that anybody could survive a fall like that—hell, the house itself didn't. But I'll tell you. It's Devil's work, that letter. For even if Robert crawled out of that wreckage, he never wrote the **Ash River Clarion,** or any other place. That man could hardly cipher. His skills were drinking money away and closing distance between us with whatever wood or iron or belt he could lay hands on." Desma shook her head. "Shot up over a pony. My God, Nora, you never could keep from showing off every little thing you know."

Anger, quick and brilliant, roared her up. "Well it's your own damn fault. What a thing: lie about your husband's death, but give everyone his real name?"

"A person don't reckon such things will follow her across a thousand mile of desert and end up in the paper, Nora. A person reckons her bosom friend won't use her darkest stories to grease her own chin—while on the opposite shore, cattle barons and newspapermen and mail carriers come heaving after every scrap she's worked her whole life to hold."

Nora pinned her bottom jaw to steady it. If it went on clattering, Desma might hear and point it out. After a time, she could speak again.

"I only did what I thought right. What I thought you would do."

Desma laughed. "How would I manage without you here to be so rock-sure of my virtues?"

"Well," she said. "Aren't I just the badman for everybody today?" This was Ellen Francis all right—Ellen Francis Volk in the flesh, resurrected here in the throat of her daughter and suddenly holding forth on the obvious injustices of life. She had not come here to be subjected to this. She was that sorry, but she had only meant to help. Did Desma, after all this time, believe otherwise? Did she think Nora would deliberately wright her harm, or cost her inheritance and humiliate her marriage? Wasn't it bad enough that she had gone days and days with no water, and was coming—peaceably, she had been mistaken to think!—to this place of safety after having endured, as no woman should, the silent vanishment of her own husband and the thankless and cruel remonstrance of her sons? Who had gone mad, by the way. Well what a mistake on her part, to think that she could find some comfort, some shelter from the confusion of the household in which she had been basely and falsely accused of being unsee-ing and foolhardy and then attacked—yes, attacked in her own kitchen, by a young man she had raised up and now hardly recognized in all his rage and gullibility. Desma might as well row in with Rob and Dolan, and Emmett too, wherever the hell he was, so they could all line up against her together.

Desma eyed her coolly. "A tragic tale, to be sure," she said. "But it's got fuck-all to do with this. You must have writ up that article weeks ago, Nora."

There. It was over now. Their anger had taken its customary course: barming up and dissipating in a flash. Already the room was growing bigger, easier to breathe in. She felt almost cool. A long silence would now elapse, and then someone—probably Nora, for she never had nerve enough to stretch a standoff the way Desma did—would say something light and mild, and the shy smiling would start. In a few minutes they would be laughing again. Well, perhaps not quite laughing. It had been a dire fight. One thing at a time, she thought. Slowly, slowly. She would apologize first. Use some endearment. And then, quite carefully, she would ease herself toward the question of water.

She tried. "I'm that sorry for all this trouble, Desma," she said. And then: "In fairness, I doubt you'll ever get another letter again."

But Desma wasn't smiling. The back of her hand touched one cheek and then the other. She went on looking at the ground.

Was it possible, Nora thought. It couldn't be.

"Oh Desma," she said. "You aren't crying?"

Comets and two-headed calves were a sight more common than this. She couldn't remember the last time it had happened—if it had ever happened at all.

Already, it was gone. Desma sat up. She was back to her stone self again.

"Don't you got somewhere to be, Missus Lark?" she said.

NOONTIME BROUGHT HER IN SIGHT OF maintown Amargo. The hills, with their few remaining headframes, were bald and flat-topped and broadly streaked with ore, black bands swooping from ridge to ridge. Rockspurs leapt up out of the sage along the canyon rim. It still surprised her to see roofs in the Big Fork Creek bottomland. Every now and again she half-expected to clear the rise and find the place restored to its primitive state: both shores thick with tents and laundry lines and gambling layouts; the nascent thoroughfare choked with wagons; the bummers hovering over stinking cookpots; sun-roasted men panning the glittering current. Most of these seekers of fortune had moved on when the silver played out. The few that got their feet under them had raised houses and bought bowlers and taken to calling each other Mister—until now.

What a thing to have gotten all the way to Desma's and then found herself too provoked, too besieged to ask for water. Never mind the elk steaks—they could be managed without. But to leave Desma's house, in the aftermath of a quarrel, feeling for the first time that she really must not, dare not, ask for anything. Well, it struck her cold.

She had fled—yes, fled—with no water at all. Now she was at the mercy of the town's mercurial cistern, and it was nobody's fault but her own.

She rode over the bridge. The faintest shadow of last year's waters dampened the creekbed below, making a liar of Moss Riley, whose joint, The Paloma House, still boasted river views from every room. It was a sin, really, how Moss had let the place fall to ruin. Sure, the sun and dust wrought their worst on everything out here, but one did not have to go along with it. He could at least freshen the place up a bit, add a dab of paint, straighten those shutters. Not everyone coming into town by this road should be subjected to the sight of all his broken tables, shattered mirrors, and stained chamber pots. What in hell was his wife about, letting that deluge pile up on the back porch? Too busy idling on the creekbank behind the hotel, it seemed, with her forehead on her knees and the last vestiges of a cigarette disappearing between her fingers, to bother keeping house. She was a loud, insipid Tennessee girl who proved incontrovertibly that a bettered station in life could not necessarily make every woman a lady, nor lighten her hand with rouge. Perhaps, by some miracle, she might not raise her head until after Nora had already moved on. But then old Bill went clattering over the end of the bridge, and up came Millie's face like a damp balloon. She wiped her eyes hurriedly with her apron. What was she crying about now? She was young enough yet, and could have done a lot worse than Moss Riley, given her starting position in life.

Millie made the grievous error of calling out. "Oh, Missus Lark." Still wiping her eyes. "How's Rob doing?"

All the rage she'd been damming since Desma's place flew out of her at once.

"What's it to you, Millicent Riley?"

The innkeep's wife had the decency to look stupefied. "Missus Lark! I was only asking after him. I didn't think—"

"Just because you're not calling down from balconies anymore don't make it fine for you to mention my son to me by name!"

"I didn't mean nothing by it! I only want to know he's alright."

"Of course he's alright!"

She might have felt less sheepish about the outburst had she not found Moss instated in his usual porch chair just around the corner. He had evidently taken Doc Almenara's suggestion about cabbage to heart in the weeks since she'd last seen him. His clothes drooped like dead sails.

Nora was already shouting, "The place looks a disgrace, Moss—I was only telling your wife, why don't the boys help you paint it up?" just in case he'd overheard her wilding back there.

Red in the face, unaided by the spectacles he

refused to wear, Moss squinted bleakly in her direction. "Who the hell is that?" he said. "Nora!" He gripped the railing and staggered to his feet. "Nora, what are you doing in town?"

"Bringing the boys their lunch—why don't I send them round here after?"

"The boys?"

"Yes, Moss, the boys."

"What for?"

Another man, a stranger, now emerged from the cool darkness of the hallway and stood on the porch behind Moss. It struck her suddenly that this man might be that rarest of all entities—a lodger. And if there was one thing Moss was likely to appreciate even less than having his young wife roared down, it was having his establishment's deficiencies enumerated in the presence of a paying customer. Though by the look of the fella, he had likely surmised them by now. It would take some effort to keep that suit looking so black at Moss's.

She backtracked all the same. "Welcome, mister," she said helpfully. "Don't mind a bit of banter between neighbors. You'll find it customary in Amargo to jape each other a little about the state of our brickwork and so on. You've chosen right—I wouldn't lay my head on any pillow that weren't my own, save for Moss Riley's."

The stranger touched his hat.

She turned to Moss. "So I'll send the boys round later?"

"Are they with you, then?" Moss asked. "The boys?"

"They'll finish up at the **Sentinel** around three—I'll tell them come by?"

Moss went on squinting.

This was when the stranger came to the railing. "Don't hold up any work on the place for my sake, Mister Riley," he said. "I don't mind a bit of noise."

"There!" Nora said. "You see? A game soul. Hope you gave him a good room, Moss."

"What's that?"

"I said: hope you've put this gentleman up in the turret, so he can see the old mines."

"Ah!"

"Indeed, he has," the stranger put in. "Thank you."

She smiled broadly through the sudden, indelible feeling that this man had not only never seen the turret, but had perhaps never ventured any further than Moss Riley's hallway. Here she was, bulling through one conversation, while all this time the two of them had been having another.

"Three o'clock all right, then?" she managed.

"Superb," the stranger said. "We'll be waiting."

Moss took a moment. "All right. Thank you, Nora. All right."

She found just about time enough to say, "All right, Moss—all right," before they disappeared inside.

What had he managed to get himself into this time? What a twitching, careless little duck he was— darting and conniving and locked in a seething contest, since the instant his boots had touched this

soil, with Walt Stillman, proprietor of The Bitter
Root Inn just across the street, over whose boardinghouse had first welcomed wanderers and inebriates.
The object of this honor was a mystery, but apparently important enough to ignite a come-to-blows
hatred in both men. Over the years, they had replaced
their respective shingles at least a dozen times, racing
each other backwards, bypassing first the foundation
of the town, the establishment of the Territory, and
the War of the Rebellion. The new steel plaque suspended over The Bitter Root Inn now read As OLD
As THE REPUBLIC—which felt like a pointed full-
stop at the end of an interminable sentence.

If Walt emerged before she moved on, she thought
frantically of japing him, too—since it had gone so
well just now. She might say, "Which Republic is
that, Walt?" Just to rile him to hell. She slowed her
horse, but he did not appear. The solitary man on his
porch was as much a stranger as the black-coat back
at the Paloma had been—a tall, lank rake with a
baroque pocket square and boots so clean they could
only be new. He kept his heel up on the porch chair
and nodded at her, standing there with his pipe
lit and his duster hanging straight. More of his ilk
moved about within. One of them was clanging out
a graceless rendition of "Laredo" on Walt Stillman's
precious piano—which, like Walt Stillman's girls,
was unaccustomed to being handled before four
o'clock. Another man stood in the upstairs window
beside a woman's bare arm.

One more of these well-clad strangers was pacing the Mercantile porch, evidently waiting on Juan Carlos Escondido to open up. To reach the cistern, Nora now realized, she would have to come past him. If today was one of the five days out of six that the lever pumped only creaking air—which seemed likely, because she could tell even at this distance that the ground beneath it was pale and dry—this hardly seemed worth it.

But her thirst, her thirst—it had made her so rough and angry already, and there was still so much of the day left to endure.

"Any water today?"

The fella looked at her and then down at the self-incriminating spout. "Don't look like it."

"Give it a try for me there, would you, sir?"

He slowly depressed the handle. It let out a blurt of compressed air.

"Please pardon it," Nora said, "it never did have any manners."

He nodded a little and went back to studying his fingernails. Still more galling than his single, hapless attempt at the pump—didn't he know the thing had to be forced?—was how immune he seemed to her charms. She was not devoid of them. A young woman yet, still mostly in color. Not so long ago, her hesitation to speak with this particular type of man, on this particular type of expedition, would have been rooted in her unwillingness to insist that she was already married. Well, fool her for making a joke. She swung out of the saddle and came up the steps, fumbling with the water bladder, which had got all tangled up in its own bindings. The fella deigned to shuffle aside and let her by.

"Sometimes, you have to give it a few pumps," she explained. She could feel him watching her as she bore down on the handle once, twice, three times. For a hopeful moment, she felt resistance as the lever caught something below, but it was only more damp air. "It knows to be fickle," she said nervously.

"Ain't it just the way."

"Suppose I'll have to try again later."

"I reckon so."

The printhouse sat just past the jail at the far end of the thoroughfare. It was a low, squat building, fronted by a crooked tract of boardwalk. Between its dismal color and small windows, it tended to remind her too much of Morton Hole. But the absence of the usual crowd on its porch waiting to buy newspapers, or complain, or post their adverts, was a great improvement.

She rummaged through her saddlebags for the lunchpails. The sun had scorched them through. She remembered suddenly Rob's inexplicable amusement with this in his more agreeable years. Whenever it happened—which was often—he would pat her on the shoulder and say: "It's all right, Mama. You ain't ruined the lunch—you just cooked it on the way!" Remembering this felt like flinging wide the door of a forgotten room. The phrase seemed so inextricable from his boyhood self—where had it been these last few years? She doubted he would recall it. He seemed to spend the balance of his life sloughing off every part of himself that predated his first shave. But she would try him anyway. She would come through the door saying: "Beans, boys— cooked on the way!"

It might at the very least stun them into a smile.

The gold-lettered Lark & Sons shingle had slipped off its hook again. She was stooping to pick it up when she noticed the storefront window.

A craw of ruptured glass was still suspended in the pane. The edges of the cut caught the entering light and twisted it throughout the office, spangling the press and the aprons on their hooks and Emmett's desk under its mountain of papers. She went in to stillness and the sour smell of ink and paper. Nobody answered her. The press was hinged wide, interrupted in its downward stroke. A composite still lay on the platen, a tumble of inky metal letters. Last week's copies hung on a laundry line from wall to wall.

She returned shakily to the window. She'd seen the wreckage of a round coming through glass, most lately at Escondido's Mercantile. This break did not have the same clean, striated outburst. And there was nothing embedded in the opposite wall. There should be, in the aftermath of gunplay: didn't

the front of every joint in town still bear the scars
of the camp's early days? The round at Escondido's
was stuck so deep that Juan Carlos had given up trying to gouge it out, and rearranged his pictures and
signage in an even more awful configuration to cover
it up.

No, this hole was much too big. Her fist fit easily
between the glass points without touching them.
Whatever had done the damage must have been
about that size. A rock, perhaps deliberately hurled.
Perhaps by one of the strangers watching her from
across the street—but to what end? An accidental
deployment of some innocent projectile was far
more likely, for she could find no further evidence in
here save for tiny, sharp shards interspersed among
the bristles of the broom in the corner, the sight of
which slowed her heart a little. Somebody had swept
up. Well, that couldn't have been her boys. They
would never have tidied after a fight. They would
have gone straight over to the Paloma for a nostrum
to numb the resetting of their teeth, and then tried
in vain to lie about it later.

The back room was just as empty as the front,
though strewn with unmistakable signs of Rob:
balled-up pages, cigarette ends (**God help us,** Evelyn
muttered, **he's some fool smoking around all this
paper, Mama!**). An inexplicable pair of decaying
boots lay felled under the chair. On the desk sat the
handwritten template for this week's front page,
outlined forward and then shakily, uncertainly, in

reverse. That Rob had lied about being able to composite without the aid of a draft was obvious enough. His frustration manifested in the dark loops of his heavily weighted script. Every few sentences saw him reversing an **R** or a **K** and scratching it out in darker and more exasperated gray cyclones.

She slid the desk drawer open and felt through the papers for Emmett's old Colt revolver. Nothing—save a poorly hidden whiskey bottle.

They been drinking, Evelyn said. **A lot.**

An ellipse of light hurried around the final brown dram at the bottom of the bottle. She could not help herself. It went down like fire, but was worth the pleasant contraction of her throat, the momentary illusion of relief.

She got on her knees to look under the desk, but found only a few scattered letters of type and a flattened beetle. A crumpled, dust-hardened telegraph slip was wedged far back against the wall. The effort of retrieving it crooked her neck.

She smoothed it out on the floor. The wobbly type of the Ash River telegraph office meandered across the page. It was addressed to the care of Misters Robert C. Lark and Dolan M. Lark. **Dear sirs,** it read:

Have received your petition formally querying Marshal Office investigation into whereabouts of Emmett Seward Lark. Lack resources at present to do the same re:

whereabouts of Paul Griggs (waterman, Griggs Water of Grayson Co.). Have forwarded your description of Mr. Lark's dray, and the location of your reported sighting near Sanchez ranch in Grayson County. Have confirmed with Sheriff Harlan Bell there exists no such conveyance on or near Sanchez property or any place thereabouts. At this time we believe no indication of foul play is evident. For further discussion we invite you to rendezvous at the Office of the Marshal Prescott Az Territory. Sincerely, Marshal Dance Prescott Az Territory.

THE UNHELPFUL STRANGER WAS STILL peacocking around Juan Carlos's porch when she got back outside. He did not seem to intuit her distress, and she stood there with her hands half-raised—whether in greeting or in demand of an explanation, even Nora didn't know.

"What happened here?" she said stupidly, at long last.

"Where?"

"There's glass everywhere, the window's broken."

"Is it?" He seemed unperturbed by this news.

"Did you see anything?"

"No, ma'am."

"Well how long you been standing there?"

"Awhile."

"You been standing there awhile and haven't seen nobody throw aught through this window?"

She knew now that she was trying to ingratiate herself to him. She reviled this tendency in herself. But even the contrivance of poor grammar did not penetrate his nonchalance. He shrugged. "I didn't see nothing."

"Well that's a wonderment."

"Sounds like you got it all pretty well figured, though. Nice work, ma'am."

It struck her suddenly that this was deliberate. He was not the dimmest man in Creation after all—he was taunting her. "Well I'll go get my friend the Sheriff, then," she said.

"Good afternoon, ma'am."

She could feel him watching her as she moved down the street.

The jailhouse door was locked. She dragged the porch chair over and climbed up to peer inside. Harlan had battened the place down at the start of his tenure as though the entire Apache nation were liable at any moment to break in or out of it. She could hardly see anything. A few bars of sunlight pooled on the fore-office floor. A belt and mismatched pair of boots were heaped by the corner basin, but it was the hat she finally recognized as belonging to Armando Cortez. Here he was, back again, sockless and sunburnt, laid out on his side and alternating his ragged breathing with somnolent utterances while the jailhouse cot creaked beneath him.

Nora called his name until he sat up. Sometimes he could seem like his old self. The man who would arrive in the cool of the evening, after walking the three miles from his place to theirs, in his good clothes, always with a loaf in one hand and some

oddity he'd picked up for the boys—a bird's egg,
a petrified pine cone, the odd tooth—in the other.
When had she last seen the old naturalist anywhere
but here? Probably before Agnes had herded their
girls into the Santa Fe stage and left him to that
empty house, with its dry well, and his tab at
the Bitter Root Inn, which only lengthened once
she was gone. Every now and again, Harlan said, the
Profesor roused up and gave the impression of having suddenly improved overnight, for good, and
Harlan would permit himself to hope it might be
true. Perhaps this time evening wouldn't find him
draped over the bar, furthering his debts while he
grew more and more agitated—the weather, goddamn them, hadn't anybody else in this town read
an almanac or history in their lives? What were they
all doing here, watching the sky, farming rock and
dust? Didn't they realize the only reliable harvest was
death? Once Armando landed on that point, Harlan
would walk over and fetch him back. Self-solution,
he reasoned, could be managed a lot more easily at
home than in a jail cell. And at least here, Armando
could weep out some of the horrors that clouded his
mind: the rot of mankind, the eventual, inevitable
death of his daughters. He was lucky, Sheriff Bell,
not to have children. He would only spend his life
imagining them dead. Nora had told him the very
same thing. And indeed, on those rare occasions
when the evening pressed in on her, Armando Cortez
was always within it. They were aligned, she and

Armando, in their thinking and in their grief, for all time probably, thanks to Evelyn. She considered herself fortunate to have learned not to think of him most days.

He finally found her with his good eye. "Nora! Back again. A head in the door."

"Where's the Sheriff, **Profesor**?"

Armando raked his stubble. "Weren't he just here after all?" He sat there in a blizzard of dustmotes, his thin legs dangling off the side of the cot. "Or maybe it's last night I'm thinking of."

"How about my boys? They come by today?"

He was an age mulling it over. "No, ma'am. No. No, they did not."

Perhaps it was needlessly cruel to them both, asking details of him in this state. He seemed about as certain as he did sober. There was room for hope in that, at least. Maybe he was wrong. Maybe he couldn't even be sure which boys she was asking about.

"Rob and Dolan," she said. "The Lark boys?"

"I know who your sons are, Nora. I'm not as far gone as all that."

He shifted to the edge of the cot and bent over the bucket Harlan had left out for him and began to splash his face. Her blood surged. Water pattered around the tin rim and the tops of Armando's feet. There it was, just two sets of bars away. She should've been the town drunk. Then it might have been her locked up, thinly slurping water from cupped hands and—goddamn him!—spitting it out.

"Where'd Harlan get that?"

"At the cistern, I reckon. You thirsty? Come in, come in."

She tried the handle again. "It's locked."

"Ah, the Sheriff'll be back in no time."

Armando sat there, looking around, his face wet and shining.

"You heard any kind of hell-raising outside?" Nora said.

"Hell-raising?"

"Glass breaking, that kind of thing."

"No, not for a while now. No more than usual." He wiped his hands on his trousers. "I guess someone was wailing last night."

"Wailing?"

He nodded. "A little while after the Sheriff got me. Come to think of it—yes. The Sheriff got me. And the wailing woke me sometime before it was light out, and when I sat up Harlan weren't here. Can that be right? I reckon so. Where's he got to?" She waited for him to remember. He waved her in again. "He won't be long, Nora. You come on in out of the sun and wait for him in here. You know I won't listen in on you two."

She put the chair back in its corner and stood on the boardwalk, looking up and down the street.

What's going on, Mama?

I don't know, honey.

Where's Rob and Dolan?

I really don't know.

Are you dizzy?

A little.

Won't you try the cistern again?

I don't want to linger around that man, Evelyn. I don't know who he is.

Maybe if you head back to Moss's place.

Moss has got himself in some bind over there I want no part of.

Then sit down here in the shade, Mama.

I will do, yes.

Are you feeling better?

A little, darling—give me a moment.

Where do you reckon they've gone, Mama? To the marshals' in Prescott?

Knowing would require me to divine what's in their heads—and that seems past my powers, Evelyn. Really. The marshals in Prescott! After Harlan's told them everything they need to know, and without a word to me.

Maybe the fight last night provoked them.

Maybe.

Maybe they figured you don't share their concerns.

That's absurd.

They did try to tell you last night, I suppose.

They were completely witless, Evelyn. What kind of mother would I be to indulge them in that state, spouting off such nonsense, wrecking the place?

But you haven't thought for one moment that some harm might've come to Papa? Not all this while?

I have, of course. But Harlan put my fears down. He was good enough to check the Sanchez place, as you see, no matter how absurd that whole line of thinking.

I suppose he's to be believed.

Of course.

I'm sure you're right, Mama.

Of course I am. The marshals in Prescott—don't that just beat all.

It's damn feckless of them to leave that letter behind in the printhouse, if that's where they're going. They'd want to have it by way of introduction.

Well, if it was Rob in charge and Dolan following, they'll be lucky to have remembered their boots.

That's true.

My God, what your father would have spared us by writing. All that needed saying was: I'm delayed bringing the water, source it elsewhere or parch.

I believe that was Rob and Dolan's point. A letter would've come by now, if Papa were well enough to write it.

What nonsense. "If he were well enough to write it." None of you remember your papa in the early days. He would disappear for weeks looking for backers or machinery or some far-flung newspaperman—this one who surely knew all there was to know about dodging insolvency—and he would be gone and gone and gone, without so much as a: Are you well, Nora? What of the children? Are you boiling in your beds, or finding water, or have the Apache cut your throats?

But it's not like Papa not to send a wire.

The Apache are always after the wires.

Bit less of that going on these days, Mama.

Not so, Evelyn. Didn't I send a wire some years back, only to learn from the wireman that the line had been cut? He said there was nothing to be done till the break was found and fixed. Said it could take weeks. I'll never forget the way he looked. All those people's words, he said, fired off and lost forever. He was saddled with having to go round telling everybody that if they wanted to apprise their far-flung dearest of recent death and illness, they must do it by post again, like the old days. Poor bastard.

I see you're feeling better, Mama.

I am now. But it'll be a killing-field evening, getting your two lout brothers to admit where they been and what they been doing. The mere prospect wearies me.

Perhaps Papa will be home by then.

Good. Let him deal with your brothers himself.

That's where they've gone then, Mama? To Prescott, to call on the marshals?

Yes. That's where they've gone.

To Prescott?

To Prescott. Exactly.

THE COLORADO

WE REALLY SHOULD GET GOING NOW,
Burke, before them people come back. They'll have
their hands full awhile, but you can bet your goddamn beard they're unlikely to forget about us. We're
watered up and rested now. It's cool enough. If we
leave before daybreak, we could still make good
time—not Camel Corps time, of course. We're not
spry enough anymore to be making eighteen miles
a day, even at our best. Faster, probably, I reckon,
when those green marshes around San Antonio
began to thin out, and we found ourselves on the
easy brown flats that would fill the horizon for
the rest of our journey. I didn't replenish my canteen
but for once, just before we turned north toward
New Mexico, right there on the shores of the
Colorado River. Those were bitter, pungent waters.
They showed me Hobb at play, a small child with
the dying sun at his back.

It was Ned Beale forever banging on about making
good time as he blazed the trail from the summit of

Seid's back. As we were in Comanche country, he'd had the decency not to engage a mounted band to play us along, but behind him hammered and picked a roadbreaking crew, flanked by cavalry and footsoldiers and trailed by his ambulances, his mule train, his geologist, his dogs and laundresses, and finally, about two miles behind, Ab in the chuckwagon and ourselves—so it cannot be said that we traveled noiselessly. Still no soul and no water crossed our path for more than fifty miles—save the dead, who watched us pass from their high-bluff caves, or from the basins where their unburied bones were scattered.

We crossed the Red and Canadian Rivers, after which our road steadily began to climb, high enough at last that the brown sheep with their knotted horns were obliged to click up steeper bluffs to get away from us. Everything was a marvel to Beale. In the sash of his jacket rode the journal in which every detail of our travel was carefully outlined: campsites, the favorability of grass, the features of every lizard and rock and arrowhead.

His geologist, Williams, was a pasty, stiff-starched fella who spent every day sweating right through his coat. Every quarter mile found him springing from his wagon to sift some curio from the dirt, upturn it meaningfully, and shake his head. Jolly, sullen and furious for having been parted from Seid, distracted himself by badgering Williams about the signs of rock and soil. Was it true, he asked, that there were forests where the gold dust had rained down for so many years that even the wild game was powdered with it? Was it true winter rains washed fist-sized nuggets of gold down the hillsides?

"I don't know, sir," Williams would tell him. "But it is my purpose to find out."

Williams was a devil for wandering off, and it was thanks to this habit that we ran afoul of any Indians at all. We had just crossed into New Mexico when the terrain sank into a succession of dry basins, yielding to his curious eye all manner of irresistible dust. One afternoon, we came upon his wagon trailside without him in it. We got to hollering after him to no avail. At last, about a quarter mile off the road, we sighted his pale little squat form frozen at the top of a ridge. "Williams!" Jolly shouted. "Come on back now." But he did not turn. We came uphill to find two Kiowa stood in the grass some ways ahead of him with their bows drawn. They were so close we could see sunlight caught in the hair of their bare arms. "Comanche!" George shouted—sounding, to nobody's surprise, as though he might hop down off Maida and fly into their embrace.

Well, at the sight of you camels, the Kiowas' bowstrings went slack. An eternity later, they backed their way and we backed ours. Afterwards, we saw curiously few Indians, and Beale reckoned word had got around, as it always did, that we were traveling with monsters.

———

Who can the people that came this way before us have been? What were their tales? How will life be altered when the camel is as unremarkable a sight in these wastes as the jackrabbit and chaparral cock? Beale asked these questions aloud, all day long, of anyone luckless enough to be within earshot. If he suspected how reverently his infantry took the piss out of him, he did not show it. Evenings found him riding with a small detachment to supply his officers with fresh game, which we could smell roasting all night and in our dreams, and which brought coyotes to the very edge of our fires. It was Beale hooked that huge cutthroat in the Pecos—remember? From the shore we saw the spangled scales of its back frothing the water, and before we knew it, George and I were rushing into the shallows to haul it out. It was a miraculous thing: the jaw drawered out to a ferocious underbite, red sails flared along the top of its back. Suddenly soldiers and packers alike were rushing to the shore to break off makeshift fishing poles. Ab got to yelling, "Fetch me another, boys! Big as this one!" We ranged ourselves about the eddies, our voices flung back and forth by the canyon walls. You camels lined up to watch, browsing the reeds as though you, too, had a stake in our catch. The sun edged higher, mirrored in blinding bolts on the water, but all I caught was some of the Pecos's brackish soul, which showed me a steamship and the dimlit streets of some town I'd never seen. All day, the river yielded no further life. In our excitement, we forgot Beale's mammoth cutthroat, which gasped out its last on the rock where we'd hauled it out. By the time we thought of it again, one of its eyes had been lost to some carrion bird, which led Ab to refuse the cooking of it. In the end, we left it lying there, a slab of twilit scales, and went back to our miserable rations.

The longer I live, Burke, the more I have come to understand that extraordinary people are eroded by their worries while the useless are carried ever forward by their delusions. This is the only reason I can think to account for the continued presence of the damnable Gerald Shaw, now leading an even larger regiment of mulepackers two miles ahead of us through New Mexico territory, and every bit as brawly under Beale's command as he'd been under Wayne's. He seemed forever torn between his derision for the camels—more and more justified each day our packtrain fell behind—and his envy for the excitement you all inspired in the fairer sex.

You'll remember this came to a head someplace outside Albuquerque. Mico and I must have driven Ab's chuckwagon into town, for it was just we three in that strange place. While Ab treated with the sutler, Mico drew my attention to a stack of dwellings, houses piled on top of houses and interconnected with crooked stairwells, the sight of which brought more joy to his eyes than I had ever thought him capable of feeling.

"This!" he cried. "**This** is more like it." Up and down I followed him while he ran about the terraces, crying: "This is a real city, Misafir!"

But the doors of that strange fortification opened only into empty rooms. An occasional lonely pot greeted us, or the dust of some cold hearth. Every time Mico pressed into a new chamber, my heart quickened with the conviction that some dead soul awaited us on the other side. But none did. I reckon the dead of those people had been laid down right, by loving hands, or were long gone and far away.

Night had fallen by the time we found our way back to the sutler's from that maze of homes. Our return was further marred by the sight of Shaw and three of his troops rattling up to the saloon on our camels. Girls were packed cheek to jowl on the balcony to greet you and Saleh, jostling with such vigor that I felt certain the whole terrace would cave under their weight.

As Mico later explained it, we only followed the men inside to correct their practice of quirting our animals. "With the flat of the hand, sir," Mico said calmly, though his knuckles were white. "They don't take well to beating."

Shaw had some twenty pounds on the next biggest man in the place, and probably as many years, but didn't need a corresponding measure of spirits to go from loudtalk to throwing punches. Two seconds was all it took. Somewhere between pinning Mico to the table and dousing his nostrils in whiskey, Shaw suddenly got that maddog look that brings to hand all possible outcomes. He might stand the offender up and brush off his coat and laugh. Or he might kill him. I was told later on that I'd begun to holler: "Come on, Shaw, for fuck's sake!" This only made it worse. Without loosening his grip, Gerald Shaw turned and pitched his whiskey-glass straight back at me. It shattered the bar mirror, which is all that particular breed of joint needs to give way. Fellas started grabbing each other and throwing fists. Somebody's arm hooked round my neck and brought me down. I met a boot and a tableleg, and, upside down and arseways, saw Mico leap shrieking into a pile of soldiers on the far side of the room.

Round about then, the innkeep got his shotgun out from behind the bar and blasted a hole through the ceiling.

"You been warned!" he roared into the suspended carnage. "Lay off them Hebes and get the fuck out!"

This set off the shuffling and slinking that precedes the coming of the law. Groans issued from under the piano. Bootheels scraped for the door. Mico climbed out of a pile of limbs and chairlegs, thumbing glass shards off the front of his garb. I never thought so highly of him.

When Beale heard about it, he gave all five of us hell. "I thought you Turks too fine and devout to get up to this kind of carry-on," he said dismally, shaking his head. "But now I see you're even worse than my boys."

———

In the wake of this incident, George fixed on the no-tion of overtaking the roadbreakers. Day after day, the rest of us were conscripted to this cause, mus-tered to break camp in the quiet dark before reveille, coaxed and berated to sharpen up our packing. I can't think why it mattered to him so, but I guess he figured it was just a matter of arithmetic. Once mounted, George would ride a half mile ahead of the column, fussing, urging us along, stretching the slightest evidence of our progress. "You see, Misafir?" he might say, seizing me about the shoulders. "See that fella, that so-and-so laying out his bedroll just there? When we drew into camp this time yesterday, he was already asleep. Why, that must mean we've gained ten, perhaps fifteen minutes! What do you think of **that**?"

What I thought was that any improvement we might be making was greatly impeded by having to wait around for Ab's chuckwagon, the caboose of the packtrain, which stalled in the ruts at least once a day and could not be freed without your aid.

George saw the truth of this. "Can you go no faster, Ab?"

"It's this fucking cornmill," was our cook's reply. "It's three hundred pounds of axle-breaking nonsense that we ain't even using."

When George identified the Little Giant as the fount of our delay, it became plain that Beale held the thing in very great affection. Our commandant referred to it at once by name, which of course complicated George's campaign against it. But we had a mandate to make Fort Tejon by October, and eventually, worn down by George's forecast of an inglorious wintertime arrival, Beale perked up to the whimsy of just leaving the cornmill there, on the malpais, for the next tribe or wagon train to be surprised by.

"I came across a printing press like that once, you know," Beale said dreamily.

"What'd you name it?" George asked him.

But even with the lieutenant's tacit permission, Ab still couldn't bring himself to heave the Little Giant overboard. "Two hundred dollars of cast iron flung out the back—all for some fool quartermaster reckoning that grinding corn would be a fit way to pass the time."

So, to George's provocation, we went on dragging the cornmill behind us like a bad leg, all the way to Rojita. A mesa there had served as a trail marker in Beale's youth, and we all stood around in the dusk while he wandered its base searching out where his outfit had scratched their names among the ancient Indian pictures all those years ago. We found nothing save a little winding path he didn't recall seeing before. It rose sharply up to where we could see a wrecked-out church the color of blood hidden among the black cedars on the rim.

"How many dead folks you think they got piled in there?" Mico whispered to me.

"Some."

In truth, there were dozens. I saw them flicker into being as the last of the day faded: kids, peering over the bluff, bright as falling stars.

We were just getting settled around our fire when the church bells rang out. Sudden music, the first we'd heard in an age. It slid slowly off the mesa and down our spines and froze us where we sat. I swear, even you camels all drew together as though you knew to be worried: who was up there, pulling them belfry ropes?

I never did speak of the dead to anyone but you, Burke, save for when I turned to George halfway through supper that night. "You reckon they're warning us away, them phantoms up there?"

"Maybe," he said. "But if not, you reckon they could use a cornmill?"

Somehow, this solution was acceptable to everyone: we would leave the Little Giant here, a benefaction to whatever good souls had built a house of God in this desolate place.

So when Beale hove out with the packtrain next morning, we unhappy wardens of the caboose dragged Ab's chuckwagon, with all its clanking ornamentations, uphill to the church.

Close up, the place was quite dignified. Papery purple vines arched over the gate. The graveyard was neatly fenced. A clutch of Indian kids in white linen were nudging hoops around the courtyard. Your appearance at the top of the rise sent one of their

ill-fated wheels sailing off into the bushes. We stalled
out there, right in the archway, with all them kids
pressing in around your legs. The dead ones were
there, too, drifting at the edge of the crowd, thumbs
in their mouths, their eyes faraway.

Down the colonnade came a bald, smiling padre
in a brown robe. He shook our hands and brewed
coffee while the kids made a climbing post of you.

George wasted no time. "Lieutenant Beale was
curious to know if you'd have use for a cornmill?"

I'd never seen a man think so hard on a gift.

"Well," said the padre. "That depends. How fine
does it grind?"

We were determined not to let him thwart our
charity, and so set about showing this ill-mannered
cleric that we'd brought him the finest damn mill this
side of the Mississippi. But our first grind failed to
impress. The padre let it run rough through his fingers and said only, "hm." Our second was likewise
found wanting. George kept forcing the wheel faster
and faster, with all Hell's curses streaming out on his
breath. Ab hovered close, useless with disbelief, fore-
seeing a future bleakly tethered to the Little Giant.
By this time, the afternoon was already cooling. The
children were filling your bridle with wildflowers,
while you just stood there, in your smug way, watching us take turns at the crank till our hands burned.

I hadn't even marked Jolly's disappearance until he
came back from someplace looking distraught. As

he knelt down to take my place at the machine, he whispered: "I just been through the graveyard. Misafir—whose children are these?"

"I don't know. Orphans, probably."

"Do you reckon they're stole?"

By the time we were on our fourth grind, he'd gone and come back again and got himself further worked up. "I think they're stole."

The padre must've overheard him, or guessed his thinking, for here he came with a comforting arm to put around Jolly's shoulder—and the next thing I knew, the two of them were strolling the little garden, together. Jolly kept trying to wedge a question in, but the padre was talking steadily, sweeping the air with a gentle hand, ruffling shrubs and bending tree branches to Jolly's nose. Before long, they'd taken to naming plants aloud.

"Limón," the padre would say. "Limón?"

And Jolly, reluctantly, would answer in Arabic: "Laymun."

"Azahar?"

"Zahr."

He was returned to us from this expedition with a gunnysack filled with some strange and fragrant herb clutched to his chest, and he stood there looking disconsolate for a long while.

"Well?" I said. "Are they stole?"

"He says they're not. Says they've been brought to Christ in this here school."

"Well then," I said.

We must have turned a hundred pounds of corn to dust only to find ourselves heaving our star-crossed contraption back into the wagon again as night drew around us. The padre shouted blessings from the gate, where he stood waving amidst that small throng of white-clad kids while we made our way back down the path. Jolly kept turning over his shoulder. "They'd know it if they was stole," he said again. "Wouldn't they?"

The dead certainly knew, buried up on that hilltop but a thousand miles from their rest.

Stole children or not, he never could bring himself to dispose of the gunnysack. The smell of that place always followed us thereafter: manzanita and sage and the bright spice of some childhood shrub, some plant whose ancient name had followed it to Spain, and from Spain to this place, this roasting rock-tower half a world away, where it had somehow managed to flower and call Jolly's mind home.

On the way back to camp, we bogged the wretched chuckwagon in the bed of an arroyo again. And so we left it among the creosotes in the red mud there, for somebody else to find, if ever a pilgrim in need of coarse grind happened to come this way.

All of George's efforts to speed us along were brought to bear just outside the little town of Bajado. Beale, with his forecamp, was rested out in the mesquite shade just after noon when we caught up to them at last to the sound of the sentry's bugle. We dispersed to pass among the resting men and then reconstituted on the llano and kept forward on the unbroken road to the next stream—the Oro, which tasted of salt.

After that, we never fell behind the roadbreakers again and led the way west through a red rock scatterland and up into the forested heights above the Devil's Fork. Another week brought us out of the San Francisco range, and into a barrens of yellow grass and petrified trees, and still further into a desert teeming with dancing cactus. Creekbed after creekbed we passed was dry and empty, and we didn't find water again until some nameless riffle that mystified even George. A pale, daytime moon hung above us.

We were just about encamped when a line appeared on the horizon. Too small for a horse, it advanced through the bright striations of sunset, pitching right and left, until it took form: a girl, stumbling and so tattered you could hardly call her dressed.

By the time Beale arrived with the roadbreakers, George had wrapped her in blankets and the two of them were stood off about how much water she was permitted to drink. She had already dispatched a full goatskin, and wanted more. He kept pointing to the bloat of her stomach. "You must wait," he said. "It'll pain you."

This reduced her to tears, in which state she threw herself on Beale's mercy. She had walked for days, she said, from the malpais, where two played-out mules and a dwindling water supply had stranded her people's wagon train.

"Whereabouts?" Beale asked.

She pointed north.

We were already so far off-trail that Beale didn't know what to make of this. Our course seemed obvious: help the wretched child. Yet we'd seen so little misfortune that her arrival seemed a likely prelude to the ambush that could disgrace us all. "Imagine the honor of any brave who rustles the War Department's camels," Beale muttered. Everybody, of course, had been imagining that very brave ever since Indianola. But here sat the girl. Someone—likely George—had outfitted her in a too-large shirt and too-long britches, and she sat sullen and dust-stained with one arm around Maida's knee.

Well. If she'd had the courage and good fortune to make that journey unscathed, what would it say of Beale if he balked at sending her people help? "An impossible but unavoidable rescue will make a thrilling addition to our chronicles," Beale said. He looked wistfully into the gathering dark. "I wish I could join you."

It was clear by morning that the girl had got so turned around on her way to us that we might as well not have brought her along at all. She had a round, windbattered face, and a mouth that might have been Indian if any of it had been visible from the scars got by her sunburn. She rode just ahead of Shaw, whose last-minute addition to our party Jolly surmised in one quiet growl: "We can't be trusted to ride alone with her of course."

George relished this misadventure. He made quick work of backfollowing her trail, pointing out the gaps where she had broken through the scrub as we climbed steadily north.

"I don't recognize none of this," the girl said miserably.

"You were delirious," George told her. "Don't worry, it will come to you."

We'd given her no chance to rest, so it was no surprise she started sliding out of the saddle. Shaw lashed her mule to his horse and put her up in front of him. Jolly didn't like that. He rode up and down the line, eyeing up Shaw, riding close and then wheeling away. "Look at him," he muttered to me, like some ancient porch-sitter. "Why's he got to hold her like that?"

When we stopped to water at a small creek, the girl became desperate. "I don't know this place," she said. "I weren't never here."

"You were." George led her into the brush and pointed out her own tracks. He even stood her in them to fit them to her feet. Seeing evidence of her passage, but unable to remember it, she cried a little. "I think I must be dead, sir," she said to me. "I think you can't be real."

I laughed, but I don't mind admitting that her words goaded me. I brought her round to you, so she could feel your breath in her hair and touch your nose and put her ear to your grumbling heart. "Do you like magic?" I opened my canteen. She peered inside. "That's water from six rivers. The Guadalupe, the Pecos, the Rio Grande, the Canadian, the Brazos, the Colorado. You ever drunk six rivers at once?"

She tilted it. "It tastes salty."

"That's the Brazos," I lied. "Drink again."

"Now it tastes of iron."

"That's the Rio Grande."

We tented your packsaddle, and she curled up below and slept through the heat. Jolly, meanwhile, seethed around the camp. He knelt to splash his face across the stream from Shaw, who had stripped down to his waist. His chest was taut and blindingly white, like some dug-up statue.

"Got a wife, do you, Shaw?"

"It's Mister Shaw to you." He rested his hands on his knees. "And what goddamn worry is it of yours if I got a wife or not?"

"Just watching you there, I got to wondering if you been recently reminded of the difference between a woman and a girl."

"I'm surprised to hear you talk of women at all. I'd have thought you would prefer that big goat of yourn."

It was too hot for the customary route of

escalation, so they left it. They slunk to opposite sides of the camp and lay up under canvas while the day whitened around us. Jolly, a light sleeper at the best of times, huffed through the next several hours. "Do you see the way he puts his hands on her when they're riding?" he said, as though we'd been talking about it all the while. "I ought to break his neck." I said nothing. That Shaw's neck needed breaking was evident to anyone who'd spent more than an hour in his company. I had just begun to drift off when Jolly repeated: "I ought to break his fucking neck."

"You ever done it?" I said.

"What?"

"Broken a man's neck? I mean, kilt a man."

"Of course." He sat up and started roughing his saddle blanket into halves. "For two years I fought in Algiers."

"I mean kilt a man who wasn't after killing you."

Half and half and half again went the blanket. "Have you?"

"Maybe." I found myself plucking at the tips of the dead sage. "It ain't the same as battle, you know. You ought to spare yourself the finding out."

Next came a sun-bleached afternoon. Miles of boiling air between us and the distant hills. We passed the midafternoon heat in the twisted shade of mesquite trees. The mercury shot up. George kept tapping the thermometer, but it kept showing impossible numbers. Of course, he found this interesting enough to grin about.

The girl tugged at my hand. She wanted more water. "From the six rivers."

"There's not enough of it to drink every day," I said.

"Please," she said. "When I drink it, I see every-thing."

I allowed her a tiny bit. "What is it you see?"

"I see my mama and my old house."

"What else?"

"Some things I don't like."

"What things?"

"Wolves."

We were dozing again when George stood and picked up his rifle. "What's that there?"

From the boiling meridian flickered into being a wide, flat shape. It grew as it came across the hard-pan, melding and tattering in all that twisted light until it became what it was: a suited Indian in an ox-drawn dray. A waist-length braid hung over his shoulder, plaited through with colorful ribbons. He shaded himself with a small black parasol. When he reached us, he raised his hat.

"My, my. Ain't you boys a sight. What do you call that there?"

"Camel," I told him.

"Ain't he handsome."

"He smells," our little girl said.

"He does indeed. Why's his back all funny like that?"

"Where you coming from?" Shaw said.

The Indian sat back down. "The fort."

"You come across a stuck wagon train up this way?" said George.

"Wagon train? No. That way? No good to be stranded that way. There's flesheaters on the wing."

He sold us water and jerked meat, then raised his hat and was on his way again. We watched after him till he disappeared, just to assure ourselves of his mortal substance. Then we went on sitting in silence. Jolly was smiling. "Hell of a day to wear a suit," he said.

Mico cut a glare his way. "Ain't that the aim of a great kingdom?" he said. "Get all its heathens in a suit?"

"I was only saying he must be hot."

"He must reckon he's a big man now, wearing a suit. Better than his brothers."

"All right."

"Or perhaps he tells himself he only wears the suit so he will not suffer. And all that while, he disdains his brothers."

"I said all right, Mimi."

"Don't call me that," Mico said.

Soon enough, he started up again.

"What fools his brothers are, he tells himself. Why don't they just wear the suit? It would stay the capture of their children. The theft of their homes. What fools they are to always choose the suffering way."

Jolly looked at him and said something in Greek. Of Mico's reply, I caught only the bilious tone and the fact that it sent Jolly back to the wordless study of the dirt around his shoes. Mico was still looking at him, smiling mirthlessly. He leaned forward. "You hear me?"

Shaw got up. "Look here, you two."

"Sit," George told him.

Mico wasn't paying attention. "You hear me, Hadji Ali? You hear me, **hadji**? You hear me, **prodotis**?"

Well, Ali jumped up. Mico was already on his feet and halfway to him. I did get one arm between them, but blows were landing left and right. A foot caught me in the knee, and we all went down together and scrabbled around till our mouths were full of dust and our faces throbbing. Then Jolly got up to find his shoe. Mico seized his hat out of a bush.

When we set off again that evening, the cousins rode in a gulf of silence. I feared the rift might be lasting.

"Don't worry," George whispered to me. "In a few days, they'll get right again."

"I don't understand."

"There are wounds of time and there are wounds of person, Misafir. Sometimes people come through their wounds, but time does not. Sometimes it's the other way around. Sometimes the wounds are so grievous, there's no coming through them at all."

"Why not?"

"Because man is only man. And God, in His infinite wisdom, made it so that to live, generally, is to wound another. And He made every man blind to his own weapons, and too short-living to do anything but guard jealously his own small, wasted way. And thus we go on."

In the morning, we reached Butcher's Canyon and the barrens beyond. Eighty miles of shimmering scald. Not a riffle of charted water, and somewhere out there, the girl's stranded wagon train.

George wanted us to travel by night, but knew we had little time. The sun shot up and fastened your shadow to the hardpan. Ahead of me, the horizon was interrupted only by the soaked linen of Mico's shirt. I watched his head grow looser and looser on his neck as the light whitened. "Hey," I said, whenever he listed a little too much.

"Not one word to me," he said. "Goddamn you."

Along came trees and flatlands and stretches of dead grass. Travois poles. Antelope ribcages and jaws. The thick curlicue of a single ramhorn. The charred remains of an Indian camp, and several hours later a roofless church whose glittering floor cut our fingers as we sifted through it. "Jewels?" Jolly asked in wonderment. George shook his head and pointed at the empty windows. **"Vitrages."**

I guess I'm trying to remind you: we been through far worse than this. Put yesterday's talk from your mind. I'm sorry I misled you. You're watered now, Burke. You're shaded. Sure you've a little shot in you, but the pain will subside. It always does. And already you're getting that leg under you. At least we know what we're riding toward—we didn't, back then.

A few hours' sleep saw us moving again to close the final stretch before sunrise. The edges of the sky were still paling, and as we rode on the stars came reeling out. Toward midnight, the girl pointed upward. We were coming into the shadow of a mesa rimmed with rockspurs. "I know them giants," she said. "I know this place."

George drew up to me. "Listen." From the foothills ahead there came a hollow, swooping note. It was still rising when another joined it, and then another. You heard it yourself round about then, and started so suddenly that I had to pull back with both hands.

"If wolves are here," George said, "we are too late."

He was right, of course. He kept the girl back when we got to the wagons. We wrapped our coats around our mouths to strain out the smell. At the foot of the mesa, we found a dry wash with what had lately been a mule lying in it. The wolves had been at it, and a grin of its rib bones shone up white by moonlight. A trail of upended wagonboxes led us up the wash and out the other side, where flurries of paper coursed into the ditch. Beneath a wagonbonnet's broken bows was visible the twisted bootsole of a man whose face was so ruined we couldn't guess his age, save by the white of his beard. We found the women shot up a little way off in the trees. There were four of them, and we covered them up as quickly as we could.

"How many were in your party?" Jolly asked the girl. All were accounted for. He did not tell her how they had perished. He couldn't decide what would be worse: to live knowing that her journey had failed to prevent their demise, or that she had been destined to escape their fate.

The wolves had gone as far as the bluff, but we could see their eyes above us while we dug the graves. After Mico had stitched the last of the bodies into a blanket, I took a final turn about the place. The hardpan was strewn with paper. There was a little creosote brake about a hundred yards off with what looked like streamers caught in the branches. That was where I saw her: a woman, naked as the plain. She was standing very still among the trees with her hair coursing down her shoulders. She looked straight at me. Then her gaze moved to you, the absurdity of you—for the dead, as you know, can still be surprised. After a while, I turned you sidewise so she could see better. Her face and shoulders were striped with thin cuts, and the knifestrike to her chest shone with some black, spectral substance I imagined must be blood. The others were there too, further back in the trees. The old man was stooping to scratch around in the dirt.

They were all moving past each other, the mother and the little girl and the old man, too—and it struck me, after all these years of seeing the dead, as I stood there holding your bridle and with your breath in my hair, that I had never seen more than one at a time, and had never realized: they were unaware of each other's presence. Suddenly, the gruesome way they had fallen seemed the least mournful thing about this place. They could see the living, but not one another. Nameless and unburied, turned out suddenly into the bewildering dark, they rose to find themselves entirely alone.

We cut southwest of that dismal killing ground and found a creek about eight miles later. It was just coming on morning. You were first to the water. We knelt on the bank and splashed our faces. The girl hung back. We were ashamed, I think, to be so thirsty in front of her, to want so urgently for anything but life itself after what we'd seen. Bending to drink, I saw one of the wolves among the trees ahead. It drifted through the stand and disappeared every few seconds so that I had to strive to find it again.

"Misafir?"

"I said: ain't he just like a shadow?"

"You ever seen anything like that before?" Jolly's face was all twisted up. "I been across the world, Misafir, and never in my life. Indians?"

"You'd think it," I said. "But all those boxes? All that paper left behind? I doubt it."

Our girl was laid up with a dull, faraway look. Nobody could think what to say to her. I made a lean-to of you, and we dozed awhile, the three of us, but she would not lie on my arm as she previously had. I slept sour and miserable, and I reckon you must've, too, but you tamped down my misery and I hope I tamped down some of yours.

You know what came next: we woke to the hum of voices. Four riflemen had come up the rise and were now leading their horses to the water's edge. The first of them was a huge, bearded grotesque who marked you straightaway. "Christ crucified, what the hell is that?"

I stood to explain myself in a hurry: we were with Lieutenant Ned Beale, bringing water to a stranded wagon train. This here was one of the War Department's camels. But my summation did nothing to avert their guns. I felt a keen, sharp awareness of your hulk behind me. You—broad as a ship, broad as any damn thing a man could hit at any distance without effort or skill. The thought sat right down on my chest, and I found I couldn't breathe.

"We don't want trouble." Jolly had sat up from under his jacket. He, too, had his rifle across his knees.

The big man took us all in. "Well, our regards to Lieutenant Beale," he got around to saying. "We can't help hearing about all the good work he doing."

Whatever had been thinning out the air now disappeared. The grotesque held out a hand, and Shaw came down to the bank and shook it. George did too, then knelt down and got to splashing water over his face. The riders set about unpacking. Saddlebags were swung down; shirts removed, pale legs freed from rumpled boots. Pretty soon, someone was laughing. The whole thing had turned companionable so easily.

That was when the girl woke and leaned herself against me.

"That's my hoss," she whispered.

"Camel, honey."

She shook her head. "No—that's my hoss."

She pointed to a slight roan one of the riders was now unsaddling. "My old hoss my papa gave me." She thought she was still whispering, but talk around the creek abruptly subsided. I could see Shaw shifting from foot to foot, deciding whether or not to go on pretending he hadn't heard her.

But it was not up to him. The grotesque's rifle went up again and he fired pointblank at Shaw. I didn't see what happened next, for I seized the girl and the two of us went crashing into the wash. By the time I'd got my bearings, you were surging to your feet and bullets were singing off the ground. Shaw was all sidetwisted, dragging himself out of the creek on his elbows. The riders had fallen back behind the rocks, and from this cover issued the thunder of their volleys. It felt a lifetime, though it could not have been more than a few seconds, for Jolly was only now springing onto Seid, who raised himself with a roar, and the two of them went churning across the water. Mico, close behind on Saleh, followed. They cut through the fireline and over the flat—and though their charge had drawn the gunfire away from us, we were now faced with the prospect of firing on our enemy with our own men among them, Jolly chasing down a reckless fella who'd decided to run, and Mico turning already to cut back through. I went on firing into the rocks, at glimpses of hat and shoulder, until one of the distant rifles quieted. By then Saleh had been hit, and, reeling, thrown Mico. Jolly now came charging back, but it was Seid dealt the final blow: we watched the last of the roughnecks crumple under the camel's legs.

Our losses came to this: Shaw was gutshot. Mico's wound was cleaner—only a ball to the shoulder—but he'd shattered ribs falling and could not be made to sit up at all. We moved camp about a quarter mile down-valley, but Mico was breathing so shallow that we were forced to stop. George feared that his broken bones were sticking his lung. Every time he was moved he howled so desolately that my own stomach began to ache. Jolly was wiping his eyes. "Mimi," he said. "Don't breathe so deep."

Shaw kept spitting at the girl. "God damn you. Didn't anyone teach you keep your mouth shut?" This earned him a kick to the knees from George, which would have silenced most. But not sometime Private Gerald Shaw. He was in the kind of froth men can't see past. He went on cursing us to a man, in varying combinations of debasement and bestiality, till George finally knelt down beside him.

"I don't know what you imagine, son, but you ain't never making it back to Beale. Quiet down while we still have the decency to keep you company till you're dead."

By sundown the trees around the wash were dark with buzzards, and the wolves had come. We could hear them by the creek, quarreling over what was left of the roughnecks. It struck me that we'd wronged ourselves more than them, not digging at least a shallow grave. When I said this to Jolly, he looked at me sourly. "Why?" After one of the wolves dragged a forearm within sight of our camp, George set off in what he guessed was Beale's general direction with the girl mounted up behind him. She looked back at us once. I never saw her again, for by the time our ordeal was over she'd been left to the care of some good-hearted woman who raised her up to prosper, and as a young lady she took a train all the way west to some safer reach, where she lived out her life in a world that grew ever more worthy of her and she never thought of us again. Or so I've always told you.

While Jolly and I were lashing branches together to make sleds, a wolf appeared on the flat. We knew it was there because you and Seid were restless, and after a time we could see the thin gray haze of its body darting left and right in the dark. It slid back into the brush only to return a little while later with two or three of its kin. They all sat down together at the edge of the trees and watched us.

We yoked you to the sleds and started off down

George's trail. About two miles out, we began hearing the wolves. Just their movement in the brush at first, and then their song. Your tail was batting madly, I remember, and you huffed like a locomotive. You kept trying to twist around to get a look at them. When one crossed our trail just ahead, you wheeled after it, and it took all my strength to keep you from overturning poor Mico. He was gray and had only uttered two words since his fall: "I'm cold."

"Will he pull through?" I said.

"Maybe," said Jolly. "If he lasts the night."

We came to an abandoned trading post and barricaded ourselves inside. The depot was a thin, hollow place. The bones of a roof were overlaid at strange angles between us and the stars. The door did not touch the ground, and the adobe walls had crumbled away leaving hollows that faced out into the dark. Outside, the wolves were singing. The boldest of them had long shadows that appeared in the gaps below the door, sometimes taking the form of men. We fired blindly into the field, but they would only go off a little way before returning again.

Shaw sat sweating fireside. "You gone leave me to them?"

"No," Jolly said.

"I don't believe you."

"We won't."

We were sitting back to back, Jolly and I, with our guns outfaced through the brickwork. Shaw had gone so pale he was almost green, and he fought hard to keep awake. Perhaps he feared that if he grew faint, we might kill him. He wouldn't go more than a few minutes without talking. "I worked awhile with a trapper up near Medicine Bow. He used to climb them Sioux scaffolds to get bodies to bait wolves with. Once we found a bunch of slaughtered Mormons in a valley, but he wouldn't take none of them for bait. I figured he didn't want the sin on him. But do you know what he said? 'It ain't me that don't want them harm—it's the wolves. Wolves can be three weeks starved but won't touch a hair of no white corpse. They's less beast than the Indians that way.'"

"You sure?" Jolly said. "Didn't seem too bothered about eating them riders back there."

He was holding Mico's head on his lap and trying to tilt some water between his cousin's teeth. I held out my canteen and Mico drank so long I had to pull it from his hand.

"By God," he said. "That's really everything, Misafir."

He sat up and looked around. "Ali," he said. "I can't believe it's this shithole I'll be dying in." Minutes later, he was back in his daze.

Shaw watched him. "Don't look like he gone pull through any more than I am."

Sometime later the first of the wolves started scratching against the door. Quick, loud scrapes, like it was already in the shack with us. Jolly fired, but the scraping only stopped for a moment before starting up again. Pretty soon, we could see the dirt flying and the shadow of its paws working quickly. "Jesus," Shaw kept saying. "Jesus." You were rocking back and forth, belching with rage. If let, you'd have broken your harness and brought the whole place down. I got on my stomach and fired straight into those fast-moving shadows. But the wolf just went on digging. Another started by the door. By this time they were so many, I thought all the world was made up of howling.

"I'm just that glad," Shaw said. "I'm just that glad you lads are here with me." Then he turned and sent his heel straight into Mico's chest.

The sound Mico made was very like a wolf. Jolly sprang to his feet. I lay there bellied while Mico drowned in blood, and I watched my friend's rifle tilting down to meet Shaw's chin. This is exactly as I remember it. Shaw lay on his back with both feet on the floor, and his whole being shook with the effort of sitting up. "Almighty God," he said. "Take me up."

"You're going no place save into the teeth of them devils out there."

"Maybe. But at least they've plenty to work on now before they get to me."

Burke—you were there. You know. Jolly stood sighting down. Before I knew what I was doing, I had turned my rifle and fired once in the direction of Shaw's head. Then everything—even the wolves—went still.

———

We wrapped Mico in blankets and buried him under the floor of that little depot, and that is where he still sleeps to this day. We got back there once—remember?—in the years afterwards, and stood listening for him, but he did not appear. It made me glad to know his rest was uninterrupted.

Shaw's body, on the other hand, we dragged for what must have been about eight miles. Then we left him there for the wolves. I didn't turn back after we cut him loose lest he touch me and get his want into me.

The wind had blown over George's tracks, so for a long while we guessed our way forward, dragging Saleh when she stalled to wait for the rider she had lost. It was three more days before we found water: a shallow stream, thin and brilliant, laid like a mirror in the dust. By that time you were frothing up and starting to list a little, left and right, and your hump had got an awful sag to it.

Jolly and I crouched together at the water's edge and cast the warm, sweet light over our faces and dwelled in the secret silence of relief.

"Imagine we didn't go back to the others," Jolly said, after prayers.

"Imagine."

"I mean it, Misafir. We could pretend to die out here. Go and find our fortune. Who would miss us?"

Well, Burke. I wonder sometimes if he really meant this. I'm glad he said it, for it betrayed the wanderer in him, the want he couldn't be rid of. I must admit I was tempted—which I'm sure does not surprise you. But I thought of George and Lilo waiting for us at the campfire, and for once I didn't run, which is how a late October evening found us rejoining Beale's packtrain on the eastern shore of the Colorado River where it left its canyons and eased down a wide wash in its finally blue course to Yuma.

Beale had got himself turned around once or twice and stalled in the end trying to find a fording place. There was no crossing yet in those days, only palisades that plunged down and vanished in deep water. Scouts had been sent up and downstream, but their news was grim: no navigable shallows having been found, it would now be necessary to swim the stock.

"They **can** swim, of course?" Beale asked, which was when it became plain to all that he'd awaited our return with the sole aim of asking this question of Jolly before he blundered all those camels into the water and drowned the War Department's entire herd.

Jolly didn't know. He paced up and down the bank, looking for the gentlest descent into the water. "Ain't you ever seen a camel swim?" I asked him.

"Where would I see a camel swim?"

The Mojave people had come up from their fields; the women, their faces ink-lined, whispering down to the kids; the lanky youths drawn together, doubting us with weary smiles.

By afternoon the wagons were across and a mule and horse had drowned. There was nothing left to do but rope the camels together and drive the first of you into the water. Jolly edged down the bank, his boots sliding. Behind him, Seid fought the drag of the scree, then gave up and eased forward. Water parted around his neck and the hummock of his back, and the white lengths of his legs flashed palely in the gloom below.

Cheers from all present, save the Mojave, who were just then turning, impassively, one by one, downstream toward another absurdity: the far-off gray wedge of a ship's stern turning slowly into this crook of the river. It was a sidewheeler, the **General Jesup**. The whole magnificent hulk of it came slowly into view. To this day, Burke, I couldn't tell you who was more surprised by what lay before them: those of us on the shore who were seeing, for the first time, a vessel in these once unnavigable waters, or the fellas on the ship, who beheld our camels dotted throughout the stream.

That river crossing was Saleh's first swim and final journey. Our detour to the star-crossed wagon train, and the loss of Mico, had all but played her out. Beale thought to leave her here to find her way—but Jolly didn't think this especially merciful. "Do as you see fit," Beale said. "Only tell me nothing of it."

So he never wrote about Jolly cutting her throat and draining her blood and butchering her there on the shores of the Colorado while the heedful Mojave looked on. He wrote nothing of how Jolly cut the meat into huge pieces and handed them, hunk by hunk, out to the waiting crowd.

By evening, all of Saleh had been given away save the hump, which Ab roasted dubiously over a spit until it was black. Afterwards we sat watching the steamer draw near and talking on Mico, his impatience and boldness and bad taste in jokes, the way he fussed over his clothes, until our hearts were full of him. Around us the silver undergrowth rustled with small nighttime stirrings. The Mojaves' fires burned on both shores.

"These people," Jolly said, when the others had gone to bed, and it was just the two of us sitting wakefully side by side again. "They don't look too bothered by that ship."

"No."

"They don't look too impressed either."

"I guess not."

"And they don't look too bothered by the camels."

This seemed to trouble him. He took some time to puzzle it out. "It's the same thing to them: ship, camel. What's the difference? There's no miracle in it. It's just another means of their end."

"I guess so."

"My grandmother used to say that when the Turks first came to her town, they built a great bridge. But nobody could bring themselves to love it. They wanted us to believe that something extraordinary had come, but we never could make ourselves feel that way about it. The miracle wasn't for us."

"But ain't you a Turk?"

He dragged a hand across his eyes. "I reckon by now I ought to be."

"Well, there you have it. You're lucky to know, one way or the other."

"Make no mistake, Misafir: so are you. In your tongue and in your very bones, so are you."

I don't mind telling you, Burke—I felt as though he'd just put his arms around me.

"Well," I said, when I could speak again. "That's something, anyway."

The **General Jesup** tied up and all that long and wondrous night and into the following morning we watched the passengers coming ashore. They were rough, unwashed traders and trappers from down-river. They had come to encroach on our sorrow with their hides and steamer trunks, their violins and whiskey barrels, the merriment of a long journey's end.

As we sat there at our breakfast, a pair of mottled calfskin boots made their way down the gangplank—and who was wearing them, Burke? You know already. Who in this weird, wild world could be wearing them calfskin boots off a steamer in the southern reaches of the Colorado River, but the wolf himself: Marshal John Berger.

I might have thought him among the dead had he not walked straight through the crowd and and into Beale's embrace.

"What's that man's business here?" I asked George.

After some reconnaissance, an answer was got.

"He's some lawman, it seems," George said. "Old friend of the Lieutenant's."

Well, I hid in our tent and slunk around with my head shawled. But that very night Berger found me at the fire. "I know you, I think," he said, clasping my hand.

Because I'd been thinking all day of nothing but our last encounter, I said: "Yes. From Fort Green." Too quickly, the words had leapt from my mouth. If only I'd taken a breath, a moment longer to speak. His brows met and I saw him wondering—if I was not precisely the man he suspected me to be, why in hell should I remember some murky night so clearly, so quickly, so certainly? I had given myself away.

"Well," Berger said. "I'll be damned. That must be it."

You can hardly blame me, Burke, for what I did—though I have wondered since how things would have turned out for you had I chosen different. Before the deed was done, I tipped back my canteen only to see the inside of some dreary gray saloon, a pair of speckled hands, a bowl of uneaten soup. The vision gave me courage. It must be myself in old age, I thought. I lay in the cameleers' tent one last time and imagined myself walking north until I fell, shriveled with thirst or full of bullets.

———

We had run so long together already—was there any chance of my leaving you behind?

Jolly was waiting for us when I led you into the trees. "Who is that man?" he asked me.

"What man?"

"The man you're fleeing."

"Nobody."

"Nobody? You're thieving one of the War Department's camels on account of nobody?"

At length, I said: "That's the man been searching for Lurie Mattie these three years gone."

Jolly stood a long time with his pipe brightening the edges of his face. "I ought to shoot you. I ought to shoot you right now." Then he took off his hat and turned his jaw sideways to me. "Strike me here." He pointed. "But take good care not to murder me."

AFTERNOON

AMARGO

Arizona Territory, 1893

ABOUT A MILE FROM HOME, NORA caught up to a dustcloud. She mistook it first for a running antelope, but when it turned down her drive she recognized Doc Almenara clipping along in his new spring wagon—a glinting marvel of a thing, almost insolently beautiful, as black as the pair of horses that pulled it. Hat raised, the Castilian was already standing up in the boxseat to call out: "Hullo hullo hullo. Hullo, the house!"

At his sixtieth birthday—or so Nora had heard—Hector Almenara Vega had been the first man on the hardwood and the last man to bed. He was tall, limber, and pinstraight, and exuded the irrepressible energy of a daddy-longlegs. A whitish scruff of beard—the last vestige of his once-glorious hair—hedged his chin. Nora had never seen him out of uniform: sunhat, coattails and cravat, blinding shoes, soft riding gloves that inspired reverence of whatever antelope had given its life to produce them. Twenty years into his tenure as Amargo's physician, with the mercury at a hundred and sixteen, the Doc still dressed for what he had expected Amargo to become: a boomtown, a real one, with a railhead whose boards were thick with similarly disposed people: people who could quote operas and speak knowledgeably about military campaigns and the value of gold—not the kind you found in the ground, but the kind that set what he mysteriously referred to as "the market." People whom Emmett derisively referred to as "snail-eating folk."

"In fairness," she once told her husband, "I'm glad of his tastes, for without them I doubt I would ever have tasted turtle soup. And he's never served us snail."

Emmett had squeezed her arm teasingly. "You needn't make **singularia tantum** of invertebrates."

The boys had come up calling him Doctor Hector. Because he'd been a friend to them—childlike himself in many ways, indulgent and playful and extravagant—they found his charms impossible to outgrow. Unsurprising, then, that Toby and Josie fell all over themselves running out to greet him, Toby with the sorry carcass of the windhover outheld before him like some magnificent prize. The Doc was making the recognizable gesture of admiration, following this up with a vigorous pantomime. Now his gloved hands framed an invisible rectangle. By the time Nora drew up, his tutorial was at an end: "And that, caballero, is how to display a dead bird."

"You're not making anything of that filthy thing," Nora called. "God's heaven, Toby."

The Doc turned over his shoulder. "The lady of the house! Were you in town? How's the Sheriff?"

She managed to overcome her surprise. "He wasn't in."

The Doc stood with his hands on his hips, shaking his head. "The young man's got a fine specimen here," he said. "It just beggars my own offering." He hoisted a towel-wrapped dish off the boxseat and held it out with ceremony. "Pan dulce."

She wished he had brought water. She eyed up the back of the spring wagon, but it was empty save for a blanket draped jauntily over the seat. Just as well—Emmett didn't like her to invite the Doc's largesse. He was forever undercharging them for his services, calling over unannounced so they could not find the pretext to refuse him. Her arm sweated around the dish while they exchanged pleasantries: the Doc's son, Alejandro, was thriving at an apprenticeship in Mexico City. His wife was back to sleeping through the nights following this latest break in the heat, and quite well, quite well indeed—an understatement if Nora had ever heard one, for she'd watched them at the Christmas social, the tall doctor and his stout little wife, mutinying the ravages of time with their lopsided polka.

Inside, Doc Almenara began his rounds with a tour of the topographical wonders that comprised Toby: his mineshaft ears, his bouldersome teeth, his acreage of limbs. "Bigger every day! They must be feeding you the world!" His hand scraped Toby's scalp. "But you're a hedgehog. Lice, was it? How long since they stopped biting?" The answer—a whole week!—seemed a cause for celebration. On the subject of Toby's eye, however, the Doc grew stern. "How do the lights look now?" Toby drew a darting shape in the air, circumscribed it with something jagged on all sides. The Doc flipped Toby's eyelid and loomed close. "How are you finding your way about?"

"Well enough."

"Why aren't you binding this eye?"

"It's too hot."

"And are you riding?"

"Not if I can help it."

The Doc shook his head. "We made a gentlemen's agreement: no riding at all."

"It's some work, doc, not riding **at all**."

"I meant what I said: one solid bump could blind you outright." He turned to Nora. "No riding, no roughhousing, no lake-diving."

"Where on earth would he go lake-diving?" Nora said.

"I don't know. Perhaps some secret spring only he knows. When Alejandro was your age, he was forever finding the impossible. He'd have had the Israelites to Canaan in less than a week." He scratched Toby's head again. "I pray this grows back to you with speed. What's the good of living with the finest barber this side of the Picketwire if she can't keep you looking fit for company?" The barber in question was twisting her red braid beamingly in the doorway. "Well, Josie? Still cutting hair?"

"When folks need it cut."

His hand rasped the shining bald dome of his own head. "Is this past your powers?"

"My papa was bald as you in his day, Doctor Hector, and I fixed it up for him with a little primrose oil."

These ongoing allusions to his hairline were either a force of habit, or an unguarded glimpse down the warren of his vanity. Nora thought it must be the latter: after all, he was the only man in town who had a gas stove—the acquisition of which he hadn't even bothered to pass off as a gift for his wife. He had gone so far as to meet it at the Flagstaff depot personally. Its arrival in town, by eight-mule team, had been processional. But Nora, standing under the awning of Lark & Sons the day it arrived—a huge, sleek hulk of a thing, gleaming in the wagonback—had felt then, as she did now, that his vices were forgivable in their frankness. No person who actually cared about what was being said could inspire so much gossip. He was himself, and himself to everybody.

He loomed over to Gramma. "And Missus Harriet. Keeping spry?"

"She moved herself again today," Josie said.

"Didn't we just get done talking about false-hoods?" said Nora.

"It's true." Josie turned to the Doc. "I was fixing breakfast this morning with my back to her, talking loud as you prescribed, real slow so she can follow along. Telling her about Montana—this place where they got a Christmas fair, the best in all the world it's said, because of the Germans living there-abouts. Only she must not've been too keen on any of that talk, for next thing I know I'm turning around and the young mister here is wheeling her back in from the porch." Josie nodded vigorously at the Doctor's surprise. "I never seen it happen myself, but I swear to the Lord it's true. Ask Toby. Happens right around the same time: early in the morning or just past sundown. Best I can figure is, these are the times she gets so overcome with who she was before being brainhurt that she gathers up the strength to go looking for herself again."

"What a glorious sentiment, Josie." He took her hand and shook it a little. "You've the soul of a poet."

"Rather than waste the Doctor's time," said Nora, "perhaps you might draw his attention to that unexplained rash on your neck?"

The Doc took the opportunity of Josie's dropping her chin into her hand to move on. "Is it true, Missus Harriet? Have you been jailbreaking?" Gramma's cheeks collapsed sourly. He looked her over, easing a line of careful squeezes along her joints, down one arm and up the other. Entreating her to smile so he could get a look at the ground-down stumps of her teeth, he lifted her lips to afford the dignified illusion that she was doing it herself. Before her stroke, Gramma had taken great care to be furtive about the way she writhed out of his grasp. As though her dignity would be diminished if she betrayed her distaste for him and all Mexicans in general. But now her very soul fought him tooth and nail. You could see it in her eyes, in every rigid inch of her being. He knew, of course—had seen a lot of it, Nora suspected, from newcomers to the territory. The harder his patients resisted, the more he seemed to make a point of not letting it dissuade him from his work. She stood by, drifting between embarrassment and the ravenous trumph of seeing the old lady fail to conceal herself.

Finally, he turned to Nora. "And you, Missus Lark?"

She was thirsty. Three boys, a slip of a girl and an invalid old lady's watering privileges outranked hers. She had gone to bed thirsty and woken up thirsty; she had passed the morning with a throat so parched it hurt her to speak; so parched she had balmed it with whiskey and bitter coffee until it burned, and she couldn't remember when she'd last had a whole mouthful of water. She said: "My head's been paining me a little."

He felt her temples. "You've took too much sun, perhaps?"

"Perhaps."

"Nora," he said teasingly. "You've not been drinking, have you?"

THEY CONVERGED AT THE LITTLE parlor table just off the kitchen. Through the window, she could keep an eye on Toby and Josie's outdoor maneuverings, which seemed, at this moment, to involve making a kind of sepulchral structure for the mummified bird. She had nothing to offer her guest save corncake, which he perched stiffly on his knee with the air of a man who would suffer it, if needs must, but not a moment before it was absolutely necessary.

"Glad as I am to see you, Hector, we haven't called you round because the burdens of this last month have put us right past our debts."

He held up a hand. "If I only tended patients who could afford to pay me every time I came around, Nora, the dead in this town would vastly outnumber the living."

"Well. If Josie's to be believed, they do."

He laughed, showing all his teeth. Out came his faded leather notebook. "When do you think you'll be solvent again?" he said. "The tenth? The eleventh?"

"Yes."

"I'll give you grace till the seventy-fiftieth." He pressed an invisible pen against the page, swirling loops of empty air. "And may God help you, Missus Lark, if you're still in arrears then."

"Hector."

Failure to sound amused at his joke earned her a squeeze of the hand. He set about cracking into the cake with his front teeth and larding on thin flattery of her cooking. She let him get on with it. Amada Rios Borrego de Almenara, when she rolled up her sleeves and routed her servant girls, was widely known as the finest cook in the entire Territory. People who fed and watered at her house only ate elsewhere to remind themselves to be thankful for the good fortune of going home.

"I suspect you're not just here to forgive debts," Nora said at length.

"No indeed." She could hear the cake sticking to the roof of his mouth. "I asked Emmett for an audience, and so was summoned here."

"Oh."

She thought she'd succeeded in broadening her smile, but this was not the case. The Doc watched her. "Ah," he said. "So he hasn't told you. Well, I'm very glad to pass the time with you till he finishes whatever he's doing."

"Did you make this appointment with him— today?"

"Last week." There was a mien of false patience to him. She could see now how effortfully he'd kept himself from looking around. "I fear Emmett may have forgotten."

"I don't know about forgetting, doc. But we might be passing a while, you and I."

"Isn't he here?"

"He's delayed resupplying in Cumberland," she said. "You know Paul Griggs?"

"Distantly."

"Well, he's been our waterman these past two years. Only he failed to appear."

"My goodness." A sour little flinch was trapped in his lip.

"Emmett thinks they've a shortage on with the drought. Or that Paul's looking to squeeze us because with the Floreses gone, he's only got one homestead to supply."

"The bastard." He lashed his pipe against his thigh. "Forgive me. Do you know what it is, to be a waterman? To be the lowest species of thief. You move into territories where people's wells are failing and bilk them for what ought be free. All the while you're nothing but a common freighter. Emmett will give him a firm booting." He fixed her with a reproachful look. "Nora—why not come to me?"

"You're just as parched as the rest of us."

"Even so. You mustn't hesitate to ask. When do you expect him back?"

"Any moment now," she said. And then, for reasons not entirely clear to her in that stagnant moment, she admitted, "Though, in truth: two days ago."

She imagined the effort he now made to keep his pitch level as a fist squeezing his gut. "He's two days delayed?"

"Three, I suppose. If you count Monday."

"Has he sent word?"

"No."

"No?"

"But that's not so unusual."

He answered this by ruffling himself excessively, like some troubled owl. "Of course not. He could have encountered delays going up there. Could have been delayed waiting on the water. Or waylaid coming back."

"And sometimes being in the thick of some great excitement makes us inattendant to the passage of time!"

"Precisely."

"And I've not heard of any trouble up Cumberland way."

"Trouble? No." He sat back. "No, the trouble's in Palo Verde."

"What happened?"

"Didn't you hear about Martín Cruzado?"

She hadn't.

"It's not cake-talk," the Doc said finally.

She got two glasses, and the Doc poured out a little of his flask in each. Nora continued to hold hers on her knee, as out of range of her nostrils as could be managed.

The Doc wafted his sternly. "Last week, Martín sent the boys out for the flock. His cousin's kids. They're gone three days, maybe four. Too long. Martín gets this foreboding feeling. You know how he is." She nodded. (She had no idea.) "So in service to his own augury, he mounts up a posse and rides out to find them. He's scrambling around up in the hills. No sign of either men or sheep. He's got a tracker with him, a Comanchero goes by Richard Night. He's looking for sign, but he says it's all confused—sheep everywhere. In the end, of course, it's the buzzards that lead them to the bluff. And there's Martín's whole flock, smashed to pieces down in the canyon." He let a little shudder pass through him. "Anyway, Richard Night figured they'd been fired on from further up the mesa and stampeded over, like a buffalo jump."

"God's heaven. Anyone live to tell it?"

"Not by the time Martín got there. One of the lads had got out from under his horse. But he didn't get far." The Doc pointed to the flask. She shook her head. "Those boys were brought into the Palo Verde dispensary after four days in that heat. You ever seen my wife's fried duck, Nora?" He raised his eyebrows and let her sit with that awhile. She wasn't sure if it was the bloat of the duck, or the way its skin blistered, that she was supposed to be imagining.

"Poor Martín. He came into town howling. Said it

looked like someone with blood-soaked hands had pulled all the stuffing out of a pillow down there."

"Poor Martín."

"Well, I'm glad to see you moved to lenity," the Doc said. He removed a parcel from his coat. Unwrapped with painstaking suspense, it revealed an adobe brick of ordinary weight and dimension, which he laid on the table between them as though it were a bar of gold. "This is the brick he threw through the **Sentinel** window late last night. He's damn sorry."

The offending missile surprised her. She had imagined it quite differently: a rock, something fundamental, something betraying an act of spontaneity, a figure stooping in the heat of passion for an object in the road. A brick, on the other hand—a brick was different. You might call a brick insidious. It had to be found. It had to be transported to the scene of pillage. There was menace to a brick—purpose and premeditation.

"How fortunate no one was hurt."

"Very fortunate." He shifted in his seat. "But then, not so unexpected. The place **has** been empty for some days now."

"What led him to do it?"

The Doc threw up his hands. "Oh, what leads people to their most regrettable moments? Drink, of course." Almost as an afterthought, he said, "But I suppose heartbreak and uncertainty played some part in it, too."

"Heartbreak and uncertainty?"

"I suppose Martín came around in the first place wanting an explanation regarding the **Sentinel**'s general reticence on the vote."

She felt hot. "We're understaffed."

"Of course—but that's why he thought the letters he's been sending and sending might find a home beneath your masthead. Emmett told him he'd give it some thought—publishing Martín's letters, I mean. In Spanish, too. And yet the vote draws ever nearer, and still the **Sentinel** remains conspicuously silent. Which led Martín to think—and I don't know, but I suppose he can't be the only one—that perhaps the **Sentinel** doesn't much care which way the vote goes."

"Doesn't care?"

"Or worse: stands with Ash River."

"That's absurd."

"Is it?"

"Hector," she said. "Come now."

He folded his arms thoughtfully. "Did you know I was a field surgeon for General Crook?" She knew. Everyone did. "I've told you something of this, I think. I drove one of his ambulances while he chased the Sioux around Montana. Anyway, one day, into the triage tent came three fellas carrying a soldier on a buffalo robe. He'd been scalped, but managed to cling both to life and a small hank of his head and hair, which I pried from his fist and was entreated to stitch back on. This I tried with what one might call uncertain results. He always went about afterward with what looked like a smashed pigeon straddling his head. But he was grateful enough for that. We all have our little vanities." She doubted if he noticed that his hand had returned to his own shining head. "About a year later, I found myself winter-stranded at a depot and the wind blew in a Lakota kid with four army bullets in him. His aunt was the sutler's wife, so you can imagine words were exchanged, and I was conscripted into saving the boy's life. Well, I did, and he recovered quite nicely. As thanks, he made a gift to me of a tanned scalp, which he had painted and done up with beads and the like. I don't mind telling you I was pretty pleased, for it was one of those curios other people seem to have, but you never think you'll manage to get hold of yourself. Only—upon closer inspection, I recognized it as the other half of the hank I'd stitched onto Crook's infantryman the year before!"

"Good Lord," Nora said.

"Imagine."

"I presume you threw it away."

"Of course not. I kept it. It had been lifted already—what good would it do in the bushes?" She didn't know what to make of this. "Well, I rejoined Crook just before Slim Buttes the following summer to find his whole regiment taking the mercury. They'd had rather a long season with only a couple of girls, and I don't have to tell you what happens in those situations. Suffice it to say, I was up to my neck. Presently in came my half-skinned friend from the previous year and hopped up on the table before me and sat there while I went about my work. I didn't think on my surroundings till I looked up to see him staring at the wall of my tent with his mouth open. After a while he said 'Hell, doc—I really reckon I don't know what to make of you. Exactly whose side are you on?' And then it struck me: I'd displayed the scalp there with some arrowheads and other mementos, having forgot completely that this was the man from whom it was lifted! I knew to overreact would put me past the powers of recovery, so I turned coolly and looked up at the wall. 'Ah,' said I. 'Ah, Mister Lansbury—I see now, the source of your confusion.'"

"That's a good story, Hector—but the **Sentinel** hasn't hung any scalps."

"But neither has it stitched any heads."

She laughed in spite of herself. "Age has considerably worsened your allegorical abilities," she said. "How is poor Martín now?"

"Sleeping off his regrettable night in the dispensary." He leaned forward a little. "Which, under the circumstances, I hope you consider a suitable alternative to the jailhouse."

"Of course. Who in their darkest moments hasn't thought of throwing a brick?"

"I'm heartened to hear that, Nora." There was a gust of obligation to the way he went about squeezing her hand. She suspected he would not wait long to continue. She was right. "In truth, however, the whole thing set me to wondering about the **Sentinel**'s intentions."

"What can you mean?"

"It occurred to me, while I was in there clearing the damage, that the presses haven't really turned for more than a week."

So he had swept up this morning. Had he let himself in? Had he been able to resist going through the drawers and reading the drafts?

"You needn't have done that, Hector."

"Well, I felt obliged. I didn't want it all just sitting there. We haven't seen the boys these past few days at all."

"Really?" Her voice faltered a little.

"I suppose it's hard to know what they're up to once they're in town."

"I came round myself only this morning."

"For the first time, I hear."

The nerve of him, counting their comings and goings like some fishwife. "It's a building, Hector, not an ailing uncle. Should I have called on it daily and brought it soup?"

"More to the point, it's a wired structure with full twice its own worth of machinery and electric works. Leaner ruins have been looted in Amargo, and in far more prosperous times." She watched him light his pipe again. Was it a result of his smoking so compulsively, she wondered, or his not knowing how to keep it burning in the first place? "If I may speak plainly?" Hadn't he been? "I find it a miracle that last night's brick was the first blow against the **Sentinel** since the county seat mess began."

"What precisely should have earned the **Sentinel** a sooner blow?"

She saw him hesitate. It was only for a moment—less, a fraction of one. His last opportunity, she understood, to keep this treaty between himself and Emmett.

"Hector," she said.

He produced a second package and slid it across the table to her. Its heft betrayed it for what it was, an envelope that had been passed from hand to hand, opened and closed repeatedly; been stored in pockets and bureaus and secreted between the pages of books and fattened over time. She let it sit awhile. If he indulged in theatrics, shouldn't she do the same? Within were letters addressed to Emmett, or else to the **Sentinel,** and on every page in Spanish or English, rightly writ or misspelled, she found the word "rebuttal."

The Doc said: "Different people, as you see, have different causes to feel aggrieved. Some are wounded that the **Sentinel** failed, or refused, to print up these defenses of Amargo—including the first envelope I sent Emmett two weeks ago. Others feel betrayed by his abrupt withdrawal from the brief and inadequate stand he finally took against the **Clarion** last week."

An unusual feeling twisted at her. "It was adequate enough to cost Desma Ruiz a great deal. Her marriage is questioned, her prospects ruined. Twenty years proving up that creekfront—and now she won't see a penny for it."

"That's the price of civic life," the Doc said.

She waved the pages at him. "All these people would be subject to the same fate."

"They seem willing to take that risk. They deserve a venue that will honor their courage."

How like her to advance a conversation and blunder right into a chastisement intended for Emmett. It was her own damn fault to be at this exasperating crossroads: side with the Doc against Emmett, in accordance with her own beliefs; or defend her husband's absurd notions in his absence. "My apologies for his not having righted all the wrongs of the county."

The Doc was unfazed. "It's no small task."

"But—you're here to tell me—it must fall to someone."

"I'm here to ask if Emmett intends to take it up. Or if something stays him."

She thought about this. "What on earth would stay him?"

"I can't for the life of me guess." He shrugged. "I treat failures of the body, Nora—not of the constitution. Perhaps he is undecided. Perhaps he is afraid. Perhaps he thinks the move to Ash River might benefit him."

"How?"

"Perhaps some offer of enrichment has given him pause."

She had thought they were still joking, at least a little. Evidently, they were not.

"An offer of enrichment—are you mad? How long have you known Emmett?"

"A long time," the Doc said. "Though not particularly well—owing to his own disinclinations."

"Hector. It's some nerve to sit in a man's house and accuse him of being a turncoat."

"I don't do so lightly. But this kind of business redraws lines of allegiance. He would not be the first indebted newspaperman to take the great bounce."

"He has not taken the great bounce."

The Doc's shrug was the most enraging in all the world. "Then perhaps he is simply uninterested in the task."

"I really cannot speak to my husband's intentions," she said. "I know only that my boys are keeping his press warm till he gets back."

"Are they? For a week now they've not shown their faces in town—while the rest of us waste time huddling on the printhouse porch, peering through the windows. If Emmett intends neutrality until the vote, then perhaps he should consider selling his newspaper while it still has a chance of doing the rest of us some good."

She laughed. "Selling it? To whom?"

He sat deliberately back.

Here—this. This was at the heart of Emmett's distaste for him. It wasn't just the doctor's "preening"—a word Emmett reserved for anyone who got up a certain way in public. It was the confidence with which Hector Almenara Vega appointed himself as the arbiter of right and wrong. She wondered if he knew what was said about him behind his back—that he had driven that poor son of his almost to madness with the weight of his expectations; that his wife took the laudanum to deaden herself to whispers of all the mistresses Hector had lined up from here to Yuma—accusations against which Nora had defended him again and again, to people all over the county, for the sake of their friendship.

And yet, here they were. All that talk of debt absolution; all the details of Martín Cruzado's misfortune. It had all been leading to this.

"If Emmett returned," she said, "and learned that I'd treated about selling the **Sentinel**."

"You mean: treated with me." He wouldn't give her the opportunity to object. "I realize it's hardly news that Emmett and I have our differences."

"Goddamn it," she said. "This again, Hector?"

"Never mind that in seventeen years, I never set foot in Emmett's house save to dispense medicine—though he has never once refused my hospitality, or my help for the shortfall in his business. And never mind that, after my tending to his wife and children, he responds to the one favor I ask of him by spouting off some nonsense about how he can't afford to take on another compositor right now, even if it's my niece."

"Hector."

"I said never mind."

"For a man who doesn't mind, you seem to keep an awfully detailed score."

"I've put it all aside, because you and I have been good friends since you alighted in Carter County. And I have great affinity for the boys. It is my continued hope that you might raise them up to make something better of themselves than just Emmett's hothead heritors." Everything went out of her mind at once. Just as well, because the Doc was still bulling on. "Now. If I were a small man—a man who holds a grudge and says, **Look—here is a gringo who insults me, who holds no respect for my kin, who won't, no matter how many times I've pressed the subject, introduce a Spanish section for the benefit of half the readership in this county—** I'd say to hell with Emmett Lark, and to hell with his wife and sons, and especially his newspaper. Why debase myself by offering to assume the responsibilities he is too cowardly to undertake?" She'd never seen a person run out of breath whispering, but here he'd managed it somehow. The top of his head glowed an angry red. "But the fact remains, last week, **The Amargo Sentinel** struck a blow against the Stock Association. It may not have had much effect, but it did hit its mark—that's plain enough. And it would be a shame to withdraw from that progress when there are so many people, like Martín Cruzado, whose lives and homes will otherwise fall to the ceaseless depredations of Merrion Crace." He cleared his throat. "May I trouble you for some water, please, Nora?"

She examined the bucket in the stagnant privacy of her kitchen. How on earth had the water dropped further? What possible reason could that fool girl have found to waste still more of it? But to refuse the Doc now would look like pettiness, and she could not bring herself to do it. She watched him drink it down with a knot in her throat. It was the longest, most luxuriant drink she'd ever seen another person take.

"Thank you," he said, when he finished.

"Hector," she said. "What is it you want me to do?"

"I'd like you to give some thought to selling me the newspaper." His boot tapped the table-leg lightly. "And should you find yourself so inclined, perhaps you might help Emmett arrive at the same conclusion. It's too vital now to squander such a resource on indecision or cowardice."

"This is why Emmett dislikes you, you know. He's always after telling me not to accept you coming over to dispense medicine uninvited. It may seem free, Nora—but somewhere, someone is running a tab."

"Most tabs, I believe, seek to draw on money you don't have rather than give you more. Not so with me."

She stood, knowing he would follow suit. "I'll give it some thought, then. Ask myself: how will this help me do better than just raise Emmett Lark's hothead heritors?"

He skated the envelope of letters across the table to her. "You may find all kinds of things sway you. Who knows, Nora? Perhaps a week from now, you'll be a rich woman and running off with Sheriff Harlan."

A single mention of Harlan Bell had been uncivil enough. A second was intolerable. "What have you got in your mind about my association with Harlan Bell?"

He replaced his hat. Its top very nearly touched the ceiling beams. "We've been very good friends for a very long time, Nora—I'll do you the courtesy of withholding my reply."

SHE WATCHED THE DOC SAY HIS goodbyes from the boiling shade of the porch. Restored to his ordinary, charming ease, he nattered with one hand in Toby's hair, the other on the small of Josie's back, interlarding his endearments with the small jokes that got folks wistful for his company. Already, even Nora herself was longingly revisiting a moment not half an hour old: his joke about absolving her of her debt, the debonair swirl of his invisible pen. What a rake, she thought. Blessed with a certain manner, one could inhabit a room long after having left it.

Emmett, too, was like this: concerned, attentive, offhandedly charming. Possessed of that rarest gift: making his every gesture seem like a benediction. People saw his passions as something to aspire to. She had always suspected this to be what Sandy Freed had recognized in him. He cleaved bull-headedly to his stances because he had taken great pains to arrive at them. Every screed against the bureaucracy of land claims or the matter of Indian sovereignty had somehow earned him more admirers than it cost him friends. Even Nora, who had grown up under the formidable shadow of the Dakota, and made a point of smirking when he called Indians the "dispossessed children of the earth," had found herself swayed by his convictions.

Of course, she had been different in the early days: lovestruck and excitable and naïve. She did not really know what it meant to homestead. She had never been lonely. Even her terrors had been communal. What did she know about Indians—their women in particular? In Iowa, they had not come visiting as they did here. She'd been in the Territory three weeks when she found herself sitting at Desma's table with a Navajo mother and two lively daughters, who, not twenty minutes before, had been mere apparitions on the plain, and were now maneuvering handily between Spanish and Navajo while Desma poured coffee and readied bags of cornmeal for them to take home. When they returned the following week, Nora asked: "I've heard of them begging like this in Nebraska—do they just go from house to house?"

"Not begging," Desma said. "This is their way."

Somewhere between Desma's sharpness and Emmett's children-of-the-earth treatise, she resolved to make herself hospitable. However uneasy, she would try.

Because hers was a new homestead, and all the girls seemed to have their favorite haunts already, no Indian visitor came until June, when Nora turned, with Evelyn sucking at her breast, to see a curious face in the window. It was an old woman—likely Navajo, though later she would ask herself what this presumption had been founded upon.

The old woman was still out there an hour later when Nora opened the door. She came in and sat herself down at the kitchen table as though she had done so a hundred times before, and began looking around the room, offering a quiet but torrential commentary on what Nora assumed must be the deficiencies of her housekeeping. The whole enterprise felt precarious. Nora spoke no more Navajo than the woman spoke English. Her youth made her naturally deferent, but she suspected her every gesture— from serving the tea without a saucer to standing rather than sitting in her guest's company—to be a calamitous insult.

But presently, without incident, the woman left.

Every few weeks thereafter she would appear at the top of the ridge and Nora would sling the kettle on the hob. Her guest talked steadily—a mercy, really, for it allowed Nora to nod along and emerge from the encounter feeling quite hospitable despite having remained more or less silent. And it was all right, even pleasant, to have another soul around the house—save for those occasions when her guest succumbed to the uninvited urge to help herself to Evelyn, then about three months old, who growled and hiccuped most hours of the day in a kitchen drawer Emmett had rigged for a cradle.

At every abrupt silence, Nora would turn to find her daughter asleep in the stranger's blankets.

"Where's the harm in that?" Desma said.

Wasn't it obvious? Suppose one day—owing to some tragic miscommunication or the general derangement of age—the old woman should refuse to return the baby? It had happened before. Desma might wave her off, and Emmett might laugh, but it had happened in other houses, to other women. Nora had read about it and felt sometimes that her fear was apparent enough to even drive the old woman to it.

It did not take her long to arrive at the solution of distracting her guest from caregiving by barter. The old woman had great affinity for sugar, but offered very little in return—trinkets, mostly, which Nora tended to keep on the porch as soon as the woman left and replace in various positions of state about the house as soon as she reappeared.

"I hope the two of you are getting along," Emmett muttered after paying up their account at the Mercantile. "I believe we've bought up all the sugar in the county this month." That was the price of friendship, Nora wanted to say—but she cursed herself for having just set a new precedent of gifting coffee beans along with the sugar. When next the old woman showed her face, Nora tried to retreat from her own previous extravagance. This led to what must have been a kind of quarrel: the woman grew very excited and pointed repeatedly toward the kitchen. Her next visit was a grand affair, at which she presented Nora a remarkable and elaborate blanket. When she tried to wrap Evelyn up in it, Nora dropped a bag of sugar into her hands instead.

Right away, she felt herself touch the line of insult—anyone with half a mind would realize that the exchange was conciliatory. Grasping that she would not be allowed to hold the baby, Nora's guest looked baffled and sullen. Nora obliged her with a second bag of sugar. When a third seemed to be demanded, Nora flew into the teeth of her own anger. "That's quite enough." She said it in English of course, but her general meaning was unmistakable. The old woman began to protest, and Nora, with Evelyn still in her arms, began edging her toward the door.

When last Nora saw her, the old woman was making her way across the ridge in the opposite direction of her customary travel. Not left and up the road to town, but right—down the road leading nowhere, right off the map and into the evening.

Next followed a plunging dread. For hours, Nora waited by the window for the old woman to return.

When Emmett came home to a cold stove and a still house, she alluded to the incident but couldn't confess the degree to which it had all barmed up in her mind. She was certain, by now, that her visitor, in her old-woman vindictiveness, would send riders from her village against the house to steal the little girl. Yes. Nora had read about it—too often, perhaps, and in precisely the kind of publications Emmett would deride, but there it was, the unbearable truth of her thoughts.

"We had an unpleasant time," she said.

"Don't worry so." Emmett gave her a little squeeze. "Old women are such bitter devils. She'll come back again next week, if only to remind you what a churl you've been."

But still the old woman did not return.

This only worsened everything, of course. The stories of Gus Volk's imagination, of Nora's girlhood, teemed with vengeful hags—woodland witches shoving pretty children into ovens, or else fencing their houses with the bones of men who had aggrieved them. A girl weaned on such notions should have known better than to insult some venerable ancient. She realized, in mounting despair, that she lacked the learning to ascertain whether the woman was even Navajo at all—there was every chance, God help her, that Nora had dismissed an Apache. And for what? The indulgence of another bag of sugar?

What harm would it have done to let her hold the child? A woman so old had probably raised a few of her own. She had probably lost some, too, to distance or ailment or the scalp hunters who ranged south of here, and had wanted nothing more than to inhale the deep, sunshine warmth of a new baby.

By then, Nora was staying up nights and sleeping

through the daytime hours. Her planned atonement grew more and more elaborate. Useless concessions sprang up in her heart: she would overcome the bedevilment of her own stupidity and conquer, at long last, the Spanish language, as Emmett had implored her to do, though the effort reduce her to tears; she would be hospitable, and learned, and she would pull herself from the teeth of her rage for all time, if only the Almighty would send her slighted guest back to her door.

But the old woman shadowed everything except her threshold. And the more time went by, the more justified Nora's dread seemed.

When she sought Desma's counsel about it, the irrepressible Missus Ruiz waved her off. "Oh, no doubt you've wounded her to her very bones. But don't be stupid. Whoever she is, she has worries that far exceed even your insults."

This hadn't gone very far toward easing her dismay. And Desma's tolerance of female absurdity had its limits. She withstood another few days of questioning, and put things to an end with a firm: "Don't be stupid."

Nora had never blamed her for that, of course. Desma did not have children. Desma did not understand the evening. She did not understand the fear that overcame Nora when Emmett left, or when any sound stirred the brush, or when that pinto and rider had appeared, some weeks later, on the hill.

AT FIRST, EVELYN'S DEATH CAST BOTH Nora and Emmett down in equal measure. They did not eat. They saw no visitors. They slept through their days and let the crops rot and the sheep wander. Ruination seemed imminent, but unimportant; for what else mattered, now that the evening—kept at bay all this time by sheer force of will, by the careful assembly of facts and mapping of environs—had finally pressed itself against the house? Nora lived, but only in her mind. Remembering that time, on the rare occasions she couldn't help but think of it, she was able nowadays to resurrect only two pictures: sitting up, some morning or afternoon, and watching Desma Ruiz weed her garden; and realizing that Emmett's beard, against which she pressed her face when she slept, had finally grown in enough to stop inflaming his chin.

Emmett's grief moved her. She had felt certain loss would make them strangers, or reveal, as misfortunes often do, the extent to which they had been strangers all along. But he took her by surprise. He saw to the house, cooked terrible stews, drew her baths, combed her hair. His passion for her seemed to deepen inexplicably, and for a while they drifted through the weeks, hand in hand, as though all that need be done was mind one another. Just under a year later, stern as a little owl, Rob came along. All Emmett's joy was restored, but Nora despaired even to look at the child, at his pink little nail-beds and whisper of hair. Again and again, her mind flew to all the ways he might be killed—considerations to which her husband seemed blissfully immune. Didn't he know the cruelty of life? The evening had withdrawn a little, but could return at any moment to consume this child as it had the last one, and Nora along with it. She began to consider flight. In one letter after another, she tried to ready her mother for her return. She felt unwell and lonesome for Iowa; the West did not agree with her at all. But Ellen Francis Volk was hesitant. What would people say, Nora? What indeed. There was no need to ask. But would it be so very terrible to become one of those women who could not endure the lives into which they had followed their husbands, and whom the townsfolk derided in whispers? Would it be so terrible to have her disappearance explained as temporary, necessary for her health? Hem Aftergood's wife had been such a woman; so had Roberto Silva's. Years had passed without either of them being heard from again, and neither Hem nor Roberto seemed especially broken up about it. But there lay the problem—Emmett would be. Unlike those other unions, the Larks' was a love-match. Hadn't he come back for her with that fistful of dry flowers? Hadn't he minded her more carefully than she had any right to expect? What betrayal to abandon him now in favor of this tiny, frowning son, who, she felt in her bones, would not survive his first year regardless of the pains she took to save him. It was as clear to her as a sign of rain: the child would die.

It's a real pity, something distant in her kept on whispering. **He's doomed, poor thing.**

She came to find this inevitability strangely comforting. Since Rob was doomed, she could regard him abstractedly—not with dispassion, but from some odd, hazy remove, as though she were merely looking in on him through glass. Her mothering got to be a little cavalier. She could ride into town with him bindled between her breasts. She could leave him in the kitchen-drawer cradle and be pleasantly surprised to find him still there, kicking and fussing, a minute or an hour later. **Ah,** the voice would say, **but next time he won't be so lucky.** Somehow, he always was. Rob turned one, and then two, bobbing falteringly around the yard in pursuit of chickens, disdainful of the brother Nora had borne him—a development which did not brighten her views about either child's odds of survival. Sooner or later—when her back was turned, or right before her eyes—some violence or misfortune, some rusted nail or ill-gained ladder or bucking horse or diphtherial outbreak would raze them both and prove her right. **It's a pity, Mama, that's for sure. But it can't be helped.**

By the time she had begun to feel like herself again—or at least, allowed her love to grow toward, rather than alongside, her boys—Emmett had gone back to trying to save the printing press. And most vitally of all, that new, curmudgeonly little voice had begun answering Nora whenever she talked to herself around the house.

She knew the voice could not belong to the real Evelyn. The Larks had never been particularly godly, but from her childhood brush with Gus Volk's religion, Nora had managed to retain that neither phantoms nor angels matured in the ethereal realms. And yet this voice—a sweet, slightly clipped little tone—seemed more suited to a child of about six than the infant Evelyn had been when she died. Nora thought perhaps it might belong to some other ghostly child—some victim of heat or circumstance, an Indian kid maybe—but its answers were almost always in step with Nora's own. No—this was Evelyn as she would have been, first at six, and then at eight, and then at eleven, as though Nora alone had been gifted a glimpse of how all of life would have unfolded had the girl survived. Evelyn Abigail Lark: kind enough, but bullheaded; pragmatic but wistful; unimpressed and a little irreverent when she

hit those turbulent years between twelve and fourteen. Somehow, she had wandered back from that
darkness into which she'd been let fall those many
years ago, and the house had stood its walls around
her and kept her safe.

Much of her wit was got from a combination of the
boys, whom she watched over in their beds as they
slept and followed through childhood accidents and
misdemeanors. She derided Nora's baking, offered a
counterpoint to ranching problems, held political
opinions that sometimes ran contrary to Nora's own.
All angles of a problem were evident to her, making
her counsel indispensable to goings-on large and
small: all improvements on the house, all livestock
decisions, all instructions to hired hands. On nights
when all the boys were away, she was happy to banter
till dawn, just to get the last word in, just to keep
Nora awake.

Emmett did not benefit from this voice. Save for
Nora's solitary mention of it a few years back, he did
not seem to think of it, nor suspect the extent of its
influence. Town life was a constant preoccupation:
years were spent acquiring books, running the printhouse, teaching his sons to composite. He was
gathering stories from every corner of the Territory
to print up, and occasionally writing his own: about
the government's relentless assault on the Indians,
about territorial disputes, about the land wars that
had swallowed his sister's ranch up north. If he was
surprised, now and again, by Nora's roughening

manner, he likely attributed it to her exhaustion from wrangling boys and constantly watching the skies at home.

They diverged according to their responsibilities: he was a man of words; she a woman of action.

Lately, it seemed he would run off to Cumberland at the slightest opportunity. She had begun to wonder if there might be a woman—a notion at which Evelyn scoffed—or if he was simply priming the entire household for a runner. After all, this, too, was a possibility. She had become a less and less forgiving companion. The boys were getting ornery in a way that overwhelmed Emmett. Rob might row with her, but at least she could take him in hand; Emmett had lost all ground with him long ago. When they argued, she was afraid they would come to blows, and that she would have to intercede on Emmett's behalf. And Dolan, always shadowing Rob's every move and mood, was not far behind.

Three days late with the water. It would be dishonest to pretend she hadn't entertained the possibility long before this. Of course, it seemed almost impossible—even if his heart, for some unvoiced reason, was worn out enough to leave them all behind, his conscience wouldn't allow it. Not in a drought.

And yet. And yet.

A few years ago, when they'd lost nearly all the flock to blackleg, and Nora had been at her wits' end, pulling mutinous boys out of every imaginable catastrophe, hadn't Emmett put on his hat and gone outside and backed the dray out of the barn and just sat in the drive in the reddening sunset? Half an hour later, hadn't she watched him stable the dray and loose the horses as if nothing had happened?

The incident was never mentioned. She pretended she hadn't seen him, and he pretended he hadn't been seen.

And what of last March? A cursory glance through the kitchen window had revealed Emmett returning from the creek, shaking with what she thought was drink. When he drew closer she'd realized that Josie, unconscious and mud-caked, was draped across his arms like a broken pelt. Sunstroke, of course. It had always been useless to warn her. Nora had put Josie to bed and directed Toby to keep changing out the cold compresses and tip water into her mouth whenever the girl came around. She had emerged from Josie's room to find Emmett and the boys holding a wistful confab in the kitchen.

"She just isn't fit for rough living," Emmett was saying. "After all, she's an Atlantic girl."

Rob slouched against the counter, worrying his hat like some dime-novel badman.

Dolan said: "If Josie and I ever come together— I mean, assuming she would, you understand, assuming I asked and she said yes. Or she said maybe. Assuming all those things. We'd probably have to stake up someplace better'n this."

Nora had been unable to restrain herself.

"What the hell for?" she shot out.

"To ensure her comfort."

"Comfort? I been living here half my life, and no one's ever asked after my comfort."

Emmett shifted in his seat. "Well, doesn't one always hope for better where one's children are concerned?"

"She's not my child."

"But Dolan is."

"I never known Dolan to be the fainting sort."

She nudged him. It was a good jape. But Dolan was too old to let flattery conscript him to her side. He looked down at his coffee.

The assembly didn't resume their talk again until she left the room. From the corridor, she listened to Emmett's voice strengthen. "What I mean to say is: hard living is for hard people. And hard women are a particular sort to which Josie does not belong."

Every part of her felt staved-in. Of course, Emmett hadn't just meant **one wants better for one's children**. What he had meant was: **one wants better for ladies—and one wants ladies, not hard women, for one's sons.**

Hadn't he considered her a lady, once?

Perhaps not. Their coming together had not been presided over by chaperones, nor impeded by any of the usual formalities. Theirs had been a love-match—strong enough, in its youth, to withstand even the death of a child. But somehow, in the intervening years, Emmett had ceased to think of her as he once did, just as she had always suspected he might. This was not entirely his fault. Nora had gone to considerable lengths to steel herself for the life into which she'd followed him. This had required hardening; she was no Libbie Custer, spooning caviar out of a tin while all around her the men were whipped for stealing ham. Even if she had wanted to remain soft, the work would not allow it. Two people at full strength could barely manage all the chores of a homestead: plowing, sowing, raising fence. And if Desma, if her own mother, if Missus Harriet were hard women, then Nora must be, too. It must never be said of her that she had succumbed to the trials of her life and had to be gentled back to some easier state of existence. Evelyn's death filled her with even keener purpose. Keep busy or go mad. Keep busy or be called mad. All the while, she had felt certain this would strengthen their union. Certain it would allow Emmett to see her better, as she really was. Not a beautiful woman, perhaps—and certainly not a delicate one. But one worthy of the life he'd put before her.

Instead, in a single kitchen musing—one of the thousands she and Evelyn had overheard and giggled about—Emmett had managed to bypass her wholesale. He not only failed to see her as a lady—he wouldn't even trouble himself with the comparison. She was a tough, opinionated, rangy, sweating mule of a thing, and the sum total of her life's work was her husband of twenty years enumerating what he desired for his sons—which did not include a companion with her qualities, but did include moving to a more favorable clime to secure the affections of a person with not one-half of Nora's merits.

Of course it did. All difficulties, in Emmett's view, could be solved by pulling up stakes. Any failing could be got away from. Failing in Baltimore, a man might move to Iowa. Failing there, he might move to Wyoming, and then to the southwest Territories. Start a flock. Start a paper.

He had made a grand adventure of his failings, and could make another when Amargo went bust.

Here, meanwhile, was Nora: thirty-seven years old and half-habited by the apparition of a child she had known for only five months, whose remaining life had nevertheless somehow unfolded in her imagination so that every beam, every mirror, every corner of this house breathed with the immutable spirit of her daughter—herself a hard person, too, hardened by death and life and by Nora's own design. She couldn't help but be.

Every guest who crossed their threshold for the month following Josie's fainting spell was treated to a long recapitulation of what had happened the day Josie Kincaid swooned. "Down went the bucket," Emmett would say, "and Josie right behind it, face-first into the mud. It was so sudden I thought she was putting me on. Of course, I got a good deal more serious about it on the run home. No mean feat, getting her up the gulch. You ever been down there? You know how far it is?"

Hearing the story verbatim for perhaps the fifteenth time at a gathering in town, Nora finally lost her temper.

"You carried a slip of a girl a half mile uphill," she said. "You're just Paul Bunyan in the flesh."

This drew laughter, of course—though not from Emmett.

"It beggars belief that you could be so jealous of a child," he said to her afterwards.

"Then we're both of us disappointed," said Nora. "Turns out I'm married to someone for whom carrying a fainting girl is an affirmation of valor worth bringing up in company."

He'd sat there beside her on the bed with his back turned, one suspender ligating his arm. It was a new habit, this going still for want of a reply. "I'm sure Harlan Bell has no need of fainting girls," he said finally, "but the rest of us mortals must stake our valor wherever we can find it."

Meeting him on this ground was pointless. You could not argue Harlan Bell with him and win, and if Emmett had felt at all inclined toward real conversation, he would not have brought the Sheriff up in the first place. She was not jealous. Nor did she believe that there was some great impropriety brewing between Emmett and Josie. Or that Josie was an unfit match for Dolan—though she suspected that if the two of them ever came together their household would be razed by some perfectly avoidable domestic catastrophe within the week.

No. She could not put words to what she felt. Twenty years ago, Nora Volk and Emmett Lark had come together in love—or in what they believed was love, and at the very least a torrential hope that they were both cut from a cloth that could turn life at the edge of the world into a grand adventure. He'd had one; she had not. And now, in hoping better for their sons, Emmett had measured and weighed their years together and cast them off as wanting.

And given the chance to reimagine his life, Emmett might not have chosen Nora for his companion at all.

This was what Rob and Dolan and Josie, and all the people harping on Emmett's disappearance did not know. If his delay in Cumberland was not owed to some terrible misfortune—and it was not, she knew it, felt in her bones that her other self was alive and whole—it might be owed to impulse. To grand adventure. She'd never felt more certain that Emmett could not have written anything on that puncheon ledge last year; that he might easily have driven his dray into the ditch, mounted up and ridden on. Past Cumberland, and past Gentry, too. Past Buford and Cruces, past the border, shedding their whole life in the blue wastes of the Sonoran night.

TOBY AND JOSIE'S EFFORTS HAD MORE
or less brought the springhouse to order. Everything
salvageable lay in a dismal heap on the table. The rest
was waste: smashed glass and fruit, the two beveled
hulls of a broken whiskey bottle. The bird carcass
had been trussed by the feet and folded in its own
wings, altared on a crate with a garnish of dead
thistles.

"Toby—will you please bury that goddamn thing?
Will you?"

He looked at her with disappointment and alarm.
"It ain't ready yet, Mama!"

She sent him inside to keep an eye on Gramma.
He sloped off, turning every few stomps to look back
at her with something like suspicion.

Josie was gathering pieces of mangled cloth in the
corner. Stinging brine still fumed about the place,
recalling the worst labors of summer: the woodstove
roasting the kitchen, the cloud of boiling vinegar,
batch after batch of steeping jars, the wet shirt glued

to her back, and Josie on her knees shoveling wood in and ashes out of the stove—for what?

"It's a wonder they didn't hear this racket all the way to town."

"I ain't lying," Josie said.

"Pardon?"

"I ain't lying about Gramma moving."

"Surely even you understand that's impossible."

"Maybe so, ma'am. But it's true."

"Your superstitions make the whole lot of us look like witless bumpkins."

"She moves, Missus Lark. I ain't lying. Not about Missus Harriet. Not about the lost man. And not about the beast."

"You ought to have been dismissed a hundred times by now," she said. "All you do around here is tell us we're haunted and feed Toby's nonsense."

"To tell you fair, ma'am, I thought I already **was** dismissed—and maybe just hadn't been apprised of it. On account of how you haven't paid me a wage in weeks." Josie squeezed the rags over a bucket, one by one. "But I surely am relieved to hear I've room for redemption."

Nora looked her over. Nothing in that heat-rashed face betrayed the kind of grit that would make this a challenge. "There's an order to things round here. Your pay's coming."

Josie believed her. She wasn't complaining. "Sure, what use have I got for money out here anyhow?"

"Is that why you left the springhouse door open? As a reproach?"

"Ma'am—that you could think so ruins my heart. We were all so flummoxed by Mister Dolan's accident, and I got turned around and before I knew it hours had passed. And there went the sun and all my nerve for setting foot outside. And that's the truth."

"You raise an important point," Nora said. "Knowing that Toby's eye is ruined"—Josie nodded; she knew well, had ridden for Doc Almenara when it first happened—"I can only fathom your desire to cosset him."

"I love him with all my heart."

"Which is why you mustn't play up to his bullshit."

"Ma'am?"

"I mean it, Josie."

"He's very afraid."

"Without cause. This nonsense about the beast only takes on a harmful cast if it's freighted with our willingness to indulge him." She wondered if Josie had brains enough to recognize that Nora had drifted into self-reproach now. After all, it hadn't been Josie down in the gulch this morning, climbing into the thicket, pretending to look for sign. Nora had volunteered herself for that pantomime entirely of her own volition. "You're a smart enough girl," she lied. "I believe you can help me disabuse him of it."

Josie thought on this awhile. "You mean lie to him?"

"I mean do your part to make him understand no beast exists."

Josie looked at her—really looked. As if she had just now realized that the two of them had been talking crosswise all along. Too late, Nora followed her to the realization.

"But Missus Lark," she said. "It does. I seen it."

Nora was relieved to find her earlier anger out of reach, scrimmed by exhaustion and disappointment and the heady smell of the springhouse.

"I suppose it flew by your window."

She knelt down and dragged the tinkling mess of glass across the floor. The whiskey bottle lolled. Something about it, she thought, should be evident to her. But there was that scrim again.

"It was exactly how Toby described it."

Nora shifted to stretch her neck. Toby had never mentioned having seen the beast. His descriptions of it were limited to the tracks. There had been vague mention of something else, too—an unfamiliar odor lingering around the chokecherry thickets that rimmed the Floreses' garden, which Nora had put down to rut-crazed elk.

"What did he say about it?"

It was huge, Josie told her. A ruffle-boned skeleton with great, folded wings on its back. A vision so improbable that even Toby mistrusted himself. Felt that his brothers were right to mock him. Only Josie had felt sorry for their rough treatment of him, and so had gone through his picture books to determine where the idea of such a creature might have first rooted in his mind—to no avail. She'd hated to leave him there like that: no longer quite believing himself, but unable to arrive at any other conclusion. So far removed from the apparition that it was beginning to feel like a dream.

"Which it is," Nora said.

"No, ma'am."

Josie had seen it. Unable to sleep, as she sometimes was, lonely for city racket, she had sat up at an unknown hour and pulled aside her curtains on a clear moon night some weeks ago to the sight of a massive black shadow moving slowly from around the side of the barn. It was bigger than anything Josie had ever seen, the huge, folded wings on its back just grazing the upper-story windows.

"I'm that shocked you didn't scream," said Nora.

"In my head, I did. All the while, I screamed and screamed, like someone was tearing out my heart. Only the sound stayed stuck in me." It seemed to Josie that not just her voice, but all the sounds of the world had been sucked up into a vast black nothing—and that, perhaps, the mere fact of her vision meant that she could no longer count herself among the living.

"Yet here you are," Nora said, disappointed.

"To tell the truth, ma'am, I'd vouch what saved me was my own determination to live so I could tell Mister Toby he'd been right. For I was that sorry to rank with the rest of you in doubting him."

"I'm sure you were. And did you tell him?"

"I did, ma'am."

"And what did he say?"

"That he'd seen the selfsame thing."

"Where?"

"At the Flores place. Only from much further away, with the sun in his eyes. And excepting one thing."

A crucial detail that had almost eluded Josie herself. Just as the monstered shadow moved out of her sight—after an hour or a minute, she hardly knew—Josie's screaming heart gave her away. Her terror shook the void. The beast stopped what it was doing and turned a huge, shining head from between its folded wings to grin in her direction.

There was significant discomfort in witnessing the retrieval of an unwanted memory. Here was Josie, cross-legged on the springhouse floor, with her face as contorted as that of a person passing a graveyard at midnight. But whatever pity Nora was meant to feel for the girl stayed behind that scrim, along with everything else save the slowly emerging notion that Toby—her Toby—had once again become part of a conference of whispers from which Nora had been excluded.

"Doesn't it seem more probable that the alignment between your vision and Toby's is owed more to what he described than what you really saw?"

"I thought so, too, ma'am. Only afterwards, I got to thinking. And I remembered that Toby never said a word about no grinning head."

"Memory is a changeable thing. I would urge you to question the substance of anything you think you may remember about what Toby said he **might** remember."

"But that leaves me with the same conclusion, ma'am. Because my own powers of observation lead me toward naught but the occult."

"Well," Nora said finally. "It was dark."

Josie folded into silence. Rubbed her sweat-reddened chin. Looked to be readying for a whipping. Maybe she should be, Nora thought.

Then the girl leapt up. "I can prove it."

SHE STOOD IN THE STIFLING QUIET OF Josie's room and watched the girl ransack the old dresser on its dilapidated legs. The heft of Nora's own presence felt monumental here, amidst the deluge of Josie's forsaken intentions: the trunk with its westbound stamps from New York to Chicago, Chicago to St. Joseph, St. Joseph to Cheyenne; the patent boots tucked neatly under her bed; the ridiculous hat, tumescent with burlap flowers, which Josie had wisely put away.

Josie returned triumphant and dropped something into her hand.

Nora turned it over. It was a bead of some kind, about the size of a seedpod or rosary, pitted and painted up with a maelstrom of blue circles. She tapped it with her fingernail.

"What is it?"

"After I seen the beast, I reasoned I'd best be quite certain before I say a word of it to Mister Toby. So I went out to the barn first thing in the morning. You can't imagine, ma'am, what it took for me to do it, fearful as I was that whatever I seen should still be out there."

"I suppose there were tracks?"

"I couldn't say, ma'am. I never was no good at reading sign." An extraordinary understatement. "But just as I was reproaching myself for not being better—having the chance to learn it off so fine a gentleman as Mister Lark—this shone out at me from the grass. Like it was set there by Providence to remind me to keep faith with what I seen."

"What is it?"

"I couldn't guess. But I never seen the like. And taking the risk that it might be unholy, I took it up and put it aside for just this moment."

The bead felt hollow. Its heft was unfamiliar. "Probably some old Indian trinket."

"But for it to appear exactly in that spot—when hours before I had watched the beast stand at the barn window, not two feet from where I found it?"

Nora looked outside. Light twanged up and down the laundry line below. She could see the stubbled backfield, and the dry snarl of the brush where it thickened toward the bluffs.

"Josie," she said. "Whatever this may be, it has undone you further." She pointed. "Your window doesn't overlook the goddamn barn at all."

SHE CUT A SWITCH FROM OUTSIDE AND laid it on the table between them. The gesture itself had often proved enough for even the boys. It was certainly enough for Josie. She wept. Nora took the opposite chair and waited.

Toby—whom she had never struck, but for whom the mere sight of a switch was likewise wounding enough—was peering through the cracked kitchen door. She could see him out of the corner of her eye.

"Let's just get it all laid out," she said to Josie, "and we'll have no more of this."

Josie sounded like someone had stuffed her mouth with wet cotton. "I laid it all out for you already."

"Why are you crying?"

"Because you so determined not to believe me, Missus Lark, and I done nothing but lay it out for you, and certainly nothing to earn this whipping."

"What whipping?"

"The one you about to give me."

"I'm just sitting here."

"Till you lay hands on that switch. I heard from

Mister Rob how you get when you of a certain mind."

Nora skated a hand across the tablecloth, smoothed it as flat as she could. There were three, six, nine, twelve blue-threaded squares between her and Josie's bloodless fingertips on the far side.

"Weren't we upstairs together just now?" she asked. Josie nodded. "Haven't you just finished telling me that you sat up in bed the other night and 'seen the beast' out by the barn?"

"I said I seen the beast."

"By the barn."

"I guess so."

"But as was just established: your window doesn't overlook the barn, Josie. The barn's clear around the other side of the house from your room."

Josie took a breath and went over it all again, more slowly this time. When she got to the end, she said: "Maybe I mistook where it was standing."

"But didn't you find that blue kernel behind the barn, because you knew where to look?"

Josie dropped her face into her hands and howled. Nora waited her out. It wasn't the lie itself she found galling. Not really. It was the flimsy construction she couldn't abide—haphazard and poorly thought-out, just like the lie of pretty much any soul who cared to meet Nora on this particular ground. Ruses too vague or too elaborate, crowned with some excremental detail that would collapse under the slightest pressure. As if Nora herself, now having to sniff out liars rather than be one, were some rube who didn't know to investigate any declaration accompanied by flinching eyebrows or twisting mouths. Hadn't she raised three sons?

Sparrows rustled in the creosote outside. A splinter that had steadily been working its way through Nora's stocking for the better part of ten minutes had become a constant and untenable prickle in the bottom of her foot.

"Come now, Josie," she said. "That's enough crying."

This brought Toby out of the kitchen. He put his little paw on her knee. "Mama," he said. "I can't see."

"A moment, lamb."

"But Mama—I can't **see**."

His bad eye still wandered, but the good one followed her finger. She sent him back to the kitchen. He, too, was sobbing by the time he'd felt his way along the wall. Having reached the doorway, he made his final stand there: rested his elbows on the doorjamb and drenched his sleeves with bitter tears.

"There's just about two ways to see it," she said to Josie. "Either you didn't see the beast. Or you weren't in your room. Take a moment to reflect on which is worse. If the former, perhaps you're just humoring my son, against my directive, out of some misguided notion about what's right and fair. But I got a ransacked springhouse says it's the latter, for you are lying up and down, girl. What puzzles me is why."

The two of them keening like this raised a sting

into her own eyes. Her nose prickled. She couldn't tell if this was owed to Toby looking such a sorry picture, or because she was still that wounded he'd thrown in with Josie against her.

But Josie would not fold. She made a muffled gargling noise whose final notes alighted, very faintly, on something about being mistaken.

"What's that?"

"I said I must've been mistaken."

Nora pushed back from the table. "When I was a girl, my mother forbade me leave the house after dark. But I had older brothers who exerted a terrible influence over me. I used to climb out the attic window with them come midnight and run down into the timber camp shanties and bang tambourines till daybreak. Well, one night Patsy Ford's old dog up and vanished, and Patsy, being a man all about the shortest line betwixt two points, accused this Dakota boy who lived downriver of making off with him." In the kitchen doorway, Toby had lifted his face from his arms. It was blotchy as a squash. "So Patsy got himself a posse and went downriver to where the Dakota boy lived, and wouldn't you know it, there in last night's stewpot, he found some fur that

he reasoned certainly did belong to old Rufus."

"Poor Rufus," Josie said miserably.

"Indeed—only I'd been out on one of my nightly jaunts and seen Rufus snatched by a coyote with my own eyes. So there I was, twelve, and more frightened of my mother than my children have ever been of me, and the only person who knew that this Dakota boy was innocent. But if I confessed, I would doom myself."

"What did you do?"

"Confessed. Said I'd lied on my whereabouts, and took my punishment, but got the Dakota boy out of it." In truth, she had spent a sleepless night mulling it over, but kept it to herself, and the Sheriff had flayed the skin from that child's back so thoroughly that the neighborhood kids were still finding pieces of his bloodied shirt in the bushes two weeks later. She hadn't thought of him in years.

"I admire that, ma'am," Josie said, both hands clasped. "But I ain't lying on my whereabouts."

"All right," Nora said. "Come with me."

Her getting up raised a fresh wail from Toby. Switch in hand, she led the way upstairs, Josie shuffling along behind her, Toby howling below, clinging to the banister as if it were the mast of a foundering ship. They went from room to room, looking through the windows. She knew the view from hers and Emmett's, of course: the brown foreyard, the corral, and then nothing but scrubland, dotted here and there with the stumps of bushes they had cut down for an unobstructed view of the surrounding plain. Still, the details she had failed to retain were a surprise: their window also framed the ruins of their first henhouse, and the wall they'd started while they were still arguing about where to put the **huerta**. The sight of these markers—at least in this fresh context—moved her. It was like looking at something for the very first time.

The other rooms held more surprises. Toby slept in the little hall nook to the right of the stairs. His window, if one could call it that, overlooked mostly the stovepipe and a snarl of the upper branches of the scrub oak now digging its roots under their foundations.

Across the hall was the comforting order of Dolan's room: quilt turned down, his good shoes side by side under the bed, his books stacked carefully in their crate, the curtains fluttering through the open window, in which were framed the corral and the garden, where yet another brazen hare was, at this very moment, laying waste to Nora's cabbages. Its transgression presented a much-needed excuse for getting rid of Toby, whom she ordered to go and chase it off. But she could hardly hear herself for his wailing. He had made it all the way to the top of the stairs, and now stood between her and Josie and declared he wasn't going anywhere.

"Suit yourself," Nora said.

Thinking back on this moment, she would wonder whether she'd been close to giving up. What was the point, she wondered, of this endeavor? But it was this refusal, this pointed throwing-in with Josie, that set her on her path again. She made for the attic.

Rob's room was musk and misrule. Clothes, like the debris of some detonative force, were everywhere. Boxes of his many keepsakes, lidless and flung about.

Wood shavings and whittling tools circumscribed his little carving table like some occult layout. A dozen or so of his tiny wooden creatures, awaiting sale in town, were arrayed in a haphazard menagerie along the window-ledge. Nora pulled the curtains aside and looked down over the yellow grass, the hills topped with knotty trees and the scattering of shingles that were missing from the barn roof.

In the doorway behind her, Josie was sobbing. Her pitch had softened from fear to resignation.

Well. Here it was after all: the only window that overlooked the barn.

Nora sat down on the bed. "Toby," she said, after a minute. "We've left Gramma below all alone—will you please?"

"I can't see," he said.

"Go tend her, please. I'll warm you a poultice in a little while."

But he still would not abandon Josie. He clung to her skirt with one hand. Josie's shoulders were still shaking, but through all her distress she seemed to have intuited the dangers of putting her arm around him now.

Lowering the switch to the floor went some distance toward reassuring Toby. He took a long while to wipe his nose, then disappeared. Nora could hear him raking his way down the banister, gouging her wallpaper with determination as he went.

"Well," Nora said once he was out of earshot. "It seems this is the place."

She looked around Rob's room. The hurricane of him. Rob, least like Emmett in body but possessed of habits through which his father's fixations and predilections shot out like water boring through fissures in a dam. Rob couldn't see right angles: his books spilled in a corner, his basin tilted here, his jug there. The toes of a stray sock peered out from under the bed. From the flung-open doors of the box he used as a chifforobe dangled, in every possible configuration, the outspread viscera of belts and suspenders and trouserlegs; an embarrassing tall hat that gave him the air of a New York dandy; a too-small Sunday coat destined, in another year or two, for Toby.

"I don't suppose Rob saw the beast, too?" Nora said.

"No ma'am. He didn't wake."

It was one thing to be accosted about Rob by an erstwhile whore in the Amargo thoroughfare—but another thing entirely to fight the vision now rising to her mind: Rob prostrate, sleeping with one arm flung above his head as he had when he was a boy, and covered half by rumpled quilts and half by moonlight, which as it streamed into the room shone silver on Josie's bare breasts beside him—which, in this fleeting and fatal vision, were small and pert and freckled, just like the rest of her, God help us. The effort to smother the thought only amplified it, as in every girlhood mass when Nora had found herself squirming in the pew, panic-stricken, while unbidden oaths—**our goddamn Father, who art in heaven, hallowed be thy** fucking name, thy kingdom come, thy goddamn will be done, on earth as it is in fucking heaven—tumbled catastrophically through her thoughts.

"What about Dolan?" she managed.

Dolan, with his neat room and his absurd notions, ghouling around the house with tools he'd disdained all his life, releasing exonerated plagues of mice into the woods behind the house. What a show he'd put on these past months, deriding Rob's intellect to Josie. And all the while: this. The outrage flooding Nora on his behalf was muddied by a distinct feeling of—what? Strange, sour vindication. Hadn't she warned him about being so goddamn eager? Perceptive indeed.

"Mister Dolan don't know yet," Josie said.

"Which of you has the happy task of telling him?"

"Mister Rob, I expect."

"**Mister** Rob." She let herself laugh. Across the room, Josie was shifting her feet. She did not brace herself against the wall, nor have the decency to look as rueful as she should. She stood there, instead, as though her rightful place were somehow in this room, among the explosion of Rob's things—as though this disarray, by which even Nora felt a little oppressed, were so familiar to her as to be invisible. And now it was Nora who suddenly felt strange sitting at the foot of this particular bed. She got up and slung Rob's denims over her arm.

"I suppose, under the circumstances, the spring-house door is the least of your lies."

Josie stood even straighter. "I must object, ma'am—they weren't lies." They had thought long and laboriously on it, she and Mister Rob, and resolved that lies and omissions did not amount to the same thing. They had taken great care to avoid provoking any questions that might force them toward falsehood until such a time as they revealed their engagement to the entire family. "I'm that sorry to be telling you like this, in his absence."

"Are you," Nora said. "Are you 'that' sorry." Josie did not look sorry at all. "Now will you tell me what happened in the springhouse?"

From Josie's innermost being now came a long sigh of resignation and relief. She had done her level best not to lie about that, either, ma'am. But she supposed it was only right to come out with it now, though she would prefer to have the others witness for her character. The thing was, the boys had spent days trying to find a way toward convincing their mother that Mister Lark was dead. They'd had to hear all about it from every soul that came in to buy the paper or post a letter—about the dray someone had seen being taken apart up at the Sanchez place, and a lot of whispered talk. Nora's refusal to press Sheriff Harlan more urgently for answers—or for that matter, why she thought it prudent to involve him at all—mystified them. Josie herself liked Sheriff Harlan just fine—he was a kind man, and he made her laugh—but the boys were suspicious of the **Ash River Clarion**'s steadfast support of his reelection.

"So Mister Rob thought: if they could just get you to see it **their** way."

To this end, they had gone into the springhouse last night together, all three of them—even Mister Dolan—to séance with Mister Lark. (How strange it seemed, Nora thought, hearing that disparity between Mister Rob and Mister Dolan now—how the former, on Josie's tongue, felt like some delicate pet name, while the latter conjured up a village spinster.)

The séance had been Rob's idea. If it succeeded, it would put the question of their father's death to rest. Josie practically had to be dragged to the shed, on account of the beast—which she **had** seen. Whatever Missus Lark might think of her, she swore she'd seen it. She had only overcome her fear and relented because it tore at her to see the boys so desperate, the both of them, in the wake of the suppertime fight. Mister Dolan was just heartbroken about his own lack of self-control—he had surprised himself as much as anyone, punching through that door, and so close to Nora's head. Josie supposed there was no way of telling it from his behavior right after, for he had hardly covered himself with glory when he had continued to shout and thrown a plate. But that had owed more to shock than anything else. He had gone upstairs afterward and just wept with disappointment. He hadn't thought he could face his mother ever again.

"I'm only telling you all this, ma'am," Josie said, "to let you know his state of mind afterwards. You know yourself what a skeptic he is—what it would take to enlist him into séance. He was that sorry, ma'am. Just beside himself. Kept thinking on how those woodchips might've gone in your eye, and he just cried."

For hours, they had sat in the springhouse together. Josie held a piece of Emmett's shirt and reached out to him. She'd called him every name he might answer to: Mister Lark, and Emmett Lark, and just Emmett—even Father, since the boys were there. Outside, she had heard distant nighttime noises coursing on in their usual way. The tapping on the springhouse roof was just the branches of the scrub oak. At one moment, something had brushed up against that blue darkness that lived in her, and she had grown hopeful it might be Mister Lark. But the spirit had not answered her. It hadn't knocked or moved the pocketwatch she put on the table.

They had given up around three in the morning, and gone to bed.

"When I saw the springhouse wrecked this morning, I did curse myself so," Josie said. "I feared perhaps Mister Lark's manifestation might've just took a little longer than it should, and we were too quick giving up on him. Maybe all that mess in the springhouse was just Mister Lark raging because he'd finally arrived, only to find us already gone. But you were right—we must have just forgot to latch the door, and it was nothing but the dogs after all."

"I take it your inability to conjure up Emmett

means he's still among the living?" This did not sound quite like the joke Nora intended. She felt as though she had flung wide some wounded part of herself in speaking, and could not hide it again.

Josie shook her head. "It don't prove much, ma'am—save that I couldn't reach him."

"Well, bully for me," Nora said. "A victory for sense and reason. Almost worth this entire episode." She folded Rob's denims once more, carefully, in half. The seams of his back pocket were fraying again. The trouserlegs red with dust. **His denims,** she thought. Here. His denims here—and therefore his suit on him. Elsewhere.

"Did he tell you where they were headed this morning, all gussied up?"

Josie shook her head. "Ma'am, I swear to you, he did not."

WHAT ARE YOU DOING BACK OUT here, Mama?

Feeding poor old Bill.

Didn't think he needed feeding again so soon.

Well, it was a hot old ride into town and back. He deserves some small reward for not playing out.

You wouldn't be hiding out from Josie, would you?

Not in the slightest.

Rob and Josie. How about that?

I don't care to think about it overmuch, Evelyn, thank you.

It just don't seem to fit. He's such good fun. And she's so forlorn—and at the same time, a little stupid. Ain't that what you always say? That God put both hands behind his back when Josie got in line?

It's doubtful I ever called her stupid.

But she ain't educated like you, Mama.

It's not a matter of education. I grew up poor, too. But your father and I took great pains to speak carefully.

Well. Even so. Growing up the way she did—it probably cost her.

I believe my word was "inept."

Still. It is some feat—keeping that hid from you under your own roof.

I guess when all your machinations take place under cover of darkness, even the most inept among us can get away with a little something.

I wonder if anybody else knew.

I doubt it. No one in this house can lie worth a good goddamn.

Save for Rob and Josie.

Guess so.

Rob and Josie. It just don't fit. I bet Gramma knew. She's always around. Always listening to what Josie's saying, 'stead of just pretending to. Bet she just knew, even if she didn't stumble onto them some night in the corridor—which she probably did, you know. Given that she moves.

Don't start.

She does so.

If it were me wheelchair bound, and suspecting that sort of thing, I would've used my last breath to let it be known around the house.

When you really get down to it, isn't it just a bit romantic?

Not a bit.

But still. Two young people, thrown together by chance in a raggedy old house. Looking up at each other over porridge and woodcutting.

What about Dolan?

Oh he'll tear the house in half. Still. Maybe he'll come around to their happiness in the end.

Happiness? I wonder if Josie has any notion of how many sweethearts of Rob's have come and gone.

There's been a few, all right.

Or how well regarded he is around town. In both whorehouses.

Papa was hardly a saint when you met him.

Evelyn. It's not right for you to say such things.

It's just the truth I'm telling. Who knows? Maybe it's for keeps.

For keeps? With Rob? Ridiculous.

THE GILA

IF EVER YOU DESPAIR OF OUR PREDICAMENT, Burke, gather courage in remembering that you number among perhaps forty living souls who crossed by land and sea from the Levant to the Pacific. You staked two thousand miles of desert road, and while your horse and mule kin were laming themselves in the barrens and wailing around the empty water barrels, you simply went on.

Even when we parted company with the corps and struck north, could you imagine the wonders you would see? You have stood on the shores of the mighty Platte, where Red Cloud's Sioux, gathered for the parley that would wright their ruin, had grazed a horseherd two thousand strong, balding the prairie all the way back to the tree line. You have seen the hunchback yuccas pick up their spiny skirts to flee an oncoming duststorm. When the wind stilled, didn't we shake out from our shelter to find the trees' ranks reconfigured, the whole horizon a changed place? You have stood on bluffs planted up with scorched saplings where the ground was pocked with exhalations, with ruts belching white gobs of mud as if the earth were breathing. You have walked the rim of a jaundiced gulch, veined high and low with bands of ore, through which the whitecaps of a nameless river went roaring. You have pulled stave carts and timber wagons and Gatling guns. You have carried ties for the men who lay rail; coal for miners; buffalo bones for the ciboleros; salt for the sellers of it.

Above all, true to your nature, you have carried water to those furthest from it. How strange that your lack of want for it should make you so perfectly suited to bring it to others. You have carried barrels full of life for prospectors and miners, for small townships whose wells had gone alkaline, for lost wagon trains and thirsty desperadoes. Men half-hung in trees wanted our water, and even the ghosts hoving after us did, as though they knew they'd died an inch from relief. Up and down the Mojave, the Chihuahuan, the Colorado, they knew us.

"Here comes the Camel Man," they said. "Here comes the great red horse to water us."

You did it then, my funny, noble friend. You did, and you will again. Get on up now before they return.

Remember Christmas Eve in Graveneck, Wyoming? I'd never seen an outpost so bleak. A corridor of falsefronts, at the end of which sat the boiling yellow windows of a saloon. The buffalo hunters had come in off the range to drink and be maudlin, and the streets were black with people. The whole place fell silent when we came jangling into town. Someone, as we passed, got up the nerve to whisper: "Well mercy. We got us a magi."

For two dollars, I agreed to stand you beside a manger whose occupant was a cornhusk doll done up to resemble the infant Jesu. And there was Gabriela, the boardinghouse keeper. My own and only love. I can see her now, young woman with black eyes and a dark braid over her shoulder, handing me an empty copper mug with a wink-and-whisper. "Myrrh," she said, and grinned when I told her I'd always wondered what the hell that was.

To our right stood a fat little donkey that blenched whenever you stirred or looked at it sideways. Playing the cow was a little buffalo heifer just outgrowing her russet coat. We stood for hours in this ragtag company while the children, with their wind-reddened faces, huddled in the barn, gawping and pointing. The bravest had just about grit enough to put pennies in our jar. Others took to wailing. Gabriela emerged, turbaned with a kitchen towel, to take up the cornhusk Jesu and rest him on her knees. I wanted more than anything to be in her good graces, and said the only thing that came to my mind: "Behold. A star in the east. Mayhap 'twill lead us to the king of kings."

It didn't land well, as we were already at the manger.

Later, the festivities moved to the Red Desert saloon. A glistening brown goose hissed on the spit. Outside, it had begun to snow. The road into town lay smooth and shining. Some Irish cowpoke was singing the infant Jesu a fireside hymn, and it cracked into me a little bit. I was still dabbing at my eyes when Gabriela brought over the boiled pudding. "And your tall friend?" she said, meaning you. "Will he have anything special for his Christmas dinner?" She looked at me with, you might say, the kind of unabashed forethought that led me to understand I had misjudged both her youth and intentions. The joke between us ran deeper than my tall friend, deeper even than myrrh, and we revisited it later in the warm silence of her room below the stairs. At first, I was wary of my own desire, afraid it would make me quick. But while we whispered to each other in the dark, I found the sadness just beneath my want, like frozen soil.

"Where in all of Christendom did you get a camel?" she said.

"Texas." There was no truer answer.

"Well," she said, after a time. "I'll be damned."

Life's happiness is always a famine, and what little we find interests nobody. What use is it, the happiness of some stranger? At worst, it drives onlookers to envy; at best, it bores them. Happiness in love, especially, has only the latter power. One good day follows the next; the wildness of early passion gives way a little; pet names are designated; small jests take root and become great kindnesses revisited in the swell of higher feeling; habits are learnt and tolerated. One's camel is stabled in the livery, and after a time, it even comes to tolerate and be tolerated by his beloved's mules, and so on. Humdrum—those were my years with Gabriela: a blissful humdrum that subdued even Donovan, mostly because I feared what the canteen might reveal to me should I give in to his want.

The most riveting things about this time are likewise the most unmentionable: Gabriela's husband, for instance, was off rallying round the flag with his Kansan brothers. She had no indication he intended to return—though that didn't stop us from jumping at every footfall that struck her porch, lest it belong to him.

With our already meager forts drained by that Baylor havoc to the south, and by war in the east, the only thing on anyone's lips was depredation. We were forever fearful that the Utes would come flying off the range to butcher us; and the Utes were themselves fearful of us, and we were none of us too keen on the Mormons generally. The town was united in occasionally glooming about you, musing that your presence might draw the eye of a raiding party. Quarrels broke out that Graveneck should not be affiliated with either of us. The Reverend Stanton began sermonizing about the ills of idolatry. He preached that golden calf bit until even the most half-witted of his parishioners understood that he was talking sideways about you. You—an idol. Well all right. And so what if you were? I'm sure you were the chief object of his derision, beloved as you were by the children and women alike. But I was, too. Few of the town's residents believed I was merely a boarder at the Red Desert saloon. I had also doomed myself by attempting, on the anniversary of Jolly's feast with the Mojave, to establish a similar tradition in Graveneck. But I was a poor curate of Jolly's religion: unsure of the day and details of the slaughter, save for the distribution of meat to the needy and the feasting, which the Reverend said reeked of sin and heathen worship.

"Never mind him," Gabriela said. "He thinks bathing is sinful. He thinks books, hats, newspapers are sinful."

Sinful or not, newspapers were how I came by the only word I ever got of our compatriots in all that time. Lazy Pie McClane, our mail freighter, came by with a note from some sutler three towns over. "Here," he said, "I can't imagine who the fuck else this could be." The letter was addressed to "The Camel Man." Inside was a raggedy clip of newsprint decrying the tragic death by sniper fire of a camel named Old Douglas in the fight at Vicksburg. Down the page, I got to reading about how Camp Verde had fallen to the Rebels—which I suppose should've been no surprise. Old Douglas had been the last of the Oriental charges stabled at that distant livery, snatched up by the invaders and conscripted as a mascot for some doomed regiment or another, until he was gunned down, woeful collateral. On the Union side, offering his thoughts on the matter—to my great astonishment and delight—was one Corporal Absalom Reading. "I traveled with Lieutenant Beale when he first staked the Mojave Road," he said. "And though the beasts were meant to be working for us, a lot of the time it was us working for the beasts. I can't say I cared for them. But I was sorry to hear about Old Doug." Ab, I thought. My old friend. So he had gone back east after all. It was the only time I ever felt ashamed for not having done so myself. But I had no people outside the Territories. No certainty, even, that wherever you and I landed would be annexed to whatever rattlebag country would be left to stitch back together when the fighting was done. So we stayed on and carried dispatches and pulled howitzers between forts and once in a while helped some small, weary band of Cheyenne move their lodges. Anytime I heard tell of some buffalo soldier regiment thereafter, I believed Ab must be among them, back out west and bound for glory.

The following spring, we were ferrying a load of salt from the Lonewind mines one afternoon when we caught the stare of a bearded, milky-eyed stranger. "You just coming from that battle?" the fella said.

"No."

"Then how came you by **this** ugly fucker?"

"I bought him at the ugly fucker fair."

He looked doubtful. "You telling me a camel lives this side of the Mississippi and ain't been in that battle?"

That scored me good. "What one?"

Well. What the hell was the matter with us? Didn't we know Sam Bishop, that maddog cavalier, had been moving freight by camelback from California to Albuquerque when he found himself trapped by the Mojave and a couple hundred of their friends out in the desert? It was all over the papers. They were two weeks besieged, Bishop and his civilian packers, unaided by military outposts and cut off from the outside world, save for their brave little courier who risked hide and haunch to carry futile overtures for help to the nearest fort.

"They're out there now?" I said.

Ah no, indeed, it was all over. The men had buried their supplies, burned their wagons, and in the profusion of ash and darkness, effected their escape by charging their camels at the astonished Mojave.

All this the stranger had heard only yesterday from a newspaperman in Santa Rosa—which proved to be a small town in a cedar-choked valley only two days' ride from Lonewind. When you and I got there, a bespectacled little clerk was just closing up the **Santa Rosa Crier** office.

"Lordy," he said upon seeing you.

Only the promise of trying you out could persuade him to stay awhile and show me the paper I wanted.

There, in little more detail than we had previously heard, were the facts as the stranger had relayed them. Mojave enraged by relentless trespass had barred the packtrain for weeks. The predicament had grown very bleak. Toward the middle of the page sat a single mention of Sam Bishop's "faithful Arabs." So they'd been there after all—Jolly for sure, and maybe even George, out in the starlight together, huddling against the cold.

We led you out into the woods above Santa Rosa and you carried the newspaperman up the road, this way and that. I'll never forget how he looked, smiling down from the saddle and waving, his ridiculous spectacles dropping closer and closer to the end of his nose with your every step. You tolerated this indignity as you tolerate all things, and I was thankful.

I was thinking, meantime, about Jolly. Had the battle claimed him? Surely the newspapers would give some word of casualties. I found myself tipping the canteen back—but it always showed only what it would; on this occasion, nothing but a cliffside above a stretch of river. So it was left to me to imagine what the waters would not reveal. Bishop, Bishop, Bishop the newspaper said. Bishop urging his men. Bishop leading the charge on a great, white camel.

What I saw was Jolly, battle-ready, cinching his saddle. There was his column in a little stand of crooked oaks. A light morning rain was falling. Somewhere, a coyote bewailed the diminishing night.

Across the field, the Mojave had formed an unbroken line. The smoke of their fires dimmed the moon. They, too, were righteous and unafraid. Then the camels, all bellsong and gunfire, lurched forward.

And where was I? Dreaming about it in a moonlit wood.

For the first time it struck me that perhaps running had robbed us of something. Well maybe it had. That feeling got into me. It wasn't Hobb's this time, or Donovan's. It was my own. My happiness began to unravel. Gabriela's, too. She'd had a letter from her husband, this one postmarked from Kentucky. He was coming home. Days were lost to the arithmetic of our remaining time. If he tarried in Nebraska, how long did that leave us? How long if he was waylaid by raids in the Dakotas?

The afternoons took on a sour glare. Gabriela and I rode you down to the whipcrack bends of the Green River and sat in shared sadness by the stream. "We could leave together," I said. "He could come back to find you vanished."

"What kind of woman would that make me?" Her voice was dulled by having asked this of herself a thousand times. "To abandon a man who has fought for kin and country? I would undo myself. And you would hate me."

It's doubtful I would have hated her, but we both wanted so much to believe me a mettlesome enough man for it to be so. I went back to sleeping in the room I had let and listened to her wakeful footsteps on the boards. Days passed. Despairing, I sent a wire to Fort Tejon. **Ali,** I wrote, so that he would know me. **Relieved to hear about outcome of battle. Am in Wyoming. Send word of yourself.** His reply followed so swiftly I hardly had time to reckon with the joy of his having survived. **Aware of your whereabouts for some time. Recently an agent name of Berger left here to seek camel man. Enroute Wyoming.**

I suppose there was opportunity then to make my life over. I might have stood my ground and waited to meet John Berger on the home plain. I might have sold, or set you to roaming—I know you would have been all right. But by then I was the Camel Man. We were bound up, you and I, in this fleet. Though it break our hearts, we had as little choice then as we have now. Only this time, I haven't the suitcase and spare pair of boots to sell. But when you're right again, when we take off, we'll run just as far.

I suppose I should admit there were some missteps. We might have done better than that raggedyman circus we wound up following through Nevada, camping night after night beneath the stars. We met good people there, but their friendship was not worth the stands filling with the nocturnal babble and mutinous smoke of half-wild crowds who cheered at the Indian beauty on a horse, and pelted the ring with apple cores to spite the clowns, and sometimes to spite you, whom they considered insufficiently impressive for simply walking the ring even with a half-naked girl on your back.

"Don't that creature do anything besides just **be**?" the impresario asked me.

It was the kind of question he asked before cutting people from the show, which is, I swear to you, the only reason I answered: "He can lift fifteen hundred pounds."

It was my saying that, I know, which invited the miseries that followed. He devised ways to make you showcase your strength. You would lift first four hundred pounds, then six, until a thousand brought the foam from your mouth. The act had little effect unless the jeerers loaded the saddlebags themselves, and I know they never failed to take these opportunities to pinch you, or nip at little bits of your hair. I've never been as sorry for anything.

Sometimes the circus camped on some lonely stretch of road, and then a woman in an apron, sometimes carrying a child, sometimes with her arm looped through a young boy's, wandered around the fire at night as though she might warm herself there. I took care not to let her touch me.

Elements of our ragged troupe were always disbanding without warning or ceremony. The half-naked girl met a chinless man of soft disposition in Camp Nye. One of the clowns took up with a couple of rustlers in Reno. In town after town, we shed performers whose dreams changed or injuries worsened, or who found sudden love casting the light a little bit further into the darkness of their foreordained lives. Whenever this happened, I was only able to resist a few days before sending a wire to Graveneck. Gabriela never answered.

So back we went to the malpais, you and I, and wandered the snaking length of the Colorado, from its floodplain to its northernmost narrows, where the river left us behind to twist between its canyons. I thought often of that water on its unseen course, coming to us from places unreachable by man. I imagined the dead, if they rested anywhere, must rest in a place like that. For they were resting in no other place, and we saw them, it seemed, in every tree, in the streets of every little pueblo, dotting the horizon in their loneliness, the unburied dead of battle upon battle, and the women and children too, always trailing along to somewhere unless they were standing very still and smiling softly at the sight of you.

Purple sunsets every once in a while silhouetted the thin smoke of Indian fires, but these were fewer now and always more distant. Here and there, the shore was crosshatched with wagon tracks. At the southern road crossing, we began ferrying water again. But our time in this pursuit was diminished, too, for they were digging irrigation ditches everywhere. Now and again, it occurred to me that though I was only thirty, I had gone the way of unbearable old men: talking all spring of the Camel Corps to Mormons and children and thin husks of pilgrims waiting on the new ferry—indeed, to anyone who would accord me the time. The wide raft moved unendingly back and forth across the stream. The boys standing guard at the ramparts of the fledgling fort on the far shore were too young to remember the old emptiness of this place: the blue of distant mountains; the Mojave, those tall river people, the first and last men west of the Missouri ever to face down a camel cavalry; the first steamship to travel this length of the Colorado rounding the crooked current with her wheel shining as it cut the water. But we remembered, you and I. It saddened me. Who would speak of these things when we were gone? So, too, must the makers of those distant fires have asked themselves as they fought the fading of their world. I began to wish that I could pour our memories into the water we carried, so that anyone drinking might see how it had been.

Drought settled over the valley and brought with it thinning souls. The doomed French rode up from the desert with their brilliant pennants. Small cavalries of dead Indians roamed the old battletrails. Their arrowheads still lay thick on the ground in the groves where they'd fought and died and won and lost. Every now and again some dead brave would pass us, hurrying home to be reborn. They reached for me once in a while, but I could not bear to let them touch me. You might disdain me a coward for it, Burke—but I could not abide it. Their want, I knew, had distilled generation by generation, and to feel how much and how little it entailed would tear my heart in two. I did not want to carry it with me forever. I had not caused it, after all. I had not, Burke. Never by my own hand.

Then came that roasting July afternoon when the drought cleaved a piece of parched mudbank into the Colorado. Down went two wagons and a tent with a sleeping prospector in it. You were grazing by the outcrop, and were caught in the slide. You scrambled, but went over the lip and into the river. I was in the water kicking against the weight of my boots before you had even righted yourself. I got your bridle in hand and drew you to me. You had that look in your eye you've had these last days— reproach, I think, as though this mightn't have happened under your stewardship. If only our whole lives had been the other way around, and so on.

Anyway, we gained the shore to a thin screech of cheers: the high banks were lined with dark figures: men and women and children all laughing and shouting in wild relief.

We must have dived into streams a thousand times thereafter, you and I. Twice a day, when the crossing crowd was thickest, we jumped side by side into the cool blue water while the music of relief erupted behind us. We gathered coin in the copper cup of our old regiment. From a peddler's wagon, I bought fine tasseling for your bridle. Tied a turban round my head and fit a shining piece of glass to it.

We were encamped on the shores of Lake Bigler one September afternoon when a pale young man with a thin face and clean hands sought us out. "So you're a real Turk, then?" he asked.

I told him I was.

He was a writer who'd come to the West to make something of its stories. He asked me what I had learned of it all, and I told him I did not know— which struck him as a great profundity. Everyone he'd met had just about one thing to say: the land was changing fast. I supposed it was, but what struck me most was how much of it was staying the same. Lean holdings, miles that couldn't be made unwild. That vast and immutable want everybody, dead or alive, carried with them all the time.

Together we hunched over his pages and crudely traced the wagon route from Indianola all the way west to the sea. I had no knack for mapmaking, and told him George would have been the better man for this job—if George drew it, you'd get every crook of every river—which of course got me wistful about George. I found myself telling the little writer all about him, about how he could speak four languages by the time we parted ways, and solve any difficulty of engineering, though he couldn't sing or play to save his soul, which had always been a great misery to him, one he would have traded all his knowledge of land and water to remedy.

"If he's such a pistol," the little writer said, "how come I never heard of him?"

"Hadn't nobody heard of Bill Cody, neither," I said, "till someone like you wrote about him."

Oh, he liked that. So I stayed up nights recounting all I could remember about Jolly and George, about Beale and Ab and the padre in that old wreck on the mesa. I saw no reason to tell him that you and I had never reached the end of the Fort Tejon Road—but he didn't have such a good grasp of time and never did put it together that we couldn't have been in California and Montana both at once. I did let him know Beale lied when he wrote our company had suffered no losses—for wasn't Mico buried out there somewhere in the desert, in a grave we could hardly remember to get back to? And I told him all about you, of course—your inclinations and appetites. I told him you were a great, opinionated, willful, con-temptuous thing, reserved with your affections but beautiful in your own way, unslowed by age and unafraid of anything. I told him you had seen corners of these deserts that few eyes have ever beheld, for no creature had ever needed water less nor yearned for wandering more. I told him about that time a flood caught us up in a painted canyon and the waters rose around us while you walked until, kicking slowly, you floated up, up past the petroglyphs and the shining, swooping walls of the canyon, and swam on a new river of rain with me on your back, all the way down, so far that when the waters fell your feet touched down in Mexico.

The little writer listened, filling page after page of his notebook.

We parted ways after some weeks together, heading in opposite directions: you and I to winter in the low country, and he to rendezvous with his people near the Great Salt Lake. For the first time in many years I felt lighthearted. There was some certainty now that we would be remembered, side by side, all of us, camels and cameleers alike.

But when I saw the little writer again, he was standing unawares beside the ghost of his horse on the road with two rounds through his back and that curious, weary look of a soul who would linger awhile before he ever understood what had happened to him. He called out to me, but I urged you onward. I did not want to touch him.

I searched the surrounding ditches for any trace of all he'd written—but I never found a word.

When I think back on George sometimes, I wonder if I didn't do you a great injustice, Burke, by talking only this nonsense about the dead to you. Riding along, George would sing to Maida. He would expound on the movement of the heavens. By the time they made Tejon, I reckon that sage old girl could count all the way up to a hundred.

And what did you ever learn from me—save to keep to yourself, and look over your shoulder? My fate was the great, unearned misfortune of your life. I knew only to gather myself up whenever the breaks turned against me. I sat all my life with my eyes cast backward for Marshal John Berger. Even when he was no longer a lawman, even when the territories we crossed schemed and bought their way to statehood, one by one, and wars were fought and Indians besieged on their reservations.

The hours I must have spent reckoning what I would say if he ever finally caught up to us. I would tell him everything. I would taunt him for having spent his life looking for me.

But when it finally happened—when, finally, in that camp outside Red Bear, he sat down at my table while I drank—what did I say?

Nothing.

"I saw your friend outside," he said. "And knew I'd found you at last." He pushed a drink toward me with a speckled hand. He'd been an old man when last I saw him, and was played out even further now. But an old wolf is still a wolf.

"I'm sorry, but I don't know you," I said.

"You know a warrant don't stand unless it's signed anew now and again?" he said. I knew. "Well, the judge that issued yours died two summers ago, and I ain't found the man to write me another. Seems you're unimportant, as killers go. Still. I knowed you was close a long time. So here I am."

"I think you got me mistook for somebody else, mister."

He leaned close. "I'd know you anywhere—even without that big ugly thing waiting on you outside. But it ain't your face that's kept me up nights all these years. It's that boy you killed. I was there before he died, when they were still hopeful to save him, and had to cut out the dregs of the eye you kicked out his head. That boy took fever and soiled himself and screamed for weeks in his sleep while you was off hooting it up, too much a coward to come back and face what you'd done. Ain't there a God with His hand on your shoulder? Don't you feel you owe Him your surrender?"

"I'm sorry, mister," said I. "But I ain't the fella you looking for."

He nodded awhile. "I been carrying you with me through Missouri. Through Texas. Through Montana and Nevada. Through California. I wouldn't say I've thought of nothing else. You weren't even the worst son of a bitch ever to cross my path. But you were a goad to me. All badmen, one way or another, confess themselves to somebody. They can't help it. Or they stay bad enough to die by enemy hands. But you never seemed to. Sometimes, I wondered if it wasn't my search keeping you alive. Perhaps, if I could just bring myself to forget you, you'd just go on and die. Well. That ain't happened. But I know who you are, Lurie Mattie. I may be the last soul living who does. And I will take you to my grave and there extinguish you with my silence."

Everything I might still have said, everything I'd been fixing to say all those long years went out of me. All I could think was: here sits the very last person who'll ever know I was a brother to Hobb and Donovan. And when he goes, whose kin will I be? I looked at that old man, soaked to his very soul with living want, and knew two things. That I must never kill him, nor be near when he died. And that, whether for spite or cowardice, I could not bring myself to give him peace.

"I'm sorry, mister. I just ain't the man. I reckon you gotta keep looking for whoever is."

Whether he believed me, I'll never know. When we rode out I glanced back once more at the dreary shambles of the saloon. I half-expected him to be standing there, sighting us from the porch. But he was only sitting in the window, looking at his soup as old men do.

After that, we moved upvalley and jumped into bleak rivers garrisoned on both shores by soldiers dead and living. We carried water where it was needed and filled Donovan's canteen, and we didn't care who shot at or was affronted by us, and we did not brook the interference of strangers and we had no doubt of ourselves.

I reckon I'm trying to say: however badly off we seem now, Burke, however angry and tired you are, we been far worse off than this. And your sullenness now over a little wound like that, and the way you went after that girl—well, Burke, it just disgraces all that. It's unlike you.

Remember last time? When that November cough slowed you? You hovered warily over your food, and a strange milky glue gummed your fine old lashes. Desperate, I let myself write Jolly at Fort Tejon: **Burke has taken ill.** But no answer came. Soon your belly was bilged with outstanding ribs, and your knees had begun to shake. A horse doctor came to rest his ear against your chest. "He must have taken catarrh, I suppose," he said. "Though what that means, I can't imagine."

He prescribed a week's rest in a warm stable, but that made no difference.

"We could try a tonic," he said next. "Though it would be fairer to put the beggar to his rest, and spare him the coming misery."

"Thank you," I said. "But no."

"Well, it's all the same to me." Before he left, he lingered in the doorway with his dollar coin, looking back at you wistfully. "What if I gave you fifteen dollars?"

"What for?"

"For your friend there."

"Ain't you just said he's all but done for?"

"He is. But I don't reckon I'll get a chance to look inside many more camels round these parts. And you look like you could use fifteen dollars."

"Thank you, no."

"You sure? The whole fifteen, right now. It's a lot better than nothing for watching him die, and having me come back here in a couple days and get his bits for free."

"I said I ain't selling."

"Suit yourself." He put on his hat. "Let no man interfere with the carers of beasts. But even so—rest him here and don't wander too far. I'll see you both again soon."

I got to thinking. If this doctor had fifteen dollars to spare on a dying camel, he might spend ten on beggared wrecks who might beat the camel's owner and steal the camel anyway. And there was no dearth of their kind about.

So we ran out on that town, too.

We had days of slow, uphill road-going. The redwoods were so high and thick their trunks made no sound even in the heavy wind. You walked slow and stopped often. Huddled under the saddleblanket, you lifted your face to smile at the windblown snowflakes when they fell. You tolerated your knees to be dusted of pine needles before we set off each morning.

I had thought to hide us, but those hills were thick with timber camps. Gaunt men wintered around their fires and peered out at us from sagging tents. From a pair of blear-eyed hardware boys I bought a bedroll and a couple blankets and fixed us up in the woods away from the creek. I'd lie there and listen to the faint sucking thud of that big heart in the fathoms forward of your hump, right between neck and the shoulder. Every now and again, I felt your lips moving drily about my hair. By then your breathing had got very shallow. You had always looked as though you were praying when you lay down. I figured you were doing enough of it for the both of us just by lying there with your knees and fetlocks both bunched together. Praying front and back. For the first time in years, I gave to Donovan's want and drank a little to see what could be known—but was shown only Jolly, and a small house with shoes and flowers on the mantelpiece. No sign of you anywhere. I bedded you down and wrapped your snout in a rag wet by the canteen water, and we slept thus through the march of days.

I feared you might grow to despise me for not letting you rest—but wasn't I right then? Wasn't I? And ain't I right now?

I'll admit I should have heeded sooner that strange feeling clenching over me. The desperadoes in that

camp kept eyeing me whenever I left the tent. By
and by one of the cookhouse boys asked, "Ain't that
big horse of yours about done dying yet?"

"He ain't a horse," I said. "And he ain't dying."

The man was bald, his clothes a patchwork of
previous summers and winters all strung together on
a whippet frame. "I can hear him in there wheezing.
Ain't you Christian enough to do right and put a bit
of his meat our way? We've had naught but hardtack
in weeks."

But as soon as that happened, didn't we break
camp and keep going till we reached the foothills
and the blue desert beyond? The nights were still
bitter, but the days were as bright and lonesome as
we liked them. We kept by the streams. Your walk
was slow and meandering, sure. You got real stubborn about leaving off the greasewood, which made
the skin hang off you in drapes and your hump
slowly begin to list. Night after sleepless night, I lay
awake and counted your breaths, fearful I might
drift off and wake to find you a shade.

But then we came through it. As I remember, we
had wandered into a canyon getting clear of a
lightning storm one wild-colored March day. We
followed the water to a burled fence that threaded
through the woods. Behind its gate sat a squat red
house with smoky windows. A bent woman with
white hair and a woolen shawl was emptying a
bucket of ground meal before a congregation of
wildly plumed black-and-white chickens.

"Well," she said. "Now there's a sight."

Dueña Maria's kitchen was cluttered with sprigs of herb and corncakes and little jars and flowers. Paintings of an old man and knitted baby boots were laid side by side on her mantel. It was only after we sat down to **posole** that I felt any certainty she was alive at all. The dead may cook, for all I know, but they certainly don't eat. Her stew numbed my lips and set my nose running. Between slurps, the old woman leaned back in her chair to get a look at the yard, where you and her murdersome shoat stood eyeing each other across the trough.

"What does it taste of?" she said.

"Can't say. I never tried eating him." She wouldn't leave off looking out at you, so I said: "And the people who mentioned wanting to ain't lived."

"You're some hero, threatening to kill an old woman what's given you the benefit of her fire and her supper."

"I'm threatening nobody, if nobody's threatening my camel."

She went back to her soup. The fire went on snapping and chattering.

"So," she said. "That's a camel."

She looked you over. Through the kitchen window, I watched her bring your big gnashing head down and peer into your mouth, rest her ear against your shoulder and listen for the whistling intake. Your breath riffled her fine white hairs. Whenever she drew you closer, your smile seemed to deepen.

For the benefit of the concoctions Dueña Maria dosed you with, I cleared her shed, threw out eons of crates and newspapers, laid siege to mice in her grainhouse. I clapped together a rickety ladder, and climbed her roof while you and she stood staring below. Years of nests sat mossed between her shingles. Acres of bracken snarled her vast claim. Every day brought some new task to light. All this toil got us two squares and a bed, and you a daily dark green poultice and a rancid nostrum you fought with all your strength against imbibing.

But it wasn't so bad, was it? Your wheezing did subside. Meat climbed back up your thighbones. By the time the fields behind the house were finally cleared, it was you pulling the plow and me blundering along behind while the old woman hollered instruction.

"I wish I'd had a tintype made up this afternoon," she said contentedly after supper one evening. "You were some sight, the pair of you."

"Folks wouldn't know what to make of it." It made me drowsy to hear the steady snap of her pipe. Outside, in a cold light rain, you and the old woman's shoat were digging yourselves deeper puddles and licking fenceposts for the salt, and spring had come.

"You know," she said. "There's a man way out in town would give his fortune to see a camel again in his lifetime."

"I'm that weary of people wanting to see camels. In my experience, all they ever really want to see is how much weight it'll take to break their backs, or how their innards are configured in comparison to horses, or what they taste like."

"Not so with this man."

In the morning she led us the twelve miles into town, riding ahead on a small white donkey whose plodding tilted her left and right like a gale-tossed ship. The April sun hung lazily between white cords of cloud. The shady sides of the hills were still thick with snow, but the weather was fine and warm. We reached the village to find the saloon crowd had spilled into the sunlit plaza and circled their chairs around a chess layout. One by one the players sat up as you came out of the trees and into the thoroughfare.

We followed Dueña Maria to a small house at the far end of the village. She sprang out of the saddle and went down the walk, hollering: "Filip Tedro! Come out and be surprised!"

The door flung to. And there—beneath a speckling of gray hair and a groomed mustache—stood Hadji Ali.

EVENING

AMARGO

Arizona Territory, 1893

"THERE'S THE BOYS AT LAST," NORA SAID.

Late evening had brought bats and dry air, and now a rider down from the road. He followed the bluffline with the sun red behind him, and worked his way through the mesquite and toward the house. A second rider had not appeared by the time he reached the trees.

It's Harlan, said Evelyn.

Josie, shading her eyes, said it almost simultaneously. "That's the Sheriff."

It was. Unsettling, how a person could be so easily recognized at a distance, not by feature or coloring, but by the composite gestures particular to himself alone. Harlan Bell was lean as a greyhound. He rode cave-chested, holding the reins loose in one hand at an odd angle. He listed to favor his right side on account of ghost pains from shot he'd taken scouting the borderlands for Crook.

"I guess there might be news on Mister Lark," Josie said.

"You'd best get that poultice warming for Toby."

With Gramma tucked away in a less obtrusive corner of the kitchen, Nora rearranged herself. Her hair was a shock, but there was little time now to do anything save fight it down flat. In the mirror, Gramma's eyes guttered back and forth, following the speed of Nora's hands.

Harlan was reining up when she got back outside. He was not a handsome man—but in Desma's words, "you'd live after seeing him." He had sparse hair and a high, wide brow and an even wider set of teeth. The first afternoon Nora met him, he had just won a prizefight at the expense of two molars. A punch had shoved the balance of his front teeth straight back in their gums. He stood, in nothing but muddy trousers and a bib of his own dried blood, calling for a spoon. Moss Riley had obliged him with one. Harlan, in full view of everybody, had put it to the backs of his teeth and pushed them forward into place with a crack that called to mind a felled tree and momentarily cost at least one observer his consciousness. Somehow, improbably, the teeth had managed to heal back to their original magnificence. He had small, quick black eyes set far back in a staved-in face, and the whole configuration came together to always make him look a little wild. This new beard, which he'd sprouted abruptly in September, softened his corners a little. But it did not suit him.

"Sheriff," Nora said. "Back again."

"You shamed me so thorough the other day for coming round empty-handed, I figured I'd best remedy my disgrace as soon as possible." He sent the lead rope over the porch rail and back around.

She hoped he was ready to be shamed again. "A brick made its way through the **Sentinel** office window overnight. Yet here you are, reining up with neither mention nor solution."

He looked grim. "First I'm hearing of it."

"Guess you haven't been by your office since this morning."

She had intended that to sound less deliberate. He stood there, watching her. "It was an early start kept me out," he said. "Not a late night."

"What business is it of mine, where you spent your night?"

His hands drifted into his pockets. "Where's Rob and Dolan?"

"Away just now."

"They due back soon?"

"Depends on what you want with them."

That she did not intend to invite him in was now manifestly clear. He had not expected to meet resistance at her door. That was a comfort. If bad news were abroad, he would have come less unprepared.

"I might have use for that cart they been looking to sell," he said at last.

"If you need a cart so bad, why don't you use my husband's? I hear it was found near the Sanchez place."

More of the same lingering. "Where'd you hear that?"

"Abroad."

"Rumor is what it is. I ain't heard it fresh since I went up there to look." If only he would glance down at his boots, or hesitate, or flinch some other way, she thought. Then she could be certain of his duplicity. But he had an earnest way, Harlan, of looking straight ahead at her, as he was doing now. "If you doubt me, I'll go back again in the morning, Nora. I will."

Without intending to, she had waited too long to answer and brought herself now to a change of subject. "What do you want with a cart?"

"Figured I'd have my deputy paint it up with my name, and drag it round behind my horse for the benefit of any as-yet-undecided constituents till the election." He took the opportunity of her laughter to hunt around his duster pockets. "And I thought you could use this. For Toby." He held out his hand. In it was a small, withered eye patch. "Wearing it awhile set my nephew seeing straight after he was born cross-eyed. I know you said your boy's eye is torn, and that's different. But I figure it couldn't hurt."

Unexpected tears blurred the outline of him. She pushed her tongue against a seam of muscle that had suddenly begun to tighten her mouth. "That's mighty of you."

"You needn't use it if you reckon it'll do more harm than good."

She took it from him and held it in her apron pocket and felt along the cracks that braided the leather. "You'll stay and have a bite of something, anyway."

Harlan followed her into the kitchen and stood in the doorway, muttering his greetings under the full blare of their household chaos: Toby raising Cain over the eye poultice, which was loose and oozing and too hot and too cold; Josie readying Gramma's supper, cutting the margins off a ham and shouting the moment he entered, "Sheriff Harlan again!—but you keep coming round here like we still need convincing to vote for you!"

"Rob said he weren't voting up Sheriff Harlan no way," said Toby cheerfully.

Shushed from all flanks, he shrank in his seat and quickly discovered something in the grooves of the tabletop worth studying. Nora sat Harlan opposite him, and the Sheriff made his way through Amada de Almenara's pan dulce in silence, one corner at a time. If he had any notion of the gulf his possible third term had opened between Larks, he didn't show it. Toby, his mood greatly improved by the arrival of his own share of the dessert, grew thoughtful.

"Won't it be queer to call you **Mister** Bell again? After you been Sheriff Bell so long?"

"Just you go on calling him Sheriff Bell for now," Nora said. She pushed a plate of ham and corncake across the table at him. "Take your gramma her supper. Go on."

He stomped reluctantly off, cheeks bulging with his last, hurried bite.

"I reckon you'll be sheriff again," Josie said. "But not with that beard."

Harlan feigned a gut wound. He twisted at himself until he was satisfied with her laughter. Then he said: "I think it rather becomes me."

"I read once that folks like lawmen to be clean shaven," said Josie. "It's more honest-looking."

"What about dignity?"

"Your beard's a bit thin for dignity, Sheriff."

"It'll thicken out."

"Do let's shave it."

He dealt her the long look of a parent already won over and merely withholding his answer. When he said, "All right go on," Josie leapt up the stairs. Returning with all her barbering implements, she stretched over Harlan to tie the bib behind his neck, and then went around tucking, shifting, smoothing, running her hands over his shoulders and down his arms. The beard, an uneven gray snarl, was further ravaged by all the evidence of Harlan's numerous attempts to shape it, which Josie was able to ennumerate in almost supernatural detail—see here, Sheriff, how you've cut it long and it ain't coming back even? see how the direction of your hair's all changed? my goodness, Sheriff you didn't really try doing this all by yourself, did you? Though, of course, he obviously had. Josie was behind him now, frowning, tongue stuck out, brow furrowed, as if her very serious undertaking had indeed warranted all this tactile investigation, and there was very good reason to lean so close and put not one, but both, hands in his hair.

"Haven't you anything more useful to do?" Nora said.

"No, ma'am. The chickens are fed and the springhouse is swept."

Nora watched those feeble, pink fingers wandering slowly across Harlan's scalp.

"Weren't you meant to get those hackberries off the damn tree?"

Josie made a noise. "I plain forgot, ma'am! I'll do it first thing."

"Now's as good a time."

The girl looked up cautiously. The pause she allowed to lengthen out, Nora realized, was meant to convey the gravity of what was now being asked of her.

"Well?" Nora said.

"But, ma'am—it's falling dark."

"Well then you better run, hadn't you?"

Josie set her scissors down. Her movements were all gallows-walk now, slow and deliberate, hopeful of a last-minute intercession from somebody. None came. Toby, unaware of her predicament, chattered without pause in another part of the house. He would not be howling to her rescue now.

The picking basket was under the sink. Josie retrieved it and shook the few loose twigs stuck to its bottom over the back step. She wondered aloud whether or not the evening had by now got cold enough to warrant a change of clothes.

"You'd best take a shawl," Nora said. "At this rate, it'll be winter by the time you get down there, and it's your frozen husk we'll be getting instead of berries."

Josie's hat went on slowly. The ribbon, which she ordinarily let fall behind her shoulders, was wrestled painstakingly into a single, and then double, knot beneath her chin. She looked about ready for a noontime picnic, but didn't smile when Nora pointed this out. With a final wounded look in the general direction of the kitchen, Josie went outside.

Harlan sat with his knees stuck out from under the blanket and examined his boot-toes. Josie's departure had left a residue of sadness in the room, and it spoiled everything. Even the splendor of those faintly purpling clouds couldn't overcome it.

"She's a nice girl," Harlan said.

"Thank God for that. If she weren't, you'd be hard-pressed finding any sign of the Almighty's design in her."

His smile was patient. "She's harmless enough."

"I suppose I shouldn't be so curt with her."

Emmett had used the word "cruel" on more than

one occasion. But Harlan just shifted his shoulders under the drape. "She wouldn't take it so hard if she put less stock in pleasing you. But ain't that how we learn to be ourselves? Failing to impress them that matter most to us?"

Outside, evening dew had opened up the smell of the grasses. The dark outline of Josie had made it just past the fence, moving quick now among all the other tableland shadows. A sudden and inexplicable weight connected with Nora's chest, momentarily displacing the realization that she and Harlan were alone. From somewhere, Evelyn's voice said: **call her home.**

But now Josie had gained the ridge and become, for a fleeting instant, just the angular silhouette of herself—hat, neck, shoulders, waist, bell-shaped skirt—before disappearing down the trail.

"AND WHAT'S TO BECOME OF ME?" Harlan said. "Sitting here, resigned to my fate, with no one to barber me?"

"I'm of no use in that regard, I'm afraid."

Harlan resettled himself and looked through the window. "Hope that girl can tell her way. Or it'll be Peyton Landers all over again."

Nora hadn't thought of Peyton Landers in years—though perhaps, in mulling on the beginnings of her and Harlan's friendship, she often thought in a roundabout way on the occasion of Peyton's demise without featuring him in it at all. Peyton had been a haggard Carolina prospector with a quick temper and a smallish claim up the creek from Amargo proper. He lived in a state of agitation, at odds with everything: the heat, the weather, the gold or lack thereof; the density of the crowds and the absence of quality people; his neighbors and their proclivities; the fact that they were so far inland he doubted a railroad would ever come their way—and if so, what was the point of staking up in such a godforsaken place?

"Hard queries all," Emmett had said, "but fuck, don't the rest of us manage to live somehow without biling on about it all day long?"

One night, back in the days when they were all still lying under canvas and counting each other by name in the dark, Peyton failed to announce himself. They called for him awhile. Waited and called again. A few of the bolder lads went around the whores' tents, but found no trace of Peyton there, either. Every spare hand was rousted to the search. The women numbered five: Desma Ruiz, riled for having to endure this ridiculous odyssey for such an unworthy soul; Amada de Almenara, thinner in those days and sundark and every ounce as methodical about this as she was about everything else; two whores, whose excitement about the variance of their usual itinerary was wearying; and Nora. Some torch-wielding authority at the point of the crowd paired her off with Harlan Bell. She knew little about him, save that he was the postrider who had scouted for Crook, and kept mostly to himself. Just that morning, he had won a prizefight.

The crowd of some twenty souls dispersed into the night. For half a mile, she watched the receding orbs of their torches dance away. Harlan led her up the mesa and into the cedars. They felt their way along, calling Peyton's name until they were hoarse, then rested up in a little glade where Nora, forgetting herself, pressed her hands against her eyes. "Oh Peyton," she said, unthinking. "You've all the chins of a hog, but none of the gumption."

Harlan's laughter was explosive and surprising. She thought of how sunstruck he'd looked that day, bloody from the fighting, wiping himself down with his shirt, and a bruise already welting his shoulder, and found herself practically grinning.

By morning, another search party had come upon Peyton's dogs barking at the mouth of a ravine, and a few swift climbers confirmed what they already knew: there he was, smashed unrecognizable below.

After the burial, Harlan had the care to find her and say, "It weren't sin to laugh nor tell the truth that night, even if did concern a dead man—just so you know." Something in her shifted to build a secret, unassailable room for him, and he still occupied it.

"Poor Peyton," she said now. "It's an age since we poured one out for him."

"Still no sign of the boys," Harlan observed.

"Not yet."

"I guess I might prevail on you to show me that cart after all."

They went outside into the cool evening. She found she did not need the lantern to make her way. Harlan rustled along behind her. She felt hemmed in from all sides, and rigidly self-aware. Foremost on her mind: the flimsiness of her unlaundered shirt and the weight of her boots. For want of a better arrangement, she put her hands in her pockets—but this caused her to slouch, so she took them out and let them swing at her sides. It had been a mistake to wear trousers. The seams, which had been pressing all day into her most conspicuous reaches, felt now like the strings around sausage. At least, she thought, it was dark.

About halfway out over the flat, Harlan stopped to look back at the shining windows of the house. He didn't stir when she said his name. He was sure he'd heard the boys, he said, their voices floating out from somewhere upstairs. Her insistence that this was impossible went unanswered. He continued to stand there, staring up at the eaves and Toby's small shadow roaming around behind the curtain, until she said, "Harlan, we're quite alone."

Then he turned around.

In the barn, he really did look at the cart after all. It was a wrecked-out old thing whose undercarriage had finally given way last summer, this time for good. For months, the Lark boys tossed around the notion of repairing it again, but then it was decided—by time, if not committee—that they should sell the salvageable parts to whoever couldn't afford to buy them new. Harlan did not fit this bill.

"I can't see the sense of you clattering around town in something so decrepit," Nora said. "Aren't you meant to inspire confidence? I thought it was your lawkeeping destined to finally make us respectable enough for statehood."

"I don't know about that—respectability, I mean, not statehood." He grinned up at her with those incredible teeth from where he knelt beside the cart. "I'm from Missouri; I know all about statehood."

The rig would take some fixing, but he could right the axles and sand her down and give her a new coat of paint. Harlan got up and wiped his hands on his thighs. "How much they asking?"

"I don't know," she said. "What's it worth?"

Harlan climbed into the wagonback and shifted his weight from foot to foot to get the feel of it. "You look like something out of a Barnum and Bailey revue," Nora said. This only plunged him into more exaggerated pantomime. He held his hands out to her and she climbed up beside him and they jumped up and down a little bit and the poor cart creaked and shook beneath them until a pin shot out of the undercarriage.

They sprang down together like transgressing children, the cart's worth now significantly depreciated.

"I reckon three dollars," said Harlan. "That sound fair to you?"

"Three dollars?" She was a little out of breath. "With all the work you'll have to do on it?"

"You're supposed to take your boys' side. Tell me: Three dollars? Harlan Bell, I do declare."

"I don't talk like that, you know. Like I just stepped off the Alabama train."

"Harlan Bell, I do declare," he went on. "Don't you know this was built by Robert Cade Lark—who growed up to be Carter County rodeo champion three years running—when he were only two? Don't you know he and his brother used to pull each other around in it long before Dolan Michael Lark got the big judgeship over in Cheyenne? Three dollars, Harlan Bell—get away with you."

"I guess you're right. Maybe seeing what a wily dealmaker their mama is might dispel some of their grievances against me."

He waited patiently for the last of her laughter to subside. "All boys got grievance with their mothers."

"Well," she said.

"Nora. Where are they—really?"

"I don't know. Best I can figure, over in Prescott."

He jumped down and stood beside her. It was an unconscious habit of his to light his pipe when he really meant to listen. "What's in Prescott?"

"They've queried the marshals about Emmett's delay."

"Has there been any news?"

"No. But they're unconvinced of how carefully you looked for his wagon."

He put the pipe down and held out his hand. "I ain't lying. I looked real careful. I been swearing to you and I'd swear it again."

"I know. They're young. They think I accept without merit the things you tell me and they accuse me of foolishness. And now, it seems, they punch doors."

"So that's what happened. I didn't think it right to ask."

"Dolan did that," she said. "Would you believe it?"

Harlan stood with the velvet smoke rising around his face. "Well. Drought times try people in the strangest way. And I can't say the entire county ain't lost its mind about this vote."

He looked around the barn, and then climbed up into the loft and disappeared. She could hear him moving things around up there in the dark: now came the scrape of wood on wood, the sound of hinges creaking, a lid falling open. She couldn't imagine what he might find. An old smoothbore, apparently, and a couple of Colt pistols. Emmett's siege arsenal. Harlan was picking the guns up one by one and turning them over.

"What are you looking for?" she said.

"Not for—just around."

"All right. What are you looking around for?"

"Anything amiss. Don't it fall to me to ensure you and yours are safely kept till Emmett comes back?"

"He **is** coming back." She had not intended to pose a question, but Harlan was already nodding. "You found no sign of a cart out there? Nor sign that he had come to any harm?"

"No, ma'am."

"If you had, your being here would be despicable."

"I know it." He swung his boots over the side of the loft and sat looking patiently down at her. They had gone over this already. He was merely waiting now for her to arrive at her point so he could reiterate his: delays happened for all the ordinary reasons, to everyone, all the time. Emmett would come home.

"Remember how long we waited for news before the wires went up?" he said. "We forget quick enough, Nora: today's conveniences were yesterday's magic."

True enough. She could well remember the dread

of separation twenty years ago. The inevitable sense
that the people you were leaving behind might never
be seen again—dead, perhaps, by evening, and their
loved ones on the road for days, weeks, even months,
believing that life was carrying on as usual in their
absence, when in fact, all that remained behind was
emptiness. It seized her up a little just to think of it,
that old not-knowing, that particular kind of evening. But then the wires had come through. Now
one's most ardent hopes or dreadful fears might be
confirmed in a matter of minutes. And having to live
with the old discomforts, for even an hour, even a
day, felt impossible.

She and Harlan had stood side by side last year
when Ash River's first telephonic transmitter, with a
single line to the Crace ranch, was installed in the
Worther Hotel. The hotelier, Walton Pickney, had
got a new purple cravat for the occasion. A choker of
sweat ringed his collar. By noon, a streetwide crowd
from three counties was pressing against the fifty
people who had managed to cram into his establishment. The fortunate among them, like Rob and
Dolan, had gained the elevation of boxes and crates.
Toby had been small enough to sit astride Emmett's
shoulders. Moss Riley and Walt Stillman—further
entrenched in their enmity by the dredging up of
their respective failures to win the telegraph company contract for Amargo all those years ago—were
moated by damp bodies. Across the room, Nora
and Harlan were wedged in so tight the Sheriff was

obliged to put on his hat to keep it from brushing against her. The scent of tobacco clouded out from Harlan, and she tilted his way to let it overcome the potent cocktail of everyone else's odors. All those souls in twelve feet by twelve, and Walton Pickney in his cravat and waistcoat advancing with the steeliness of a tightrope walker toward the machine where it sat in state on his new desk. He assumed the chair and laid his hands on the table. Then he put on his half-moons, turned to the device and lifted the cup to his ear. He cleared his throat. "Good afternoon, Mister Crace, sir. Here is my message: **must I with my base tongue give to my noble heart a lie that it must bear?**" Wood flies barmed the shelves and ticked against the sweet-lipped candy jars. Then the horn crackled to life, and back came the miraculous, rough-soft voice of Merrion Crace, distant and a little broken-up, but sounding every bit like the man they could all imagine hunching over a similar contraption many miles away. "Walton? For God's sake, it's not the telegraph—a simple 'good day' will suffice."

"Oh—good day, Mister Merrion Crace!"

"Well done, Walton."

Poor Walton Pickney. He would later confess to Emmett, after a few too many, that he had spent the better part of the week choosing this ill-fated first utterance. But his disgrace went unremarked; to the breathless assembly in that room, all was miracle and magic.

Afterwards came the obligatory barn dance, a great

bright jolting mess of boots and dresshems that grew progressively more rancid as the evening wore on, until Nora could no longer stand it. Harlan found her taking the air. The hills above town were constellated here and there with the orange lights of miners' lanterns, and the music of their work came down and broke up the skirl of fiddles and racket of feet.

"I've the strangest feeling," she said.

"Fitting enough for strange times." Harlan stood near and lit his pipe. "Ten years ago, it was invisible flashes flying through the air that staggered us. Words traveling at speeds so incredible that all a man had to do was write a notion on one side of the country for it to appear two thousand miles away, almost at the speed of his own thinking." How impossible. Harlan had sat a good many years staring after those steadfast teams of men planting the telegraph poles. Wood and wire, and suddenly the whole horizon of human thought was altered. It had made him wonder what else might be coming. What else might be possible. "And now, sure enough." He pointed back to the Mercantile. "The human voice."

Nora thought about it. Hardly a day went by, it seemed, without the newspapers touting some remarkable discovery that upended the truth or convenience of living. Miracles of every variety: buildings so tall they could only be summited by electric conveyance; pictures captured on metal. From Atlantic state palaces of learning, educational revues were making their way slowly inland to share the latest scientific advancements: anatomical marvels and wonders of automation. Put together, these all had the effect of drawing things closer to one another, of illuminating that grainy twilight beyond which lay the landscape of a new and truer world.

And then there was Josie, who despite all of Emmett's questioning was fixed in her belief that spirits, occupying the selfsame plane as their living counterparts, could announce themselves by script or knocking. That they could be summoned from their heavenly abode just to appease human frailty and frivolity. Called down from the hereafter for confessions and parlor tricks. What an absurd and unholy notion.

But on the daylong ride home from Ash River, Nora fell quiet. She couldn't leave off wondering about what Harlan had said. If electromagnetic pulses could fly through the air; if giants with shin-bones the length of her entire body had once roamed ancient seas; if the world was plagued by legions of creatures so minuscule that no living eye could see them, but so vicious that they could lay waste to entire cities—was it not also possible that Josie's claims, however exploitative and preposterous, might hold some truth? Might the dead truly inhabit the world alongside the living: laughing, thriving, grow-ing, and occupying themselves with the myriad mundanities of afterlife, invisible merely because the mechanism of seeing them had yet to be invented?

She had come home feeling affixed to her fate.

There in the kitchen sat Josie, gracelessly shucking the last of the summer corn.

"Do you want a drink?"

"Ma'am?"

"Whiskey?"

She watched Josie struggle through a few tentative sips. It took strength to drink without wincing— Nora mustn't forget that, no matter the debasement to which she might now willingly subject herself.

"Josie," she said. "How are you able to call faraway spirits down?"

"Ma'am?"

"Well, when Mister Crace asked you to call Fint Colson down," she said. "Remember?"

The girl did. "He never answered though."

"But where did you call him from? He can't have died near town."

Josie lapsed into a long, ruminative stare. "I'm not sure where they come from, Missus Lark. I call out to them, and they answer or they don't."

"Do they answer more readily if you call out from the place where they've died?"

"Sometimes."

"And do they answer more readily if you call out from where they've lived?" She could see the girl was not following. Nora wasn't entirely certain of following all that well herself. She tried again. "Would a séance, for instance, held within the home of the deceased be more favorable?"

"Of course. Well. Not always." Josie frowned. "I

wish you would just go on and ask what you're cir-
cling around, ma'am—I feel I'm answering you
wrong, and it makes me that fitful to be around
you when I think you're mad."

Briefly, Nora considered giving up. But there was
something so eager, almost pleading, in the girl's
upturned aspect. And she had one foot in the mire
already. "I suppose—do spirits move, Josie, or are
they fixed to one place?" What did she mean? "If a
spirit were about—if it haunted a house, for instance.
Would it be fixed to that house for all time, or could
it move away?"

"It could be made to leave, of course."

"But could it be made to **follow**?" She pressed on.
"Suppose a family moved—could the spirit move
with them?"

Josie brightened. "That would depend on the spirit."

After a time, she took Nora's prolonged silence
as evidence of the conversation's end. She began
picking at the cornsilk meshed between her fingers,
adding to the mountain already heaped on the tablecloth like the rent-apart wig of some scarecrow.

"You know I had a daughter."

"I know," Josie said. "She died of the heat."

"I guess I'm wondering—is she here?"

They closed the kitchen door and extinguished all
the lights save the candle in the middle of the table.
All the room's shadows slid languorously from the
corners and darkened the floor so that Nora could
not even see her own feet. Everything filled with

haphazard slabs of darkness. Josie did her the courtesy of dispensing with the usual turban and bangles.
She sat with the planchette before her, and closed
her eyes. The silence grew until it seemed to sit down
at the table beside them. Josie asked whether Evelyn
Abigail Lark was attendant to them—could she hear
her? For a long time, there was no answer. Then
something ticked against the window. Nora could
not bring herself to turn her head. Evelyn might be
there, looking exactly—or not at all—as Nora had
envisioned her all these years.

Josie called again to the darkness, and again the
tapping came. She invited the spirit of Evelyn into
herself. This was, Nora realized, perhaps her last
chance to let her invention live on unaltered. Wasn't
it enough to know what she knew of Evelyn? What
if the ghost who slid into Josie and opened her eyes
to look on its mother for the very first time did not
resemble that soul whose presence, real or imagined,
had nevertheless followed Nora through life?

But it was too late. Josie was stiff and far-seeing.
Her pencil had begun to scratch wide, looping
shadows.

"Your daughter is here," she said. "She found
the dress you picked out for her christening very
beautiful."

Nora could not remember that dress. She leaned
closer, but by darkness the etchings did not resemble
words at all.

Josie went on. Evelyn had a lot of opinions about

improvements to the house—most of them agreeable, now that she had learned to navigate them. It
was difficult to learn new maps of the living world.

Nora said nothing. The Evelyn of her
imagination—radiant, tall, like Nora's mother—
had never liked the new layout of the house, either.
She thought the porch too small. She did not
understand why they had built around and then
up, and not simply raised a new house when the
present one became insufficient to contain them
all. She was keenly aware that a room had not been
designated for her—and Josie said this now, in a
moment of sudden alignment: "She is glad to know
she would be old enough to marry—for where
would she sleep otherwise?"

The window rattled again. Nora looked. Outside,
the moon was standing clear of low clouds, and tracts
of darkness hurried over the quicksilver plain.

"What else?"

Well, Evelyn was glad that Emmett had stopped
calling her "birdie." He had always called her that
when she was very small, and it had made her cross
with him. But now he referred to her as "Evelyn" on
the rare occasions he did bring her up, and she considered this a great improvement. She could feel him
thinking of her in those moments as she really was—
not as she had been—and it pleased her.

"She is full of forgiveness," Josie said.

Nora nodded so she would not have to speak.

"And the Indians," Josie said. "The ones who rode in and drove you into the fields where she died. She forgives them, too."

The girl went on, but Nora didn't hear the rest. The candleflame swam. After a while, she held up a hand. "That's enough—that'll do." On her way upstairs, she blew out the light.

If there was one thing Evelyn—the real Evelyn—would surely know, it was the circumstance of her own death. The Evelyn of her imagination knew it; rarely spoke of it, but was frank when she did so. Left the Indians out of it, for she knew the truth.

This shade conjured by Josie—whatever it was—did not know.

The only other soul who really did was Harlan.

And he was standing now with his hips slung forward and looking at her in that old, grim-soft way. "So the boys think Emmett's kilt?"

"And that the Sanchez brothers were involved."

"But why?"

"I don't know."

She sat down on the cart. "I guess a few days' silence seems an eternity to them. Ain't that funny. They were quite small, and don't remember when it was a common enough thing to go full two months with no word whatsoever from their father. I'd worry one day, rage the next. So that by the time you rode over, week seven or eight, with a letter from Denver or Cheyenne or wherever he was at the time,

I wouldn't even read it. Remember? Just set it there on the table while we had our supper."

She had a sudden memory of sitting across from Harlan on one such night. He looked like his present self in the memory—beard and all—which was impossible. But she could see the plate, with its blue rim, and his food divided neatly on it. Peas here, potatoes there, meat carefully trenched in its spot and not a lick of sauce traversing these separate zones. She had teased him mercilessly about this, and it shamed her to remember, and so she said the only thing that fell to mind.

"That beard really does make you look awful mangy, Harlan. It won't do at all."

SHE GOT THE BOYS' TALLOW SOAP FROM Dolan's room. Harlan sat very still, looking down at his hands, while she greased up his face and whet the knife. Ordinarily, she preferred to start in front; but standing behind the chair offered her an unobstructed view of the window, through which she could watch the road for any sign of visitors or returning parties—Josie, or the boys, or worst of all, Emmett, who was liable to overreact to this particular tableau. She scraped the first of the oil from his cheekbones. She was dismally out of practice.

"By God, I don't know about this," Harlan muttered through a nervous grin. "You seem a little unsteady."

"Only on account of your talking."

"I'm only talking because I ain't had a dry tallow shave in ten years, and I don't reckon my skin can stand it. It don't spring back like it used to, Nora."

"Let's leave it, then."

"No," he said. "Go ahead—go on. Please."

How gratifying to learn she still knew the contours of his face by heart. Why should this surprise her?

Weren't features as memorable a topography as any other? Hadn't she shaved him a hundred times before, back when they would come together after dinner with the fire banked and nothing between them but the quick scrape of the blade and the occasional wet zip of the razor against the bowl's tin rim? She always worked the same way: lip first, chin next, followed carefully by the sides of his face and neck so that he could rest the weight of his head against her shoulder while she finished. The first few times her hands had shaken so badly she cut him—once on the chin, and once quite broadly below the ear. It should have been sign enough for anybody: nothing so ominous as throat-cutting to ward a man off. But he'd proven obligingly cheerful about it.

"Go ahead and slice me a few more times, while you're there," he'd said, examining his blood-soaked towel. "My trade don't often earn me a wound this impressive without proper risk to life."

All this had begun some years ago—five, she'd been telling herself for so long that it was now closer to ten. Before Ferdy Kostic, back when Amargo had no post service at all—just Harlan running the only freight contract in town and occasionally bringing the mail. A stretch of prosperous years tracking rustlers all over Texas had put him in good standing with local cattlemen, who could always be counted on to make a bloodhound of him for two or three months at a time. When work was slow he wintered in the Amargo mining camp. But after getting deputized to assist in the capture of the Foxbow gang, he figured he ought to put down roots, just in case a shot at elected office might be in his cards. He filed on a claim two lots over from the Larks— a craggy little tract where not even Rey Ruiz could divine water—and took to calling around when Emmett was away.

Harlan would ride over in the afternoon with mail and sundries and gossip from town. One chore or another would keep him there till suppertime, much to the disdain of Rob and Dolan—who, at the ages of eight and seven, considered themselves expert on a host of household undertakings about which Harlan dispensed terrible and needless advice. Harlan, to Nora's delight, was unfazed by their contempt. On summer evenings he would follow her and the boys down to the stream, where they cast shabby lines into the warm mud of the creek and listened, with helpless beguilement, to stories about his traveling days. He had helped stake two hundred miles of rail. He had lived four years with the Sioux. Though he was not, by his own admission, much of a shot, he had backed Page Starr and Armand Gillespie in gunfights and lived to tell about it.

"Got a warrant out on you anyplace?" Rob had once astounded Nora by asking.

"Yes sir," said Harlan, without hesitation.

"Where?"

"Bullhead City."

"How come? You kilt a man?"

"I always heard it said the only men leaving Bullhead City without warrants on them were kith and kin to the Devil—and for that reason I consider my warrant a badge of honor."

Later, when Nora asked him to elaborate—having suddenly realized that if she was going to allow her boys to hear talk of warrants and gunplay, she ought to get full measure of the case; was there a woman in question, for instance, a consort or betrothed that Harlan had simply failed to mention?—he obliged. In his lawkeeping capacity—sometimes deputized, often as a range detective, occasionally as a mere bystander—he had countenanced the very lowest people. Suffice it to say the depredations of the men he hunted were not limited to cattle or property. It weighed on him that he might have been over-zealous in meting out justice now and again, but the overturning of warrant after warrant against him kept his conscience clear. Then a woman had disappeared, he said, somewhere in New Mexico. She'd had two daughters. That the boy he apprehended was only a kid, and not the primary architect of what had happened to them, did not concern Harlan. The judge disagreed. And of the four warrants out against Harlan, only this one was still outstanding—which, he felt, was as it ought to be. He wasn't sorry for what he'd done.

He reminded her of men she'd heard about in Cheyenne. They lived by their own unflinching laws, often subduing misrule by their mere presence. She had no doubt that Harlan's aspirations for Carter County sheriff would come to bear. But they did not. Amargo—backward hole that it was, den of small-minded misers and fishwives—reeled at the prospect of a hothead young bachelor, devoid of familial foundations, wearing the tin. He worried that it might be something else, but she was able to convince him after a while.

"If you were married," she said. "It would have gone differently."

"I know," he said. Then he kissed her hand for the first time.

She began to notice the letters Harlan brought her were sometimes two or three weeks delayed. He was keeping some of them back, she realized, in order to justify his visits in the intervals she received no correspondence. "How droll," Desma had said, without really seeming to mean it. Nora considered telling him not to worry about pretext. Neighbors could call on each other for the simple sake of being neighborly. She felt almost sure of having read a passage about that in Scripture. But she said nothing, because to name this strange, fragile thing—this whatever-it-was that kept him appreciating her middling cookery and laughing at the occasional humor of her small cruelties and even touching her fingers now and again—might break it.

Moreover, she knew well her own part in all this. She did not make a habit of shaving any of her other neighbors' faces. She did not laugh when their jokes were terrible, nor consider their near-illiteracy charming. She did not count down the hours until their arrival, either; nor let them linger past midnight before the fire so they could regale her with stories about scouting for inept brigadiers. If they happened to squeeze her hand, she did not thrill for days afterwards. And if she had brought them into her bedroom to attend to a stuck window, she would not have hovered in the doorway like some faint novice, feeling strangely warm and unable to keep from touching her own face.

So for as long as things did not need saying, she said nothing. Ecstatic, unbearable—this charade went on for years.

Even so she had thought it a happy time. Everything had felt a little easier, as though life were slowly righting itself. The Evelyn of her mind was about nine, chatting ceaselessly in her ear, occasionally even praising her for getting the hang of ranchwork. Emmett was making headway with the newspaper and still cheerful about their odds of squaring Sandy Freed's mountainous debt. There were no other newspapermen coming to visit—odious creatures, she thought, always plotting how to make something bigger or meaner or more worrisome than it was.

Of course, not all of it was happy. If watching Emmett leave distressed her, facing his return after weeks with Harlan was harder still. She would fill up with dread, lose her appetite, argue cruelly against everything. Emmett, believing it a reaction to his long absences, withstood it with surprising patience.

The closest he ever came to reproach was when he compared coming home to entering a snake's nest—and even then, his complaint turned only into a joke at his own expense. "I have to place my feet very carefully," he'd said, tiptoeing toward her.

She laughed, but felt the urge to say, "Try breathing with half a lung."

For that was how it felt to be torn from the comforting routine of possibility, the momentum that seemed to bring herself and Harlan inevitably closer to a precipice. At any moment, Harlan might make his overture and change everything. The promise of this had carried her through the days—carried her on from Evelyn's death, and the upbringing of her mutinous boys, and the knowledge that she might be stuck here until Emmett failed or succeeded, which could happen today, or next week, or twenty years hence, when she was played out and old.

But a person could get used to doing without. Gamblers did, and so must she. For six weeks—or months. A year, sometimes, during which her only reprieve might come at some loud party where the density of the crowd would thrust her and Harlan together in some quiet and exciting corner to carry on a conversation interrupted months before, which both nonetheless seemed to remember. She counted them all, and out they came, dancing into view as the seasons changed and the years went on, full of comings and goings.

Then came the winter of '89—a soul-hollowing winter that drenched them in downpours and ate away the mountainsides and buried whole ranches and swallowed up those poor men who were still trying to coax some flake out of the played-out canyons, all of it so catastrophic she wondered if there might not be something biblical in the works after all. If she could only get through it, she thought, Harlan would come back from his latest job in Texas, and Emmett would head for the annual gathering of newspapermen in Denver.

A few weeks into March, however, Harlan returned in the company of a woman whom town gossip quickly established to be Missus Harlan Bell. Wild rumors eddied around her: she was a Confederate loyalist; some desperado's widow Harlan had been forced to marry; an heiress of the Blackwood logging company. Nora didn't believe any of it. One look at the woman told you everything you needed to know: she was a thin, blond, bird-boned thing; but no amount of Atlantic breeding could mask that Doric forehead, that jaw so robust you'd be forgiven for thinking she ate rawhide four squares a day. Her consonants dropped like stones, leaving little room for doubt that her ancestors had been present at the sack of Rome. Harlan, it seemed, had met her in Texas, fallen hard, married her before the judge, and managed to keep the whole thing secret until she came clicking into town behind him in her little black gig, signing the guestbook at the Bitter Root Inn as Emma Konig-Bell.

The few facts that emerged about her over the following weeks were firmed up by her handmaid, Sara Wright, a slight flint of a girl whose daytime terseness stood in stark contrast to how loose-tongued she became after one or two glasses of whiskey after hours. Missus Emma Konig-Bell was from Minnesota by way of Texas. She liked this mining camp only a little better than the one where she had met Mister Harlan. A jewel the size of your head was sewn into the hem of one of her dresses. She drank beet elixirs twice a day. She had always set her sights on marrying an upright fellow with lawkeeping ambitions, but would live at the Bitter Root until her new husband had made his homestead habitable for one such as herself.

The town ladies had some theories about what kind of person preferred to live in a hotel rather than in a home of her own keeping. Nora had thought herself above such cruelties—but something brittled up in her. Having gone so long without naming whatever it was between herself and Harlan—which had now, seemingly, died—she could not name its aftermath. And unable to name it, she could not root it out.

Nights at the dinner table, she tilted the soupspoon and forced thin dregs of sustenance between her teeth. Again and again, she woke from hazy dreams to the conviction that her house had been robbed.

By the time Harlan rode out to her place again—it was a year; she had counted (not that it mattered, but she had): November to March, during which time she had blithely thought everything was all right while Harlan was falling head over heels in Texas; and then March to the big spring celebration in May when she shook Missus Emma Konig-Bell's smooth, light hand for the very first time; May to August of course, oppressive and interminable; and then finally August to November, which had once been their season—Nora was four months along with Toby. Emmett was in Denver. The new Missus Bell was visiting cousins in Minnesota.

Nora stood on the porch and spoke—she believed—softly, trying all the while to suss out any appreciable change married life had wrought in Harlan. He looked a little played out. Anyone fool enough to marry a German would be, of course. His gauntness spoke volumes about the woman's cooking—or lack thereof, for what kind of cooking could a woman possibly acomplish within the stuffy, wallpapered confines of the Bitter Root Inn anyway? Harlan, meanwhile, stayed mounted. He meandered through news of weather and crops and his recent failures at joinery and the conversations he'd had of late with Mister Merrion Crace, who was unexpectedly civil and encouraging of his intentions to run for sheriff—though it had been difficult to parse whether Crace was sincere or just over-polite.

"You know the English," he said.

"It's an affliction," said Nora.

He looked her over. "What's the matter?"

"Nothing."

He climbed out of the saddle and went on looking at her, passing the lead-rope from one hand to the other. "It does my heart good to see you, Nora. It's been too long."

"Don't be absurd. Weren't we both at the Hallows fair only just last week?"

"Well." Caution stifled his voice. "We didn't hardly speak at all."

"I don't know about that." She stuck her hands in her apron and looked down the road. "You told me all about Missus Bell's ambitions to instate a vegetable garden once she's moved out to your place—I reckon that's more than we've said to each other in months."

"Missus Bell **does** intend to instate a vegetable garden."

"I'm pleased to hear it."

"More to the point: there **is** a Missus Bell."

Her heart jumped. "I know that."

"Of course. I only meant. You understand the impossibility."

"Perfectly. I understand it's fine enough for you to come riding over here night after night, with your mixed-up letters. Hanging about till it's too dark to ride back home. But now that there's a Missus Bell—oh, how the sanctity of blessed union comes rushing to the fore."

She had him on the back foot, but not for long. He went red.

"There is also a Mister Lark."

"What a ridiculous thing to say."

"No more ridiculous than pretending we're strangers when your husband comes in the gate, and then expecting me to come calling again the moment he's gone."

All this, as she had long suspected, was what came of naming fragile things.

Years of thin handshakes and cursory nods across crowded rooms followed. When she remembered days that now seemed past, she saw the scenes from outside herself, as if she were observing them third-person, as if all along they had happened to somebody else. In twisting flashes populated by faceless people, she sometimes dreamt that they were still friends. She sometimes dreamt they were more, too, which was far worse. "Are you ill?" Emmett asked whenever she woke weeping—a rare enough occurrence these days, but so common back then that Doc Almenara had finally outlined the benefits of laudanum. He was cautious about prescribing it. He would not offer much, and only for a little while. She was glad of this interlude, for his gentle suggestion was all she required to get herself upright again. Laudanum indeed. It was just a little heartsickness, nothing the task of living couldn't overcome. What did he take her for—some wilting, Atlantic-state hotel wraith?

The new Missus Harlan Bell left town the fol-

lowing September. Desma came riding over to tell
Nora all about it. Apparently, the lady had packed
up without a word to anybody, taking the servant
girl, Sara, and heading east to Texas to take the
waters. There was an assumption she might be in
the family way, but Desma wasn't so sure. People
living within earshot of the Bells said there had been
quarrels. A lot of nights spent abroad. It did not
seem to be an ordinary curative trip.

Harlan was just beginning his tenure as sheriff. It
was to be an interim position. His predecessor, Mac
Calwell, had taken two rounds in the thigh putting
down a couple of rustlers near the border, and Harlan
had stepped in for him while Tucson physicians
debated whether or not Mac's ham of a leg could be
saved. Amargo recapitulated all the reasons it had
elected Mac Calwell in the first place: Harlan didn't
spend enough of the year local to possibly have the
full measure of the town's inner workings; during
the last election, Harlan had seemed flexible on the
question of range-fencing; and though he was now
married, wasn't he bound to be a little reckless, what
with the wife gone abroad for the season? To make
matters worse—for Nora especially, this smelled of
spite—Emmett printed an article arguing that the
Territory, being up for statehood, must generally
resist the ascension of elected officials whose lawkeeping record could not be verified. Harlan Bell,
the **Sentinel** insisted, was friends with a lot of particular interests all over Texas, and woefully unready

to contend with a jailhouse then overrun with desperadoes. What could he possibly do with the four souls sharing a cell at the far edge of town (a duo of prospectors who'd attempted to gun each other down, and two bedlamites who had reneged on wagers at the Bitter Root and come to grief at Walt Stillman's hand)?

The jailed desperadoes shared this outlook. They welcomed Harlan on his first day with a rousing chorus of "Garry Owen"—and soon enough made the reason for their mirth evident, attempting a jailbreak just after Harlan went off home that same evening. But this was where the story turned: the new sheriff, unbeknownst to any of them, had rigged the outer adobe walls with bells. When the men started digging, the whole jailhouse went off like Easter Sunday. Two o'clock in the morning, and people came out in their shawls and stood around in shock while Harlan coolly waited in the street with his shotgun aimed at the presaged exit. Nora didn't see the incident herself, but it was acknowledged to be the most marvelous arrest everyone else had ever witnessed.

The two of them warmed up again right around election time. Nora happened to pass by one afternoon while Harlan was standing on a box in the thoroughfare, staggering miserably through a speech that was intended to put to rest some of the questions **Sentinel** readers were still asking. She drew up and listened, fanning Toby's tiny bald head while

he squirmed in his wrappings against her chest.
Harlan Bell was categorically against cattle fences;
unequivocally in favor of maverick branding;
the author of more than fifty arrests all over the
Territories. His opponent's support of fencing
homesteads seemed like a ready solution to the rustling problem right now, but it would go a long way
toward breaking up the fabric of their community,
the trust and care with which Carter County cattlemen treated one another, knowing that any steer
might graze on anybody's land at any time and not
fall prey to the dangers of dishonest profiteers.

Harlan sweated. His voice faltered. Never had a
man so suited for the job been so inept at this—the
only means by which to obtain it. She wanted to
laugh, to commiserate. She wanted to tell him it
would be all right.

Toby fussed and kicked and fell asleep and woke
up again. At the oration's end, Nora raised her arms
over her head and applauded with all the zeal she
could muster.

Bertrand Stills made his pendulous way over to
her. From beneath that oil-slick moustache, he asked
whether Nora, as the wife of a pillar of the community, might tell him how the Lark house was now
disposed toward the incumbent.

Nora answered without thinking. "Ensuffraged
Larks will naturally support Sheriff Bell."

This endorsement would prove unnecessary, of
course. All anybody could remember or talk about

was the thwarted prison break and how it had felt to stand in the street and bear witness to something the grandchildren would surely never believe. Damn near every ballot went Harlan's way, and not even an amputated foot could garner Mac Calwell enough sympathy to make the contest remotely sporting.

But the print-up of Nora's remark in the **Clarion** led to one of her and Emmett's most bitter and enduring battles.

"My vote spoken for," Emmett cried. "And promised to a low-down range detective."

"He's a lawman."

"Have you any notion of how many people he's strung up, Nora, all over the Territories?"

"That's just nonsense cooked up by his opposition."

"You know what they call him in Texas?"

"Sheriff Bell, I'd imagine."

"They call him Harlan Knell."

"You can damn well vote any way you like when you're in the box. No one will know."

But Emmett would not make a liar of her. And in November, he was obliged to stand before the Ash River photographers and grin to the point of rupture while the moment of his one and only vote for Sheriff Harlan Bell was forever immortalized for the benefit of strangers. That a daguerreotype of this scene now hung above the Mercantile cash register—beside a picture of Merrion Crace with Wyatt Earp—had proved a raw and lasting insult.

———

A last gleam of tallow still clung to Harlan's face.

"How does it look?" he wanted to know.

"Marginally improved," she said. "But then I'm not a magician."

His hand wandered over his chin and then across her fingers where they rested on his shoulder. Ten years ago, this would have been a gesture to decipher, long for, visit and revisit again and again over the interminable stretches of his absence. Not so now—not at all. Here they were, friends and still unscathed, still the keepers of each other's deepest confidences. Betrayers of no one, having wounded neither bystanders nor each other. She thought of Harlan sometimes as a fellow combatant with whom she had resolved never to speak of how close to disaster the battle had brought them. That they could be sentimental of the unspoken truth of their friendship was enough. And if his visits were less frequent now, they were also less fraught. And if they sat further apart at the kitchen table, it did not feel an excruciating privation. And if he spoke of his wife—with whom he did not expect to reunite, though they would stop short of a divorce on account of his office—Nora did not feel all the time as though she were being doused in freezing water. And if her skin tingled a little where he touched it—well. It was only flesh and blood remembering.

How strange, then, to find his hand had moved down to her knee. The whole world had gone mad today.

"What's got into you?"

"Nora," he said. "Listen to me."

He looked at the point of tears. "Good Lord, Harlan—what's the matter?"

"Listen."

FROM SOMEWHERE DOWN THE CORRIDOR came the skirling of those dreaded chariot wheels. Nora lowered the mirror. Harlan was already sitting up to wipe his face when Toby rounded the corner in the wake of Gramma's chair. He edged the old woman over to the window where she could sit in the cool. Then he sat, squinting suspiciously at Harlan, who had managed to fight down whatever emotion had been rising in him and replace it with an ordinary, if unconvincing, grin.

"Why ain't you ridden out to Cumberland and see if my pa is there?"

"We're undermanned," Harlan said. "But we've looked elsewhere for him."

"Well you're here," Toby said, "so I guess you ain't looking now."

A heady snort cracked out from the depths of Gramma's wheelchair. She looked as surprised as anybody to have emitted it. Her eyes shivered from Toby to Nora, from Nora to Harlan.

"Well, it's dark out now," Harlan said. "Not every-one is fine in the dark, like your pa."

Toby looked down. "No one's fine in the dark with the beast about."

"What beast is that?"

Toby looked at her. Out it came: the beast whose tracks he'd seen up at the old Flores place when he'd been grouse hunting. The tracks—"Josie can tell you herself: Josie!"—were very, very strange. Toby put his fists down on the table, one beside the other, so that Harlan might countenance the sheer dimension of a single footprint.

When Toby paused for breath, Harlan said: "There's a bear been breaking into springhouses up and down Narrow Creek."

Toby put this down flat. "It weren't a bear."

"Well, then," Harlan said, leaning conspiratorially forward on his elbows. "Perhaps it's that ghost horse put itself through them prospectors' tent down the gulch at Shelley's Point about a month back." Had Toby heard about it? By his open-mouthed silence, Harlan could tell he had not. Nora's attempt to intercede here went unnoticed, and Harlan plowed on. It was Sal Abregado who first told him about it, maybe a month or two back. He'd gone fishing down on the Blue Fork in late summer when there was water still, and come across the brush all torn up, like a big herd had gone charging through it. Spoor trail and thick clumps of hair snagged on every branch. Well, Sal Abregado had never let fear turn him away from anything in his life, and wouldn't start now. He went up into the thickets and through the gulch, all along this game path that had been torn until he got to a little clearing below the ridge, where a couple **buscadores** were encamped. Only when he got there, the camp looked like a stampede had come through. The tent was ripped in half. The hearth was trampled. Pots and pans everywhere. Some of the horses had pulled up their pickets and run off. Sal Abregado's pals had met the rough end of this surge. One had an arm already slung up, and the other was trying to splint his twisted foot.

"Sal offers them water, and then says **que pasó aquí**? And he can tell, grateful as they are for the water, they'd rather not bore too deep into what had **pasó aquí** and what had not. Sitting there looking at one another with all their gear flung about. Nothing, they tell him, just a little disagreement. But Sal's no fool. He don't let up. He asks again: What kind of disagreement? Don't they know it ain't right to fight your brother?

"You know how Sal is," Harlan said to her. Nora nodded. All she could remember of Sal was that he was a charming and easily distractible sportsman who would watch two snails crawl up a stalk of grass if somebody deemed it a race.

"Well?" Toby said. "What was it?" He had slid all the way down the end of the bench, abandoning his poultice in an oily pile on the table.

"It was a huge red horse," Harlan said. "Big as a

house, with dog's teeth and a lion's mane. All night they'd heard it howling about in the brush. The two of them sitting there under their canvas, shoulder to shoulder, pistols drawn but scared to look out. When it came time to defend, they were powerless. It went ripping through their tent and rolled them up in it like they was dolls, and dragged them twenty or thirty feet together, howling all the while. All they caught of it was a handful of red hair and the glimpse of a huge, white head and black eyes before it lit into the trees and disappeared."

Nora could see it now: the avalanche of this story engulfing Toby, the sleepless nights that would follow. She charged into the silence.

"And then those two rowdy **buscadores** were clapped up for lying. The end."

Nothing about Harlan's smile indicated that he had heard her, much less caught her drift. His hands lay on the table within inches of Toby's.

"It didn't hurt them?" Toby whispered.

"I guess it roughed them up pretty good. Tossed them around in their tent."

"That's just like what Josie saw," Toby said. "The lion's mane and the white head. She'll tell you." He began calling her name again. "Josie! Where **is** she?"

"Must be upstairs," Harlan said.

Nora trailed them to the banister as they started up. Toby led the way, bugling Josie's name. Harlan's dust-scuffed boots followed. It heartened her so much that he was willing to play up to the boy like this. She watched them scrape around the landing from room to room, Toby checking himself against the walls, Harlan opening doors and looking behind each, disappearing first into Dolan's room and then into Toby's. He reemerged and looked up at the next flight that led to the attic. "Farther along, I guess," he said, and went upstairs. His hand was on his holster—force of habit, she imagined. His footfalls faded with each step, and the rafters shook out a little of their dust. Rob's door banged open. She heard it thud against the rear wall, and then come creaking back. Harlan's boots scraped from window to window. Then came two consecutive thumps— the sound of his knees on the floorboards, she realized, and she could see him, just as clearly as if she were in the room herself. He had gotten on his knees to look under the bed. What the hell for?

Toby was still on the stairs below. Josie's name had become a two-syllable warble emitted at intervals regular enough now to be truly agitating. JOH-ZEE, JOH-ZEE. Devoid of all meaning. Between those outstretched vowels and the sudden swooping sensation between Nora's ribs, Evelyn's voice rose clear:

Something's the matter.

Upstairs, to some unknown end, Harlan was opening Dolan's wardrobe. She could hear the hinges groaning on their stiff pins. She could hear Harlan's fingers sighing drily along the length of the landing wall as he came back down. Every few steps, he stopped to knock on the boards.

He came into view again. He looked grim.

"Harlan," she said. "What the hell are you looking for?"

He said something about the boys again, but this was lost to the panicked tremor of Toby's voice. "Mama, Mama—where's Josie?"

Only then did it strike her: the girl had not come back at all. "Down in the gulch, honey," she said.

FALLING FROM HORSEBACK LAST MARCH, Toby had made no sound. The horse in question had been a pinto bronc recently broken by Rob and destined for a quick sale. The bronc had pink nostrils and an uneven white blaze down its face. It had spent the balance of a month charging around and snapping its corncob teeth at the dogs. "He's well broke now anyway," Rob had insisted, though all of them knew it wasn't so. But it was unlike Nora to keep open score on how often she was right and others mistaken, so when Rob boosted Toby into the saddle, she said only, "Mind him, now." It all went softly enough at first, the little man and the bronc lifting velvet purls of dust. As she passed them on her way to the springhouse she saw the bronc's back legs go up—just barely. An exploratory bump. Rob was shouting instructions about heels and reins and posture from the corral fence. He said, "Don't lettim get away with it"—whatever that meant. Toby did whatever it was he thought was expected of him. This gesture, unseen by Nora, sent the horse's back legs into a vault. Toby went down. Rob—unaccustomed to being moved for—didn't move. The bronc was a rangy, thin-legged thing. It stilled the same instant Toby went flying, perhaps because its only aim had been to shed the weight that harried it or perhaps—as Rob always insisted when it came to horses—because it sensed itself responsible for something unworthy. It hovered with its foreleg curled away from the boy. Toby lay stunned. **A real pity, Mama.** Nora could tell that all the air had gone out of his lungs. His mouth opened and closed soundlessly. Then he caught the air and sucked it in, loud and ragged like a belch reversing course, and Nora found her own aching breath. He stood, a little shakily. Rob, still at the fence, was saying, "Take the reins and get right on up now. You hear?" Toby went for the lead-rope, missed and fell forward again. This set her running. By the time she reached him, a crooked trail of blood had left the corner of his mouth. She would not remember, despite promising herself otherwise, to search the dust for his lost tooth later. Toby ran a hand across his face, spreading the blood up toward his eye, so its source was unclear to her once she'd swept him into her arms. All the while it was the silence that terrified her most. She had seen a boy brainhurt before, back in Iowa, and all this felt familiar: as if the body, half-remembering some well-learned map of living movement, had floundered out in one final gesture and been silenced.

None of that compared to the weight of Toby's silence now. Even Harlan took a step back.

"Well, Josie's only been gone a few minutes," Nora said.

"Well," said Harlan.

"Not long at all, lamb."

"Maybe she got turned around in the dark."

Toby dragged a single, dry sob. "Mama, I can't see."

Harlan looked at her. They struggled toward the same conclusion together. A few minutes? The sky had still been alight when Josie left for the gulch. The two of them had lingered in the kitchen awhile longer, gone out to the cart, spent unaccounted-for minutes in the barn, come all the way back. Nora, in the grip of some desire to preserve this sanctuary of calm, had decided to shave Harlan's beard—and he had let her, and again that strange bittersweet urge to stretch the moments kept her from quite paying attention to how long it had all taken. Long enough for Toby to return. Long enough for Harlan to tell the story of the ghost horse. Long enough for him to scout the upstairs rooms—for what?—itself an episode that felt foreveraway and longago, though it had only just happened.

So though Harlan insisted once again now "it hasn't been long at all," it occurred to her that this could not be true. An hour had gone by. Perhaps more.

Harlan put on his hat. "I'll go have a lookround."

He hurried out into the cool darkness. Paused for a moment just outside the door, lit up from behind by the yellow glare of the windows. From the tilt of his head, she could tell that he was checking his gun. Then he slid out of the light, and became just another imagined movement on the sageflat.

"Toby," she said. "You sit put and wait awhile."

Emmett's old Colt was in the mailpile. Four bullets were chambered—the other two lost to whatever nonsense went on about the place when she wasn't around.

"What's happening, Mama?"

"Sit put right here, and don't you move. Not for anything."

SHE HAD EXPECTED IT TO BE ENTIRELY dark by now, but a last, tightening slice of light still clung to the hills. A few pale clouds were unraveling into the eastward dark. Her knees shook the dew-spray ahead of her into the sage. Halfway out across the field, she looked back at the house, the haze of fat, pale moths ticking against its windows. Toby was perched where she had left him, wavery through the glass, still and straightbacked on the kitchen chair.

She kept the plow to her left and made for the slanted black bones of the outer fence just ahead. The only sign of Harlan was the smell of his tobacco. She said his name a few times, and then Josie's. Bats swooped overhead, clicking. Once or twice, some unseen bramble in the grass caught and almost sent her sprawling.

Harlan was in the barn. She could see a faint, orange orb drifting evenly past one of the upstairs windows. Then it disappeared. She stood still, listening. Soon followed the sound of his footsteps—or at least what she thought were his footsteps, for here and there between them came Evelyn's voice again. **What's he looking for? What is it?**

What had he meant to tell her? Everything had been going sideways all day, and Harlan's arrival had brought the first promise of some familiar stillness. Now even that seemed to be falling away. Her throat was burning again. There was no reason for her presence out here, save for the sharp guilt of having forgotten the girl—but even now, Josie was less on her mind than was Harlan, whom she could see coming slowly down the ladder with his lit pipe orange between his teeth. Looking for what? Not the girl. He already knew she wasn't in the barn.

Looking for something, Evelyn said.

Harlan emerged on the far side of the outhouse and went up the slope ahead of her, thin and raw-boned in the moonlight. At the top of the rise he sprang up onto the jackfence and stood shouting Josie's name downhill. Nothing came back. After a while, he called again.

"Reckon she's still down there?" Harlan said, once Nora reached the fence.

"I expect so. She never could tell time, the goose. Probably found a few spirits to dance with."

"Right kind of night for that."

And it was. The moon was just clearing the bluff above their little patch of forest. By its light, the contours of familiar trees and stumps and the tumbledown perimeter wall looked quicksilvered and faraway. She stood with her arms slung over the palings and mulled over the prospect of having to find her way down to the stream among all these twisted shadows.

"Won't you go indoors, Nora?"

"What the hell were you looking for upstairs?"

"Josie."

"That's not so. You knew she wasn't back yet."

"I reckon I forgot."

She couldn't see his face. "And what did you set out to tell me?"

"Please go on back to the house."

"You don't even know where you're going," she said, and set off for the trailhead.

The slope was far more treacherous by night. A steep, narrow grade, almost entirely scree. The crumbling embankment on both sides was shot through with rattail roots that snagged her fingers. She braced herself and slid one foot in front of the other. Rocks went crackling away from her downhill.

From somewhere behind her, Harlan bellowed: "Josie!"

The eruption of his voice was a shock. In answer to whether or not he intended to give some indication when he was fixing to do that again, he met her only with a blinding grin and she felt that greedy, nostalgic weight between her ribs like a bird resettling.

It was another quarter mile, maybe a little further, to the wash. The air was already cooler down here and thick with mosquitoes. She slapped at her

forehead and fought the slide of the scree where the
trail steepened just before easing out into the trees.
There, her outheld hands met the undergrowth. A
cobweb went into her mouth and she peeled at its
invisible tendrils till Harlan took her hand and
pushed swiftly through down to the beach.

They stood together with the dry wash before them
and the black tanks along the shore shining with
mud. Bluff to bluff, the beach was empty.

"She would've gone clear around that way," Nora
said. "Maybe she got turned around."

Harlan moved her to the wall. "This is far enough
to be playing hide-a-seek for three," he said. "Don't
you wander off now. I can't go looking for more than
one of you at a time."

She watched him feel his way along the bank, calling Josie's name. The cane rustled and jerked wildly
wherever he touched it. On the far shore she could see
familiar forms, the ragged lip of the mesa, above which
the stars sat in their whorled millions. The bluffsides,
banded over with ore and stuck about with newborn
scrub, all shadowed together. Nothing seemed much
itself except the creek. From here it looked like water
still, and she moved her tongue unthinkingly through
the tanks of thick spit that had collected behind
her teeth. To be an animal now and drop one's chin in
that slow, red mud. Moonlight had forged a second
course along its surface and shone like hammered steel
between the rocks. Toby's fishing place sat midcourse,
domed and still as a long-dead tortoise. Eddies came

foaming in toward her along its little jetty of stones, and disappeared among the reeds.

She tried once. "Josie!"

The bullfrogs were at their nighttime frisk. Their bloated calls moved up and down the wash. The cattails rattled all together, a long line of them like nodding spearheads broken up by a long, dark sandbar lying slantwise across the stream. A mud turtle was making its silhouetted way along this obstruction, one clawed foot sinking ahead of the other.

"Harlan?"

There was no answer.

She stood awhile, trying to remember what those stones looked like by daylight. She freed her soles from the sucking mud and eased down toward the water. Her shoe met something and sent it skidding away. She found it again a few feet later, and bending with her hand outheld, touched the coarse weave of Josie's basket. There were brambles inside, and a rancid foam that stuck to her fingers.

She heard Harlan at the bend. All the lightness had gone out of his voice. He was calling her name as if he thought, perhaps, she might not answer.

"What is it?" she called.

"Stay there."

"What is it?"

And what was there in the reeds? She didn't remember having seen this sandbar in the daytime at all. It looked more like a toppled line of rocks that had knocked some of the cattails down. A gentle roll pinched its middle. The slow mud had pushed up around it, and foam had caught between it and the streambed, and it seemed to move a little with the reeds, though she could not be sure. She looked down its length again, from one end to the other. It was wearing a boot.

Harlan was coming back, crashing around in the cane. She tried to stand, but everything in her had gone very still and sour, and here came the blood to her head again. The mud sucked at her boots. She teetered where she knelt. Harlan dragged her to her feet and held her up, but she couldn't look away from it, the broken reeds and the boot. Harlan saw it, too. He shoved her back up the bank and said Josie's name—very differently now, harshly, as though he were speaking to a child caught red-handed in some calamitous game. He went down into the reeds and made a sound.

When he lifted the girl's head, streams of mud came coursing down her face. He overturned her and carried her up the shore, struggling against the drag and the weight of her clothes and the stiffness of her limbs. Nora slid down toward them on her knees, and opened the girl's mouth and listened for breath. "Josie?"

Rolled over and slapped, she continued to lie still.

Then she groaned.

"Jesus," Harlan said. His hand left a trail of darkness across his brow. In their moonlit mud calderas, the frogs went on singing.

　　　　　✳

"WHAT HAPPENED TO YOU?"

"It struck me all at once."

"What struck you? What did?"

"My head hurts awful," Josie said, and fell away again.

"You've all your fingers at least." Harlan opened his fist to reveal a crumbling of thin yellow fragments. "These ain't yours, merciful God."

"What in hell are those?" said Nora.

"Knucklebones. I found them over yonder."

"What's happened to her?" A shoulder dangled loose in its socket, and down the length of Josie's body one of her boots was twisted the wrong way around.

"Leg's just about broke in half." Harlan stood looking away downstream. He turned and took in the whole length of the beach. "She didn't just fall. Something did for her mightily."

He crouched back down. She wondered at the purpose of whispering. Hadn't they just been shouting and joking up and down this hill together?

Joking she thought, joking while Josie lay here in the mud. Not to mention the racket they had raised getting the poor girl out and breathing. If something were lying in wait for them, hadn't it wised up to them by now?

A mudbubble bloated the edge of Josie's lip. Nora wiped it with the edge of her sleeve. Through the fabric and swollen lips, she felt gaps in the sharp line of Josie's incisors.

"Some of her teeth are broke."

Harlan slid a finger under Josie's lip and felt around. He did this without looking at her, staring straight ahead into the dark.

"Bear," he said. He shifted around, folding Josie's arms one over the other. "Must've come up on her in the dark and got startled and brought her down in the creek when she ran. A sow with cubs'll do that—kill a man without eating of him. Jim Wainsbrouk up in Fort Hollow run afoul of a sowbear last summer and she took his eye and broke his every rib and left him there for dead."

"I remember." Bertrand Stills had found him and written about it as though he had fought the sow off personally with nothing but his caustic wit.

"She don't look bit."

"Poor Josie." A dark and exsanguinating realization made its way forward through her fear. "What will I tell Toby?"

"You ain't telling him a thing less we get ourselves back to the house in one piece."

She patted the mudlogged little head and steadied herself against the ground and waited for him to plan their way out. Toby. If only there were some evidence to point to the fact that Josie's mishap—as she was already resolving to call it—had only just befallen her just this second. Some way around the fact that Toby's dearest friend had been lying there for an unknown length of time, crushed and disregarded, like dead timber only good for going past while his unthinking mother took the air with a sheriff loathed by the household.

"All right," Harlan said. "I'm gone carry her up. You follow along soft as you can."

"I'd like to spare Toby the sight of her."

"Don't be ridiculous."

"Harlan."

"The barn then."

For a moment she feared he might sling Josie over his shoulder like a ham. He lifted her instead as if she were a child and started up moving crabwise over the beach until he met the hard flat of the imbricated rocks.

They went up the hill diagonally together, bending low with their hands outheld to feel ahead. The rocks were huge, abraded and wedged upstream by some extinct current, but the cracks between them were deep and treacherous, might easily swallow an ankle or a leg. She thought she knew them. She did not. She fell and fell again. Every time she got back up, Harlan was a little further away. Josie's crooked boots swung and clacked against the rocks. They reached the bajada, the once-shore of that ancient river, and straightened and moved sideways, searching the bluffline ahead for the chevron that marked the cliff trail. Ahead lay the ruffled darkness of the trees.

She walked in the wake of Harlan's sweat. He was breathing fast and whistling through his nose. Then he stopped.

Something stood a little ways ahead of them. Too close already to be wary of now. At first, she just thought it was a very tall thicket, but then it shifted, and its movement was accompanied by thin metallic song. What looked like a long, articulated post peeled slowly from the massed haze of it and braced up in the dirt behind. A leg. Fore or hind, she couldn't say—but it did not belong to a bear.

The sixgun was in her pocket. As her hand met the barrel blindly and overturned it, she thought of the old adages about territorial standoffs: Arizonans, she'd read someplace, always shoot through the pocket. The clarity steadied her. She was calm enough to think of how strange it would be to shoot a bear in the dark through her own pants. But this entity—whatever it was—stood eight feet at the shoulder and stank like a trench, and it was not a bear. Harlan evidently had yet to realize this, for here he was saying "Hey bear!" breathlessly, lest their presence come as an unwelcome surprise.

It looked up abruptly. Its head, snakelike and bob-bing, was free of armature. Not a bull elk then, either, nor a steer. It was something much bigger, with a ragged outline and a webbed, periscoping head from which emanated now a long, malodorous belch. It shouldered a tree aside, thumped out into the open, and rushed them.

In the brief moment before Nora moved or was pushed out of its path, she looked up, up past legs and neck and a web of tackle and saw the black sockets and bared teeth of some screaming rider as the animal tore downhill. Then her hands clenched, something struck her in the ribs, and she and Harlan fell in separate directions.

When she sat up, the animal was rounding below. This angle made it look more familiar. Something about the slope of its shoulders, and the way its back swayed independently of its front. It turned back up the hill and rushed straight over the hole where Harlan lay. Then it lit into the treeline. For a long while, they could hear it thrashing around in the undergrowth. It was moving up and sideways, away from the path, away from the house.

"Harlan—are you kilt?"

"Not quite."

"What then?"

"I'm twisted up some."

She went over to him. He had dropped rather ridiculously down among the rocks and sat grasping his left leg. His trouser was darkening. A little ways up from him, Josie had fallen in a crumple of skirts and limbs that made her look like one of those twisted fair freaks whose parents folded them into tiny barrels to keep their joints from setting. Nora rolled her over and righted her. She came to once more, blinked around, and was gone again.

"What in God's hole," Harlan said.

"I don't know," she said. "There was a rider."

"A what?"

"A rider."

"Well fuck him, then."

Harlan was trying to stand. As soon as his foot met the ground, the knee buckled. He sat back down again.

They came now to a reckoning. He wanted to leave Josie here while they went up, and return for her with help. "No, please no," Nora said, shaking her head, and saw that he had merely been waiting for her to say it.

He tried the leg again. This time a black upwelling bloomed out and hurried down the cloth.

"I'll take her up," Nora said. "And then come back for you."

She gave him the gun and tried to lift the girl sideways, as he had. Josie's legs slipped and thumped on the ground. For a moment Nora imagined herself grappling with a bird of improbable size. How often had she called this very same child a goose? She caught the head and tried to work around the twisted arm. All this time, she had thought herself taller than Josie. It had certainly seemed so. But there was a good

six inches between them, with Nora at the dis-
advantage.

Harlan was staring her down with worried impatience. "Get rid of her skirts."

He slid down the boulder and began undoing Josie's
dress. Nora cradled the head between her knees,
watching the thin white frill of Josie's underthings
widen under the blue fabric, the little waist muddy
and broken. At the third button, she brushed away his
fingers. "Turn around." He swung both legs over the
boulder and sat with his back to her, wiping his hands
on his trousers.

Some of Josie's buttons were missing. Nora undid
the rest and pulled open the caked neck of the dress.
The shoulders gave her trouble, and for a moment
she thought she might have need of Harlan after all.
But then she stood and tried again from the opposite
direction: pulling, as in life, was easier. Having managed to secure one pale arm, she freed the other. Half
out of her dress, the girl looked like a split-open
seedpod. White ruffles fleeing a stiff casing. Evidence
of her previous mishaps met Nora's fingers: a huge
bee-sting; a razorwire cut Nora herself had sewn up
last summer. She didn't remember the gash being so
long. Its meandering stitchline surprised her. Could
such careless work be her own? She would disavow
it were it not for the clear memory of heating the
needle and assailing Josie to keep still, goddamn it,
when the thread pulled her flesh.

Standing back Nora dragged down the stubborn
morass of skirts. Josie's left shoe came off in the
effort, but the right foot was crooked and hopelessly
swollen, and Nora could not shift the boot even having unlaced it. Gathered up, the dress must have
weighed twenty pounds. She wrestled it down into
the scrub. From somewhere in the stiff tangle of
fabric, a hard weight met her hand.

The right pocket was empty. The left yielded a
small, four-pronged woodpiece—a buffalo, she realized. One of Rob's.

Fear of Toby had so stupefied her that she had failed
to consider Rob at all. **Well**, Evelyn said. **He loves her.**
It felt strange to know this now and realize still more
hazily that she had never imagined the woman Rob
might love. Or perhaps, in truth, had never imagined
that Rob would love a woman at all. Always in her
mind she had seen him a wanderer. Resigned herself
somehow to the fact that sporadic letters would take
his place in her home. All the love he might get in life
would have to be got before he crossed her threshold
toward those hard nights of road living and dimlit
Montana saloons and blue northern reaches. It had
weighed heavy on her, the inevitability of his solitude,
all the while without her realizing that some other life
had been possible for him.

And here she was, the girl Rob loved—sitting up
dazedly. "I'm helping."

"Lie still now."

"All right."

Before long, her eyes had guttered closed again. Nora dragged her upright and put her over her shoulder and started up.

What a trick it was of the darkness to sharpen inclines and soften the memory. She came through the trees and groped with her free hand along the canyon wall. The crumbling earth fled her fingers and showered, pattering, around her. She could hardly hear for the rustle of petticoats and thought now what a horror it would be to invite the beast's return—betrayed by the rustle of underwear. The scree slid under her and she fell a few times. Dropped Josie once. Her hands were stinging by the time she cleared the rise. There stood the house in its middle distance, still lit up with the jagged woods and the darker mesa rising behind. No sign of ambulatory bushes anywhere. She ran with the damp stickiness of Josie's body burning down her right shoulder. She imagined now how it would go with Toby: the terror and crying, the blame. She could not do it alone. She veered.

In the barn, she found a dry place and laid Josie down across the crates and covered her with a clean tarp that didn't smell too badly of anything. It took some shaking to bring her round again.

"I hurt awful," Josie said.

"Your head?"

"My leg. My shoulder. Everything."

"Lie put."

Scraping back down into the canyon, Nora sang a

little. "Caroline"—or some such ancient ditty whose words she couldn't remember. Harlan picked up the notes somewhere in the darkness below, and that was how she found him. He had managed to maneuver up through the trees a little, not very far, crutching his way from boulder to boulder.

"Can you stand?"

"Hardly."

When she got her shoulder under his, she could feel him shivering. They three-legged it the rest of the way, pausing now and then for him to catch his breath. She had not expected him to give her so much of his weight, though she could feel him trying to move it off her. He was lying, she realized, about how badly he was injured. A man didn't sweat from a little twist of the knee.

"I wish to God I'd been a better man than to ask you for that shave," he said quietly.

"I wish to God there were two stone of petticoats to lighten from you."

Side by side, they fit themselves into the mouth of the trail. The wall scraped her shoulders. Earth crumbled into her hair. An outcrop caught her knee, and the pain sang through her body so that she wanted to double over. Her mouth had split and she could feel the sting of sweat in its corners. Near the top, where the incline was steepest, she was obliged to fall back and push him like some stalled mule. She felt, then, that he did not sense how close she was to playing out.

At the top, they rested. The breeze had gone cool and the clouds had cleared. They went on again toward the house through the grass. About halfway over the field, she met the smoke wafting from their stovepipe and smelled charred meat.

Voices floated down to her. Emmett, she thought. Never mind her having to explain Josie's condition, or being under Harlan's arm in the dark—it was Emmett at last.

But as they came on, she saw no sign of the dray.

Instead, a horse she did not recognize was hitched up out front.

THE HOUSE WAS THICK WITH ROASTED air, the smell and sputter of meat frying. Twin skillets smoked on the stovetop. Toby was where she'd left him, still obediently in his chair, his face half-obscured now by a black rectangle he held pressed over both eyes. Though she had knocked down a stack of books bringing Harlan through the narrow corridor, he did not look up at their entrance. Neither did Gramma, who was at that moment sitting with her jaw all but unhinged to dispatch a hunk of beef, pink and dripping and speared on the end of a fork held by a stranger, a stout, dark-haired bull of a man who sat on the footstool before her. He looked up at them and stood, lowering the empty plate. He wore a striped gray suit and clean boots, and in all that heat his sunbrowned skin shone without a bead of sweat.

"Missus Lark. Sheriff." He smiled. "We were in a wonder over what had become of you."

Toby looked up. "Mama!" he said, and held the contraption out. "Look."

She shifted her shoulder under Harlan's slump. "What is it?"

"A streptoscope."

"Stereoscope."

"It's got pictures in it from all over the world." Nora made an appreciative noise, but Toby caught her pinched tone and looked worriedly at her. Then, panic-stricken: "**He** gave it to me."

"Don't point, Tobe."

"Well I don't know his name—he ain't said it."

"That's Mister Merrion Crace, honey."

"The limey carpetbagger?"

Crace was good enough not to let that sit too long before casting a smile her way. "It's far better than what I expected in this house, Missus Lark." He pointed the butt end of his fork at Harlan. "Best get that leg upraised, Sheriff. No matter how agreeable your present position."

She helped Harlan over to the table, and he steadied his boot up on the adjoining chair while she got the scissors to cut away his trousers. She was relieved to find the wound sieving only a little bit of blood now, most of it black already, save for the yellow shard of bone jutting ostentatiously from just below his knee.

Toby, still clutching the stereoscope, was torn between very different fascinations. "What's happened, Mama?"

"Nothing but a little stumble," Harlan said.

"Where's Josie?"

"Gone for the Doctor." It was no small thing, dispensing with his question so handily. That bill would come due soon enough, of course—but she weighed the balance and found it worthwhile, for the time being.

Crace meanwhile had wet a rag with whiskey, and was offering it to her. She was trying to find a way to ask him what he was doing in her house, but couldn't get around his fussing: there was something lodged in that wound, so where did she keep her styptics, her needle and thread, her pincers? When she did not reply, he brought a cup of flour and stood at her elbow, peering down while she wiped Harlan's blood away.

"That's bad now, but it ain't the worst," he said.

"I can feel something in it, right there," said Harlan.

"A rock, I'd say. Who pushed you?"

"I did," she said.

Crace grinned and nudged him. "Well, Sheriff. That'll teach you to forget yourself."

All the way up the stairs, she could still hear him. Even with the door closed. He was grating on about the weather, the crops, the outcome of that morning's altercation. You could always tell when Merrion Crace had arrived at a gathering. His consonants were just that bit too loud for any room. All day, she hadn't drunk and now the very last of her water would go toward dousing a wound. And all day, she hadn't eaten a thing, and now the smell of the steaks was overwhelming her. She wondered if she would be able to steady her hands. By the time she returned, Harlan and Crace were well into the whiskey. She got a small pot boiling and tonged pincers and knife in and out of roil and flame, water and flame. Gramma watched her, tonguetip protruding between her lips.

When it came time for the drawing, Crace did her the courtesy of getting out of her light. She could hear him behind her, rattling dishes.

"Come here to me lad—do you know how we come to call the English 'limeys'?" he asked Toby, who didn't. "In wayback days, English sailors were forced to eat limes to safeguard against scurvy."

"What's a scurvy?"

"A skin-bleed that twists you up and won't quit."

"Does it kill you?"

"It does indeed. You come here young man, and keep looking this way."

She could see the rock, black as a leech, sitting in the thick muscle below Harlan's knee. She put the tip of the pincers against it. His leg jolted, and his breathing caught like an uphill train. Behind her, Crace was shaking the pans, one at a time, loudly. More meat dropped onto the hissing iron.

Toby was still getting his head around the notion of scurvy. "How'd they take sick with it?"

"Because they were packed all tight together, with naught to eat for months but hardtack and jerked meat."

"Are **you** a sailor?"

He was not. He said so.

"But you're something," Toby decided. "You talk funny."

"We're all branded with the traces of our upbringing. Yours perhaps will be that eye. The kind of inevitable war wound that befalls a boy who grows up breaking horses. Now mine are a distaste for gloomy weather and these wonderfully rolled vestigial **R**'s."

"Like Coyle Williams!" Toby said.

"Another Englishman."

"Or John Johnson," Nora put in. "Yet another Englishman."

"Yet another Englishman—whose deeds are vilified in the public imagination."

The rock came out whole. It slipped from her pincers and she heard it clatter away somewhere under the table. Harlan eased the belt out from between his teeth and set about straightening the leg against a kitchen spoon she'd provided as a splint. Already, he looked improved. She poured him a whiskey, splashed and floured his leg. The blood gummed up in its white coating. When she turned to wipe her hands, Crace was looking at her, rolling an obscene pat of butter around the skillet. "Really, Missus Lark. From myself to John Johnson in the same sentence."

"I thought we were naming Englishmen. I really couldn't speak on whether or not the similarities between you stop at your vestigial **R**'s."

"They do."

"For all I know, they might extend to Johnson's tendency to decant howitzers into women and children."

"Surely that had less to do with his being English than with his collecting scalp bounty."

She tilted the whiskey bottle over one palm and then the other and dug under her nails with the kitchen towel. Her hands were still the color of thin tea. "I wouldn't presume to know."

"Is that right?" Crace had the huge, furrowed black eyes of a bloodhound, and he stood gazing woundedly at her. His voice was so soft she had hardly heard him, though he was as near her now as he had ever stood, and giving her a keen sense of his size and focus, and of how faraway Harlan really was—not just owing to the distance from the stove to the table, and the table to him, but his injury and the four generous whiskeys it had taken to numb him.

"If you've a yearning to disprove my opinion of you," she said, "you might find it in your heart now to ride for the Doctor."

Crace looked puzzled. "What a vote of no confidence in Miss Kincaid—she's not been gone an hour!"

Nora's stomach tumbled. Here was her lie, eating its tail. She muttered something about the dark, Josie's poor sense of direction, the wisdom of perhaps sending a second rider in case the Doctor was occupied. Already Toby was talking about the beast again—the beast, she thought! God's heaven what a cruel turn!—a few shrill syllables about everyone needing to stay put exactly where they were. Crace steered her back toward the table. "You've fixed the Sheriff up so handily. What's left for the Doc to do besides administer laudanum and change his dressings? Rest yourself now, and we'll have our supper while we wait for them. I reckon the Sheriff's up for something to settle his guts."

The moment she sat down, Toby was on her. He wanted to know how Josie would fare all alone out there in the dark—and when she wrangled him away he came back to her with the stereoscope. "Here, look." She gazed into its foggy interior. Toby changed the slides and grated on about what she was seeing: now the zoological gardens of Paris, now the Palace of Horticulture. And here was the great train station of Philadelphia! Before her eyes flashed blurry gray columns, webs of metal, glimpses of distant gardens. He showed her a preposterously tall animal, speckled with square blotches, and her mind had almost dredged up its name—what was it? Emmett had showed her something similar in a naturalist's handbook a lifetime ago, and suddenly it came to her, the name of that thing in the gulch. She said "camel" aloud—"camel!"— but Harlan didn't hear her. Toby looked inside, laughed, and said "Naw, Mama, that's a giraffe!" and slotted the next picture into the frame. He showed her a stone beast in the desert: it wore a square hat and lay buried to its shoulders in a velvety sandbank. Next came the lustrous, blank gaze of an enormous severed head. Beside its cheek sat a grim, dark-faced man, shawled head to toe and leaning against its nose. She kept saying, "I see." But all the while she thought **camel. Camel. Camel.** How could anyone have guessed?

Crace meanwhile was moving around her kitchen. Opening doors and laying out plates. Casting a suspicious eye over the smudged ends of her cutlery.

"I do the washing-up," Toby said helpfully.

"I believe it."

He eased steaks and drippings onto each of their plates. Three more remained in the pan. "Will we wait for your young men?"

At first, she did not know whom he meant.

Later—much later—she would remember that Harlan roused himself to say: "No."

They ate in silence. Toby as though he'd come forty days through the desert to get his hands on this huge, fat-rivered piece of rump. Harlan, ghost-pale, tilting uneasily at his red-puddled plate. Crace as though he were sitting at the Golden Hind, right in main-street Cheyenne, with an awed hush humming all around and the world's every lens trained on him. He finished in six smooth, symmetrical slices, and sat back smiling at Toby.

"Young man. What good fortune has the miraculous Josie foreordained to you?"

Toby got around his mouthful. "She don't tell fortunes."

"I thought she was a spiritualist."

"But she only talks to the dead. What she calls 'the other livin'."

"Ah." Crace lapsed into a long silence.

It had been a terrible mistake to leave Josie out there in the dark. Suppose she were headhurt. Suppose she sat up and started calling for them—wouldn't that take some explaining? Nora would have to find a pretext to go out there, and soon. The meat on her plate had begun to cool and resist her knife. She did not dare look up from it in this freighted interval. She half-expected Crace to turn Toby's way and say **Josie's broke in half, and all thanks to your mama**—though he could not know this, for there had been nobody else in the gulch to see it save the camel, and no one had been standing on the porch when she had come uphill with Josie on her shoulders. Nobody knew save herself and Harlan, and all the creekside eyes that cared nothing for life got or lost.

And the rider, Evelyn said.

The rider. She hazarded a glance at Crace. Is that where this shitheap of a day might lead—Merrion Crace, the architect of all her miseries, charging around in the dark on a camel like some phantom bandito? **That's your thirst talking, Mama.**

"Have you had milk, Toby?"

"We haven't any."

"You must have something."

"I ain't thirsty, Mama."

"I might drink some tomato," Nora said. She stood and split the top of a can and took two gulps of the reddish water. It stung going down, and stung coming halfway back, and stung still more going back down again. "Toby," she gasped. "You must have some."

"No Mama." Toby shook his head. "No."

Crace looked stupefied. "How unusual," he said. He held out his hand for the can and she gave it him, watched him grapple with what she hoped he would interpret as merely a strange domestic custom. She was fading in ways she had not expected, reeling at the edge of some precipitous place. She did not want him to know it. May two sips of tomato restore her.

"Can't say I care for it," Crace was saying. He slid the can back across the table to her. "You know, Toby, I never did meet a dead person who was all that eager for carrying on with talk," Crace said, as if their conversation had been ongoing all this while. "It's a wonder to me that Miss Josie can make a living from it."

"Josie talks to all sorts," Toby said. "There's a Navajo girl in the Simons' orchard what died a hundred years gone, back before there was oranges here at all. And in the square Josie met a gallows-hung fella who mistook her for his daughter." He grew excited. "And ourselves, we got a man in the springhouse right now. She calls him 'the lost man.'"

"The springhouse?" Crace said. "Goodness."

Nora had the eventual feeling that his refusal to meet her eye was deliberate. She crossed her knife and fork. "Well," she said with what she hoped was an air of conclusion. "It was mighty of you to bring supper."

It was his pleasure, his privilege. "Word round town is you been waiting on steaks."

"It's a lean week when word around town regards my larder."

Wedges of meat stung the gums between her molars. Crace apparently faced similar discomfort. He began picking the back of his mouth.

"Well," he said. " 'Around town' ain't a fair truth, really. More accurately: I was over at Desma Ruiz's earlier. And her failure to provide the promised steaks featured last among her many, many other regrets. So she sent these around—elk she said, but see here, where the skin is scorched? That's a brand. So it's likelier to be what you might call 'slow elk'— and probably one of mine." Crace went on, but she did not hear him. The beef had suspended in its slow, abrading drag down her gullet, and for a moment she thought it, too, would make a return as potentially calamitous as the tomato juice had. By the time this feeling eased, he had already turned in confidence to Harlan. "Did you know that Desma had a mother still living in Oklahoma? Ninety-four years old."

"God bless her," Harlan said. He was drunk.

"Imagine the stories she has to tell." Crace sat back and rubbed his thighs excitedly. "My own ma was only thirty when she died, and even her stories were enough to turn you inside out."

"Well she'd better sleep soundly tonight," Nora said.

"Who?"

"Desma." She paused. "If she doesn't—if something happens to her, for instance, slow elk or not—you would be the last person who saw her."

"I doubt that very much, Missus Lark. All kinds of people been riding up and down the Amargo Canyon Road these days."

"I know you been sending riders to her place to harry her."

"What a thing to say, Missus Lark."

"Like you sent somebody up here last night to drain every last bit of our water. Well. Desma better be alright. Because I'll swear before a judge to seeing you here, in front of the Sheriff, confessing you knew something about it."

"I ain't sent nobody to your water, Missus Lark." Crace looked appreciatively at Harlan. "And well— the Sheriff don't mind. Wouldn't be the first time he's heard or seen something that slipped his mind later on."

She caught Gramma's eye across the room. A slow, inner roil had furrowed the old woman's countenance. She was frowning, Nora realized. Frowning at Crace with her whole being.

Toby had gone quiet. Nora nudged him. "Well past bedtime, I think."

His look drifted from her to Crace and back again. He was stuck between his desire to witness whatever was now unfolding and the knowledge that such situations only ever resolved themselves in his absence. "Just a bit longer."

Bedtime, she said, but he went on sitting. And now Crace put a hand on his shoulder and said, "Let the young man stay. This concerns him, too. Perhaps more urgently than anyone."

In one swift motion, Gramma shot out a hand and seized Toby by the arm. It was quick as a viperstrike. So fast that Nora barely saw it, and perhaps might not have believed it had the hand withdrawn. But there they were: five thin, green-rivered fingers clasped around Toby's arm, and Gramma leaning halfway from the wheelchair. Not, as Nora thought for a moment, in a wild tumble from her seat, but holding herself up entirely by the strength of that grip while Toby looked down in delighted surprise, as though magic had left every other corner of the world and all gathered here.

He turned to Nora. "Mama," he said.

"I see."

Syllables roamed Gramma's throat. Mm-hm-n. Her mouth spasmed. Mm-hm-n. "Come along" was the intended gist.

Toby wrapped his fingers gently around hers and got up. His arm was around her, easing her slowly back into the chair. Her hand was still on him, her fingers ticking tenderly against the sunbrowned skin of his arm.

After he had gone, wheeling Gramma away before

him, the rest of them sat in wretched silence for a
long time. She was trying to think on how to extri-
cate herself to the barn when Crace said: "I hear you
ain't had the **Sentinel** running since your husband
up and went off."

"The boys are managing it."

"It must take considerably less manpower to print
up weather reports than falsehoods."

She grew irritated. "We don't print falsehoods."

"All right."

"What you read in our papers may not suit you,
Mister Crace. And God knows I've pled the case
round here for harder treading. But lies they are not."

He sat with this a moment. As though actually
considering what she had said.

"You ain't been printing much of late at all."

"There's no denying we're undermanned."

"And yet," he said. "That big Washington press
continues to nip at your pockets, day after day."

It was a burden they had carried a long time, she
told him. They were well used to it.

"It always did astound me. How people can commit to something that's fixed to just keep costing and
costing them more on top of its initial price. You
get the press, and that's debt enough to its previous
owner or whatever wiseman gouged you for it at its
last port of call. In your case, that bank in Flagstaff—
and all right, now you've bought yourself a printing
press! But then comes a joint to house it in. Men to

work the levers. Paper, ink. If you're serious about the endeavor at all, you're at twice the cost already, for every few months' work puts it in need of repair. Gears stick. Joints need greasing. Meanwhile, new and better presses keep getting made out in Chicago, and their leaves are flying at twice the speed of your own. And still you're bleeding money like a Sunday hog—but wait, now a roof leak! Or a broken window. Money lost and lost. Not to mention peace of mind."

"Well," she said. "I'm sure you know yourself, with the **Clarion**."

"Can't say my familiarity with the **Clarion** is too profound, Missus Lark. From what I understand, it's a paper in Ash River."

"It holds a mighty favorable view of you."

"Shouldn't somebody?"

He was looking at her. She wondered if she was meant to laugh. If this was his idea of a joke: to pretend that his stake in the **Ash River Clarion** hadn't turned it from a foundering camp rag to the hammer it was today. She could well remember the day he shored it up. Emmett had gone up to Ash River for the ribbon cutting. There was a picture of Merrion Crace and Bertrand Stills standing side by side, smiling, in Emmett's words, as though both of them might not make it to the outhouse in time.

"I imagine keeping cattle is no different," she said eventually. "You buy a heifer—but now you've got

to water and pasture her. Hire men to herd her.
Protect her from wolves. By and by she catches
blackleg and dies—and what did she ever do but
cost you from the day she came bawling into this
world?"

"That's a—that's a fair point," Harlan broke in
hazily. He was sweating like a choleric. She got a rag
and wiped his brow.

Crace was sitting forward with one arm slung
across the table. "There is a difference between newspapers and cattle," he said. "Cattle ain't like anything."

He sat back and waited. The right reply eluded
her. Cattle were like a great many things.

She was growing nervous now about Harlan.
She had gone so deep into the lie about Josie that she
had to remind herself that none of what was unfolding here could be blamed on the girl—as everything,
for months, had been. No: Josie was shivering in the
barn, her head lolling on a hopefully unbroken neck.
Doc Almenara was at home, asleep and unaware that
he was needed here. Nobody had gone for him.

"Unless you intend to murder the Sheriff by neglect,
Mister Crace, I believe it's high time now to go for
the Doc."

"Let's give Miss Kincaid another minute," said
Crace. She should tell him. Why not? Call a truce in
whatever inadvertent parley seemed to be simmering
here and say: I've left the girl in the barn so as not to
upset my son, but now you must be decent and go

for the Doctor. Crace would be a man of enough character for this. But true to himself, he had already started up again.

"My mother went to a fortuneteller once, you know. A real one back in London. Her people were shipyard folk, and she wasn't but sixteen when she married my father. So she went to a gypsy woman who was the succor of young mothers at the time and asked what was to become of the baby in her belly.

"The gypsy told her that if I didn't die by ten, I'd be a king. Imagine. A young girl, a dockman's daughter, hearing that kind of thing. Taking it at its most literal meaning. Coming home through those dark, narrow streets to my half-blind father and telling him: Albert, our son will be a king."

"MY FATHER—FOR ALL HIS FAULTS WITH whiskey and darts—was a gentle man. Easily swayed, eager to please my mother, for he was tender about the twenty-five years' gulf between them. He treated her always as though she had alighted by accident in his life, and hadn't yet realized it, and might fly away at any moment.

"They took the gypsy's soothsaying about my prospects real literal, the both of them. Even went so far as to tell people around town—which couldn't have helped their standing much, God love them. Just two mad Catholics walking up and down the docks, and me in the finest pram they could buy or steal, decked out as if I belonged to some other family. Ladies used to come up to my mother and ask her whose wet-nurse she was. That's how fine the pram looked. She never flinched. It wasn't in her to feel shame. Our son will be a king, my mother kept saying, and my father indulged her, though it surely earned him an earful in the pubs. When my brothers were born it was my old shoes they wore, and my ragged and outgrown jumpers. And all the while 'twas me in the new knits and caps, me in the polished shoes, me in the parks where the children of the gentry played because she'd got it into her head that the only way for a child of our standing to be a king was to marry a princess—and true and fair to her logic, she kept me in gentrified company. Her son, the king. When she died, I wasn't but nine years old—and it must have terrified her more than anything to think that with her went all the prospects of my future. For though my father loved her, he was an easy and unambitious man, and she could hardly fathom that he would rouse himself, alone now and saddled with four children, to keep after the future foretold for me. There were a lot of late nights at her bedside, I suspect. A lot of recapitulated promises.

"Nothing much came of them for some years, of course. My father was a teacher. By and by, we moved to a country parish—still further from my mother's onetime schemes. I was about twelve then, and feeling the weight of my brothers' hatred. They never forgave, as children do not, the fact that less esteem had come their way than mine. We fought like heathens. Came home black with mud and blood-clabber. Farmers who found us squalling in their barns dragged us home by our ears. Said: Albert, can't you do nothing about these monsters after all? My poor father—weeping at the hearth as he mended the clothes we had torn off each other's shoulders. He used to say he never remarried for want of there being, in all of Christendom, a woman so fine as my mother. But in truth I suspect Christendom was short a woman willing to brook such mongrel sons, even if the gentlest man who ever drew breath came in the bargain.

"At fourteen I was brought on as a groom for Lord Ellsworth, up in Devon. The kind of jobs gypsy folk were doing—and we hated each other handily, the gyps and I. They because I was better treated, and I because I had grown so ashamed of the 'king' business by that time—which my brothers never let me forget—and was happy to blame the people who'd lied to my poor dead mother for tenpence and a laugh.

"But we got on for the sake of the horses. What fine animals they were. The Lord stabled thirty, and people were always coming from upcountry to look at them and praise them and linger and ride. Ladies in such fine dresses, with such pretty faces, you'd be blinded if you stared for more than a minute.

"I never was much of a rider. Too firm in the thighs, people said—though in horsetalk, that just means fat. Is that a smile, Sheriff? You know well what I'm talking about.

"Lord Ellsworth was a fine enough man—so horsemad that if he got you in a corner, he could talk studs and hands all evening without drawing breath. But he liked the cards almost as much, and he liked the bottle too, and those things don't mix. When his fortunes began to falter he got to selling off his horses—which was how I came to find myself shipboard and Texas-bound, with a brood of mares he'd sold to a cattleman, Mister Sam Mulvaney. Duns and grays were the mares, and they didn't care for the water or the rolling or the other people on the ship. My father had gone to pieces ahead of the journey, for he'd lost brothers to America in years previous, and he knew what it could do to a young man. All of a sudden he fell thrall to my mother's wishes: remember, Merrion, he kept saying, remember America don't look too fondly on kings. No one's tried being king in America with any great success, remember that.

"I was to see the mares to Galveston and come straight home.

"But then—Texas, Missus Lark, in 1858. Christ, such a place. Whole swaths of nothing, and a smell of horses and rain, and a green-gray sky, and all the young blood of the world riled with talk of slavery and statehood and secession. I set my boot on that beach and knew I weren't going back across the water not ever again.

"I took up with all manner of folk. Prospectors bound for California. Enterprising men who were fixing to stake roads across the prairies. Weren't much point in committing to any one thing, so I drifted along. Worked in saloons and assayers' offices. Worked for the telegraph awhile. Wound up wheelwrighting in St. Joseph. Thenabouts Mister Sonny Asterfield brought me in to ride for the Pony Express. Ain't a more dangerous line of work in the whole world, son, he said. But if you make it through your first year, you'll have lived enough life for ten people.

"And ain't that the point of life, after all? To feel yourself living it?

"You all right there, Missus Lark? Someone at the door? I hope I'm not boring you. No?

"I was a year riding for them. You'd light out, one station to another, playing out horse after horse, riding so hard that every tooth in your head would rattle. Got through it mostly by thinking to myself: my mind's here, but my body ain't. My body has gone on ahead of me, and I am riding to catch up with it and get whole again. So when those Cheyenne or Crow would hove up out of the trees, I'd stare straight on and think to myself: there I am, in that cottonwood stand, or on that hilltop, or at the next waystation, and they, seeing only my ghost-self, would give up and fall behind.

"It was through that work I come to appreciate secrets. Every few nights, after I got done lancing saddlesores, I'd give myself the pleasure of opening just one letter from my mailbag. I'd spend hours choosing which. Looking at the penmanship on the envelope and asking the horse: Do we feel like a love letter tonight? Or more like 'news of the family'? I'd slit the letter near the top careful and hold it by the fire and read aloud. People were going about their lives here and wanting other people elsewheres to know all about it. John, your sister's on the mend. Sally, your mother and I are very happy for you.

Tim, your pa died yesterday—those were always the strangest. Knowing the truth of a life that weren't even your own. Poor Tim, somewhere ahead of me, living as if his pa was still on the right side of the grass. And me riding hard to bring him the truth—as if the whole dark of night were mantled out behind me, and this time, this firmament, was unbounded both forward and back.

"And then I would hand over my letters to the postmaster in San Francisco and go to a little place in Chinatown and sit myself with a pipe and think on it. Me, a vessel of other people's secrets. And people elsewhere living without knowing that their private lives were known to me. I used to dream about what it would be like to recognize someone from the letters on the street. I'd say: Charles, I carried a letter from your mistress. And wouldn't your wife like to know about that? A powerful feeling. A man who knows your secrets is a man who knows you whole—and nobody wants to think of themselves laid out entire before a stranger.

"I went away from that job feeling like I knew more of the world than was ever meant for one man.

"Fascinating is exactly what it was, Missus Lark. Yes, thank you.

"Exactly so.

"I might have gone my whole life in that line of work. But then came the telegraph, and afterwards the war, and I went north and hunted buffalo awhile. That was damned work. Mostly because the men drawn to it were mirthless and mad and cold, and it wasn't any kind of living sitting in some gloomy shack with your hands scalded by hot rifle-sides and dried blood in your nail-beds and hair.

"How you doing there, Sheriff? You look a little pale. Can't think what's keeping Miss Kincaid. I'll go for the Doctor in a minute now.

"Let me tell you what happened. When I came back down the Missouri in the winter of '65, the war was done in name alone. Militias were still in the hills, and people came pouring onto the plains with fresh urgency. Life itself had caved somewhere behind them, and there was nothing to do but walk the sage-flats till you came to either your death or something new. Of course with the Kiowa and Sioux and Comanche all rightfully livid, the former was far more likely. So many on the move that the army was throwing up forts along the Platte and the Yellowstone as fast as they could cut the timber. Fixing ferries and building bridges.

"I got the sense that everybody had found out what I had known for years: the West was too fine a promise to waste. They were heading there with their wagons and sheep and their trampling feet to make life that just bit harder and more crowded for folks like me who had known and kept this secret for years.

"It does that to you, you know. Like no place else. Does it to every man woman and child. The plains were fated to it the moment the first man hauled himself up a good hillock, took one look at the countryside unrolling in every direction, sucked in deep, and told himself that all was designated for his own, solitary soul. Told himself: the sublime lives here, and I am the only one who sees it.

"And thank God for that first bastard. Without him, we'd none of us be here.

"He should thank us too. We keep him alive.

"I hope the story ain't too boring, Missus Lark. I am just shy of my point, I promise.

"Anyway. I didn't know if there was still wilderness for people like me. I kept overhearing again and again the song of Texas. The war had orphaned thousands of cattle there, unbranded and unremarked. All a man had to do was herd them up and make them his own.

"That's what I did. So did dozens of others, but there was room and stock enough for us all. Ten men could ride into a pastureland in the morning and by midday be the stewards of a herd so vast, its endpoint could not be marked on the horizon.

"Once you had them, of course, you had to pasture them someplace. My old partner, Simon Velman— how he did press for Dakota Territory. Good grass up there. Good, mild summers. I knew well—I had seen it on my journeys. But in those days Red Cloud's Sioux were raiding up and down the Powder. I told him, if you want to die so bad, why not just hitch yourself to a rope, and I'll kick the chair out from under you so you can stand before the Good Lord and look Him in the eye and say truthfully that it weren't self-solution? It'd be gentler than having some Sioux wildman tear your arms off here and your legs off there, and string your prick on a necklace to give his kids.

"Apologies, ma'am.

"So we came southwest to the Mogollon. People told us: ain't no water, ain't no grass. And if you think the Sioux are bad, wait'll you meet the Apache. The whole place is just dizzy with Mexicans besides, and they been carrying on with the Indians every way imaginable for damn near two centuries now. Somedays they're marrying and swearing blood oaths. But then it goes sideways, and they're stampeding stock and snatching each other's children to raise up as their own, just out of spite, just as a fuck-you to their enemies—whom they'll be back to kissing and handshaking before the year is out, and all that slaughter for what?

"I tell you, there were days when we crept through the canyons without so much as a clink out of our tackle. Even the cattle knew not to breathe heavy.

"Simon Velman caught fever drinking from a muddy creek and it didn't take him three days to expire. That was a surprise, and it hurt me. Felt like maybe if we'd gone his way, he might have made it to see whatever pasture we fetched up on. But as with Moses, so with any Jew worth a damn. He never saw what he set out to see.

"And I went on. Just me and the steers and a few cowhands who were hungry enough, or didn't care which way their lives went, or were dead-set on out-running whatever wife or warrant loomed over them back east. This was where I renewed myself, Missus Lark. Riding with the cattle clinking along afore me and behind, nothing but yellow dust and horn. That sun was relentless save for when it got covered over by driving rain. It rained so hard sometimes that full rivers came tearing into the canyons, like they'd been switched on in whatever place underground all rivers sleep.

"You seem determined to get rid of me. I'm coming to my point, Missus Lark, and will go for the Doctor then, though it break poor Miss Kincaid's heart to meet me in the road and learn how little faith you have in her.

"My point is: nobody believed it could be done. But I did it. I got those cattle over the barrens and came here to the greenest pastures and bluest skies, and I laid down my walking staff—same as you. Before me, there was no Ash River: only a handful of tents on a hillside that had no name.

"You will argue with me, as your husband has, that you was all getting along just fine without me. Raising up your corn and wheat and losing your children to heatstroke.

"But before me, there was no **aguaje** where a traveler could water his horses. Before me there was no stage route, no postmaster, no sheriff, no stock association. There was nobody in Flagstaff gave a good goddamn about bringing law to this place. People rustling cattle and people falling down cliffs and calling both an accident.

"Before me, we were all the way inland.

"You don't get a railway in these parts unless there's cattle bound for Chicago. So if I say it's Ash River destined for that blessing, that's how it will go. For when the railway comes, it'll be my money christening it and my steers riding it.

"When the **Phoenix Sun** sent up a kid to report on men proving up this valley, it was me they found. Myself. And when they asked me what it was made me choose **this** place, I told them true: I knew that the eight months a year when this was the harshest scald on the face of God's earth would keep out everyone save the true and the good. I was pleased about it: the people who surrounded me were only the greatest and the best, baptized in sweat and blood. And we would share in our triumphs together, for they too had lost limbs and loved ones and sometimes even the edges of their minds. They too had overcome the harshest test a soul could face, and we shared in those struggles though we might never say a word about them to each other. We didn't need to. You could look a man in the eye and know. English, Negro, Slav, Mexican. Don't matter to me. We knew what it took to come home to this place, and we were for and with each other.

"But you can't have that with dissent. You can't have it with people clinging to a valley what's played out. You can't have it with every goddamn soul feeling free to divert a watercourse or build a fence, just because it please him. You can't have that with one side calling every poor man a saint, and every rustler a friend.

"You can't have it with Emmett Lark calling me 'limey carpetbagger' because it suits him to say it's me doing the wrong because I call the law and strike the beggars down.

"You can't have it with Desma Ruiz pleading seniority, or with you clutching to your house for it don't suit you to move thirty-five miles to Ash River, thankyouverymuch.

"I am mad with love of this earth and sky and water. It's mine, same as yours, and no fence you build and no letter you write to Washington will send me slinking with my tail tucked. It's my work that raised this place up. And I'll be damned if I'll sit here and let you say that I don't belong to it.

"But—you're a mother. If a gypsy had told you in the wayback days that your son would be king, even you would have hoped and willed it so.

"Even now, to think of my own mother receiving the **Sun** and opening it to find those words—'Merrion Crace: The Cattle King of Carter County.' I could weep just thinking about it.

"Perhaps that's why I came here myself tonight, Missus Lark, instead of sending my men as some think I should.

"Give me your hands. Don't worry, Sheriff Harlan don't mind. It'll do his heart good to get a little stab. Give me your hands. Lord, look at your fingers. It's like you tried to crawl out a grave. Are you much hurt? What will the Doctor think of us—disregarding your injuries to cosset the Sheriff here in his whinging and writhing over so small a thing as a broken leg?

"Missus Lark. Nora. I ask you to mark once more that I am here personally, free of associates, or any lawmen, because you **are** a mother—and doubtless love the very bones of your sons. They are young men still, and have a chance yet to be kings themselves.

"This morning's trouble need not be the death knell of that chance. In fact, I would prefer the opposite. I would prefer to think of this morning as the moment our friendly little rivalry burst its banks. Let us see it sink into the surrounding soil.

"To that end, I am here to treat with you. To offer sensibly on the easement of your burdens, in the hope that you will shake my hand.

"It has come to my attention that your husband's debts on the **Sentinel** press are considerable. Cost upon cost—as we said. Incalculable monies have surely been spent to keep it in good repair. With your blessing, I would like to settle that account for you, tonight, once and for all. To the tune of, say, three thousand dollars.

"The machine's true worth makes fuck-all difference to me—I'm sure the balance will spend in time.

"I make this offer on the condition that you put the **Sentinel** to rest. You need not remand it to my people, or destroy it, or indeed even remove it from your store. On the contrary. It would please me most if you revised its career as an instrument for printing announcements and placards. Perhaps even books, someday.

"Anything but the so-called newspaper. That should be left to more well-equipped folk in Ash River, who are closer to the truth.

"Consider this a gift of freedom, if you will, in the grand tradition: I am not buying your press, but liberating it from the bondage of **The Amargo Sentinel**. Let it turn instead to more leisurely and pleasant pursuits, and spread no more lies about me and steer no more good Amargo folks from progress toward better things.

"And we will consider all our past disagreements settled, and this morning's unpleasantness square."

AFTER A WHILE, HE TURNED TO HARLAN. "I see she's got no notion of what I'm talking about."

Crace had managed to roll up his sleeves and shed his suspenders and hang his coat off the back of his chair. His hands had grown warm around her fingers. She was beginning to suspect that by now, two shallow, even holes had bored down where his elbows rested on the table, and that tendrils of new mesquite had begun to coil about his ankles and probably her own, and that Harlan's leg had gone sour and Josie—poor, poor Josie—would at any moment come staggering through the door with an accusatory look, unless she had already given up and gone to God. For who could blame her? This was what happened when somebody like Merrion Crace got going—for they all had stories, didn't they, just like this, interminable and essential to the world's workings. This was what she had been thinking when he began to talk about the morning, and the morning's unpleasantness, and some part of her, half-hearing, had assumed he meant the incident with Ferdy Kostic at Desma's.

But no aspect of that matter would cause Harlan to look as he did now, perched at the very edge of his chair and staring down at the floor.

"You been here how long?" Crace asked him. "And ain't told her yet."

"I was fixing to, in my own course."

"For a man who's so dead-set on delivering news personally, you sure take your fucking time."

Harlan looked at her. "There was a dust-up this morning at the Sanchez ranch."

Crace snorted. "Dust-up."

"An ambuscade. Two men with dogs put down Pedro Sanchez and his brothers. By the time I got to the field cabin, they was all kilt save Pedro himself. Do you know him?" She did not. "Before he died, God rest him, he counted his killers by name."

"What a stroke of luck," she said. A strange cold shake had crept from her toes and up her calf. Her knee was jumping a little, and she feared the movement might keep advancing up and through her until her whole body rattled like cane. A nail on the underside of the table was digging into her knee.

"So I must ask you once more, Nora: do you know where your boys are?"

"In Prescott."

"When did you last see them?"

"Last night—as I said."

"So you can't be certain." The effort of sitting up further twisted his face. She could tell by the way his leg lolled on the chair that all the feeling had left it.

Perhaps his toes had gone blue. They might be blackening already. "If I were to scour every inch of your place. Look under the floorboards and in the springhouse. There'd be no trace of Rob or Dolan?"

The realization, now, of what all his earlier prowling had been toward pushed that cold feeling further up her body. "Well I reckon if you haven't found trace of them in the many, many hours you been pretending to be here on a social call, Harlan, you won't find them now." She had the sudden urge to kick the chair out from under him and send all that blood thudding back to his leg. "I take it Pedro Sanchez mentioned my sons."

"By name."

"Mighty convenient. Almost takes the sport out of your work."

"I'd rather it didn't," Harlan admitted. "And I wish I could tell you Pedro was dead when I got there, and it was some third party said Rob and Dolan's names to me, for I know you're hoping it was so. But I was there myself, Nora. I heard him say it."

"What a use of his last breath," she said. "To waste it on a fucking lie." He sat and watched her. He had come fully sober again, sober enough to wipe the sweat from his own eyes anyway. "They'd never do such a thing," Nora said.

"Would they not? They been all over the county every damn day accusing everybody who looks at them sideways of killing their father." He pointed to the hallway. "Didn't you just get done telling me how Dolan punched through the door last night—because he thought Emmett was kilt, and the Sanchez brothers to blame?"

"Had I known what you were after, I would never have told you so," she said. "I wouldn't have let you within a mile of the place."

"No," Crace put it. "But for lending a considerate ear, it seems the Sheriff **did** get a mighty close shave."

She thought of the shave—the talk, the precious hour wasted, Josie in the ditch with her shoulder torn out and her ankle twisted back, for what? a vestige of some belly-flutter, some reduction of loneliness nobody should ever admit needing—and that reliable Volk rage came roaring. She turned to Crace. "Why are **you** here?" she asked. "If there's truth to any of this, it don't concern anyone save my sons and the law, with the possible exception of Pedro Sanchez's widow."

"I rode point ten years with Pedro. The dead have a right to be spoken for."

"May we all leave such a friend in this world—someone who'll use our blood to bargain for the decommission of a weekly newspaper."

Crace bit back a smile. "Pedro wasn't the kind of man who asked terms. He knew that whatever is done is done for the good of all."

"Nora." Harlan sat forward and leaned across the table toward her. "If Rob and Dolan run off now—if they don't come forward and admit themselves to the law—they'll be wanted men."

"But if they confess to something they did not do, and I decommission my printing press—they can come home?"

He looked at Crace. "If they come forward and make a full confession, we can begin to talk about settling the matter peaceably."

She sat back. "You know, Harlan, when people kept on about how you were in Merrion Crace's pocket, I laughed them out of my house. You might have started by telling me all this the moment you set foot at my door. Before the printing press came into it."

For the first time, she saw anger in his face. "I was working up to it, Nora. It don't come easy to tell a—friend that her boys are outlawing themselves while she sits at home waiting for them. But then I was felled in the gulch."

They sat now in a silence so wretched she could hardly find her breath. Air came to her in little bursts. She could not remember how it felt to draw deep breath. Poor Josie, she thought. Breathing through broken ribs in the barn.

"I tell you what," she said. "How about, instead, I wire every soul I know in Cumberland what was said here. And when Emmett gets back, he prints a full recapitulation of every detail—including that the Sheriff, in the midst of reelection, attempted to coerce a defenseless mother to force her sons to confess a crime they didn't commit?"

"Foremost," Crace said, "calling you defenseless would be a singular joke. And second: I doubt that

Mister Lark will have much to say about this situation. Busy as he is in California."

"California?"

What now? Crace was lifting his coat from the back of the chair and feeling around in the pockets. He would've been faster getting flake out of a vein. From some deep inner pocket, he finally extracted a square of yellow paper, and unfolded it with exaggerated ceremony. His spectacles soon followed it out of the coat, and she sat in silence, watching him adjust them on the bridge of his nose.

"This is a letter," he said, "from Mister Emmett Lark, formerly of Amargo, Arizona Territory, received by the **Ash River Clarion** two days ago and set for printing in their next issue."

He read it aloud to her, and she sat there picturing the words. "Dear Mister Bertrand Stills. I thank you kindly for your letter of last month, to which I have not had the opportunity to respond owing to the journey I have lately made to the town of Los Angeles, California. Perhaps you may be aware of Mister Merrion Crace's intention to assemble a county council to begin remedying some of the difficulties of these past few redoubtable months in Ash River and the surrounding areas. Though I would be honored to accept Mister Crace's offer to chair such an assembly, I feel it is my duty to inform you that I hope to make the excursion I am currently undertaking a permanent one. While I will be back and forth every so often to Amargo in the coming years to make arrangements for my family to join me, I feel that my withdrawal from the community will leave me inadequately informed to decide on the important issues at stake. I would be grateful if you would do me the honor of taking my place on the council. I await your answer eagerly in Los Angeles. Yours respectfully, Emmett Seward Lark."

"My husband didn't write that," she said.

"It says right here that he did, Missus Lark."

But her mind had come to rest on the bulbous contours of that familiar word.

"I wonder if you can tell me what the word 'redoubtable' means?"

"Pardon?"

" 'Redoubtable.' What does it mean?"

"Why—it means dubious, I believe. Or full of strife."

"Whoever wrote this letter may not know what it means, Mister Crace, but my husband certainly does. You never made such an offer to him. And he didn't write that."

"All the same, it bears his ink."

He held the page out to her. It was typewritten, and scrawled at the bottom below Emmett's respects were a looping signature and the stiffly scratched initials ESL.

"If Emmett signed this, I am Libbie Custer."

"Really?" Crace sat back with his chin in his hands. "If only we had something for comparison. If only we had—I tell you what." He laid his fingertips on her hand. "If only we had the letter he wrote me **last month**. The one outlining his sincere promises that, owing to certain compromising facts I admitted to knowing about his wife, his newspaper would never actively campaign against moving the county seat. Now of course, the **Sentinel** reneged on those promises by publishing the work of Ellen Francis—so one might call both Mister Lark's word and signature worthless. And I doubt that anyone here cares to relive the unpleasantness of the details contained in my exchange with Mister Lark—a child's death and so on—especially given how unsurprised Emmett seemed to hear what I had to say. Almost as though he knew it already. But fortunately for our purposes here tonight, that letter can continue to remain a rumor. As was Mister Lark's trip to Cumberland for water, it seems. For here he is"—he patted the paper—"in California, after all."

The sudden exhaustion that moved into her now was familiar. She had felt it before, standing on the street in Cheyenne and watching the whole street burn and telling herself, don't worry, when this is all over you can get some rest at home, and realizing in a rush of darkness that no, she could not—for here was home, on fire like everything else, and what she wanted, among so many other things, was now impossible.

Papa's dead, Evelyn said. **He's dead, and he's been dead, and you're the only one who hasn't known it.**

How strange to know it so suddenly. Perhaps at

one time there had been opportunity to learn it, grow used to it, but that was all past now. She felt as though she'd stepped into a field camp only to find it deserted and realize that all the people she had been expecting to see there had already moved on. Rob, Dolan, Toby, Desma, even Josie—their sign lay all around her in the trampled grass, but she could not tell how long they had been gone, or where to, or how far behind them she was. They might be days away, years. Perhaps she might never catch up. Beyond lay the dark: flat and unrelenting, unpeopled, absolute. Somehow it would drain her out of herself, while at once crushing in all around her. She had seen it before, but could not remember the way back from it. But then—there, just on the other side, a single lamp at the window. A gravel drive and a massif of slanted roofs; her own footsteps on the boards, and here she was—at the hearth of her rage. It was still here. She had grown up in it, let it contain her all her life, and she knew it, its margins and oddities. She was still herself, after all.

She pressed a hand to her chin to still it. "California really must be as miraculous a place as folks say," she managed. "If the dead can write letters to the living from there in an entirely new hand. For he is dead, my husband—no matter what that letter says."

"Is he?" Crace turned to Harlan. "You found any evidence of that, Sheriff?" Harlan sat, white-knuckling his kneecap, and did not reply. "You found a wagon? A bloodtrail, a riderless horse?

Anything at all to invite the butchery those boys visited on my men this morning?"

"I found nothing," Harlan said. "You know damn well."

It required looking right at him to keep herself from crying, even if her gaze went unreturned.

"Now, Missus Lark. You mustn't be too hard on our good Sheriff. Men with bleak pasts in Charlesburg and Dodge City don't often rise to hold office. And they certainly don't get reelected. Men who know how to proof a wrecked little adobe cell against jailbreak because they've broken out of so many jails themselves are useful. But they don't need the provenance of their skills shouted from the rooftops in an election year." He smiled at her. "But you know that already. Of course. There are no secrets between you and the Sheriff."

Harlan made a sudden, flimsy show of standing up, but Crace's fist came down on the bad knee. Some very distant part of her was amazed by the simple efficacy of this—but in truth she watched as though it was happening elsewhere, to people she did not know, as though the Harlan now sinking back with his face drained of all blood were a stranger.

Crace went on. "You know who else keeps a man's secrets?" he said. "His wife. A funny thing, matrimony. Never found much solace in it personally, but I'm given to understand that it supersedes everything of consequence—pasts, friendships. Not in perpetuity, of course, which is what makes it so dangerous. For the end of such a union turns each spouse into a vault of the other's secrets. A kind of unopened letter, if you will, waiting for the right reader. Sometimes, the release of its contents is motivated by money. But often, if the heartbreak is profound, spite is plenty enough. For nothing injures the soul quite like infidelity. Even the uncon-summated kind. Perhaps especially so. Imagine then, the injury of the wife of a man who cannot mask his love for some other married woman." Harlan was saying something—her name. She could hardly hear him from whatever thick place had swallowed up her hearing. "Imagine how necessarily such a wife might unburden herself to a confidante. A handmaid, for instance—and how that same handmaid might unburden herself to strangers, at home and abroad, who care enough to keep buy-ing her whiskey and letting her talk. Think of the things she might say: 'God, but our Sheriff was so enthralled to that Arizona shrew—he wouldn't leave off about her. He felt sorry for her. He felt she was some poor thing needed rescuing, for wasn't she already a half-broken soul, carrying around the burden of having kilt her own child? Had the whole town believing it happened because she was hiding from Indians—but wasn't she just fool enough not to be able to tell the difference between an Apache brave and poor Armando Cortez, who was only riding over with—what was it? A loaf of bread? My God. Can you imagine such a terrible thing?'"

He stood and picked up his coat. "So, Missus Lark. If you intended to say that the Sheriff will hold up your side of these matters—well. I hope I've put any such notions to rest." He nodded a little. "I'll ride for the Doctor now."

"How did my husband die?"

"What an absurd thing to say—he is in California."

"I'd like to know."

"Suppose he **was** dead—of what use would the details be to you?" Crace took his hat off the peg by the door. "I was at my father's side when he passed, some twenty years gone. And I was alight with all my worries and fears. Was he cold? Could he feel his own pain? Did he think of me? Of my brothers, my mother? Was he, in his final moments, the person I remembered, or just a garble of thoughts all drawn together from odd corners of his mind?" He shrugged into his coat and straightened out his collar. "Save for the sense of having fulfilled my obligation to sit with him, I gleaned not one satisfactory answer to any of my questions."

"You fulfilled your obligation, at least."

"Depending on your point of view—yours being that the Sanchez brothers were responsible for your husband's death—you might very well say that your sons have fulfilled theirs."

"What about my obligation, Mister Crace?"

"That remains to be seen. You have an opportunity

now to decide where your obligations lie." He held out his hand. "Believe me, Missus Lark, it is my sincerest wish to face no further strife from this house." His hand was warm, and not unpleasant. The edges of his face held the faintest trace of resignation, as if the two of them had committed some grand crime together and were reminiscing about it one last time before going their whole lives without ever seeing each other again. Of all the times she had been menaced by men, she had never felt so pointedly like one herself. "My offer stands. That I've made it at all, given the many ways I could bring you ruin, shows at least some of the esteem in which I hold you. I said as much to your husband: I am under no illusion about the kind of fight you might put up, but a fight is not what I'm after. I do not wish to besmirch you with talk of your dead child. I'll tell you this, Missus Lark: I was surprised to find Emmett so **un**surprised. To find he already knew what I had to say about your little girl. So I beg you to consider. If you refuse, all you've lost will have been for nothing. Your boys will be hunted up and down this country all their days. You'll have only the one little lad left. We all know how dangerous it is to be down to just one. And he was so keen on the stereographs—even if he only could see down one side of them. I reckon he'd relish the chance to see some of those sights with his own eyes, in time." Crace didn't say ma'am, and he didn't tip his hat. It was honest, at least. He called into the kitchen. "Come along, Sheriff."

For a long while afterward, she could hear Crace readying the horses in the dark outside. Harlan got himself to his feet and stood braced against the table. He was just about managing to look at her again. But he wasn't moving. Did he expect her to come round and help him?

"I meant to tell you straightaway," was what he said. "About this morning, I meant to tell you. Took a moment too long to get to it, is all."

How strange, she thought. She had hooked into a heightened order of sensations along what felt like every lateral—she was aware of the ball of her foot, for a pebble or similar entity was goading her through the sole of her right boot, in and of itself already paining across the toes because she had spent the entirety of this hot, wretched, bewildering day in gift boots she had not wanted to admit to Emmett were too small; she was keenly aware of her thirst, of course, so matter-of-fact now that it was hardly worth noting, but there all the same, always and irrepressibly there; she was aware, too, of a growing discomfort in her stomach, not pain, but something that might turn eventually to it, for the steak was not sitting well in the wake of this rather turbulent supper; she was aware of the sweat cooling beneath her armpits and hair and of the smell of rancid fat off the pans that would linger, probably, for days. What a remarkable thing of one human body to receive all these simultaneous impressions, and be able to center on each alone, and all at once.

And how strange that a body capable of such feeling might now make no association between the man standing before her and the words coming out of his mouth. They might well be the last she would ever hear from him, and they were about Josie.

Josie.

He would make sure the Doctor came for Josie.

"It ain't true I felt sorry for you," Harlan went on. "I never said a thing like that. Not to anybody. I never did."

Then he braced himself to the door and went outside.

Crace was a while getting Harlan mounted up, and a while after that getting them both from the wan light of the open door to a distance from which she could only hear their horses moving through the grass. She stood in the doorway while they loped past all of Toby's little rock towers: twenty yards at the corral; thirty at the barn. She might be able to hit Crace, even in the dark, as far off as fifty yards, with at least enough accuracy to bring him out of the saddle. The rest would have to be done point-blank.

She went for the shotgun behind the door. But having it to hand was one thing; raising it another entirely.

If she raised it, she would probably fire. She knew herself enough to feel certain of this. But what then? Crace would fall, pulling the horse down with him. Roll onto his belly or crawl for cover and return fire from the bushes. If she wasn't killed right off, she would eventually hit him—even with Harlan backing him, which might easily happen, for who knew what haunts slunk through Harlan's life, what deals and debts bound him? But she would be killed.

And who the hell would back Nora in such a gunfight? Toby, from some upstairs window? Josie, with legions of the dead at her command? Or would it be Gramma, perhaps? Wouldn't that be a dose now: to realize after all this time that the old lady couldn't merely wheel herself about and grip arms, but handle a rifle, probably better than the rest of them combined? She might as well be capable of flight.

Perhaps it was worth seeing.

But then, Nora knew, the cool draft of regret would go through her, as it always managed to one way or another. Even if she survived, how would she get on, dragging Crace's corpse into the gulch, or burning it, or burying it, and then battening down for retribution? Perhaps Harlan would take her directly to jail, from whence Crace's men would drag her some night before week's end and string her up, probably next to Desma, if Desma wasn't swinging already thanks to that slow elk, and the two of them would hang there with their boot buckles shining in the torchlight and be called madwomen and whores to their children's children.

What if she missed? Merrion Crace would wheel his horse and come back shooting. And all his men, probably dotted throughout the bushes, would mount up and back him.

And if she let him ride away? What then? In the barn lay Josie, improbable survivor—hopefully, still—of an ordeal that seemed, even now, to have happened such a very long time ago. Upstairs, sweaty and dream-tossed, Toby was growing hair more slowly than anyone she'd ever known. Somewhere her other sons were camping by firelight. Passing the whiskey bottle. Taking turns at the watch. They were thinking about what they'd done—the lives taken. The lives avenged. Emmett's hothead heritors. Her killer sons. They were thinking about their father. Thinking about her, in this house, imagining her asleep. Perhaps even some of the dogs were with them still. She pictured the old lusty one, resting its gray head on Dolan's boot by the fire—improbable, she thought, for even the elation of surviving a gun-fight could not have moved that ancient cur to keep pace with fleeing horsemen. For that's what her sons were on this, their first night as outlaws—and what they might yet be for the rest of their days. Rob and Dolan Lark. Fodder for some future boy's dime novel dreams.

Ah, it's a pity, Mama. But I guess it can't be helped.

Indians, she had said after Evelyn died. Five of them, on horseback. She had repeated it, and kept on repeating it, even after Emmett, with a few of the neighbors, rode out and found no such trail. Five of them, she said. Apache. She was certain of it. She could tell. She knew. Otherwise she would not have hidden in the field for so long, lying flat under that boiling sun, praying they wouldn't set the whole place ablaze.

She had left it up to Doc Almenara to explain the rest to those who cared to know: little by little, the baby girl had grown overheated. Eventually, she sun-drowned.

It had been summer. Their first house just about built. Emmett was gone somewhere, driving the flock. Evelyn was sleeping in a bindle between her breasts while Nora ferried water back and forth to the house, keenly aware of her solitude, watching the horizon, when a rider came up over the ridge. Just one man. A dark rider on a spotted horse. There was no road in those days for him to come by, only the twisted, ungovernable brush of the mesa through which she glimpsed leather and mottled horseflesh. Dark rider. Spotted horse. She thought **Apache** because the word had been growing in her like an illness all her life, but especially since the cavalry had raided that rancheria about a month back, and word of their doings had drifted to town with all the usual directness: buffalo fat and a bonfire that climbed and whistled and singed even the edges of the dead While her neighbors mulled over when and upon whom the Apache would visit retribution, so swift and so very disproportionate, Nora had sat quietly and thought: disproportionate? I'd do it to you, too. Your tongue and your eyes. Your guts pulled out in streamers, if it were my children cut down and left to dry in the sun.

And still she had chastened that woman. That old, ordinary woman who wanted nothing more than to hold her baby, smell Evelyn's milky breath and kiss the fat little knuckles, perhaps because her own children had been cut down in some Apache camp, long ago or yesterday. Still she had chastened her. Why had she lacked the fullness of heart to let her hold the baby, just for a while?

When she saw the rider there on that pinto, Nora thought she had stumbled into a death foretold to her every day of her life. This was what happened to unbounded people. This was what the evening contained. Her blood lurched and went thin in her.

She was in the field, running through the long grass, running till she went flat on the ground under that boiling sun. Eyelevel on the hot dirt with the yellow bones of a mouse or vole. Evelyn's breath was warm and quick on her neck, until all that surrounded her was the sound of those small gasps growing faster and faster. Whimpers every now and again—but somehow, inexplicably, miraculously, never cries, though she pulled her skirt up and over her to make sure no sound escaped that depression in the earth where they lay. Eventual hooves in the distance, somewhere near the house. A man calling hullo hullo hullo—in English, she'd realized, to lure her out, deceive her into showing herself. Hullo hullo hullo, in a voice she did not recognize because she was wild with terror and imagination.

By the time he had gone, Nora's eyes were bloodshot with the sun, and Evelyn was hot and fretful. Asleep already.

Her fever had not broken by the time Emmett returned, nor by the following morning. When Doc Almenara called around, he undressed her and held her on one arm in a basin of cold water and smoothed droplets around her neck and over the little tufts of hair she had begun growing. Nora was not allowed to touch her save to do the same. In her final hours, though her skin was a furnace, Evelyn had looked herself. The grim little face and the clenched fists, still and always in a huff.

Two days, or a thousand years later, they buried Evelyn on the hill behind the house.

And the women from town started coming around with their pies and their empty regrets and, when they judged enough time had passed for such a thing to be deemed acceptable, their questions. What happened? What happened, Nora?

She'd had to hide. She'd had to keep still.

There had been Indians. Five of them. Apache.

Then in October, Armando Cortez came to pay his respects. He was holding Nora's hand when he said, "My God, if I had only known what trouble was coming your way. If only I'd known to ride out a little later—not when I did. I mighta found you home. I mighta been there."

And then she understood. A dark man on a pinto. Not an Apache at all, but this man, this man here, who now stood weeping into her hand. He had little girls of his own, and was imagining himself at their graveside. She was imagining it, too. Wishing fiercely for it.

If it hadn't been for Emmett, whom she loved, she would have tied herself a noose that same afternoon. And the next. What had the women of her youth called it? Self-solution. She thought of it whenever visitors left her alone and the house sat empty, or her husband gently put down any talk of going home, going wherever the evening wasn't, to Iowa, or any other place where children did not boil in their own skins. Whenever Armando visited thereafter—and he came often, because he now lived a part of his own life in her lie, lived day after day counting the cost of his decision to venture out on his innocent errand a little too early, a little too late.

Sometimes she wanted to tell him. Release him of the burden of believing his fate was so horribly tethered to hers. Instead, she kept saying only: Indians. Five of them. Apache. Of course she was certain of it. Of course she knew.

She knew, and was believed more absolutely about this than she had ever been about anything before. A liar after all. And the lie, so easy in its time, a kind of evening in and of itself, was carried forward. Out it went, in the mouths and minds of women and freighters and soldiers, to some unknown amalgam of harm, a greater evening, so vast, so abundant, that every now and again, when she thought about it, she could convince herself it must be something else. How could there be so much of something so evidently poisonous?

"Do you think any other people came to harm because of what I said?" she asked Harlan, when she finally told him the truth entire.

His gaze toward her, unchanged by her admission, was full of faith and love. "No," he said. "No, I don't think so. No, of course not."

Well. Here was her lie already begetting another. One need look no further than Armando Cortez's slow fall into terror to know it wasn't true.

And elsewhere, further abroad? She shuddered to think of it. Luckily, most days, she had managed not to.

So take the water and take the land. Take the years they had built here together. Take Desma Ruiz and the Doctor and Josie. But my God, she thought—this is the house where my daughter lives. What if her entire being is tethered here, and forbids me to leave? And if I go—what if I never hear her again?

＊

IT'S COMING UP ON DAYBREAK, MAMA.

Looks like it might be fixing to rain.

I do wish you'd put that gun down, Mama, and check on poor Josie before Toby wakes up.

You know I only told Harlan the truth of what happened because poor Armando Cortez was going to pieces. And I was too damn flimsy to carry the weight of my doings on my own.

I know.

It was wrong enough to cost my child's life for being a coward and a fool. But being a coward twice over—too much a coward to admit I had been cowardly. That damn near drove me mad.

I know, Mama.

And your father couldn't be told, of course. A man has the right to live protected from some heartbreaks.

But he knew, it seems. He knew and loved you just the same.

Don't that just beat all.

I don't know, Mama. I always thought it evident enough, in a way.

I never dreamed Harlan would tell another soul.

That ain't the truth, now, in fairness. It kept you up nights when you first got word of his wedding. You were jealous all right—but not near so jealous as afraid that all your secrets would out.

Well. Suddenly there was someone for him to tell them to.

But then you thought about all the things you don't tell Papa, and it seemed reasonable enough to feature that everybody keeps some part of themselves hid away. Even from their beloveds.

I thought he wouldn't tell a soul.

We were both wrong, I guess. Put that down for a rare curiosity!

I don't mind people knowing about me so much, Evelyn. Knowing that I was so wretched and afraid that the sight of a mestizo on a horse scared me half to death. When it was only poor Armando coming with some bread and a story. I don't mind them talking about me, darling. They do anyway. But I do mind them talking about you. Like you're some poor wandering soul who had the misfortune of being born to a mad mother. I don't want you known that way.

It don't matter to me.

This is how I know you're not a real spirit.

How, Mama?

You're good to me—disproportionate to what I've earned by you. Every which way I go wrong, you forgive. Real spirits don't. Neither do real children.

I guess you're right.

I know I am.

You know what Rob and Dolan wouldn't forgive?
You giving up the Sentinel **to get them cleared of**
avenging Papa.

Don't care if they forgive that. I care that they don't
spend their lives running from the law. Sleeping in
caves and catching bullets.

I guess if they get wind of how you gained their
pardon, they won't much care to come back.

That doesn't matter to me.

I guess in a way it don't matter what you want.
They made their sacrifice. It'll be a worse betrayal of
them to give up the Sentinel **and pretend Papa ran**
away to California. Imagine them forgiving that!

What choice do I have?

You could take the Doc up on his offer.

And then what?

Leave and pray you find each other, I guess.

And you? If I leave here—will you come with me?
Or will you have to stay?

*

JUST AFTER DAWN JOSIE CAME AROUND
once more. "I'm so thirsty."

"It'll have to be tomato, I'm afraid." She propped
Josie's head up, and the girl drank obediently. One
of her eyes was bloodshot, the other purple and more
or less swollen shut. But both looked straight ahead
in unison when Nora asked her to follow her finger.
"I don't think you're headhurt, thank God."

"It was the beast, ma'am."

"I know, honey. I saw." She found the buffalo
carving in her pocket and closed the girl's hand
around it. "The Doc is on his way. I only left you out
here so as not to upset Toby."

"That's good, ma'am. I'm glad of it. I wouldn't like
him to be upset."

"I know. Are you cold?" Josie wasn't. She continued
to hold Nora's hand. After a while, Nora said,
"Emmett's among the other living now." The girl's
eyes didn't open. She was listening. "Killed up at the
Sanchez place, I believe, just as the boys said. On
Merrion Crace's orders."

"I'm that sorry ma'am. I am that sorry. I'd hoped it wasn't so."

"Perhaps when you're well again, we might sit down with Emmett, you and I. I've some things left to say to him."

The girl squeezed her hand. "Someone's here now, you know." She smiled. "He sat with me down by the creek, talking till you came. But it ain't Mister Lark. It's the lost man. He's right beside you."

It would be stupid to look around, Nora thought, but she did it anyway. No one was there. "He's got his hand on your shoulder."

"I feel it," she said. She felt nothing, of course. She turned Josie's hand over and tried to scrape the dirt out from beneath her nails. "When we get the water in, I'll fix you a proper bath. Are you cold now?"

"No, ma'am."

She brought the girl another blanket all the same and then went back inside. There was still no sign of the Doc. The edges of the mountains were just beginning to drink up the light. It rained uselessly a little east of them, and then the clouds moved over and made clear a beautiful morning.

When Toby emerged, wheeling Gramma, Nora woke uneasily in the chair. "Why haven't you lit the fire, Mama?"

"I fell asleep."

"Where's Josie?"

"Still at the doctor's."

"Where's the men?"

"They're all gone."

He stood beside her with that worried look, stroking her arm. She couldn't lift her head from her fingers.

"Did you see Gramma move?"

"I did indeed."

"I knew you would," he said. There was no triumph in his tone—just stern and obliging forgiveness. He let her put an arm around him and draw him against her. He kept very still all the while, forbearing the indignity. "I'll go out and get the stock fed."

"Don't. I'll do it. You go ahead and get the fire lit and fix up your Gramma's breakfast."

Outside, the sage was weighted with dew. It left whips and curlicues of darkness on her boot leather. Through the window, she could see Toby moving back and forth with the wood, the bright red flare of the fire gorging itself on new kindling. He was chattering absently to Gramma. The old lady sat as still as ever and followed him with her eyes.

She would never move herself again, of course. They would watch for it in the coming years, but it never happened, and thinking of it afterward Nora would come to wonder why substantiation always seemed to kill the things that had survived so long on faith alone.

When Nora came outside with the bucket of chicken feed, Toby had moved to the yard. He was sitting cross-legged on the ground with the stereoscope pressed to his eyes. The gray, inflamed expanse of his head and his sun-roasted eartips. Lost in the world of its pictures.

Behind him, coming noiselessly down from the trees, was the camel.

The sheer size of it was a shock. The high branches of the pines parted in its path, and it left the brindling of the treecover and came out into the grass. By early daylight, it was nearly red, though some of that was owed to the dust that matted its hair. A dark hackle coursed from between its ears down the slope of its neck, where it thickened out into a hanging shag full of burrs and chollas and smashed leaves that had turned to powder over time.

The rags of a rotted bridle hung around its pout.

Its ribs were bilged by a cinch that cut blackly into its sides and held in place a saddle, whose dead occupant lay pinned in his blue coat by a circumscription of ropes as thick and frayed as vines.

THE SALT

MY POINT BEING—IF WE HAD HEEDED all your sulling and wheezing back then, Burke, we would have given up in that dismal timber camp all those years ago. You've played at being a rogue all your life, you bellyacher, you beautiful trickster. It's no different now—naught but a little shot. If it didn't stop you damn near killing that poor girl by the wash last night, I don't see how it's slowing you now. If you had strength enough for that, you've strength enough yet.

Didn't we think once before that nothing was left for us—only to find our second run? Only to find Jolly?

For there he stood, bracing himself in the doorway of his little house. Our faces were damp by the time he crossed the yard to embrace me.

The afternoon drew out. Chess in the plaza was abandoned. Men gathered instead to marvel at you and hear us revive the past. Trudie—Jolly's wife, his **wife,** thought I, a woman he had married, a short, pretty-eyed Sonoran girl with a Yaqui lilt and a pianist's fingers and a cross around her neck—laid out a feast, and we hovered in the garden talking until the shadows grew long. By and by, Jolly retrieved his horned saddle from somewhere in the house. You suffered him to rig you out and the two of you went bounding around the plaza, Jolly clicking and shouting while you loped in what looked to me like true delight.

Evening rain sent us indoors. The cabin walls were papered over with Jolly's drawings. To his already fine collection, my old friend had added miniature scenes of strange camps and headframes; mesas and clusters of flat-paddled cactus and yucca; here and there, studies of the camel's skeleton; eyes and arms and portraits of George and Beale and other members of our late company, the catalog of his life entire. Trudie took one down and brought it up to my face with a condolatory look. "Don't despair, Misafir," she said. "So go the ravages of time."

Trudie and Jolly spoke little English together, meeting most often somewhere between **limón** and **laymun**. They had a bustling, tender manner, as though they were always in each other's way, but glad to be. After she had gone to bed, the two of us sat outside. I remember the clouds in their gauzy herds hurrying over the hills. You lay folded up in the fore-yard, a little damp, but content to raise your head every now and again to follow the thin clank of the wind-stirred trees. We felt at the end of something.

"Why'd the Dueña call you Filip?"

"It's my old name. Filip Tedro."

"You took it up again?"

Jolly nodded toward the house. "We could hardly have married otherwise."

"What about your hadj?"

"I reckon it stands, so long as Allah hears my devotions."

"Can you remember them all?"

Jolly got to his feet. "Let's see how badly you been running this fine fellow down."

He went over you with careful hands. Your teeth and joints were in good shape, but there was weight to be gained back yet from what he guessed must have been a long illness. You were favoring your right leg some— I should take care to more evenly disperse your load. "And your old saddle," he concluded, "is rubbish."

"I didn't expect such poor marks."

"If only you'd stuck around long enough to become a proper cameleer."

"Some cameleer you are, with no camel. Where the hell is Seid?"

Dead, he told me. Felled, at long last, by a younger bull in rut—a consequence of their having been penned together by Fort Tejon soldiers who didn't know one damn thing about them. The other camels had been dispersed during the war. Some were loosed. Some were sold. George, as fastidious with his purse as he'd been with everything else, was the only one of Beale's cameleers who'd put enough aside to secure a few camels of his own. For a while he and Jolly had a freight contract between George's little place near Rancho La Brea and the surrounding mountains. Lilo helped, but then grew homesick and set off back east with a wagon train some years ago and hadn't been heard from since.

"Did you ever find those woods where the critters were all powdered up with gold?"

"Maybe." He laughed. "There was some mining business after the war." He lit his pipe. "I scouted for the army. Worked as a teamster—though mules never did suit me. Wretched things. I struck a rich vein at South Pass, lived there for a while—but it went quick. Then Trudie came along and got pretty firm about my giving up that kind of way."

I envied him, and told him so. "You've managed to see the Pacific **and** find a wife who can stand to have you around."

"I guess so." He had this faraway smile. "But you see, Misafir, there's so many parts to everything in life and it costs you to learn all the little details. And people who've learned afore you take advantage. They don't point out your mistakes, just so they can delight in watching you make them."

I reckoned that was true. "What've you learned?"

He sat smoking beside me. I watched him, sitting there with that faraway look of his, and for a moment time cheated me and I felt myself fall backwards to some other way of being. If a bugle had sounded, in that moment, from somewhere ahead, my bones would have known to stand and break camp, saddle you, mount up and head for the westward dark, and all the shadows of the desert would have met me as friends.

"I learnt that a man must always be a little discontent," Jolly finally said.

"Well that's easy enough," I said. "In my years I learnt a man more or less can't help it."

He laughed. "But that's as it should be, Misafir. Too much contentment is apt to make you think you can have more. And worse, make you wonder: when will it be taken away?"

"What do you fear being taken?"

"Trudie."

"How do you keep yourself discontent?"

He turned a little to see my face. "I stay here."

That was a good year. I doubt even you would say otherwise. We were a little battered, sure, and getting up there, but we made the best of things and got used to the pleasures of coming home. All told, we must've helped Jolly run ten tons of salt along the Gila corridor. Mining towns were springing up all over the Chihuahuan in the dry beds of ancient lakes. We carried water in and salt out. I filled my canteen in the Colorado, the Yuba, in spring arroyos and strange inland pools where huge starfish lay locked in stone.

Out and back we went, month after month, and for the first time since Graveneck we spent more nights at our own hearth than we did under the stars. And it was all right.

And Trudie and I became good friends. After I'd built our shambles of a house, she helped me get twenty acres broken and planted up. She stood around with her hands on her hips once I'd wrecked all our tomatoes before even the first crop, and I could tell by her that she was ready to take me on for whatever learning I needed, and for however long it took. She must have reckoned that if I stayed, Jolly would have an easier time staying, too. Carrying heavy that summer, she fanned herself through the boiling afternoons and brought out a little girl, Amelia, who came early while we three heroes were knocking around in the salt flats. The baby was already set up in her cradle like a pink little gnome when we returned, the house utterly unchanged, save for her big-eyed presence haunting it. Used to hear her hollering over at their place through the night, and that was an all right kind of music for home.

She had a long, ill-tempered stare, Amelia, and shared her father's suspicion of most things—though naturally not of you. She just about tolerated you to be near her, and you just about tolerated her to be pulling at your chin hairs, and between you there ran a kind of grudgeful truce that everyone felt all right about.

Amelia turned Jolly superstitious. He uttered so many **ma'ashallahs** around her that people thought it was her name.

I barbed him about it, knowing myself as guilty of such nonsense as he was. Hadn't I grown wary of filling my canteen, lest it show me something terrible might befall her? Giving in to Donovan's want now, didn't I pray to see nothing of what might come, and look only toward the past, to my youth and yours, till the faces I saw resembled Jolly's drawings more than they did our raggedy selves?

A year without running. A good year after all. And then another.

It must've been right around the time Amelia turned two when a couple of prospectors came into town with a story to tell. Over three nights while they slept in some distant gulch of the Salt River, their camp was visited by a presence, heard but unseen, that wilded the horses. The more superstitious of the two fellas convinced the other that they should not, on their very lives, try to see the creature while it groaned and scraped around outside—but on the fourth night, his friend's curiosity got the better of him. So quietly they lifted the tent flap. And what should they see besides moonlight?

"An ugly fucker to end all belief—just like the one you got here!"

Well, this got Jolly all worked up. Now and again he'd heard of old survey camels sighted west of the Colorado—but such tales tended to be well-worn by the time they reached him. This particular encounter, on the other hand, might be a sign that one of your cousins had finally found its way deeper into the Territory. We got the map out right away, and decided quick enough there's little strategy to divining where a wild camel might turn up. Best we could figure was to lie up at the creek nearest where the prospectors had survived their strange visitation, and wait.

"Just think," Jolly said. "What if there's more than one? We could have ourselves a real little caravan."

What did he want with a caravan? We were only two men, after all. And you'd always preferred your own company to any of your kin.

But once this kind of ambition had got hold of Jolly, it only grew. We'd catch the prospectors' camel and any friend traveling with him, and we'd broaden our work north and east, maybe even get a freight contract with the railroad, summon George from California. I reckon you didn't like the sound of any of that.

Neither did Trudie. I was patching a roof leak the night before we were set to go out and try for these so-called wild camels when she came down from the house to hold the ladder for me. I was awful wary of dropping something on her head, but she didn't even look up whenever some clay gob peeled off the end of my blade and went sailing past her. "That's Filip for you," she said after a time. "Two years gone, he didn't dream he'd ever be laying eyes on another camel. Now only three will do."

"He's just excitable. I don't reckon we'll find any."

"Even if you don't, it'll be something else soon enough. Anything to keep him called away."

"I'm sure that's not his thinking."

She looked up at me. A great believer in points made by silence, Trudie. I started to wonder if she ever intended on letting me climb back down.

"Don't you reckon he's done more than enough wayfaring for one lifetime?"

I didn't—but then it turned out I didn't know shades of Jolly's early days like she did. I didn't know he'd been called "happiness" by his mother for only a few short years before he was stolen away from her. Or that Jolly believed, but couldn't be sure, that it was his father who'd done the stealing—though he traveled with strangers a long time before he realized his father no longer numbered among them. Afterwards, the only thing his old people and his new ever agreed on calling him was "captive"—and when he'd had his fill of that and earned by pilgrimage the right to be called Hadji, the cousins he'd left behind called him traitor, which was what he suspected they'd been thinking all along anyway. Fellow Turks riding with him into Algiers could never quite bring themselves to grant that he was their own, and so called him Izmiri. Only the Arabs called him Turk, and not for very long— for then he came here to be called Arab by everybody, and resign himself to life as Hi Jolly, a name that meant nothing to anyone he'd ever known.

"It means something to me," I said, feeling an awful burst of fear. "Ain't I called him that every day since we met?"

"I reckon that's all right," she said. "He says he don't call you by your given name, either."

But after all that, here her husband was: Filip Tedro once more, rid of his hard-gotten name and so solitary in his devotion to his God that he had hardened around it till it couldn't be got at by anybody—even if there were anyone to share it with, even if he weren't the only Mohammedan in the whole world.

"Why don't he preach?" I said.

"He says he's not learned enough. And the more time passes, the less certain he is of what he knows."

"Well," I said. "What's there to religion? Following rules and admiring the weather."

Her point was: what had all his wayfaring got him that he was so damn keen to keep on with it?

"Well," I said stupidly, "didn't he get you?"

Trudie frowned. I thought she might shake the ladder. "Well what's he fixing to do now, save keep right on going?" she said. "You know, my father was similarly disposed. He was a real serious, practical sort, save for one thing—he reckoned the fact that he found himself this side of the Rio Grande the day they redrew the maps was a sign of Providence. And by God, he would reap whatever rewards came on the back of it. He used to say to me, **Trudie— have you ever noticed how folks say you're off to seek your fortune? Not just any fortune—but yours. Your very own. Like it's out there with your name on it.** Well, he sought his in the mines and he sought it in the cardhouses, and in the rail towns, too. And in the end, the only thing with his name on it was the cross we planted him under, a hundred yards from where he was born. But he never stopped wanting after this or that. People get it into their heads that it's always just around the corner."

I felt a little affronted, a little foolish.

"Well," I said. "What if it is?"

We did catch two camels the following spring in a dry wash just south of Oso Negro. Both were dromedaries—though smaller than you, thinner and a good deal less agreeable. We had a hell of a time trying to guess their provenance. They were deaf to Turkish and Arabic, and unmoved by any of the commands indigenous to the Beale expedition. Because Jolly believed camels did not forget, he surmised these new recruits must be strangers to us, pack animals brought privately over for work in the mines or bred from that old Beale stock.

"Imagine if we got two more," he said.

I didn't know about that, but it was nonetheless a much thanklier task running salt with three camels. We got a good bit of money under us, and I'd say you must have welcomed sharing the load after all. We were still going, and the going was good. The journeys were shorter, mere flicks of the wrist on a map from the home we always returned to. And every place we went was something new and astonishing.

Jolly was still immune to the draw of the cardhouse. He had settled into thinking that whatever riches he would get would be got on his own, no matter what.

Which was how we came to be hired by the Blacklake expedition.

———

Mister Frank Tibbert and Doctor Lloyd Beecher came to know us when Jolly and I were working for Rockwell Mining Company of Huerfano. We'd been four months out in the Chihuahuan desert, about twenty miles east of Bullhead. It was just about the furthest place I could imagine. I'll be damned if I caught more than an hour of sleep on any given night. Dead miners roamed the streets and the little graveyard on the hill, singing their strangled lullabies. An eastern wind raised oblivion from the desert wastes and swept it nightly over the bowl, and the dust hung yellow between the avenues of tents. Bar-goers slapped it from their hats and thighs as they came into the Santa Sangre saloon.

One evening this haunted wind blew in Frank Tibbert and Lloyd Beecher: pushed them right through the door and directly to us. Tibbert was a youngish man, short and bearded and fastened into a suit too good for his face. Beecher was huge and smiling. He liked to pretend he was shadowing other people when in fact you could tell in two seconds that anyone in his company was merely his mouthpiece, just as sure as if he'd perched them on his knee. A huge gash bisected his eye—not just the browbone, remember, but the soft of the eye itself.

"We're geologists," Tibbert said. "We hear you're the people to see about carting precious cargo a long way from water."

No man had ever bought five minutes of Jolly's time by offering him a drink, but my friend couldn't say no to talk of precious cargo. Three glasses were filled and refilled while they told us their tale: there was a mountain, they said, way out in the Chihuahuan. It had fallen in a burning arc from the sky one evening about two thousand years ago, and in its heart sat the richest veins of gold and quartz anyone had ever seen. The Indians talked about it in their stories, but no civilized person had ever laid eyes on it.

"We been twelve years trying to reach it," Beecher said, pressing his big thumbs together. "But we been faced with the insurmountable: there ain't a drop of water, not within a hundred miles of it."

"We'd all but gave up hope," said Tibbert. "Till we come upon some miners up in Sweetwater County talking about there's two Turks down this way who got themselves pack animals can go a week without water and carry a thousand pounds."

As they talked about the size of the mountain, Jolly's eyes grew wide.

"I don't like it," I told him when we bedded down. We were sat under that rickety old ramada the mining company had given us to house you, for Jolly scoffed at letting you all sleep untended out here. He was smoking and had that old look in his eye he used to get whenever anyone told him he was the only man for the job.

"Imagine," he said. "Being paid in diamond flake."

"I been paid in flake. It's fancy dust."

"Where do you think it fell from—the mountain?"

"I don't think it fell from anyplace, Jolly. I think

it's a load of horseshit. They're going to lure us out there and kill us and steal Burke and Charley and Georgie. Amelia's gone grow up saying my daddy was killed for a falling sky mountain."

That gave him pause enough for a while. But day after day there he was, talking to the old-timers who sat around the mines, asking them had they heard of such a place. Most of them had. They'd heard about a glass cliff, too, somewhere up in Wyoming, and a hole in the ground that could bring you out on the other side of the world just like a dumbwaiter. "Geology, my son, is God's most apparent miracle," Bright Joe, the oldest man in the camp, told him confidentially. "And ain't that all we are? Geologists to a man?"

It was a lot of gilded talk, Burke, and I was suspicious of it. Not because I didn't want to see—but because that look in Jolly's eyes, the way he got when people spoke of mineral as though it were the face of the Lord, well it struck me wrong. But then I got to thinking—don't we all got a thing makes us get that look in our eyes? All of us who ever said, let's go, let's go on, who starved for the sight of something new? Perhaps it ain't the same.

We left Castle Dome Landing in late September, due west for a malpais that swallowed the sun. We carried two waterbarrels apiece—or should I say, you and Charley and Georgie carried six waterbarrels between you. I think that was around the time you were beginning to favor your left hind a little, and I'd started trying to work out your age. You were getting grumpy and showing more white around your chin. We'd been on the road together a long old while, and of late I had begun to wonder how long a camel might be expected to live. "About thirty years," Jolly said. Then he smiled. "Or fifty. Depends on the cameleer."

Tibbert and Beecher were good enough company. They rode along at the head of the line, stretching out maps and holding up compasses. When they hadn't killed us by Mesquite, I got to thinking perhaps I'd misjudged them. Perhaps they were only batty stone-breakers after all, as tickled by this adventure as Jolly was, all three of them riding together and pointing at the horizon like none of them had ever seen it before.

The mercury sat between 105 and 116, so after Tiburon we got to riding only by night. The gray ground stretched flat in all directions. I'd seen deserts before but this was so much itself no living thing could be out here but you. The night was silent save for the **thomp thomp thomp** of your feet. The **slosh slosh slosh** of our slowly diminishing water.

We watered at Huerfano Creek and turned northward for the mountain. It would be six days without resupply, and I remember filling my canteen and thinking about all that desert silt falling into the quiet darkness, and whether we'd be mad by the fourth day and tearing off our clothes and holding each other at gunpoint and gnawing each other's shins. The canteen gave me no answer; all it showed me were distant mesas. "If I die," I whispered to you, "you get away quick as you can. You can live anyplace. Go on and on and on."

A camel without a cameleer might even make it sixty years.

Tibbert and Beecher's horses were whining, wheezing nags who rooted in place sometimes and wouldn't move for anything unless they were allowed water, and for this chore we had to stop often, which always led to rough words. The days got hotter and the words got rougher. By the fourth day we weren't speaking at all, just seething along. My mouth got so dry I couldn't force myself to eat even after I'd watered. We slept in blinding sunlight. Often upon waking I feared I might still be asleep, and so would drink from the canteen, just a little, to get the taste of all those rivers in my mouth and remind myself that Donovan's want was still with me.

We came by darkness to the rim of a deep plain, a caldera whose floor was white with snow. "My soul," Jolly whispered. "God is great." Well, He was. We went down to the valley floor. What we had mistaken for snow turned out to be salt—thick, glittering whitecaps arrested by the sudden disappearance of some great sea. It was coming on morning when we reached the far side. The whole place flooded with purple light, and as we climbed up the bank I thought I heard the sound of rushing water behind me, and turned. Perhaps you remember it differently— perhaps you will tell me it was a dream, but in the haze of that purple dawn I watched the valley roil, and the waves of that hidden sea returned from shore to shore until we stood looking down on a great, heaving mass of water. Jolly saw it, too. There were tears in his eyes. Not the Pacific, true—but a more substantial sea than anything I had ever dreamed.

You knelt and I went to the water's edge and drew back wet fingers. I filled my canteen with those spectral waters. Say what you will of my superstitions, Burke, but I know I did. I carry them yet.

On the sixth day, to much rejoicing, we came upon the mountain. At first it was just a blue shadow, like all the rest of that endless place, but then it firmed up. It was as Tibbert had said: a fist flung from the heavens. While our geologists argued about how to begin, Jolly and I took a turn through the surrounding crater. Little curling plants had taken root in the shale. In the depressions of our footprints, the floor shone white.

"Just imagine," Jolly said. "Ours might be the first tracks on this ground."

"They very well might," said I, though I doubted it.

Tibbert and Beecher argued for a whole day, and then another. They set up a ramada to house their beakers and boxes, and they scraped and hammered and peered at the ground. They dug a mysterious hole under the mountain, and Tibbert's knees could be seen sticking out of it every hour of the clock.

"Where are the rich veins?" Jolly asked after four days.

"My boy," Beecher said, taking him amiably about the shoulders. "Everywhere."

"We'd best get some flake off them, then, and soon. It's many days back to the nearest water."

It became very apparent that Tibbert and Beecher, for all their navigational know-how, had failed to properly time this expedition. On the fifth day, their ramada was still up, their boxes full of soil and little scrapings of dirt, and they were standing about with their hands on their hips and pointing at various parts of the mountain. When our water began running out, they got to quarreling with us about the camels. "Can't we halve their rations?" Tibbert said irritably. "I thought they could go weeks without water."

"Days," I said, and pointed to your sagging hump. "It's very plain when they start suffering."

The men packed up reluctantly. Back into their bags went the boxes and the bottles, strange cuts of rock wrapped carefully in burlap, sacks of glittering sand. The evening before we departed, Jolly said: "They got a lot of weird stone—but what do they intend to pay us with, Misafir?"

When he raised it with Beecher, the huge man looked puzzled. "Your pay is imminent, boys! Don't trouble yourselves for another moment."

I knew at once it was a lie. I know now that we should have threatened to strand them there—though I don't doubt they had planned for that if they planned for nothing else. I could see Jolly coming to grips with it, too. They had permitted him to dig and hammer away at the rock, but had taken all his findings for themselves and stupefied him with names they had likely invented, betting on the inevitability that all he wanted was gold.

When we got back to Huerfano Creek, the geologists began talking excitedly about their next course of action. They would ride for Los Angeles, there to exhibit their findings and secure more funding for the next trip.

"Fellas," Jolly said. "Our pay."

"Pay? Now? But we are only at the beginning of this great venture! The greatest riches are yet to be discovered within the mountain itself. We will have to return! Come back with a larger party and proper equipment. The materials we gathered are just preliminary study, my lads. And we owe it all to you."

Jolly fumed as only he could. "That was not our agreement."

In a last-ditch attempt, they wrote us bank checks for fifty dollars. They were conciliatory, but there was nothing to be done. In the morning, they would ride for Los Angeles with their magic rocks, and we for Arizona with our slips of paper. In a few months, they would find us again at Huerfano and enlist us to the task of greater enrichment once more. I expected Jolly to fly into a rage. This was, after all, exactly the thing that most galled him: a failure to admit and rectify wrongdoing.

"Will you imprison them now, as you did me?" I joked, but he was in as foul a mood as I'd ever seen him.

By morning, however, he had changed his tune. He shook their hands sportingly, assured them we would be in Huerfano again the following spring. "Good luck with your findings, gentlemen." They rode away from us with a warmth of feeling, a joyful wave before they dropped below the horizon.

"What's got into you?" I asked him.

He was riding along and smiling. I'll never forget his face. It was a look of complete triumph, and when I asked him again—"Ali, what've you done?"—he opened his saddlebag to reveal a perfectly round black rock shot through with rivers of gold.

Well, that assayer in Chubbuck couldn't make heads or tails of Jolly's rock. Neither could the prospector in Rice, nor the hermit in Parker to whose abode we were directed by both previous men.

"In my opinion," the hermit said from behind his quivering and malodorous beard, "its worth is only that it is not of this world."

By then we were arguing a great deal. Something about the rock troubled me.

"Oh," said Jolly, "because you're above thievery yourself." He pulled his old **nazar** off its chain and flung it at me. I hadn't seen it in so long, and the feel of it in my hand reminded me so of Hobb's want that I almost gave over trying to convince him. But I remembered, too, what it had felt like to be in its grip. "These things are cursed," I told him. "We become indebted to them."

He did not care. "Misafir," he said to me. "All my life some fool has promised me this or that. My father promised me manhood, but all I got was capture. The French promised me gold, but all I got were a couple of camels. Beale promised me pay—do you know he never had me enlisted? That I am entitled to nothing—no backpay, no pension? He never even put in the papers to make me an American. That's why Lilo left. He said, 'If it couldn't be achieved by the kind of journey we took, well then, what will it take? Shall we have to fly to the moon?' Ten years I worked for that man, and learned only that I might as well never have existed." We were sitting by night in a clearing full of supplicant yuccas. Their twisted shadows played an odd game with our fire. Jolly looked a hundred years old. "I'm no fool, Lurie," he said, catching me soff guard. "Even if Tibbert and Beecher find us again, they will take us there and back a thousand times and never give us half of what's owed to us. Better to take their rock and see what we make of it ourselves."

"Ali," I said. I intended to tell him what his wife had said about his wayfaring. I meant, too, to tell him about the dead, about their want. Maybe someone's had gotten into him, and he just didn't know it. But he looked at me so long that I forgot what I wished to say. I held his **nazar** back out to him. "All right. We'll see what your rock is worth."

But it was not to be. For all that waste, and all that solitude, news travels quick among **buscadores**. Word got out that there were two Turks out there who'd stolen a priceless rock from the wasteland of the gods. It was worth more than any goldstrike, more than any claim. Drop your pans, the call sounded from Yuma to Hesperia, and join the search.

That these two men were rumored to be accompanied by camels did not help matters one bit. We were fired upon in Reno, and pursued by a small posse outside of Jackson, California. We managed to lose them in the Sheephole desert and spent days there, wandering among the yuccas. It was a good wander, though we damn near died. Only the bees saved us. Our flight always took us to places where it was impossible for others to follow, away from water, and for that we have only you to thank. Jolly grew listless. He stopped eating and sat with his head in his hands a great deal.

"Misafir," he said one night. "I fear I've made a grave mistake."

"We made it together, you and I."

"The next posse comes upon us, I'm going to give them the rock."

And so he did. They were a group of young men not much older than we'd been when we first met. At the outset, they did not believe the prize he handed them was the one they were after. A redheaded boy with shaking hands stood us down with a sixgun while his Mexican partner searched our saddlebags. For a moment, I thought he might take my canteen. I said, "It's a sin to strand a man without water, son," which made him throw it back to me. A few hissing drops struck the ground and disappeared.

Jolly's relinquishment of the rock was a graver mistake than stealing it had ever been. The most outrageous rumors are always the hardest to shed, so the news that we were rid of the cursed treasure did not seem to take. Every few days saw us outrunning or explaining ourselves to some unlikely posse. When Jolly's face appeared on the board outside the Red Bank jailhouse—WANTED: HEDGY ALLIE: CAMELEER!—we decided to separate, set loose our camels in opposite ends of the desert and join up again in Peres. By that time, we had neither of us seen Trudie nor Amelia in almost a year. I wondered what they would say to see us, so thin and gaunt were we.

"Not so thin nor gaunt as our excuses," said Jolly miserably.

We were mounted at the Palo Santo crossroads. He would go three days north, toward the Colorado River, and I would take you south to the border and leave you there to your fate. I believe he thought the tears in my eyes were for our parting—his and mine, I mean, and I suppose to some extent they were, for when we rejoined we would be cameleers without camels, and what would that make us? What would we have left to say of ourselves, when the Camel Corps was truly no more, only a reminiscence, and we became old men who talked about a long-ago time we had gussied up for the benefit of disbelieving youth?

For the tears in my eyes, he squeezed my shoulder and put the old **nazar** back in my hand.

"Have courage, Misafir," he said. Then he turned north and rode away.

I meant to take you to Fortuna, and there lose you to the Mexican wilderness. My apprehensions were terrible. I would have to turn you loose near enough dwellings to be able to walk myself back to town. But this would leave you vulnerable to depredation. While we rode, I put it together that I would remove your trappings but leave the bridle on you—so that if any hunters came upon you, they would think twice before firing, lest it turn out you belonged to someone. Though you had belonged to no one, not even me—unless it was the belonging friends make of each other, scarcely existing without traces of themselves in each other's memories. I had thought my selfishness would overwhelm me, and that I would be thinking of myself as I readied for our parting—imagining what it would be like to live without you. But all I could imagine was your life, Burke, and the things you'd seen on your travels locked away forever in the stores of your own patient mind. Things you might still see. The silence and secrets of wild living. And one day—perhaps in three years or thirty—some passing party would find your bones and wonder how on earth you had come so far, the furthest-flung camel in the world, and perhaps by then the tales of our adventures in the desert would be so well known that whoever found you would recognize what lay before them, and gather all that was left of you into some precious box and hand it down, father to son, running you on for all time.

We went as far as Beulah together. It was springtime

in the high desert, and the brilliant blossoms burst from every cactus. The good dry air put a spring in your step that made you look like a meadowed fawn rather than the old rattletrap you were. In a burned-out canyon where the thick little shoots of new life greened the bluffs, a rainstorm overtook us. It was the briefest relief, hot and cold at once, and I uncapped my canteen and filled it there for Donovan, and for all the want that was left in me.

We were crossing a malpais before our afternoon rest when I heard the crack of a rifle and the first bullet came whizzing past. By the time I'd got you wheeled around, a black column of riders was advancing all in one thick cavalcade over the rise.

And so it was that six horsemen caught up with us on the llano that day, Burke, and for all my efforts I could neither save us nor be believed. "You're that Hadji Ali," they kept saying. They were young men, blood-drunk. Mad enough when they found my gear empty to send kick after kick into my face and ribs. Where was the rock? Where was the gold-veined treasure?

After a while, rage and disappointment stilled them. If I wasn't the man they were looking for—the little robber Turk whose face was all over them posters—then what the hell was I doing with a camel? And what the hell were they supposed to do with me?

They mulled this over around their fire that night. My leg was all shot to hell, and my whole chest was beginning to stiffen under my bonds, but I thought it quite a miracle that we were still alive. How long that would continue was uncertain. It was one thing to kill a man outright; but to be stuck with a dying one raises up a kind of superstitious dread in even the sturdiest badman. And as none of them boys looked brave enough to put one behind my ear while I slept, I knew it would be long and slow for me. The trouble was, their whispers were already turning toward the inconvenience of you. Was there someplace a camel could be sold, they wondered, or would it be better to just butcher you here? What might be done with the skin? Which of them would take the head?

"I'm a wanted man," I called out from where I sat tied up among the trees. "Got a bounty on me far greater than the one Hadji Ali does. Just take me in, you'll see."

"Is that right?" they said. "Who the hell are you?"

"Lurie Mattie, formerly of the Mattie gang."

I can't say I didn't care, one way or the other, about saying it—but it wasn't in my mind to confess it now, to some eavesdropping firmament, before it was too late, either. I only knew this was the last time saying it would ever matter. Not because they'd heard of the Mattie gang, of course. But because they were young, and prone to be turned by details that sounded true and overbold.

"What kinda thing you got hanging over you?" they said.

"I kilt a boy in cold blood—though you'd do well

to tell the man you take me to that I also did for a mulepacker named Shaw. It's the truth, and it'll get you more money. He'll believe you."

"And who would he be?"

"Man named John Berger, out in New Mexico," I said. "But you'll have to bring my camel along. He don't know me without it."

In the morning, I was lashed to your saddle for the journey. They were taking no chances, these little roughnecks. The rope was wound about my shoulders and my legs and crosswise, then stitched back and forth around the pommel again. In places where my blood had dried, my shirt stuck to my chest. The leg was hurting something awful, too. I'd be dead by nightfall, I thought, and where would that leave you? I could just about see your head hanging over some gloomy saloon door, or your bones laid out in some curiosity tent. What an end for the pair of us, I thought. Goddamn, Burke, but I wished it could've gone any other way for you.

Just then, as if you'd felt my want, you blenched. The boy holding your reins jumped back. That great, curdled roar came surging out of you, and you busted through their feeble line and lit out across the sageflat.

They couldn't have chased us for more than five miles. I can't be sure, because I couldn't turn back in the saddle, only sit upright and stare forward. You were damn smart about our escape; went right into the barrens. The edges of the world had begun to dim and shimmer. When I woke, the distant mesas were closer, black bluffs against the first roiling flickers of sunset. By and by all gradations faltered: the reds turned gold and then gray and then black. Your head before me continued loding on through the darkness, a shadow foregrounded against the outflung blanket of stars.

"You're a good sort, Burke," I said, uncertain I had ever said it outright. Your ears twitched back to the sound of my voice.

With the morning rising palely to meet us, you stooped to drink at a gulch riffle. I got my finger around the lead-rope and gave a small pull, but it was fastened too tightly. The strength in my hands was gone and I listened to the siren babble of the water recede as you rose and rolled on. Soon enough it was just your steady footfalls thumping dustily along the track. We climbed out of the caldera to see a distant rivercourse of camp lights. "There," I tried to say, "there." Your ears twitched back again. You closed distance toward this familiar yellow luminescence. I thought if we could only reach some camp, someone, anyone, would cut me down. We arrived in the wee hours and climbed the hill to the tents. By the fire sat a lank-haired kid of no more than thirteen, striving joylessly on a bone flute. His horses mutinied at the smell of you, and my calls of greeting were drowned out by the racket of campdogs and general riot, and then gunfire. You took off into the shelter of the thin trees and down into the creek, and after a while the voices faded. When I woke again, the pain in my chest was sharp, and we were standing at the edge of a milky white river beyond which the trees groved as evenly as summer clouds.

We passed other camps, other towns. Always in the distance hovered the wavering lights of some possible resting place, and sometimes you strove for them and sometimes you did not, staying in the barrens, bending your neck back and huffing with concern, trying to see me. A smell began to haunt us. Sometimes, when you stooped streamside to drink, a flense-headed buzzard would land nearby and wait.

In the wake of a retreating thundershower, we came to a small town on the plain and crossed in darkness from one end of the thoroughfare to the other. Pools of lamplight shivered in the rutted street. I called out, I think: Hello, **salaam, hola**! Your ears were upraised and bent forward. A windowcurtain rippled. Sometime later, a porch door opened for a thin-legged child. She stood, still holding the latch, in the white shock of her nightdress and stared across the plaza at you.

She's afraid, I thought, she'll stay where she is. But out she came, padding softly toward us. From here, I thought, we must look nothing but a shadow to her. A few more steps, and she'll hear my voice, broke as it is, and go fetch her pa. She stopped in the middle of the street, swaying on her toes. "Little one," I said, "it's alright."

I'll never know what drove you to stand in that

instant. But you shifted to rise, and the girl turned and ran back to the house, deaf to me.

And as for you—well. You moved steadily through town and out into the dark and haven't stopped moving since.

Birds followed us from water to water. They sat in the treetops like black bells, so determined by then you could no longer shake them off. Still I kept thinking: if only you'd drift into some camp where they'd hold off shooting long enough to cut me down and give me a drink. I could hear my canteen, **ssss ssss ssss,** Donovan's want slung over the saddlehorn. I didn't care much to see what might be coming. What I longed for was to see less dimly all the things that had been.

I came round one morning not too long afterward in a wakeful dread. There I was, standing beside you, though I could not remember how I'd got free of my bonds, or managed to dismount. All around me, the edges of the world had gone very soft. Muffled and faraway, as if I were looking up from underwater. It was from this halflight that I watched you move past me with the gray arm I recognized as my own hanging limply from your saddle.

I called after you, knowing already that your ears wouldn't spring back to the sound of my voice again. I don't care to think often on that moment: watching you start uphill without me. You didn't get far before you stopped, and that big, worried head came twisting around to get a look at what lay behind.

Something troubled you; but it was only my absence you felt, not my hand on your neck, nor my voice in your ear. Then you turned away and kept on up the hill.

What else was there to do, save follow you and keep on calling?

I can't say how long we've been adrift like this together. Long enough for you to grow white with age, anyway, and for the chollas stuck to your legs and sides to sink their roots in you and begin to grow. For birds to nest and hatch and die and fledge in the hollows of my coat. The dead, I know, must be all around us, though I've never seen them. I've seen only the living in their distant towns, whose yellow lights, once so sparse, have brightened more and more of our black nights. It made me mournful to see them. Somewhere, in just such a town, Jolly was growing old. Perhaps with Trudie still at his side; Amelia, too, and other children, whose faceless forms hurried around the house I found myself less and less able to remember. Perhaps my friend had gone home believing me a victim of my old way; running on, as I always had. Or perhaps he felt my absence, as you did, and spoke of me now as a man of the past. Perhaps to his children. Or perhaps to George, who by now must surely have come through from California to sit at Jolly's hearth and call me by name into the midst of my living brothers.

Of this I'm certain: if the Jolly I know still breathes, he does so believing you and I might ride into town at any moment, and some small door of his soul is forever open to us. I've never quite left off thinking we might stumble through it after all.

But you've been too wary for people. For many years now you've stayed hid among the trees, or vanished yourself against the pale, bald hills at the first sign of passing riders.

I'll admit, Burke, that sometimes when the sand-storms cast their great, roaring clouds around us, and the grinning moon spun away into the dark, I have wondered if we mightn't both be wandering a world devoid of anyone but ourselves. A man gets lost inward, going so many years unremarked-upon and unseen. It's hardly reassurance enough to skirt a camp every once in awhile and see the dogs sit up and come to the fire's edge and bark at our passing. We did once cross the path of a prospector, who dropped his shovel and fled. And he did reappear a few days later with a carrot and a length of rope, and a slurry of soft words you only withstood for a little while before backing into the thicket.

He wouldn't give up, that fella. Kept dogging us for days, and it took you losing your temper and rushing him to finally put him off our trail for good.

Of course, that taught you to rush anyone coming within a half mile of you—miners, mules, that poor girl and the people who came for her—but I'll admit I was pleased to see him go. For a torn moment I'd feared he might cut me away from you, and that you would go on toward his life, leaving me behind in the desert alone. It set me thinking that coming up on Jolly might not be so bright a day after all. Oh, he'd recognize us, to be sure, and be relieved to have some old questions put to rest. But there would still be unknowns. The full truth of what had come to pass would always elude him. And what could Jolly do for us any different than what a stranger might? Free you of me. Pull us apart. And then what? He might not shoot you for sport, nor hang your head above his door. But having weighed the extent of your diminishment, he would put you down. Bloodlust or mercy, the result would be the same: with both of us dead, we would wander alone, each unable to find the other again.

The dread of this has sheltered in me for a long time—though never quite as badly as now, Burke. Of course, I know you won't live forever. Though to me you remain the handsomest old man on four legs, I see those clouds in your eyes, and that sag in your hump. I know the hitch in your step has worsened. All summer long, you've moved from dry wash to dry wash till we found ourselves back at the redrock wastes we first crossed so many decades ago. Even before that woman shot at you from the window, the drought had all but hollowed you out.

But every day we go on is home.

Why else would I go so long without answering the girl? Wasn't hers the only human voice to call out to me in all these twenty long years, back when she first touched the edges of my mind and said, "Who are you?" And when I didn't answer, "Are you lost?"

She looked without seeing me, but I could feel

the press of her unquiet mind. All kinds of things gusting around in there—fear and love and melancholy. "Do you know you're among the other living?" she said.

"I know," was all I ever told her.

But she wouldn't be satisfied. She pressed me about my name, my demise. How long had I been wandering? I couldn't bring myself to answer, for by that time you were damn near played out, and I feared she might break into me and see the truth, see us bedding down in that abandoned house at the top of the mesa; see us making our way, night after wretched night, around the outbuildings and down to the dead creek in the hope some faraway rain might have thickened it.

We should've stayed put and not gone off looking for water. What little you found over at that other place was not worth getting shot for—and anyway, hadn't there been water all along, right up here, in the springhouse? All you had to do was heed me, and wait awhile longer for them all to disperse. For the girl to stop feeling around with her mind, and the men to ride down to the wash and away from us in the moonlight—and all the dogs with them, in the bargain, and you free to drink to your heart's content, unheard and uninterrupted.

No matter. A few more hours and you'll be right enough to go on again. You'll see.

"But, Lurie," you'd say to me now, "why are you pressing me onward, when not two hours gone, you told me you had changed your mind? Before the girl showed up and called out to you again, hadn't you come around to my way of thinking? Hadn't you just got done telling me how shot up and old and played out I am, and how my pain wounds you worse than any fear you may yet carry—and that it was perhaps time, having borne the wants of so many, to heed your own? Hadn't you wanted to let me rest?"

And then I'd say to you, "That was last night, Burke. Now all is changed."

And you'd find me with that long-dead stare. "How so, Misafir? How has it changed?"

"Well," I'd say. "What about the girl? Ain't you just put down the one solitary soul might've helped us, understood what we were asking? I feel more lost than ever now."

And you would say, "Don't feel lost, Misafir."

"But who will put us down together, Burke, now that the girl cannot?"

And you would say, "We'll find us someone, Lurie. I don't doubt we will."

MORNING

AMARGO

Arizona Territory, 1893

THE CAMEL STAGGERED ALONG ON JOINTS
that seemed to fold in all the wrong directions. Out
in the open now, dusted red and drenched in sunlight. Its hair, all but invisible between the overgrowth
and the distintegrating adornments, was white—
thin and iridescent, as if each strand were a single
thread of glass. What Nora had mistaken for shadow
back while it was still among the trees was in truth a
wide band of blood and shot blackening its right
flank and tightening its stride, so that it rolled forward arhythmically, pausing to rest the dragging leg
and breathe through the foam around its mouth. It
had come all the way down the hill like this, and was
almost in the yard. Every once in a while it seemed
to find her with its ancient, gray-fogged eyes, but it
was clear enough now that it looked without seeing.

If it had hands, she thought, it would be feeling its way along.

Mama, Evelyn said.

In later years, she would remember wondering where her fear had gone. There had been no dearth of it in the gulch last night, and that was before she had taken full measure of this bedraggled mountain, this overgrown wonderment and its shriveled, grinning rider.

An old and sudden sorrow joined her instead. She felt it arrive as though some distant friend, long unseen, were calling from just outside the house, and she need only go toward that familiar voice and open the door. Its spell changed her sight, and the impregnable morass of cloth and brush that burdened the animal as it came toward her seemed not only knowable, but familiar. She knew the reins, their weight and texture, the sharp way they frayed between the fingers. She knew the bewildering topography of that hump, the warmth rising off the saddle. The flat cool of the few discs still dancing along the bridle. She wanted—what? Her vision blurred. She wanted to be here always. She wanted never to be here again.

The wind shifted, and the camel's sulfurous pungency astounded her. Moments later it astounded poor old Bill, who thrashed free of his lead-rope and went screaming across the corral. This was when Toby finally lowered his stereoscope.

"Don't turn around, Tobe."

"Why, Mama?"

"Keep on looking at your pictures."

At the sound of her voice, the camel stilled. One thick, tattered foot lifted and thumped back down. Slight spasms jerked its head left and right. It couldn't quite get a fix on where she stood. Its sides distended and fell. She was counting its breaths, and had got up to six, when she realized she had moved up the porch and was already easing the shotgun from behind the chair. Its heft felt foreign, odd. She broke it open.

Toby heard it snap back into place.

"What's happening, Mama?"

But he stayed obediently behind the stereoscope, in that pale half-world across the sea, or under some dazzling archway, while she stood out here in her yard, in the sun, in this daze, and brought the rifle up.

"Stay as you are, Tobe."

She was a poor shot. Always had been. If she missed, the camel might trample Toby on its way to her. Why, then, was she aware, through a scrim of feeling that seemed not entirely her own, that her foremost fear was not for her son, sitting here in the dirt with his back to the beast that wandered his dreams; nor for Josie, whom it had already overwhelmed? In the path of what should have been her terror was another, broader, more urgent one: that the camel, if she failed to hit it, might find itself ongoing. Veer off into the woods and disappear again, as it had before. This time must be different. The sorrow of its suffering journey—what the hell did she know of its suffering journey?—rushed into her like a dream of the abyss. There was nothing at the bottom.

She fired. A spurt went up at the junction of neck and shoulder, but the bullet was slow to wake that numb, ancient flesh. Then it stung, and the camel reeled back half a pace, tack singing, and turned her way. It took one, two, three impossibly long strides, and then came thunderously down onto its knees and fell forward. A detonation of dust lifted from its back, like afterquake shale leaving a mountainside, and went on purling.

Toby sat frozen with the stereoscope still pressed over his eyes. "What is it, Mama?" He began to cry.

She was crying herself. After a while, she gave over trying to take the stereoscope from him and left him sitting there in the dust and went up the slope to where the camel had fallen. Huge, jellied ticks had left craters in its hair. Paste from its thick-lashed eyes had run black rivers down the sides of its face.

The dead man's coat was buttoned and crusted stiff. Below the rotted throat clasp she could see slim yellow rib bones, with their sheath of petrified skin, disappearing into darkness. Mattings, which she realized were hair, lay glued back against the saddle. One of the hands and its opposite foot were missing. The rest was contained in the ropes in more or less the same configuration as had been ordained by life.

"What is it, Mama?" Toby was still sitting with his back to her.

"Come and see."

"I don't want to."

He felt his way up toward her with his eyes shut tight. Every so often, he pressed a closed fist against them as though he wanted to sear even the possibility of whatever lay there from his vision.

"It's a camel, Tobe."

"What's that?"

"A huge horse. Just as you said."

"I don't believe you."

"Open your eyes, then."

"It smells awful."

"It was very old, I think."

She tried to coax him closer, but he continued to hang back with his elbow crooked over his eyes. Finally she took his hand and led him, little by little, to where the huge head lay in the sage. She lowered his open palm into the soft, thick curls of its brow.

"Is it real?" he said.

"Sure is."

Toby's fingers found the ears and the thick orbital protrusions above the eyes. "What's it doing here?"

"I really don't know. I think it must have come a very long way."

He would only agree to look at it after he'd gone inside and climbed upstairs and was safely standing in the window of Rob's room. Nora shaded her eyes to look up at him. She could see his little head behind the glass, and now she could see him from within the room, from behind, standing on tiptoe amid the wreckage that was Rob, amid the wood shavings and the thrown-about shirts, as though all the deluge of Rob's old life was now watching Toby unlatch the window.

He leaned out and made a face. "It don't look anything like they do in the books."

"Well," she said. "They never do."

"What's that on its back, Mama?"

"A saddle," she said.

From this distance, the rider must be just a blur to him. Toby leaned his bald head against the window-frame. She could see him standing there ten years from now, Rob's height or maybe a little taller. If they stayed—if she gave Crace way, and the boys were allowed to return—he would want this room for his own one day so that he could look out and be reminded of this sight, his mother standing over this odd and impossible kill, the strangest thing ever to happen in his life made all the more precious because his brothers had missed it, and in no time at all he would be its only living keeper.

Toby pointed to the road. "I think I see the Doc coming."

"Good. You get your Gramma fed and presentable."

When Toby disappeared from the window, she turned back to the dead man.

What was she meant to do with him? All the certainty of the last few minutes had gone out of her. Nothing had replaced it. Then she thought of

Emmett laid up in some vast, forsaken gulch, with the sky cloudless overhead and the birds already gone from him, waiting for some stranger to open his coat and ask the contents of his life—who was he? To whom did he belong? And the answer, necessarily, would come: to somebody unknown. Might as well be nobody.

She opened her knife and began cutting the ropes away. The rider fell out of his bonds in pieces: the shin and thighbone sliding out, one after the other. His trouserlegs were white with bird droppings, and ragged with long-ago monsoons. As she cut, the man's hand slid out of its pocket and crumbled, and she marked the tips of his fingers so she would know where they had fallen when she returned later to gather him up.

The Doc was rounding the bend, the red dust of his horses rising constantly in twin plumes as his wheels churned the road. He would be at her door in a matter of minutes. He would rein up and ease himself out of the boxseat, pretending they had not, for a moment yesterday, become strangers. Pretending, perhaps, that nothing on his mind needed answering. He would follow silently along when she led him into the barn, where his coldness would fall away. And once Josie was safely upstairs, they would turn to this new, impossible task together, working through the day, through all the Doc's exclamations and conjectures, till the sun went down, by which time he would certainly have grown impatient enough to return to the question of the newspaper. What would her answer be tonight? He would not ask her a third time.

When the ropes were all cut, she took the coat by its lapels and dragged what remained of the rider out of the saddle and onto the ground. A woodland of pine needles and sap stained the empty seat. She could see the saddle panels laidbare by the body's vacancy. They were glossy, as though someone had spent a lifetime polishing them. She unbuttoned his coat and the stained yellow linens of his shirt beneath. He was there—or most of him, anyway. Dry skin stretched like bandaging. One hand, one arm. The hollow turnkey bones of his pelvis.

Straightening up made her dizzy. She felt the sudden want for rest.

The dead man's pockets were empty. In the saddlebag she found only a mess of waterlogged papers whose words had pooled along the pagebottoms in brown and yellow fans a lifetime ago. He wore no tags, no jewelry.

Strapped over what remained of the saddlehorn was a tin canteen, marked with the crossbraces of some nameless legion. When she pulled it loose she heard—the strangest thing—the singing tumble of water.

The cap held firm awhile, but crumbled eventually between her fingers. She had merely intended to satisfy her disbelief. Just a little water flashed against the black insides, but, yes, there it was—singing in the darkness. Rain and river. Iron and salt. How many years, she wondered, had it been carried along? She shook it, and it sang again. Brightly, cleanly around its course. Somewhere behind and above her, Toby was asking a question. She had no answer. She had no answer yet, but she put the canteen to her mouth and saw, yes—a house; their house and its mesa, their stream and its water, and seas; seas and chimneys; the distant funnel of a greenblack hurricane; coins, buttons, buckles, dizzy blue beads and this canteen; this canteen, and this camel, and Coyote in his winter coat; a long unbroken road, a line of misshapen shadows, and men all around laughing at, no, laughing **with** each other, laughing around the fire, resting on their camels; a girl, small, thin-legged child of the desert, with her hand outheld; and water—the roar of rivers leaving their canyons, rushing over land, over cliff, over the thicksalted bed of some strange dark sea; and now her house again; camel and rider side by side in the brush, folded side by side in a deep trench—no, grave; both in the grave together, and the blinding flash of a camera; passersby shouting, "hey is this the place?"; yes, this is the place; this is the place—until it isn't; her house—until it isn't; no water and therefore no house, no paper, no town at all, one way or the other, no matter what; but then some other town, some other house, some house elsewhere, some new house in Wyoming; and Evelyn there—Evelyn with her in the new house, after all; and Toby; little Toby stacking his towers; Toby again, but older now, his hair grown back and brown, not blond as she had expected; brown-haired Toby reading a book; Toby, brown-haired and leaving that other house, leaving Nora and Evelyn for Denver; and Desma swinging an ax; Desma swinging from a tree, or in a porch swing; and Rob swinging, swinging around to look at her from among the goblins; swinging through the Sanchez ranch gate in his Sunday suit, swinging the shotgun into his hands; swinging Josie around the hardwood; and Josie; Josie walking crook-footed, crook-footed forever; Josie forced to wear a brace, forced to wear glasses, always-dizzy Josie; always-dizzy but alive, run-over by a camel and lived to tell it Josie; Josie and Rob in some distant town, in some unfamiliar church; a shower of rice and a small child; no—two children; a house somewhere in the blue north; tarot cards on a felt tabletop and graying Rob in overalls and some strange contraption in his driveway; and Dolan; little Dolan resting his chin on folded hands, watching the silk of the sieving line darken; Dolan, by firelight, stitching up his brother's arm with bandaged hands; and now walking arm-in-arm with a dark-haired woman through a city that must be San Francisco; and Nora, taking the train; taking the train past singing waters, taking the train to rock with her bare foot the cradle of a solemn little girl-child; Dolan and girl-child in a green park; no—churchyard; child laying flowers down, child waving to Dolan from the schoolhouse steps; Dolan's scarred knuckles braiding all that schoolgirl hair; and Nora in some new house, alone; or in some new house with Emmett— and Emmett gray, Emmett old, Emmett aging alongside her, as Evelyn had; Emmett from room to room in his slippers; Emmett holding her hand in sleep; his sleep and hers; and Evelyn; Evelyn in the new house at twenty; Evelyn at thirty; Evelyn on the Denver train; Evelyn in the theater seat beside her, holding back tears for Toby, brown-haired Toby taking his bows onstage; taking his time at the lectern, taking a turn through the lamplit neighborhood with a tall young man; and Evelyn's hand in her own in the kitchen; and Emmett laughing with Evelyn on the porch; on their porch; on the porch of some new house, theirs but not this, not this one at all; not this sundrowned farm with its camel and rider sleeping side by side together beneath the roasted earth; not this house, with its puncheon log where the words were written, where they had lived once, and yes, been happy—she saw everything, she saw it all.

ACKNOWLEDGMENTS

A great number of incredible people have come into and bettered my life in the years since my first book was published. That they stuck around while **Inland** was being written is a testament to their love and generosity. They know who they are, and I am grateful to them all.

I'm also grateful, beyond words, to my agent Seth Fishman, and to Rebecca Gardner, Will Roberts, and all the big hearts who make The Gernert Company home; and to my editor, Andrea Walker, as well as Maria Braeckel and my Random House family.

Writers keep writers going, and I am lucky to be kept humble by some of the most talented and hardest-working on earth, a few of whom were kind enough to read early drafts of this novel. Thank you, Parini Shroff, Jared Harel, Andrew Fitzgerald, Jill Stephenson, Bryna Cofrin-Shaw, Rachel Aherin, Catherine Chung, James F. Brooks, Daniel Levine, Alexi Zentner, and Noah Eaker.

I thank my lucky stars for Michael Ray of **Zoetrope: All-Story,** an unrelenting supporter of all writers, who keeps reminding me that short stories are my first love; and for my students and colleagues at Hunter College.

Without the support of the Dorothy and Lewis B. Cullman Center for Scholars and Writers, and the National Endowment for the Arts, of course, this book would never have been written. Thank you for all you do.

It was beautiful to watch the Camel Corps enjoy a kind of return to the national consciousness even as I wrote this book. **Inland** is, above all, a work of imagination, but the journals, letters, and reports of the men who were a part of at least one aspect of this history, especially May Humphreys Stacey and Edward Fitzgerald Beale, were indispensible to its writing. So was the work of those historians of the American West who have amassed the far-flung details of this weird and fascinating episode, particularly Eva Jolene Boyd, Lewis Burt Lesley, Chris Emmett, Forrest Bryant Johnson, and Gary Paul Nabhan, not to mention the irrepressible Tracy V. Wilson and Holly Frey of **Stuff You Missed in History Class**.

I am thankful to my family, in the United States and Ireland, for all their love and support.

And to Dan—the source of all things good and true. You make everything possible.

ABOUT THE AUTHOR

Téa Obreht's debut novel, **The Tiger's Wife,** won the 2011 Orange Prize for Fiction and was an international bestseller. Her work has appeared in **The Best American Short Stories, The New Yorker, The Atlantic, Harper's Magazine,** and **Zoetrope: All-Story,** among many others. Originally from the former Yugoslavia, she now lives in New York with her husband and teaches at Hunter College.

teaobreht.com